EARLY PRAISE FOR

"One of the richest supernatural wo[...]
are about to hit the jackpot as Cla[...] ...energize
this amazing series. Searching for layered plotlines and complex characters? Look no further, as Clamp truly delivers!"
—*RT Book Reviews*

PRAISE FOR THE SHAPESHIFTER NOVELS OF
CATHY CLAMP *and* C. T. ADAMS

"I read the book in one sitting. . . . [It] has some new twists in the werewolf's tail that were very cool."
—Laurell K. Hamilton on *Hunter's Moon*

"This incredible novel is inventive, totally riveting as well as surprisingly tender. Adams and Clamp are a powerhouse team that has opened the door to an amazing new world."
—*RT Book Reviews* (4½ stars) on *Hunter's Moon*

"Adams and Clamp are adept at writing intensely sensuous, hot lovemaking scenes, but where they really shine is in the creation of an unforgettable world where secret shapeshifters live, love, and scheme. Laurell K. Hamilton readers will enjoy this edgy world."   —*Booklist* on *Moon's Web*

"Adams and Clamp score another winner. They continue adding new and interesting branches to the greater shapeshifter hierarchal tree; with so many animal species to choose from, the sky is literally the limit in their imaginative and complicated mythology. There's also a nasty set of power-hungry villains whose characters and sinister agenda will literally make your skin crawl. Exciting and very readable."
—*BookLoons* on *Captive Moon*

"Is it good? Oh yeah. Adams and Clamp just keep getting better and better with each book, and they've made it easy for a new reader to jump in at any point. Whether you like urban fantasy or paranormal romance, this is a series worth picking up."   —*SF Site* on *Howling Moon*

"By focusing on complicated pack politics and on the difficulties of balancing a human and an animal self, Adams and Clamp have created a fascinating but credible world. [Characters] confront fairly complex issues related to leadership, community, and individual freedom. This makes for a thought-provoking but riveting read. It also results in characters who are far more multifaceted than the average superpowered paranormal creations."
                    —*The Romance Reader* on *Moon's Fury*

FORBIDDEN

TOR BOOKS *by* CATHY CLAMP

Forbidden

BY CATHY CLAMP *and* C. T. ADAMS

THE SAZI
Hunter's Moon
Moon's Web
Captive Moon
Howling Moon
Moon's Fury
Timeless Moon
Cold Moon Rising
Serpent Moon

BY C. T. ADAMS *and* CATHY CLAMP

THE THRALL
Touch of Evil
Touch of Madness
Touch of Darkness

WRITING AS CAT ADAMS
Magic's Design
Blood Song
Siren Song
Demon Song
The Isis Collar
The Eldritch Conspiracy
To Dance with the Devil

LUNA LAKE • BOOK ONE

Forbidden

Cathy Clamp

A TOM DOHERTY ASSOCIATES BOOK

NEW YORK

FORBIDDEN

Copyright © 2015 by Cathy Clamp

Hunter's Moon excerpt copyright © 2003 by Cathy L. Clamp and C. T. Adams

All rights reserved.

Title page image: iStock.com

Designed by Mary A. Wirth

A Tor Book
Published by Tom Doherty Associates, LLC
175 Fifth Avenue
New York, NY 10010

www.tor-forge.com

Tor® is a registered trademark of Tom Doherty Associates, LLC.

The Library of Congress Cataloging-in-Publication Data
is available upon request.

ISBN 978-0-7653-7720-3 (trade paperback)
ISBN 978-1-4668-5460-4 (e-book)

Tor books may be purchased for educational, business, or promotional use. For information on bulk purchases, please contact the Macmillan Corporate and Premium Sales Department at 1-800-221-7945, extension 5442, or write to specialmarkets@macmillan.com.

First Edition: August 2015

Printed in the United States of America

0 9 8 7 6 5 4 3 2 1

ACKNOWLEDGMENTS

As always, I want to thank my wonderful and supportive husband, Don, and my terrific agent, Merrilee Heifetz. I'd also like to give a huge written hug to editor supreme Melissa Singer, awesome publisher Tom Doherty, and all the people at Tor for their continuing faith and belief in the Sazi reality.

Special thanks to new romance author friend Tamara Morgan for her help and great sensory input in locating and creating the town of Luna Lake. Thank her by buying her books, listed on her Web site: www.tamaramorgan.com.

I'd also love to give a shout-out to the residents of Republic, Washington, and the rest of Ferry County. You're home to bits and pieces of everywhere I've ever lived (the mountains of western Colorado; the Burlington, Colorado carousel; the Native American lands of the Four Corners; and the mines of both Colorado and Texas), which totally rocks! I hope you'll welcome your new fictional neighboring town and quirky residents. Ferry County looks like a very cool place to live, and I hope to someday visit and wander around all the businesses I got to know on your chamber of commerce Web site.

CHAPTER 1

Fear wasn't something Claire Evans thought she'd ever feel again, but an all-too-familiar buzzing filled her ears while bile rose into her throat. Adrenaline raced through her veins, and her muscles flexed involuntarily, as though striking at an invisible foe. The sensations were hardwired into her from that time, long ago. But now she was just a passenger in a car in rural Washington, with no enemy that she could feel or smell. Yet she was alert and wary.

"You feel it too, don't you? The dark tightens around your throat like a hand." Danielle's tremulous whisper beside Claire made her start and turn her head to look at the lovely African-American woman driving the car.

She tried to shrug it off. "I'm a Sazi . . . a wolf. The dark doesn't scare me." *So why is my heart pounding like it's going to leap out of my chest?* She stared out the windshield where the bright headlights barely held the night at bay, looking for something . . . anything that would explain what she was feeling. *Analyze the fear, Claire. Force it to reveal itself.*

Danielle Williams's laugh held just a touch of hysteria. "It's not the dark, girlfriend. It's what's *in* the dark. Strange things live in the forest here. Stuff that even scares those that hunt at night. It's why I'm the one driving you tonight."

Claire turned in her seat to face Danielle more squarely. "Come again?" Before the other woman could open her mouth to respond, Claire took a deep breath through her nose and knew abruptly why fear had been tightening her throat. It wasn't her own fear filling the air . . . it was Danielle's. Underneath the thick scent of feathers that she expected to smell from an owl shifter was the unmistakable sour scent of near-panic. An owl scared of the dark? That was wrong on so many levels. There had to be something deeper at work. "What's wrong, Danielle?"

A long pause followed. Claire let it grow until the other woman couldn't stand the pressure anymore. "It's my . . . little sister and . . . brother." The words were choked out with long gulps of air between. Claire didn't have to ask their names; though she'd just met Danielle tonight, she'd done her homework on her host family. Nineteen-year-old Danielle was the oldest biological child of John and Asylin Williams. Ten-year-old Kristy was the youngest and fourteen-year-old Darrell was in the middle. But the Williamses weren't content to raise only their own children. They'd opened their home to more than a dozen orphans from the plague and raised them as their own. Many "after-plague siblings" of various races, families, and shifter species had come and gone through their massive, hand-built home during the last decade, making it the perfect place for Claire to stay and to gather information. Danielle snuffled and wiped her nose on her sleeve. "Kristy and Darrell have been missing for three days now. Nobody knows where they are. I left college to come home and help search."

"Oh, man! What happened?" Three days? Why hadn't she been told yet? Or did Wolven not know about the disappearances?

"Kristy was supposed to spend the day at a friend's house. When dinnertime rolled around and she hadn't come home,

Mom sent Darrell to get her. When neither one made it back after another hour, Mom called Isabelle's family. They hadn't seen Kristy all day. Hadn't seen Darrell either." Danielle drummed her fingers on the steering wheel. Claire felt the speed of the car increase and began to push magical energy out in a wave in front of the car to hopefully warn any prey animals to avoid the roadway. The last thing they needed was to hit a deer and wreck the car.

Danielle kept talking, the words tumbling over themselves in a rush. "Mama should have called me that day. I would have come to help look for them. But she didn't want to *bother me*. Damn it! Kristy's only ten and Darrell's not much older. They haven't even shifted for the first time." Tears glistened in the orange light from the dash. Danielle wiped them away with an angry hand before clutching the wheel again, wrapping fingers around it like talons around a snake.

Claire reached out to touch the other woman's shoulder. "I'm so sorry, Danielle. I understand just how you feel." In fact, she understood more than Danielle could imagine. She had once been one of the missing. Worse, to many in her hometown, she still was. It's why she was the perfect person to send here to investigate.

I wonder if there have been other disappearances. Is that why nobody is talking to Wolven? She was young to be part of the Sazi law enforcement branch, and only a few people even knew she was active. But the agent on duty in Luna Lake didn't seem to be sending in reports of anything abnormal . . . or at least, nobody admitted to getting them. She was being planted in the town by the Sazi Council to find out what was happening. Her primary task was to find out why people were missing from the official reports, even though the town leaders claimed everyone was accounted for. While it was likely just a clerical error, it could be dangerous if someone was hiding something. Thankfully, because she was bound to the

Texas wolf pack, she could mentally contact her pack leaders, Adam and Cara Mueller—Wolven agents and police officers both—in a crisis. She had to work hard to make the connection work and it gave her a bad headache, but it was better than nothing. "Is there anything I can do? Once we arrive, I mean."

Danielle put up a helpless hand. The wet scent of sorrow filled the car, smothering the sour panic. "I don't know. Maybe. We can use every set of eyes. Maybe, as an outsider, you'll see something the rest of us are missing."

An outsider. It seemed strange to be considered an outsider in a town that was all Sazi. No shifter should ever be considered an outsider. That was the whole point of the encampments that had been formed after the plague: to welcome and protect Sazi of all species. Claire tried hard to project confidence into the car. The gift of empathy was still new to her and she wasn't very good at projecting emotions yet. But the healer back in Texas had told her it could be a valuable tool for investigating once she was more skilled. She only knew she was succeeding when the hot metal scent of determination rode up over the musty damp smell of fear.

"Anything I can do," she said firmly.

They went back to watching the dark landscape slip by in a blur while Claire struggled to keep Danielle's fear from overwhelming her. She couldn't afford to become an amplifier of someone else's negativity. She tried to concentrate on the bits of roadside that were highlighted in the headlamps for brief seconds: a speed limit sign, which they were presently exceeding by at least ten; then red and yellow leaves that whisked into the air, swirling around the hood and over the roof; even a bright bit of metal in the grass, shining silver before disappearing. But it was no use—the more silence that passed, the more time she had to dwell on possibilities, and the greater the fear grew. Claire needed to take Danielle's mind off the situation. "Tell me a little about Luna Lake. Where might the kids have spent the day if they didn't go to their friends'?"

Danielle shrugged. "I've been wondering the same thing. There's not much to the town. There's no arcade or anything and no mall. The nearest town is Republic, but it's too far to walk. There's an ice cream store but that's the first place Mama checked. S.Q.'s a sucker for little kids with wide eyes. Gives them so many free samples that they wind up sick in the morning. Of course, that means every kid in town hangs out there." She must have realized Claire didn't know the people in town, because she explained. "S.Q. Wrill . . . with a *W* . . . owns Polar Pops on Main Street. She's a nice lady but you'd think a falcon would have more brains. I swear she'd forget her head if it wasn't attached."

"S.Q.? That's her real name? Just initials?"

"It's sure what I'd call *myself* if I had her given name. Everyone blends the letters and calls her Skew. Her mama should have been ashamed." Danielle shook her head as the road slipped by. She didn't continue until Claire prompted.

"Which is?"

"I'll have to spell it. S-e-n-s-a-b-i-l-l-e. Her middle name is Quille, with an *e* at the end. I mean . . . *really?* Her mama must have been high as a kite when that poor girl was born." She tsked, clucking her tongue like a chicken, and then sighed.

Claire struggled not to laugh out loud. *Wow. Sensabille . . . Quille . . . Wrill. No kidding, poor girl.* But this was all great stuff. Not only would learning about the people in Luna Lake keep Danielle occupied, but Claire would learn a ton about the town. Already the scents in the car were lightening. "Interesting. What else is there to keep kids occupied? Is there a playground?"

"Oh, sure. Back behind the school. The whole town pitched in to build it. Monkey bars, teeter-totter, swings . . . even a climbing wall. But they keep it fenced off so nobody uses it after school."

Claire let out a small laugh. "Fences never kept me out when I was a kid. I'd climb over, slip under. Nothing could keep me from the swings. Made me feel like I was flying."

The owl shifter flicked a glance her way. "Oh, swings feel *nothing* like flying. Trust me."

There wasn't anything to say to that, and Claire was grateful beyond measure she would never know. Her life would have been totally different if she'd gotten wings instead of fur. Totally, frighteningly different. She fought to keep from shuddering. "But the kids had never shifted, right? So they couldn't just hop over the fence?"

"*Puleeze*." Danielle's voice held scorn. "Sazi designed the fence. We have birds of all sorts, cats that can jump two stories high, wolves that can dig through near-solid stone. You can't just *hop over*. It's no ordinary fence. You'll have to see it to understand."

Danielle slowed the car, flipped on the blinker, and made a turn onto a much narrower paved road. There were no shoulders and no striping. But there was a sign, the only indication of where they were. They would arrive in Luna Lake in ten miles.

Claire asked, "Why bother to block off the playground? It's not like the kids will get hurt. They'll heal." It was the longstanding saying among their kind. Nearly anything would heal. No wound was too bad. Head and heart both had to be damaged to kill.

Danielle's voice was surprised, but the underlying scent that rode the air to Claire was haunted, filled with sorrow, fear, and pain. "Nobody heals since the plague. Where have you been? Hardly anyone heals better than full humans. We're really cautious because we lost our healer last winter. We don't know why she died."

Wow. Claire struggled to wrap her mind around that. When the Sazi were attacked, nearly a decade ago now, by family members who had created a magically-charged chemical that "cured" shapeshifters and made them human again, it became a plague, devastating their kind. Exposure to the cure was like a toxin and had killed many and caused madness in others. But what would it take to kill a *healer* short of major injuries? "In Texas, the kids run around like wild animals. It's a rare day someone isn't digging cactus spines from their legs and arms, or getting treated for snake bites." Like Luna Lake, the Tedford Compound was remote, but they had the luxury of several healers nearby and most of the pack was healthy. "Have you applied to the Council for a new healer?"

Danielle let out a snort as she turned on the wipers to knock a layer of dead bugs from the windshield. "You must have some sort of magic potion down there then. That's not how it works up here. We've applied for a new healer dozens of times. I don't think the Council even remembers we exist. We haven't had a Councilman visit or call in years."

Again Claire felt a moment of shock. A member of the Sazi High Council was through her town every few months. Was it really that different up here, or were the townsfolk in Luna Lake being fed a line? She couldn't smell or sense any deception from Danielle. On first impression, it appeared she really believed that they had been set adrift by the Sazi hierarchy.

"Of course," Danielle continued. "It's not that different from the human government. The area struggles. So we have to be pretty self-sufficient. We're on the only road close to town that doesn't need repairs. You need a jeep for some of the back roads. We do the best we can with the money we have." She paused and then sighed. "But it would be nice if we could get a doctor. We can't take the kids to the hospital in Republic. What if they did a blood test?"

We'll check into it. Count on it.

Claire faintly heard the voice of her pack leader, Adam Mueller, in her mind and it made her feel better to know they were there and could still hear through her ears, even though the contact made her temples throb sharply.

She knew both Adam and Cara would take action on what she observed. But Danielle . . . in fact, none of the people in Luna Lake could know it was being worked on. She steeled herself for the pain that made nerves scream through her skull and replied to her pack leaders the same way. *Please be discreet. Otherwise, it did no good to send me here.*

One word rang through her mind, bearing the distinctive Tejano accent she'd come to know from her surrogate mother. *Duh.*

It nearly made her laugh and Claire had to struggle not to let her amusement show in her face or scent. So she immediately concentrated on what it would feel like to have a child in the house who was injured where they couldn't go to a human doctor, and a Sazi one was days or weeks away. "Sorry to hear about your healer. Are there a lot of elderly in town? How many kids?"

Danielle nodded. "A fair number. We just have one school in town, K through twelve. There's about fifty students. There's probably two hundred total Sazi in and around Luna Lake, scattered around. About half of the adults are over forty. It was bigger right after the first attack, but not everybody's suited to life up here. The people who came from big cities wound up moving to other compounds, closer to sewer systems and grocery stores."

Claire nodded in agreement. "Yeah, same problem at the Tedford Compound. Not everybody is up for the heat and cacti, or boiling well water to drink and wash in, or using outhouses where we can't even put in septic systems."

A flash of light outside the car caught Claire's eye and she pointed out the windshield. "What in the world is *that?*" The green glow seemed to pulse with a life of its own. It swooped and danced in the black sky like dragon dancers at Chinese New Year. It disappeared and reappeared through the towering treetops along the road.

"Ooo!" Danielle slowed the car and moved to the side at a spot where there were fewer trees and they could see the sky. "It's the northern lights. We don't see them often, and they always seem to be green when they appear this far south."

Claire had seen videos of the northern lights, but had never seen them in person. It was surreal. Once the car was fully stopped, she opened her car door, which made Danielle nervous. "We can't stay more than a second. We really need to get to town soon."

"A second is all I need. I just want to see it without the glass." The image drew her, pulled her to stand up, one foot still on the floorboards of the car. The scents of the night hit her nose in a rush, adding to the frozen moment. The air was so incredibly *clean*. Crisp, powerful, filled with pine and apples, and with a hint of far distant snow on the wind. A variety of animal scents made her turn her head this way and that, but she never took her eyes off the dancing lights. Deer in the deep brush, birds in the trees, along with musky plant eaters she had no name for yet. Possibly elk or moose. Or maybe even bear. She'd never smelled them before.

After a few moments, she was satisfied and started to get back in the car. But movement in the darkness caught her eye. Whatever was pushing against her senses was large—as big as the car, at least. But though she tried, flaring her nostrils and inhaling deeply, she couldn't smell a thing. It was as though the rest of her senses were lying to her. Claire hadn't been born a Sazi; she'd become one after she'd learned to rely on senses other than her nose. And what her eyes and the prickling hairs on her neck told her was she needed to leave. Now. She slid back inside the car, grabbing her seat belt on the way down. "We need to go. Hurry!"

"Wha—" But apparently the look on Claire's face, her scent, or maybe she'd accidentally pressed onto the owl shifter a bit of her own urgency . . . something was enough to silence Danielle. She slammed the gearshift down and hit the gas, hard enough that it threw Claire back against her headrest.

The car lurched sideways when something impacted the back door on the driver's side. Danielle let out a small screech and tightened her grip on the steering wheel until her knuckles were white. The car leaped forward. Claire felt her own fingers tighten on the armrest. She kept checking the rearview mirror, but there was nothing to see in the darkness behind them. That didn't stop her heart from racing or a low growl from building in her chest. The wolf part of her wanted to turn and fight. The human side knew that anything capable of making a moving car swerve was nothing to mess with. She glanced at the instrument panel. Their speed was sixty and increasing. The little car's engine wasn't very powerful and eighty was the best they could hope for. That should have been plenty fast enough to outrun any animal on the planet, and any Sazi short of a Council member.

It wasn't.

The tires squealed against the pavement when an unseen something hit the back bumper, pushing them forward and then sideways. Danielle turned into the skid as though on an icy road and they shot forward again. They were only a few miles from town now. Most predators, human or otherwise, wouldn't risk continuing an attack where they could be seen. "C'mon, c'mon. Move, you piece of junk." Danielle was whispering but the words seemed loud to Claire.

The landscape whizzed by as seconds passed. The sour,

bitter scent of panic burned her nose every time Claire inhaled.

Just when the lights of the town appeared around a bend,
an unearthly howl filled the car and the world upended in a
rush of metal, glass . . . and pain.

CHAPTER 2

The phone rang once, then twice, dragging Alek from a deep, dreamless slumber. He slapped around on the nightstand until he found the portable and pulled it to his ear. "'Lo?"

The tired baritone that spoke made him groan and want to hang up. "I'm sorry, Alek. I am. I know you're tired, but is there any chance that—"

"This is the first night I've had off in a week. I'm not tired, Lenny. I'm *exhausted*. I know you're busy and I know the kids need to be found, but if I don't get a few hours' sleep, I won't be any good to anyone. I spent the last two hours working on Mrs. Wilson's computer and I still don't have the spreadsheets run for the city Council meeting." Alek yawned so wide his jaw popped painfully. He buried his head back under his pillow, taking the phone with him. He wanted to hang up. A quick press of the button was all it would take. But his finger wouldn't move. He had to find out what the problem was first. Was this going to be his life after the police academy too? Never a moment's rest? Always responding to everyone else's problems?

"It's not the search, Alek. It's Denis."

Crap. He really should have hung up. Whatever it was

would serve his stupid, egotistical brother right. But . . . "Is he hurt?" He bit his tongue before he added *this time* to the sentence. He threw the blanket and sheet off and swung his feet to the floor. He wouldn't be able to close his eyes tonight. No chance.

Lenny's sigh sounded frustrated over the speaker. "He's fine. But he was picked up about an hour ago, tagging the wall of the bathrooms at the lake."

Alek ran fingers through his hair and padded toward the closet, feeling sick to his stomach—both from the lack of sleep and the knowledge of what lay ahead. "Which means a curfew violation too. You going to charge him with vandalism?"

"I don't have any choice, Alek. He wasn't arrested by us. A county deputy was on a call of nature and startled him . . . got a face full of paint for his trouble." Alek winced and groaned as Lenny continued. "Denis was caught red-handed. Well, black-handed. Literally. He was still holding the spray paint. He's damned lucky he didn't get a charge for assault on a police officer."

Alek's mind started working at top speed. Curfew was a pack regulation, not a county one. The vandalism was on town property. But the lake was a county recreation area. So . . . was it county or town property? It could at least be argued to be town. But if the deputy pressed for assault . . . yes, it was only a Class C felony. But it would mean time in a county jail. At least a couple of months, with *humans*. And while Denis hadn't yet shifted for his first time, he came from strong wolf genes. He was sixteen, so his first shift was overdue. It could happen anytime. Especially if he was under a lot of stress. Like being in jail.

Crap.

"Was he taken to the county jail? Is he in Republic?"

Lenny's sigh was one of relief. "Thankfully, no. Their

jail is full right now from the big festival this weekend. They didn't have a cell to spare. I got the impression the deputy didn't have time to do the paperwork for such a minor offense, so he turned Denis over to me and told me there wouldn't be any *county* charges." There was a pause, where Alek started to feel his heart beat again. But then his hopes were dashed.

"But I can't sweep it under the rug this time, Alek. The deputy actually stressed the word *county*. They're going to be watching to see what I do. You know everyone has been watching us more closely, especially with all the rogues lately. They're starting to believe there's something odd going on here. I'm going to have to bring at least misdemeanor charges against him. You can bail him out, but he'll have to go to court, and have a few weeks in jail to think about things. But I can keep him locally and seal the records since he's a minor. We'll make sure nothing . . . *unfortunate* happens."

"You want me to come down and pick him up?"

"He told me to call *you*. Not John or Asylin. Told me you'd drop everything to come get him."

That spoiled brat. The worst part was, he'd been right every previous time. Alek had promised his mother as she was dying that he'd take care of Denis. He hadn't anticipated it would be an all-consuming lifelong task. Alek looked up at the clock. It was nearly midnight. "Yeah. I'll get him. But tell him you couldn't reach me. Let him stew for a bit."

"No problem." Lenny paused. Alek started pulling on a pair of black jeans and a sweater. "We'll make sure he gets some food and a cot. And Alek . . . I'll do what I can to keep this low-key. The background checks they do at the police academy won't find it."

That stopped Alek cold. He'd heard Lenny say he couldn't sweep it under the rug *this time*, but it hadn't fully sunk in. Could he be rejected at the academy because of his brother?

It hadn't occurred to him that Lenny had swept other things under that same rug. But thinking about it—it should have. Damn it! "No. No, Lenny. I don't want you to hide anything or bury it. The last thing I want to do starting off a career in law enforcement is fixing crimes. The human cops would just reject me. Wolven would do worse."

Lenny made a snorting sound loud enough that it reached Alek's ear from where the phone rested on the bed. "I *am* Wolven in this town, Alek. Wolven won't take a strip of hide for protecting your brother."

Which is one of the things I want to change if I make the cut. But he couldn't say that to Lenny. He put on a heavy sock and boot, his fingers almost too numb to make the motions, his eyes burning with the need for sleep. It was on the police chief's watch that the humans started sniffing around. Lenny might think the sheriff and state troopers weren't terribly bright, but Alek knew better. There was a good reason why humans were the dominant species on the planet, and why the plague had successfully killed off half the Sazi. "I appreciate your support, Lenny." He did too. Denis would probably be in prison by now if not for the older man. But he wasn't doing anyone any favors by treating Denis like a mischievous little boy. He was nearly a grown man. Pretty soon, tagging and smoking dope would lead to meeting the wrong people. Denis claimed to love the "rush" of sneaking around. But soon small rushes wouldn't be enough.

"Why don't you just go back to sleep, Alek? I'll keep him overnight. He'll be safe here. I'll have Mary bring him some of the venison roast she made for dinner tonight." Fatherly, kind. But far too willing to bend the rules. It made Alek crazy. He'd come from a similar environment in Chicago and it had nearly meant Denis's death when he was only six. He'd much rather have Wolven agents who led by example and made people toe the line.

"I might just do that." Might. Not will. No, he was going
to the lake to see what he could find. He wanted to get some
pictures of the tagging . . . in case it vanished by morning. He
hated to think Lenny might do that. But he wouldn't put it
past the older man. "Thanks for calling, Lenny. I appreciate
it. Bye." He hung up without waiting for an answer, his usual
habit with people in town who couldn't seem to stop talking,
asking for one more thing, even though the call was over.

Alek's muscles protested as he filled his pockets with wal-
let, keys, and other sundry things. But he kept moving; if he
stopped, he would probably drop to the ground and sleep
where he fell. So many hours of searching for Kristy and Darrell. But he'd keep searching until he found them. They'd
been his sister and brother for the past decade. They were
family.

Wait.

His mind started to replay what Lenny had said. Denis was
at the *lake*? And he'd been snuck up on? But there should
have been a dozen people out there, just like the past two
nights. Unless they'd been called off . . .

Why did he always have to think of things just a split second too late? If he called the chief now, it would look suspicious. It had been obvious from recent conversations that
Lenny already thought that Alek was overly curious. Would
he get out to the lake just to discover a dozen people there
and no vandalism to be found? Maybe.

Would Denis lie about the facts to cover his own butt? Absolutely.

The only thing Alek could do was hurry.

Before he left, caution made him look out the window.
Somehow he was not surprised to see a police car across the
street. Parked with its lights off, it was running, the tailpipe
drifting exhaust into the breeze. So, he was being watched.

He pulled his keys from his pocket and regarded his motor-cycle, parked in full view of the squad car.

Was Denis even *in* jail, or was this all some sort of setup? Was Alek himself under suspicion? He *had* been the only one to discover any evidence in the Williams case—adult footprints on the roadside next to tracks from a kid's bike tire. They'd found no sign of the bike itself, but Lenny had congratulated Alek and said he'd have photos taken. Had that happened? It was times like this he wished he was more powerful, that he could sit on the town Council and have access to more information.

He tossed his key ring in his hand while he thought, the jingle sounding like chimes against the wind outside. Yes, he could probably manage to sneak out. But not only would it seem really suspicious, it would also leave a deputy sitting alone in his car all night. It wouldn't solve anything and Alek had nothing to hide. No, better to let the deputy follow him and realize there was nothing to see.

Alek slipped on his leather motorcycle jacket and put on his fleece neck guard before picking up his helmet. It wasn't winter yet, but the night wind against his bare neck would give him a sore throat in the morning. He longed for the days when he could heal anything. He used to love cold weather, the wolf in him reveling in the sensation of his nostril hairs freezing with each breath. He remembered broken bones healing almost overnight when he was a kid. But no longer. Not since . . . that night.

Pretending not to notice the police car, Alek walked out of his apartment, straddled his bike, put on his helmet, and eased out onto the main road to the highway. As much as he wanted to hit the gas and lose the squad car on the unpaved back roads where his bike would have a definite advantage, it just wasn't worth it. Not yet. Determined not to think about it, he concentrated on carefully driving the used 750cc bike around the sharp curves of the road, watching carefully for wildlife.

He rounded the corner to the lake, where starlight twinkled, reflected in the water, and noticed the northern lights for the first time. He hadn't seen them for ages, and he always marveled at them. After a moment's pleasure, he lowered his gaze to look for flashlights of searchers. He didn't see any.

A light in the distance pulled his attention away from both the lake and the eerie green glow above. It was a spotlight, at about head height, near the highway, jumping and moving like it was on a trampoline. No, wait. There were two lights— one on top of the other, though they had to be headlights, given their location. Alek slowed the motorcycle, not caring whether the cruiser was still behind him, then turned toward the highway and sped up. That was when he heard the first scream. It wasn't a call for help—it was the sound of pain. Another followed, in a different voice.

The light bar came on behind him—the deputy must have heard the screams too. As he neared what he was certain was a wreck, Alek realized he wasn't looking at a flipped car that had hit a deer or elk. The car was being attacked.

He couldn't make out what it was, just that it was big and it kept smashing into the car. The vehicle tipped over as another scream filled the air, and the lights were suddenly side by side. The relatively small distance between the beams told him it was a small car, a compact, while the way the lights dipped up and down made him think the car was on its roof now.

Alek was puzzled. Despite his excellent night vision, he couldn't see the attacker clearly, couldn't even tell if it had skin or fur. Only a dozen feet away, he started honking his horn. The reaction wasn't what he expected. Instead of the animal turning tail and running from the attention, it turned toward the approaching vehicles and charged.

That's no human and it's too big to be a wolf. It could be a cat shifter or even a bear, but it was so freaking *big*! Alek remembered in his youth when Sazi Council members would visit the hotel where he lived with his mother and the rest of the Chicago pack. This beast reminded him of some of the bear Council members. Was it a rogue Sazi who'd gone insane? It wouldn't be the first since the plague.

It was sure fast enough to be a Sazi. It closed the distance between the overturned car and the two oncoming vehicles in just a few lopes. One long arm reached out and Alek barely managed to leap from his bike before the motorcycle was swept from the roadway and thrown into the air with a screech of metal. The animal didn't seem to break a sweat at the effort.

The police car roared forward as Alek went flying across the road.

Alek's last thought as he impacted with the ground was, *He has to see that thing! Why isn't he stopping?* Then his arm slammed down onto the uneven, rocky ground, sending a shock of pain through him. Gravel ripped through the heavy leather to embed in his arm and neck. Bright stars exploded in his vision as his helmeted head bounced off two rocks, then three, as he rolled and slid down into the drainage ditch.

Screeching tires and the smell of burnt rubber were followed by an unearthly howl. Alek forced himself to roll hard and fast, coming back up on his feet. The black animal was gone. His motorcycle was upside down against a tree, no longer running, and missing a front wheel. The squad car had stopped at an angle across the road, the front quarter on the passenger side badly dented. The damage was bigger than could be caused by a deer . . . bigger even than an elk hit he'd once seen. What the hell was that thing that it could walk away from that kind of impact?

But there was no time to think. That thing could come back at any moment. He had to see if everyone was okay. He went to the squad car first and found Ray Vasquez out cold behind the wheel. The air bag had gone off; Alek pulled open the door and carefully leaned Ray back, away from the air bag. The deputy's pulse seemed steady. Alek saw some swelling around one eye—that would be a doozy of a black eye in the morning—but the air bag had done its job.

He hurried to the small car. As he drew near, he recognized the scent of the person driving, but couldn't believe it. Pulling a small flashlight from his pocket, he shone the light into the car. It was Dani! He hadn't known his sister was coming back from school. Her face was a mass of bruises and scratches, turning the chocolate skin purple and red. Whether it was from the animal or the accident or both, he didn't know. Unconscious, she was hanging upside down from her seat belt. Blood dripped slowly down her forehead to land on the tan roof liner and the remnants of her car's air bag. He checked her pulse. It was thready and she was wheezing with each breath. Alek frowned, knowing she needed medical attention. She wasn't anywhere close to an alpha, so even though the full moon had just passed, she had nearly human healing abilities. Damn.

He had to lay flat on his stomach to see the passenger. The woman was half out the passenger window, as though she'd been trying to get out of the car. He studied her back and legs but saw no movement. She didn't look like she was breathing and a gash on her scalp was oozing blood. He could smell that she was barely alive though he could feel magical energy rise from her. But it was weakening every moment.

He started around the front of the car, trying to remember his CPR training, then stopped. First he needed to get some people headed this direction. Racing back to the squad car, he reached past Ray's unconscious form to grab the radio's mic. "Dispatch, Eighteen Siska here. Come back." He'd been given an employee number during his work on the suicide hotline. It was easier to call in emergencies to the surrounding hospitals with an official designation. But was there a signal here? It was always hit or miss the farther outside town a car traveled.

"Go ahead, Eighteen. What's up, Alek?" Good. It was Marilyn Bearbird on shift tonight. The golden eagle shifter was a former combat medic in the Army and had been acting as the town's nurse for about a year now.

"We've got a multi-car hit and run on southbound Black Creek Road, about seven miles outside of town. Vasquez is out cold but stable. Additional casualties with unknown injuries. Get an ambulance here, stat. I'm going to start CPR on the passenger now. Come back."

"Ten-four, Eighteen." It was Lenny's voice now. "Marilyn's getting her gear and is dispatching to your location. What in the hell happened out there?"

He told the truth, at least as much of it as he was willing to discuss over an open radio line. "Not a clue. Just get here fast. We're right on a blind curve. I don't have time to dig out and set flares if this woman's going to live. Eighteen out."

Alek dropped the radio and checked Ray's pulse again. *He'll be okay when he wakes up.* He looked down the dark roadway. Hopefully the flashing red-and-blue bar and the squad car's headlights would be visible at the road's sharp turn. Hopefully nobody was joyriding out here tonight. Sighing, he headed back to the passenger side of the little Toyota.

The woman's hair was matted with blood from multiple scalp wounds. Thankfully, whatever that animal had been hadn't managed to crack her skull open. Despite the bleeding, the cuts seemed superficial as far as he could tell.

Unfortunately, he had no idea what sort of internal injuries she might have. And she wasn't breathing. That had to be first. As carefully as he could, he removed the weeds and debris from her face.

Underneath the blood, she was stunning. She looked to be in her early twenties with wheat-blond, shoulder-length hair. Her face was pale but perfect. She was medium height and slender under black jeans and a simple red pullover sweater. The scent that rose from her was wolf but unfamiliar, a type he'd never encountered. It was intoxicating, made his head spin. He caught his breath, held the smell in his nose, let it pour over him like honey. Even the roots of his hairs prickled, like they were moving to music. Nothing like this had ever happened to him before.

His mind tried to define the scent that captivated him. It was cinnamon and chocolate, with snow on the wind and hot coals. She smelled like those moments right after sledding, when you race inside to sit beside the fireplace with a mug of hot chocolate, and can smell the apple pie baking in the oven.

It wasn't a scent that should be covered with blood on a roadside. The discordance of his reaction and his surroundings froze him in place.

The breeze shifted and the overpowering scent of feathers, fear, and pain from inside the car washed over him. Alek shook his head and began to focus. He took the woman's pulse and checked her airway. There were no visible wounds on her torso and her ribs didn't seem to be broken. But he couldn't risk doing heart compression until he knew if there was damage to her spine. He leaned down to begin mouth-to-mouth. The moment his lips touched hers, he seemed to sink into a pool of molten heat. The sensation stole the very breath he'd planned to give her.

Alek pulled back sharply and stared at the woman, his heart racing like nothing he'd ever experienced. He felt shaken and disturbingly aroused. Good god! This woman was unconscious, needed his help. What was he thinking?

Fighting his reaction, he took a deep breath, pinched her nose shut and closed his mouth over hers again. Same reaction but this time his fingers started to tingle. He blew the life-giving air into her lungs and tried to concentrate on the mechanics of resuscitation.

His world narrowed to inhale-puff-inhale-puff as dizzying sensations washed over his skin. There was no response. He was starting to get worried.

Where was Marilyn?

CHAPTER 3

Light and pain ripped at Claire's mind as she struggled to breathe. She felt warmth on her mouth. The scent of male wolf, mingled with cologne and fear, filled her, even though her nose was plugged. But she couldn't seem to take a breath . . . couldn't control her muscles. She felt blackness closing around her.

Claire. You have to breathe. Inhale, niña.

She wanted to obey her Alpha female. She did. But she couldn't seem to make things work.

No. Hell, no.

That was her Alpha male's voice, faint but clear. She felt magic try to press through the pack's mental link. It was just a thread, but it came just as soft lips pressed against hers, pushed another bit of air into her lungs. Claire grabbed both ends of the lifeline, using them to pull back into herself.

Her eyes snapped open, her fingers clutched the dried grass under her as she dragged in a great gasp of air. A cacophony of voices filled her ears. Red, blue, and yellow flashing lights reflected off the green glow in the sky.

She inhaled again, deeply, and nearly choked on the overlaid scents, so many that her mind couldn't sort them. She stopped trying and focused on the wolf she'd smelled before, who could only be the dark-haired man whose face was inches from her own. His eyes were the color of the night sky, with scattered gray flecks that glowed with magic like tiny stars. He tried to smile, but the slack face and bowed head told her he was nearly too exhausted. "Welcome back."

She opened her mouth to reply but he put a gentle finger to her lips. "No. Don't try to talk. Just breathe and heal." Magic flickered in that finger, creating sparks against her skin that made it hard to think. He pulled his hand away and stared at his finger, then her.

But she had to move her lips again, ask the question that burned in her mind. It was the barest whisper, so soft he had to move closer to hear her as she mouthed the syllables. The tingle that flowed from his skin to hers made her shudder. "Da . . . Danielle?"

He nodded, and muscles she didn't realize were taut relaxed just a little. "Dani will be fine. They're working on her now. Has a collapsed lung, a broken rib, and she sprained her shoulder. It'll be a while before she flies again."

That made Claire sad. Danielle's voice when she said flying was nothing like the swings had held wonder and joy. "Me?" Another whisper and part of her didn't really want to know. He'd had to bring her back from the dead, after all. She knew that—had felt her own life fading. And everything hurt. Primarily her head, but her insides didn't feel quite right.

He ran fingers through hair that was thick and wavy on top, but cut close on the sides. "The . . . *something* tried to crack your skull open like a walnut. You've got cuts and scrapes and probably internal injuries." He gave her a scolding look. "You weren't wearing your seat belt."

"Was," she disputed in a whisper. "Until . . . attack. Tried . . . fight it."

He gave a little growl but it was only mild rebuke. His scent was filled with pride and admiration.

A woman moved into Claire's field of vision. She smelled of bird—a snowy owl. Claire knew *all* the owl smells. "Alek, go have Marilyn check you out. You need to have some of that gravel dug out of your neck before the skin heals over." So the wolf's name was Alek. Claire's gaze flicked to his neck and she noticed the tattered remains of a scarf and the caked blood on his ripped leather jacket. She felt her brows lower in concern. He quirked his lips in another tired smile before the woman—a nurse, Claire guessed—made shooing motions at him. "Go. We'll take care of . . ." She looked down with calm, professional, hazel eyes. "What's your name, sweetheart?"

Feeling a little stronger, she managed to raise her voice above a whisper. "Cl . . . Claire. Claire Sanchez. From the Tedford Compound." She'd almost used her real name instead of the cover that had been so carefully arranged by her pack. *Hellfire and damnation,* as her grandmother used to say.

The woman nodded like she'd already known the answer even as she readied a syringe of clear liquid. "Thought as much since you were with Danielle. I'm Roberta. We'll call your pack leaders. Let them know what's happened."

She nodded, even though her pack leaders already knew. *Let the doctor work on you. Relax,* niña. Claire nodded again, letting the warmth and concern of her pack fill her as the needle pricked her arm to deliver her into soothing, pain-free darkness.

CHAPTER 4

Alek squatted down next to the front of the police cruiser, straining to find clues as to the kind of animal it had hit to cause the crumpled fender and bumper. There should be blood and lots of it, as well as fur or skin that could be tested. But it was clean.

"What'cha looking for, Alek?" Lenny's voice came from behind him. It sounded casual, but there was tension behind it.

Trying to keep his voice just as casual, Alek shrugged one shoulder, keeping his hands in his pockets so the chief wouldn't see the latex gloves on them that he'd borrowed from the ambulance. Secreted in his pocket were also tweezers and several plastic baggies to gather evidence. "Just seeing what there is to see."

"I've already been over the bumper. Got blood samples and tissue. We'll get it tested and see who was responsible. You have insurance on the bike, right?"

Alek nodded. "Of course. It just seems strange there's so little evidence for such a large collision." He'd been trying to keep the passenger alive and had been getting rocks picked out of his shoulder for the better part of an hour while the chief had been gathering clues. Why would it be so clean? No blood, no hair, the bumper was so squeaky clean he could see his own reflection and the scent of window cleaner still hovered in the air.

"Not really so strange, if you think about it. It was probably a bear. They have damned tough hides. Even regular bears can take a lot of damage without bleeding."

That made Alek pause. What Lenny said was true, but it didn't fit with what he remembered. "Are you thinking it was a rogue?"

"Nah, probably just a big grizzly. Might have been a mama protecting a cub."

Alek's gaze flicked to the shredded metal that used to be the driver's door. There was no way in hell this was caused by a grizzly. They were tough. No doubt about that. He'd seen photos of the interiors of cars ripped to shreds when a bear was looking for food or got trapped inside. But not like this . . . like the sheet metal of the car was aluminum foil at the bottom of a pan of lasagna that got cut into ribbons by the spatula. "I've never seen a grizzly that could cause this kind of damage, Lenny."

A firm hand landed on his shoulder and then patted him. "You're still young, Alek. You haven't seen a lot of things I have. You still have a lot to learn."

Also true, but condescending as hell. It deserved no reply, so he didn't give it one. Instead, he glanced to his left and saw that Ray Vasquez was finishing getting patched up on the rear bumper of the ambulance. He worked the gloves off of his hands by rolling them along the inside of his pockets before removing his hands and used his palm against the bumper to get the leverage to stand. He turned to face the chief. "I should go see how Ray is doing. When will you need my report of the accident? I thought I might get a little sleep before I came to the office." Alek used the back of his hand to rub his eye. Yep, his fingers smelled of chemical cleaner.

If the chief noticed what Alek was doing, he gave no sign.

But his eyes narrowed and his scent was the burned coffee smell of anger. "I guess you should have thought about sleep before you hopped on your motorcycle and started gallivanting around the county in the middle of the night."

Alek felt cool air on his eyes as they widened in surprise. He raised his eyes to meet Lenny's—in direct challenge and couldn't stop the anger that punctuated the words. "If I hadn't been *gallivanting around*, those girls would be dead now. It was a damned good thing I was out here, don't you think?"

The other man shrugged, pursing his lips briefly. "Maybe they would, maybe not. But I know if you'd stayed at home where you belong, I'd still have a working cruiser and you'd still have a motorcycle."

"Are you *serious!?*" Alek seldom raised his voice to the town's Second, but his outrage slipped out. "We're talking about two *lives*, versus a couple of vehicles. They can be replaced in a few days. You can't possibly think they're even worth talking about in the same sentence."

He stared at Lenny, waiting for a chink in the armor. The taller man finally spoke and they were the right words. "Of course, you're right. I'm glad they're safe. Money's a little tight right now, but the car can be replaced." But while the words backpedaled, they were only words. There was no metallic scent of ozone that would mark relief, nor the warm, musty scent of gratitude. Just burning scents . . . coffee, metal, water, pepper. He didn't care at all about the girls and was pissed at Alek for being here. Why? There was something going on and he would figure it out, with or without the chief's help.

"So, what time do you need the report?"

Lenny stared at him for a long moment. "Just give a witness statement to Ray while you're cleaning up this mess. He can write it up. And make sure it's done before people need to get to work in the morning. I don't want anyone calling in a report that there was an accident. We don't need the county or state people involved."

Alek took a long look around. Debris littered the scene, and while the road wasn't used by hundreds of people, a few dozen cars would be coming this way to get to work at the mines in the area. And while Alek knew this was Lenny's way of punishing him, it wasn't Vasquez's fault. "You can't seriously expect Ray to bend over to pick stuff up with that lump on his head? He could have a concussion. And I can't use one shoulder." He looked down at the sling that Marilyn had insisted he wear so the wounds that needed stitches had a chance to heal. He was supposed to leave it on for at least a day, maybe two.

Lenny shrugged and then turned to walk back toward his cruiser. "I guess you'll be doing all the picking up while he supervises. Work it out. I'm going to bed, but I'll be coming back at dawn and it had better be done. If it's not . . . well, let's just say a little cloth sling won't be enough to fix what will be wrong with you."

Alek shook his head in disbelief, too angry to decide how to respond.

Ray Vasquez put a light hand on his good shoulder. "Let it go, Alek. He's been a pissy S.O.B. for the past month. I have no idea why, but it's just best to stay off his radar right now." When Alek looked, Ray's face was a mass of angry red and one eye was already being encompassed by purple bruising.

Lenny smacked a palm against the side of the rescue truck. "Get this heap moving, Roberta. Marilyn will need your help back at the clinic." He got in his car and turned off the light bar, plunging the area into darkness, punctuated only by the vehicle's taillights.

The woman scrambled to obey. She pulled one item out of the back to set on the ground before slamming the back doors shut. She jumped in the cab of the truck to follow the chief's cruiser back to town.

Ray let out a sigh. "Crap. That sucks."

"What's that?" Alek was sort of glad to see the retreating lights.

"I'd hoped the rescue truck would stay. We could really use the headlights to pick stuff up and the flashing lights would probably keep the bear at bay while we clean."

Work it out. The words took on a sinister new meaning as Ray's words sank home. The darkness seemed to close in around him. While he could see just fine in the dark to walk, picking up bits of plastic, glass, and metal from the vehicles with no light was going to be a challenge. He only had a small penlight in his pocket. He pulled it out and flicked the button. Thankfully it still worked. Alek shone it around the area, the narrow beam lighting on the object Roberta had taken out of the back of the truck. He let out a little laugh. "I owe that woman a bouquet of flowers."

Ray smiled just a bit, his mouth crooked where the swelling had claimed the muscles. "I'll buy the candy."

Alek had never been so glad to see that little red-and-black box. The emergency LED light tower from the rescue truck would give them plenty of light to work for at least five hours and more if they conserved. It would hopefully also keep the creature that attacked them, if it was still alive, at bay.

"We'd better get started before our muscles start to seize up," Ray said heavily. "I'm not looking forward to pushing the cruiser all the way back to town, especially with a flat tire."

"Pushing—?"

That's when it occurred to Alek. Their only option to clean up the scene was to put everything inside the police cruiser and Dani's car, including the remains of his motorcycle, and push them back to town.

"Bastard."

Ray snorted. "He was, you know. Lenny's mom screwed her boss and wound up pregnant. The boss refused to acknowledge him and skipped out on support." He paused. "But I never told you that."

Alek laughed before bending down to pick up the pieces of the shattered headlight of his motorcycle. The sharp pain from the movement made him suck in a sudden breath. He'd almost forgotten the cracked rib and swollen hip until then.

It was going to be a long night.

CHAPTER 5

*T*he scents of clean cotton, pine, and cinnamon brought Claire to slow, lazy consciousness. Her eyes flickered open. The ceiling above her was planked with hand-hewn boards stained the color of honey. She was definitely in a bedroom, not a hospital, but where? Tentatively stretching various muscles, she was surprised at the pain. She normally healed quickly, which told her the injuries had been severe. She was dressed in a long-sleeved, old-fashioned cotton gown with lace and tiny roses sprinkled on the white cloth. It was warm and comfy and would have been far too heavy for any time of year in Texas. But here and now it was perfect. She wanted to snuggle deeper under the quilt and try to sleep more. But no, it was time to get moving. No rest for the wicked.

She made the mistake of sitting up.

The sudden pain in her head was so intense that she had to struggle not to vomit. She put her hands to her temples with a gasp of shock and discovered a crown of gauze over veins that pulsed frantically. She lay back down and the pounding eased slightly. *Great. A concussion. Just what I didn't need to start this investigation.* The EMT couldn't have known or they wouldn't have let her sleep through the night. Or, they figured she was Sazi enough to get over it. Technically, that was true. But it wasn't going to be pretty.

Moving her head slowly, Claire looked around the room. Most of the furniture was handmade and there were personal touches scattered around the room, probably mementos of the owner's former life. A crystal sculpture of a unicorn threw rainbows of light across the polished floor, a Mets ball cap hung on a hook over the closet door, and a graduation announcement from Richmond Hill High in Queens was casually pinned to a corkboard mounted on one wall. There weren't any wolf packs in New York, and few cats. Probably birds.

She inhaled again, slow and deep, and listened closely. Whispers now beneath her feet, too low to make out. The fluffy, warm scent of owl down. She was probably at the Williams house, then. It was where she was supposed to stay, after all. She wished she knew how she'd gotten here. Or what had really happened last night. All she could remember was a hulking dark creature that could outrun a speeding car, and the star-filled black eyes of a wolf named Alek.

And oh, that smile, even a tired one. He must be a local, so she should be able to run into him again. She'd like to make a better second impression. . . .

Hello? Mind back in the game, Claire . . .

She wasn't sure whether that thought came from her pack leaders or her own mind, but it was true. She wasn't here for dating opportunities.

Showering was a pain in the tail with the bandages on but the moment she touched her head and arm, the pain told her they needed to stay until a healer looked her over. That left her hair, which was stringy and slightly pink below the snow-white gauze. She solved it by lathering floral shampoo into her palm and then balling her hair into her palm so she didn't pull on her scalp. It felt like there were stitches under the gauze but didn't know the extent of them. Rinsing the hair was tough without getting the bandages wet, but she managed. Sort of. The shampoo probably didn't rinse out completely, but oh well. At least it wasn't bloody anymore.

The short sleeves didn't hide the gauze wrapped around her bicep, snow white against her darkly tanned skin. But that was actually good, because they didn't press against them either. She tucked her Army knife in her back pocket, determined she'd keep it close while she was here. She was just trying to find a way to put on her shoes without bending over—because she'd discovered bending over brought back the sensation that she needed to upchuck—when there was a light knock on the door.

"Claire? Are you up yet?" It was Danielle.

"Just finishing dressing. Come on in."

The door opened and Claire winced at the sight of her new friend's face. "Ouchie. That looks like it hurts." Swollen nearly beyond recognition, Danielle's face looked almost grotesque. Her eyes were narrow slits. Several cuts on her forehead and cheek had been stitched, giving her a Frankenstein appearance.

The other woman shrugged the shoulder that wasn't in a sling. "It doesn't hurt as bad as it looks. The nurse said the swelling should go down in a day or two. Sounds like you got it worse than me." Her scent bore out that Danielle wasn't in much pain but a burst of tangy fear made Claire raise her brows. The owl shifter carefully closed the door behind her. "What *was* that thing?" she asked in a whisper, like nobody was supposed to hear.

Claire shook her head, realized that too was a bad idea and then held up her hands, palms up. "Haven't a clue. I couldn't get a good look at it and for the life of me, Danielle, I couldn't smell a thing." That was embarrassing to admit. She was a wolf and she couldn't *smell* an attacker? She felt heat in her face.

Danielle looked like she wanted to come farther into the

room, to offer or receive some comfort, but was giving her guest careful space. Claire patted the bed next to her and the other woman nearly lunged forward and sat down, relief in her body and scent.

"Thanks for the clothes. I presume they're yours?"

Danielle smiled a tiny bit. "You're a little smaller than me, but luckily long jeans are in this year."

They stared at each other for a long moment, and from the roiling scents in the air, it was obvious neither one knew where to start. Finally, Claire made the decision to be honest. She let out a small breath. "I was never more terrified in my life, Danielle. I'm still amazed I'm alive."

Danielle nodded, tears beginning to brim her eyes. She hugged Claire gently. She was snuffling a little when she pulled away. "Me too. Oh, and call me Dani. Everyone does." She paused for a long moment, as though trying to decide what to say. "Thank you."

That took Claire aback. "For what?"

"It was at the driver's window and it grabbed my arm. I was the target, not you, and we both know it. But you grabbed the steering wheel—"

"And threw us in the ditch," Claire said with chagrin. "I'm responsible for your face and shoulder, you know."

Dani made a scoffing sound. "Girlfriend, what you're responsible for is throwing it off balance. I saw it face-to-face. Its teeth were as long as my forehead, and those eyes . . ." She shuddered visibly and suddenly smelled of fear. "I've never seen anything like it and I've hunted with nearly every species of Sazi. Trust me, flipping into the ditch was definitely better than the alternative."

Claire breathed a sigh of relief. She'd been afraid Dani was going to blame her for the accident. Since she *was* to blame, it would be deserved. "Any news about your sister and brother?"

Dani shook her head sadly. "Nope. And Mama said people have been out searching every minute. I'm worried the police are going to give up soon. It's been four days now. They can't ask for help from the human police agencies, of course, 'cause what if the kids just happened to have their first change and they're in animal form out there? Owls aren't known for mimicking speech."

That seemed unlikely. "It would take a heck of an alpha to shift without help on a first change. Have either of them shown any signs of alphic abilities?"

Dani shook her head, then let out a little laugh. "Well, Kristy *does* run around in circles flapping her arms in the backyard every day. Does that count?"

Missing kids were no laughing matter, but Claire understood the need to relieve tension so she chuckled as well. "Who knows? Maybe she's up in a tree right now, looking down at the house, and she can't change back until the next full moon."

"Hope so. I really do." They sat in silence for a moment, until Dani slapped her palms on her thighs. "Well, we need to get going. I want to join the searchers. Are you ready to meet Mama?"

As ready as I'll ever be. "Sure. Hopefully, there's something to eat downstairs. I could really use some protein."

Dani's mouth turned up on one side and then she mock-whispered. "Never say you're hungry around Mama. She'll fill your belly so full you won't be able to walk." Sunny citrus filled the air to blend with the cinnamon and pine.

A woman's voice drifted up from below their feet. "Did I hear someone say they're hungry?"

Claire started at the coincidence. Dani gave her a mock punch in the arm and stood up. "See? Mama can hear that word a mile away."

Had she really heard it? Had the woman heard everything

Claire and Dani had just said? She'd have to remember that for the future. She put on a smile that hopefully hid her worry.

"Always hate to disappoint the cook of the house." Claire followed slowly as Dani leaped and bounced down the stairs as though she hadn't been in a car wreck the night before. Claire wasn't so lucky. Looking down the stairs made her head spin. But moving slow gave her a chance to look around.

The house was roomy and well-lit by skylights and tall picture windows. Whoever built it was quite a carpenter, based on the elaborate carving on the bannister rails and overhead beams. Flowering plants were set on ledges and tables in nearly every sunny spot in the front room, filling the space with wonderfully complementary scents. Bright, abstract art dotted the walls. Claire could actually imagine herself being happy here if circumstances were different.

"Mama! Our new sis is up and around. Come meet Claire!" Dani grabbed the end cap of the bannister with her good hand and in a practiced move, pivoted around it to land on the long runner rug next to the staircase. A few quick steps took her out of Claire's sight, into a room that was likely the kitchen, given the scent of bacon and eggs emanating from it. Claire's stomach growled audibly.

Following the same path very slowly to avoid her head spinning, Claire found herself in a large kitchen. The only occupant other than Dani was a woman at the stove who turned her head to look at the newcomer. She tried to smile but her eyes were swollen from too many tears. Still, she was doing her best to be welcoming and kind. "I'm sorry Danielle woke you up, Claire. You need your rest after that wreck. I'm Asylin, by the way. I think we talked on the phone. It's nice to finally meet you."

Claire shrugged, a little embarrassed to be imposing on the

family at such a difficult time. "It's okay. Really. I was already up and showered when Dani knocked. It's nice to meet you too, and I'm sorry to hear about what happened. Please don't do anything special or treat me like a guest. If you need to be doing things, do them. If you need *me* to do something, just tell me. Honest. I'll do anything I can to help out." She meant it too. Her goal wasn't to be an imposition on a family struggling to find their kids. Sitting down in the nearest chair, one of many set around a large kitchen table, she decided to just blend in and watch how things played out.

Asylin turned back to the stove and flipped the bacon, not saying anything but nodding slightly. Claire could tell she was crying from the wet scent of sorrow that drifted across the room, stronger than even the bacon, but the worried mother was trying not to let anyone notice. Dani saw it too. She stood up and rushed across the room to embrace her mother from behind with her good arm. "We'll find them, Mama. We will. They're out there. They're just waiting for us to find them." Asylin reached one hand back to stroke her daughter's hair and bent over slightly, her back shaking with quiet sobs. Dani started sobbing as well.

Claire felt her own eyes tearing up. "And they're praying to God that you'll keep looking. That you'll *never stop looking.*" Claire was surprised at the force of her own words, and when the other two women turned and stared at her with something close to alarm, she felt her face burn. "I'm sorry, Mrs. Williams. That was uncalled for. It's not my place to butt in."

To her surprise, Asylin broke away from Dani and rushed across the room to kneel in front of her chair. The older woman put a firm hand on each of her shoulders and looked her in the eye with embarrassment and worry plain in her scent. "Claire, you have nothing to be sorry about. *I'm* the one who's sorry. I shouldn't be throwing these kind of emotions in the air at you. Not with your history. I promise. We won't stop looking. I swear it."

With my history? Claire believed her promise but wasn't sure why she'd phrased it the way she had. At least, not until her Alpha female whispered in her mind with an accompanying throb in her temples. *I had to tell her,* niña. *She had to know about your past in case something you saw there triggered another episode.*

Episode. What an ordinary word to describe the night terrors that had haunted her since she'd been abducted and tortured. It was her Alpha who had rescued her, who had come to her room at night when she'd woken up screaming to hold her, kiss away her tears, and sing to her until she fell back into an uneasy sleep. Her surrogate mother had made sure that when she started shifting, she didn't harm anyone accidentally. It was hard to fault the woman for continuing to try to protect her.

"It's okay." She offered a shaky smile. "It's not your fault." Dani stared at them like she was missing part of the conversation. And she sort of was. Claire decided it wouldn't do any good for only one person in the house to know. Dani would likely find out eventually anyway. She looked over Asylin's shoulder. "I was kidnapped when I was ten."

Dani's hand raised to her suddenly open mouth and a gasp escaped her. After a long moment, she took the hand away and let out a slow breath. "I'm sorry, Claire. But at least you were found. So that gives me hope."

She didn't want to discourage Dani and looked to see whether her mother knew the truth. The look in her eyes said she did, but the scent that rose pleaded with her not to reveal it. So Claire shrugged and gave a little smile, which brightened Dani's face. Asylin, on the other hand, did her best to swallow back the soggy scent of worry, because Claire had not been found. Not then, and not by her parents. She remembered little about her life before her abduction and what she did remember, wasn't worth returning to.

A choking cloud of smoke abruptly enveloped them. Dani immediately turned around and started to cough at the roiling black that rose from the stove. "Oh no! The bacon!" She awkwardly grabbed the heavy cast-iron pan from the stove and moved it over to the sink.

A head-splitting wail filled the air from the smoke detector on the wall, forcing Claire to cover her ears in pain. Asylin started shouting orders. "Claire, open the back door!" She raced to obey, bearing the pain from the noise as she fumbled with the lock before flinging it wide open. The older woman took the pan from the sink outside. Dani started opening windows, one-handed, and then closed the door to the rest of the house to keep the smoke in just one room.

But the door opened immediately from the other side and a dark-skinned balding man rushed in, followed quickly by a fair-skinned teenage boy with blond hair that hung down in his eyes. "What's going on in here?" The man yelled over the din, just as Asylin came back inside. He reached high on the wall and pressed a button on the white detector and there was immediate, blessed silence.

Asylin coughed lightly and started using a dish towel to fan the smoke toward the door. "My fault, John. We got to talking and I forgot to turn off the stove. Lord, what a stench!"

The teenager stared at Claire like it was somehow her fault the smoke was in the room. But not all the burning scent was in the air. A big chunk of it was coming from the boy. He smelled angry and suspicious of her. He also smelled human but she knew from her research that he came from wolf blood.

The older man turned to Claire with a smile. "I'm John, the papa bird of this nest." Claire knew the former military officer was, like Dani, a snowy owl. He motioned to the teenager, who had wormed behind the table and was sulking in the chair in the corner. "This is Denis." Claire offered a little smile and wave, which was met by a glare from under hooded eyebrows. John let out a small noise. "Denis, mind your manners. Say hi to your new sis."

He let out a scoffing sound. "She's not *my* sis."

Asylin turned in a rush. "What did you say?" Her voice had turned from warm and concerned to stern and unyielding. Her hands went to her slender hips and she stepped forward two paces, eyes flashing—her scent cold-metal determined and burned-coffee angry. The boy's eyes widened. "Denis Siska, you apologize this minute! Every person who walks through that front door to live with us is family and you know it."

Claire moved to lean against the cabinets near the door where the air was a little clearer. The lingering grease smoke was making her head pound. She tried to wave it away. "It's okay. Don't worry a—"

Danielle picked up the banner and turned on Denis too. "So, what? I'm not your sis either? I'm not a Siska, and you're not a Williams. I guess picking up after you and making your lunches for ten years doesn't mean anything?"

Denis finally held up his hands in surrender. "Okay, *okay*! Sorry. Jeez . . ." He turned his head to Claire and sighed deeply. When he spoke, his tone was polite, if not warm. "Nice to meet you, Claire. Sorry. I just had a sucky night. I'm not in the best mood right now."

"Yeah?" asked John, with sarcasm thick in his voice. "Well, using our food budget to bail your butt out of jail didn't put me in real jovial humor either. I don't think *you* get to be in a bad mood."

Asylin didn't say a word, but her lips thinned and her eyes flashed dangerously. Dani gasped loud enough that it was obvious this was news to her. "*Denis!* What did you do?"

Denis tipped his chair back until it was on two legs. He spread his legs wide, bracing his weight against the table legs, and crossed his arms over his chest. He wouldn't meet Dani's eyes, instead staring down at his knees. "Totally bogus charge. Besides, Alek was supposed to come get me last night so you didn't have to bail me out, Papa. He totally blew me off."

"No, Denis." John leaned down and slapped his palms down on the table to get Denis's attention. It worked. His chin lifted immediately, but he couldn't hold John's glare for long. "Alek isn't your legal guardian. *I* am. It's not your brother's job to keep you in line. It's mine, and apparently, I've been falling down on the job. But that ends today. You're grounded, young man. We're going to have lots and *lots* of time together to figure out how to fix your attitude."

Now the youngster's scent and look shifted to angry embarrassment, and he risked a glare at her. Somehow, Claire knew he was going to blame her for everything that was happening. But John either smelled or saw the reaction forming and pointed a long finger at Denis. "Hey, don't look at her. This has nothing to do with Claire. Just so you know, Alek didn't come to get you because he was in an accident last night."

All of a sudden, Denis looked shaken. He looked from John to Asylin and back again. "What? On his bike? Is he okay? Where is he, Mama?"

Asylin shook her head, both sad and angry. She sat in the chair next to Denis's. "Did you not even notice Dani's face? Just look at her, son. And poor Claire's head, all covered in gauze. Alek saved their lives last night when a wild animal attacked them. Dani's car was torn apart." She laid a gentle hand on his bare arm and the simple gesture broke down his last defense. The surliness slipped from his aura and Claire saw that he finally took notice of the woman who had been his AP sibling for the past decade: swollen face, thick black stitches across her forehead, eyes brimming with tears. Worry washed from the teenager's pores. "Dani . . . I . . . Are you okay?"

Danielle shrugged her good shoulder. "I'll heal. Eventually. Claire saved my life when we wrecked. Then Alek had to save hers. He gave her CPR until Marilyn got there. So we're family now, the three of us. We protected each other, just like people did after the plague. The big question is whether you are too. Are you family, Denis?"

Denis didn't respond for a long moment. Claire understood what was happening but she wasn't sure how she felt about Dani making her into a bludgeon. Her nose told her the kid was already embarrassed about being arrested and having a total stranger witness him being berated by his family. She decided to offer an olive branch. "I'm sure Denis would have helped if he'd been there."

His gaze flicked to her and he seized her words like a rope in a raging river. "Sure. Of course I would have. You know I'm family, Dani. I've been helping search for Kristy and Darrell. I'm not a jerk."

Dani looked to her parents for confirmation with raised brows. They both nodded, staying out of the interaction between the siblings. There must be a reason why, but Claire didn't know it. Too many emotions rose from Dani and the others for Claire to sort out.

"Are you, Denis?" Dani asked sadly. "Sometimes I wonder if you even know what a family is." Denis's reaction was clear—his expression shifted from stunned to angry and new scents rose into the air. Dani sighed and turned away. "Look, I've got to get down to the police station to see if they have my purse. And the nurse should probably look at Claire's head."

Claire couldn't think of anything she would like more than to leave the house for a while and get away from the tensions swirling about the family. "That sounds like a great idea, Dani. You can show me around town."

CHAPTER 6

No good deed goes unpunished. Alek forced his exhausted leg muscles to push the remains of the Toyota up next to the police cruiser on a tarp they'd spread out against the fence of the impound lot. Although "impound lot" sort of implied that the police actually impounded vehicles, the fenced-off area generally contained the remains of junkers strangers dumped in the wilderness. The problem was that none of the larger city police departments would take them and there wasn't a crush yard for a hundred miles in any direction. Oh, Lenny went through the motions of entering the vehicle identification numbers in the system—when he could find one—but mostly the cars were wrecks with no particularly interesting history and no known owner. "Okay, that's the last of it. Can I *finally* go home and get some sleep?" He was pretty sure he'd ripped out his stitches, but he was too tired to care.

Ray Vasquez pulled the remaining broken car parts from the backseat of the car and tossed them over Alek's head to land in the tall grass. He snorted. "You wish. Wanna bet how many people are lined up at your door wanting you to do something for them? There were three when I went by while you were finding a tarp."

Alek let out a pained sound. It was probably Mrs. Wilson wanting her computer back and Courtney looking for the flash drive with the spreadsheets. Who the third one was he had no clue.

"Don't worry," Ray continued. "I chased them away for the moment. Sorry you got sucked into this, but you know the rule around here—first responder gets the cleanup. At least you get to go home. I still have to go back to the office and write reports, with a splitting headache. Air bag, hell. I'm pretty sure I did a face-plant on the steering wheel." Alek was pretty sure he was right.

He shook his head ruefully. "Yeah, I don't envy you that. But this rule thing, it makes me feel like I'm back on prom committee . . . first in, last out. Almost makes me not want to stop for the next one."

The older Belizean panther shifter rolled his eyes and let out a small laugh. Citrus drifted into the air to join the scent of dripping antifreeze and oil. "Like you'd let people bleed to death. It's no surprise you're going to sign up to be a cop. It's in your DNA. You couldn't be an innocent bystander if your life depended on it."

Alek shrugged. He couldn't deny it. He'd wanted to be a cop since he could remember. "You're probably right. But the part I'm not going to enjoy is the paperwork. I've really got to force myself to sit still for hours on end."

Ray stepped forward and clapped him on the shoulder before steering him toward the gate to lock up the wreck. "It's a big part of the job, I'm afraid. No report, no record, no conviction. Trust me, it's no worse than what you do now for the town Council. My advice is to pretend you like it. It makes the process easier, and eventually it might even become true."

It was Alek's turn to chuckle. "The triumph of imagination over reality, huh?"

Ray shrugged. "Never hurts." He bent down to pick up a

file box at his feet. "Don't forget to let your sis know we've got her purse and stuff. Shame her luggage didn't survive, but the passenger's did. If you run into her at your folks' house, let her know everything's at the station."

The passenger. Alek looked back at the wreck, at the crumpled quarter panel and deep gashes through the metal, and shuddered. Thankfully, the beast hadn't come back while they were cleaning. But it was still out there somewhere. The individual claw rips through the car had been caused by something far bigger and stronger than any bear he'd ever seen. Hell, it was bigger than any *Sazi* bear he'd ever seen and he'd hunted with several. Four tears covered the entire height and length of the car, as though it had been standing still and slashed the car as it drove by. It wasn't just the outer sheet metal damaged either. "All the way through the frame. S'blood."

Out of the corner of his eye, Alek saw Ray staring at the same damage. The scents that rose from his pores were peppery with anger and awash in honest fear. "I wish I could say I saw it. But it was just *dark*. Like a black hole that the headlights couldn't penetrate. I don't know what the fuck that thing was." The next words were quiet and voiced Alek's own dread. "What if that *thing* got the kids, Alek? Maybe we haven't found them because there's nothing left to find. Maybe they disappeared into that darkness."

Alek didn't answer. There was no need. Because in reality, any animal, including a Sazi, if hungry enough or insane enough, would prey on humans. "We'll find them." They had to.

The officer shook his head, then stared out into the woods. "Dude, we've had the best trackers in town looking for those kids. Four separate Ascension champions have searched a dozen miles in every direction. What can we do that they couldn't?" Ray looked as frustrated as Alek felt.

He felt himself shrug. "I don't know, Ray. I just—"

"Alek! Hey, bro!"

Alek turned and saw her. He couldn't seem to tear himself away from the startling blue eyes walking toward him. He couldn't think, couldn't breathe. She smiled under her crown of bandages and his heart began to race. A surge of adrenaline that made it hard to stand still. But he didn't want to scare her, so he just smiled and said, "Hey."

The blonde's smile broadened until little crinkles appeared at the corner of her eyes. "Hey yourself."

"You doin' okay?" He couldn't help himself—he ran his fingers along the white gauze that wrapped her head. "Those were pretty bad punctures," he said, frowning. "They're starting to bleed through. You need to see Marilyn."

Was it his imagination or did she lean into his touch a little? All he knew was that her eyes were firmly on his, making his heart beat even faster. Surely she must be able to see his pulse trying to jump out of his neck.

"We were just headed there."

His fingers lingered for a moment on the silky strands of her hair. He inhaled deeply, drawing in the scents of soft fur, musk, and flowery perfume. In the background, he heard someone speaking, as though far away. "Oh, the swelling? It should go down in a day or two. Thanks for asking. No, no. It's okay, I don't need any help. Alek? Hello!"

Oh. Good point. "That's right, we haven't officially met. I'm Alek. Alek Siska." He lowered his hand to take hers, marveling at the coolness of her fingers. As his other senses returned, he noticed the woman was wearing just a short-sleeved T-shirt and form-fitting black jeans. And what a form they fit. Goose bumps rose on her arm, making the nearly invisible hairs stand on end. A swift glance told him she had no jacket. "Are you cold?"

She shook her head, then sent shivers through him when

she twined her fingers with his. "I'm a wolf. It's a great temperature. I'm Claire Sanchez. Nice to meet you, Alek. And thank you; I probably wouldn't be alive if not for you."

"Claire. That's a nice name." Didn't he already know that? It felt like he'd heard it before. *Claire*. Solid and real. A blush came to her cheeks along with a small, almost shy smile.

A low chuckle sounded in the distance, followed by, "Don't bother, Dani. He can't hear you. Can't take his eyes off her. C'mon, I'll give you a lift to the station to get your purse and bags."

The voices faded, and then there was just the sound of her breathing and the pounding of his heart. Heart. That was the shape of her face. It didn't seem like a wolf's face but her scent confirmed her nature: some sort of sweet, musky wolf. "I'm just glad I was there. You had me worried for a while. I thought you might have given up. Gray?"

She squeezed his fingers and gave a quick shake of her head. "Red, from Texas. I almost had. Given up, that is. But you were persistent." She paused and shrugged one shoulder. "I like that. Persistence."

"Always." He couldn't help but smile again but at the edge of his vision, he noticed the spot of red on her head was bigger. Now he smelled the blood and urgency pushed him to look up and around for the quickest route. "We need to get you to Marilyn to take a look at that. The bleeding's getting worse." She reached up and touched the red spot. She winced and he felt a moment of panic speed his heart as he turned her toward the medical clinic. "C'mon, it's on the other end of town, but that's only a few blocks."

"Right. That's what Dani told me." Claire looked around in bewilderment. "Where's Dani? She was right here."

He shrugged and looked around. Ray was gone too. "Dunno. I didn't even notice she was with you. We'll look for her on the way. I'm sure she hasn't gone far."

He offered his arm and she looped hers through it carefully. Realizing she was moving gingerly because of the bandage on her arm, Alek quickly shifted around to her other side. She smiled gratefully. Even though his instinct screamed for speed, his mind knew that hurrying would increase the bleeding. He forced himself to walk slowly. *It's not that far. Just keep moving.* To keep from just picking her up in his arms and starting to run, he forced himself to point out some of the local businesses. "That's Hansen's Grocery. It's not really much of a grocery. There's some canned goods and dairy. Mostly, though, we use it for meat storage for deer and elk."

She nodded. "Yeah, we have a big building where we have our freezers. But I really do prefer meat right after a hunt. It loses something in the freezer. Y'know?"

He turned his head in surprise. "You *hunt?* Really?"

Claire gave him a very odd look and even her scent was confused. "Um, sure. Why? Don't you? How else would you get your meat? You don't *buy* deer, do you?"

He was about to respond when he heard a familiar voice behind him. "We tend to split the duties here, miss." Alek turned as Claire did, to find the mayor and police chief standing behind them.

"Oh? How so?" Claire's voice suddenly grew tense and her scent had overtones of distrust. *Why?*

Mayor Monk smiled and tipped his trademark white felt cowboy hat. "Well, we're in an area where there are a lot of natural predators. I'm sure you can see that it's important to guard the children and homes while the hunt is happening."

"Of course," Claire said with a slight nod. "My family assigns someone to stay behind, to watch the kids and lock all the doors. That doesn't explain why people would be surprised that I hunt."

Lenny tried to explain. "Here, women tend to stay home with the kids while the men go hunting. There's nothing more dangerous than a mama protecting her young," the police chief said with a smile. "It's kept our kids safe since the night of the plague."

Claire's expression grew bemused and her scent was slightly incredulous. "You're kidding, right?" She looked from face to face but they all shrugged. "Okay." She paused for a moment and then let out a little laugh. "Guess I'm glad I don't have any kids. 'Cause I like to hunt and plan to. That's okay, right?"

Lenny and Van looked at each other and both smiled before Van responded, "Of course. It's a free country." He held out his hand. "By the way, we haven't met. I'm the mayor-slash-Alpha, Van Monk. I'm guessing you must be Miss Sanchez, our new guest from Texas." He motioned to Lenny. "And this is Police Chief Lenny Gabriel, who is also our Wolven representative."

She held out her hand and took his and shook it firmly, her eyes still slightly narrowed. "Claire Sanchez. I'm looking forward to spending some time here. I know you must think of Luna Lake as a small town, but we're pretty far out in the wilderness back home. I need to get to know how to handle myself in a bigger community of people."

Lenny put a hand on her shoulder with a broad smile. "Speaking of that, we need to get you registered. You know how it is with Wolven—there's always paperwork to be filled out on a new pack member, and we need to get your statement about the accident. How about you come along with us over to the police station for a few minutes?"

Claire flinched at his touch, then looked at Alek with concern in her eyes and scent—as though he was her savior. He fought back the urge to growl, confused by the strength of his reaction. It made no sense. "Um, can this wait for a few minutes, guys? We were just on our way over to see Marilyn. See the blood on her bandage? She might have popped a stitch."

Both men stared at Alek, neither looking at Claire, until Van said, "Oh, this will just take a few minutes, Alek. No need to worry. If the bleeding gets any worse, we can have Marilyn drop by my office." He raised a finger, like something just occurred to him, but his scent didn't match. "By the way, I was heading over to see you because Fred at the post office said you got a registered letter today . . . from the Siberian pack leader."

Siberia? *Siberia!* It had been nearly a year since he had written to that pack, asking them to check if his sister had been transferred there after the plague. The urgency to see what they had to say warred with his need to stay by Claire's side. He felt his muscles twitching, not sure which way to turn. "There's a letter? Really?" When Lenny nodded firmly, he had no choice. "Claire, I'm really sorry, but I've *got* to get that letter. I've been waiting for it for over a year."

She looked a little confused, then shrugged. "Um, sure. If you need to go, that's fine. I guess I'll be at the police station, answering questions."

He felt the tension in his shoulders ease a bit. He wasn't sure what he would have done if she said no, please don't. He wasn't sure why it mattered. "Great. I'll just pick up the letter and meet you over there." *She'll be fine. She'll be fine.* Yet he found himself taking off at a dead run down Second Street toward the post office. The farther he got from Claire, the more he started thinking about the letter. *This could be it!* It was the one place where Sonya might be that nobody would have found her until now. The Siberian pack was very reclusive; they lived far from civilization, which is why they had been spared most of the effects of the snake attack and plague. He remembered that Sonya had spoken fluent Russian as a child, better than the rest of them, and she'd usually resorted to that language when she was scared. In the aftermath of the attacks, anyone finding her alone might presume she was Russian. She might have been sent to that pack.

In the years since the plague, Alek had written to every pack he'd heard of, anywhere in the world. There had been no sign of Sonya. But the Russian pack had never responded to his inquiries. How many letters had he sent? A dozen? Twenty? He'd lost count. *Please! Let them have taken her in!*

The old brass bell above the post office door jingled as he entered. Fred Birch was sitting on a stool behind the counter, wearing the same red plaid shirt, with scissors tucked in the pocket, and the same tattered wool hat as always, pulled low over bushy eyebrows. No blue postal uniform for him. The pipe in his hand filled the air with cherry tobacco smoke. "Hey, Alek. You here for your letter?"

"Absolutely! I can't believe it finally got here."

Fred started rummaging around under the counter. "The postmark on it is nearly a year old. Hard to believe it took so long to get here." He pulled out an oversized envelope, covered in tape, stickers, and official-looking stamps. "Ah, here it is." A few seconds was all it took to scan the bar code and enter it into the computer.

Alek's fingers were actually trembling as he signed the screen and accepted the envelope. Scents rose from the heavy dark manila covering, mostly mildew and chemicals, with lingering faint male wolf musk. It was stiff, like there was something inside other than paper, and the address was written in Yupik, the Cyrillic alphabet—and again in English, probably translated at some point in its journey. "Thanks, Fred. Really." Smiling, Alex turned to go.

Fred called out, "Hope it's good news, kid. You've had enough of the bad stuff in your life. See you at the meeting tonight?"

The last sentence brought him up short and he turned with his hand still on the door. "Meeting?"

"Yeah, at the Community Center. The mayor said it was mandatory. Some big announcement. Maybe they found the kids." He shook his head with a worried expression. "Hope they're safe. Cute kids, those two."

Alek felt his brows furrow. "Really? That's weird. I just saw Van a minute ago. He didn't say anything about a meeting, or about Kristy or Darrell."

Fred shrugged. "He's been going from store to store, telling people. Don't know why he forgot to tell you. But anyway . . . it's tonight at seven o'clock. I'd be there if I were you. They don't do mandatory meetings very often."

True. Very true. The last mandatory meeting was to announce they'd caught a snake shifter in a stolen car trying to sneak into town on a back road, nearly a year ago. Good thing they'd caught him too. The car had been filled with knives and ammo made of silver. Deadly to their kind. But he'd been turned over to Wolven without violence.

"Thanks, Fred. I'll be there." He'd tell Claire too. *Maybe that's what the meeting's for.* It would make sense to introduce a new town resident to everyone at once. Yeah, that seemed logical.

The image of the splotch of red against the white bandage flashed through his mind. What if she was seriously hurt? What if they didn't notice until it was too late and she collapsed?

Alek wrenched his mind away from thoughts of Claire. First things first: the letter. It had taken nearly a month to learn enough of the Yupik language to write the first letter to Mikhail, Siberia's pack Alpha. He'd painstakingly copied each letter onto the page, not even sure if the grammar had made sense. Then the Omega in his old pack in Chicago had read it and corrected some of his syntax. Yurgi had told Alek he hoped that Sonya wasn't there. He said that being a woman in the Siberian pack was a hard life and he would help do whatever was necessary to bring her home if she was there. Nikoli, the wolf representative on the Council, said through Yurgi that he would also help . . . if there was proof she was there and was being held against her will.

In other words, he wouldn't confront Mikhail unless negotiations failed. The Siberian leader must be one tough S.O.B. for the head wolf to not want to get into a fight with him.

Alek fought with the strong shipping tape for nearly two minutes, finally resorting to using his teeth before he realized he was going to destroy the contents if he ripped the package open using Sazi strength. Defeated, he returned to the post office to find a grinning Fred standing just inside the door, holding out a pair of scissors. "They use a lot of tape over there. Figured you'd need these."

They were sharp, like twin razor blades, but it still took multiple snips to get through the packaging. Alek handed the scissors back before slowly removing a cardboard file folder from the envelope. A slim stack of pages lay inside.

Alek closed his eyes. Was his little sister found at last?

CHAPTER 7

Claire was definitely in a cat lair. The back office of the police station where she sat, waiting for the chief and the mayor to finish talking in the front room, was thick with scents and none of them were good. Granted, she had expected the lingering scents of fear, anger, and worry. Those could be expected in any law enforcement office. But aggression? Pain? Blood? No, there was definitely something wrong here. The thing was, she couldn't seem to reach her Alphas in her head. Maybe the Alpha here was just strong enough that she couldn't get through his magic.

Hopefully they were listening in.

The door behind her opened. She pretended not to notice and continued to fill out the generic form that requested information about where she had been and what her skills were. It was like a job resume for a Sazi employment agency. Even without looking, she could now recognize which cat was which by the smell. The police chief was a cougar—not a predator to be messed with. The mayor was one of the smaller mountain cats, maybe bobcat or lynx. She didn't know all the great cats by smell, but she'd know him in the future. She tapped the pen at the bottom of the form after signing it and passed the clipboard back to Chief Gabriel. "Okay, I think that's it. Is there anything I need to fill out for the school, or will they give that to me on Monday?"

She wanted to give the opening to the mayor and chief to see if they knew her background and what had been set up by her pack. She had graduated from an online college with a degree in teaching and was certified to teach in Texas. She'd been told it would be easy to transfer her credentials to Washington. Her pack had applied for her to take a position working as a teaching assistant since she could gather a lot of information easily through talking to people. The town leaders should know that. But pack leaders who weren't in touch with their pack might not have a clue what was going on.

Chief Gabriel nodded. "Yeah, the administration over at the school does their own paperwork that has to be filed with the state Board of Education. But before we do that, we figured we should . . . *chat* with you."

The word had a high-pitched snarl at the end and the stink of aggression filled the air. Claire looked up sharply, frowning. Her muscles tensed involuntarily as she looked from one man to the other. "Is something wrong?"

The chief filled the room with magic enough to sting her skin. "Well, not so much *wrong*. It's just that you don't really look like a Sanchez. I don't know a whole lot of blue-eyed, blond Mexicans."

Ah. So that's where this was going. She was immediately suspect because her skin wasn't the right color for her surname. Fortunately, that was the first thing her pack leaders had schooled her on. But it was hard not to be antagonistic, just by their tone. "The preferred term is *Latina* for a woman or *Latino* for a man. They're pretty sensitive about that where I come from, since a lot of people aren't specifically from Mexico . . . but just for the record, there are actually quite a few fair-haired Mexicans. Still, to answer what I presume was a question, I was legally adopted by my pack leaders after the plague. I lost my parents." In a manner of speaking it was true, so there would be no scent of deceit for the cats to pick up.

Most Sazi she'd met let the topic go after that, but the moment the police chief opened his mouth, Claire knew he wouldn't be one of them. "Sorry for *offending* you. So what was your surname before the plague? What pack were your parents attached to?"

He wanted to check her out further. Why? In the packs, the plague had become a dividing point. Before and after. After was all that mattered for those who'd survived. It wasn't information she was willing to give him, so she gave a sad smile and shrugged. "I was an attack victim. I'd rather not talk about it."

That had better be the end of it. It was the height of rudeness to ask an attack victim to relive their first change. Most were formerly human, many didn't survive it, and those who did were usually mentally scarred by the experience.

Like her.

She brought her gaze up to meet the eyes of the big cougar shifter, trying to keep her scent and body language firm but respectful. She felt her fingers clench on the denim covering her legs and breathed slow and even. It seemed to work. Chief Gabriel's shoulders relaxed a bit and the tiny dip of his brows and the light scent that drifted to her nose held more sympathy than distrust. He didn't look at the mayor for his opinion—he hadn't deferred to the mayor once since she'd first encountered them, on the street with Alek. She was starting to wonder who the Alpha here really was. "Sorry." The one word was gruff, seemingly filled with images and memories that he wasn't willing to divulge. He picked up a random stack of papers on his desk and tapped the edge several times to break the tension. "So, you're a teacher?"

"Hoping to be. Working with kids is all I've ever wanted.

I am *so* excited to be here." It was easy to gush about her life's dream and the smile came without any forcing. "I hope I can show your principal that I'll be a great teacher. Every child deserves to *love* learning, y'know?"

Whatever they were expecting her to say, that wasn't it. They both looked genuinely surprised at her reaction. It was the mayor who spoke first. "Well. That's . . . good. Um, glad to know you're excited. We do have great kids here."

Claire kept smiling, keeping them off guard by her sheer cheerfulness. *Happy vibe, girl. Don't let them in your head.* She'd been taught that the most successful undercover people were those who could live the part of their assignment and focus their minds so even the best alphas couldn't break through. "So who do I check in with? I'd like to get the lay of the school and maybe observe a class."

Chief Gabriel took a deep breath and let it out slowly before picking up a pen and starting to write something on a notepad. "You'll need to see the principal, Nathan Burrows. But that's for tomorrow. For today, you'll need to write up your version of what happened in the accident last night and then get ready for your first challenge. It'll be at sundown."

Challenge? "Excuse me? What sort of challenge?"

The mayor smiled, like this was an everyday request. "Well, we have to establish your place in the pack, of course."

Claire's chest seized and her stomach felt as though lead had been dropped inside. "You want me to *fight* on my first day here? I thought my Alphas explained where I stood in the pack." She'd never actually had to face a dominance challenge. Her Alphas didn't believe in fighting and most of the members were content with their place in the hierarchy so disputes were rare. They'd told the leadership here that she was fifth in line of the females—high enough in the pack to be respected, but not high enough to be threatening to those already here.

"And that's fine for *your* pack. But we aren't a normal pack here in Luna Lake." The smile was closer to a sneer. No warmth and enjoying her confusion. "We're packs and prides and flocks, all doing our best to live together safely." He stepped a little closer, invading the hell out of her personal space. "So you can see where everyone needs the chance to meet you . . . see your talents firsthand. Right?"

While it *did* sort of make sense, she couldn't help but shiver. "I guess."

The mayor raised his hands, shrugging his shoulders at the same time—as though everything was out of his control. "And today just happens to be Ascension Day. Since it's already happening, we just decided to add you to the roster."

Ascension Day? What in the heck was that? But Claire didn't want to sidetrack the conversation. The *what* didn't matter as much as the *why*. "But I'm injured. That doesn't seem like it'll be a very fair contest."

"Well . . ." Chief Gabriel's tone told her he'd considered the same thing. "The others on the roster are omegas. Even injured, you shouldn't have any problems."

That revelation shocked her. "I'll be fighting *omegas*? Dear Lord, someone could get *killed*!" Omegas were the Sazi with the lowest magical ability in the pack. Without help from their pack leaders, they had trouble even shifting on full moon nights. It could be a painful existence unless the whole pack helped them. Many omegas Claire had heard of were depressed and angry at their lot in life. Some had even committed suicide rather than live that way.

The chief was quick to speak. "Oh, no, no. There's no actual *fighting*. These are tests of skill that show the equivalent of fighting ability. If we had actual battles, everybody would have died years ago. We don't have many alphas, so the Ascension Day challenges lessen aggression in a safe way."

Oh. Well, then. That didn't sound so bad. "What kind of tests? What do I need to do?"

The chief stood and walked around the desk. "Let's go downstairs. We'll get started."

He held open the door. The mayor led the way, followed by Claire. The chief took up the rear as they headed down the hallway to a metal door that was scarred with deep claw marks that bulged the door outward, toward them. What the hell?

She stopped cold in the dimly lit space as her nose picked up the scent of fear and feathers coming from under the door. The whisper of a female voice below their feet made her catch her breath. The door opened and she felt a sudden shove against her back. Then she was falling down and down, couldn't seem to stop herself. The doorway dissolved before her eyes, to be replaced by cool, damp rock walls.

She was back in the cave, huddled in a foul, ammonia-scented corner of her cell. *It isn't real.* It couldn't be. People didn't just transform into birds. But they were. Dozens . . . maybe hundreds of boys and girls in cages, scattered through the underground complex. They were all bound with shiny silver manacles around one leg or both arms, bolted to the solid rock. Clarissa stared at her bloody wrist. How many times had she tried to slip out of the cuff while screams echoed through the air? Her shoulder hurt from where she had tugged and yanked in a sobbing frenzy, trying to get loose when she thought they were coming for her. But the next cage was the target, Justin. He was just eight, with freckles across his nose and wide green eyes.

Clarissa's fear had turned to leaden knowledge that she would die here when Justin had been dragged back down the hall, his head thumping hollowly against the uneven floor. He was horribly deformed from trying to make the shift to bird form. She'd watched the guards' eyes as they dragged him, not even trying to hide the result of the forced change from the others. There was no feeling in those dark eyes.

Poor Justin, with thin bird talons where his feet had been, and his arms hanging limp, covered in feathers. One eye was still green, the other round and amber. Both stared unseeing, dead, as they pulled him down to The Room.

She tried not to think about The Room, but she'd heard about it in the whispers of those who had been here longer. The dead fed those who had survived the shift. The birds didn't think like people anymore. They ate what they were given, even if the meat had once been a cellmate or a sibling.

Hours became days, then weeks, then months. If fear was a tactic to whittle down the will of the captives, it worked. Soon there were no screams, except from the new arrivals. Nobody wanted to be the squeaky wheel, because the loud ones were taken first. Clarissa had thought she would trudge to her fate like the others . . . sure in the knowledge that there was nothing that she, a skinny girl from Kansas, could do to stop these alien beings who could become a giant bird or snake, at will.

But when her cage door opened and the two burly men came inside to take her away, she was surprised to find an inner strength. She started fighting for her life. She kicked and punched and bit while the guards hit her and yanked her arms, trying to keep her still. She managed to slip from their grasp and run. Tripping and falling over stones toward the small patch of daylight in the distance, slipping on black-and-white bird feces and other, worse things. She didn't care.

The light grew in size as she ran, the air began to smell less like choking ammonia and more like trees and dust. Her chest heaved, trying to get in enough air to keep moving.

Almost there. Almost there!

Then, inches away from freedom, the light was shut off—

blocked by a snake, black as coal, that filled the entire entrance. He made short hissing noises, as though amused. "Oh, you are a feisty one. I like that."

The guards finally caught up and grabbed both arms tight enough that she cried out. They bowed their heads to the black snake. "Apologies, Lord Nasil, she surprised us. We wouldn't have let her escape."

The snake shrunk down to human size, became a man with dark hair and intelligent eyes. He turned those eyes, narrowed in anger, to the man holding her as she continued to yank and pull away. "She already *had* escaped you. But she won't escape *me*. Will you?" He put one finger under her chin and then gripped her throat so fast that she couldn't breathe, couldn't move. His fingers were stronger than the iron shackles. His voice older than the stone. "No. You'll never escape, never be free again." The amusement in his voice became a threat. "You are *mine*. My feathered guardian, my warrior, my *slave*, little Clarissa. Do you hear me?"

He released her throat, but she still couldn't breathe. Because she believed him.

"Clarissa? *Clarissa*? Do you hear me?" The voice changed, became softer, feminine. She gasped for air and sat up in a rush, looking around wildly. She was on a carpeted floor, not rock. The walls around her were painted in pale peach.

A dark-skinned woman had one firm hand on her shoulder. She smelled strongly of owl, and looked . . . familiar. "Do I know you?"

"Only from your dreams." The woman's dark eyes grew haunted. "You were back there just now, weren't you? In the cave. You said his name . . . Justin. I remember him too. We sang songs to each other."

Claire searched the other woman's face for a long moment. The shape of her jaw, the slope of her nose, the full lips, and yes, a tiny scar at the corner of one eye. The words came out of Claire's mouth in almost reverent tones. "Rachel? Rachel Washington? I thought you were dead!"

Rachel smiled, showing broad, white teeth and Claire knew her. The years fell away and she was suddenly staring at the little girl with beaded braids and a smart-ass attitude in the next cage over. "Pfft! I come from Eight Mile in Detroit, girl. You think a few snakes with glandular problems and a little apocalypse can keep me down?"

"When they took you, I never saw you again. I thought they had taken you to The Room." Claire needed to stand up, get her legs under her again to shake off the memory of that time and place. Rachel helped her to her feet, then led her over to a plush couch in the corner of the windowless room. "They turned you? Were you in the battle?"

Rachel couldn't look at her. She stared at her own hands, pushing back her cuticles with one manicured, blue-tinted nail. "Yeah. I was turned. Nearly killed when the wolves came. As owls go, I guess great horned isn't too bad 'cause I flew higher than the others and made it to safety. It's better than being a burrowing owl, I guess. No more caves for me!" She chuckled nervously and finally looked at Claire. "But you . . . look at you, girl! Smelling all wolflike. How did you pull that off?"

It was Claire's turn to shrug. "They took a bunch of us away to a different location—all of us who had been attacked and showed signs of healing, but hadn't turned yet. We were rescued by the Tedford pack and some Wolven agents during the Four Corners battle. I got cut up by one of the birds guarding me and was stitched by a wolf healer who was still bleeding. I guess she thought I was already a shifter so she didn't try to protect me from her blood. Apparently, I was meant to be a wolf because I'd survived four bird attacks without changing, but one dripping doctor and I'm furry."

"And here we are: Rachel and Clarissa . . . survivor sorority sisters, trapped in Nowheresville, Washington. Who'da thunk?"

That perked Claire's ears. "I go by Claire now, by the way. You don't like it in Luna Lake?"

"Eh. It's okay, I guess." Rachel stood and walked to a table across the room where cold drinks and chips had been set up. She fingered the edge of a soda can but didn't pick it up. "I just wish the Equal Opportunity Act applied to Sazi."

Claire felt her brow crinkle. "What does that mean?"

Rachel opened her mouth to reply just as the door burst open and Marilyn Bearbird raced into the room carrying a large sachel, with the police chief hot on her heels. When she saw Claire sitting on the couch calmly, she turned on her heel to face the chief. "I thought you said she was *dying*. She looks fine to me."

He held up his hands with a surprised expression. "She fell down the stairs and hit her head. We couldn't wake her up."

"Was pushed," Claire corrected.

Marilyn turned back to her while the police chief glared. "Excuse me?"

"I said I was *pushed* down the stairs. I didn't fall. I very distinctly felt a hand between my shoulder blades."

The healer turned and raised brows at Chief Gabriel. "Is that true? Did someone push a woman who was just in a car accident, who might have a concussion, down a flight of stairs?"

He shrugged and didn't give anything away in his face or scent. "That's not the way I remember it. So, are you going to check her out? She needs to be ready for Ascension at dusk. Rachel, c'mon. Let's get you back in your own *meditation room*."

Rachel raced across the room, bounced onto the couch, and enveloped Claire in a bear hug. It was so unexpected that they fell backward laughing into the cushions. "It's so good to see you again, girl!" Claire smiled and hugged her back. But while they were disentangling and sitting up, Rachel hissed, fast and harsh, into her ear. *"Don't agree to anything, Claire. Don't trust either of them. Tell them you want a mentor. Ask for Alek. He's not one of them. Remember—Alek Siska."* The owl shifter pulled away, all smiles, without a hint in her face or scent of the whispered instruction. "See you at dusk. It'll be a great time."

A uniformed man appeared at the door and swept his hand out for Rachel to precede him. Was she a prisoner? She shrugged off a hand on her shoulder from the cop like it burned.

Marilyn stepped forward and sat down on the couch next to Claire. "Okay, then. Let's get those bandages off and see where that blood is coming from."

Chief Gabriel stepped toward the door. "Just make sure she's ready for Ascension. Knock when you're ready to come out."

"Will do, Chief."

"Chief?" Claire made sure her voice sounded casual and friendly. He turned and cocked his head in response. "We never did get a chance to talk about what's supposed to happen tonight. Could I get someone to walk me through the process? You know . . . like a coach? A mentor or something?"

Both Marilyn and the chief of police froze in place. Claire could hear Marilyn's heart speed up until it was a counterpoint to her own. Both fear and amusement rose from her pores when she spoke. "Well, you heard the woman. She wants a mentor."

The chief's eyes narrowed in barely contained fury. "So she said."

"And I'm not a wolf," Marilyn continued. "Neither are you."

"How about Alek Siska?" Claire struggled to keep her voice

light and not react to the obvious discomfort around her. "He seemed nice when he was showing me around town earlier."

Chief Gabriel ground his teeth and clutched the doorknob until his knuckles were white. "I'll see if he's *available*. In the meantime, I need you to look at one of the prisoners, Marilyn. Let's leave Ms. Sanchez to get some rest."

Marilyn looked up, astonishment clear on her face. "She's *bleeding*, Lenny. Let me at least get her bandaged up again."

"*Now*, Marilyn. There'll be time for bandaging later. *After* the challenge."

So. She'd struck a nerve, hard enough to have a Wolven officer let her bleed.

Don't trust either of them. At this point, Rachel's ominous words sounded like great advice.

CHAPTER 8

*A*lek slammed a fist down on the table, making the computer monitor nearly topple over. He caught it in time, but felt like throwing it against the wall. He couldn't read the letter from Siberia. It was in some sort of alphabet that he couldn't identify. He'd been searching for hours, using Fred's computer in the back room of the post office and still wasn't any closer to deciphering it. It wasn't Cyrillic or Greek or any other alphabet he could find, including Sanskrit. He knew the pack leader there was old. Could he be using a dead language with no known key?

He picked up the photograph that he'd found in the file folder, of a raven-haired teenager standing in what looked like a tavern. She was wearing a plain, black, knee-length dress and a white apron, with her hair pulled back severely from a heart-shaped face. She had an uncomfortable expression in the photo, as though having a picture taken was something to be worried about. Could it be Sonya? He just couldn't tell. She'd been so young the last time Alek had seen her, just six. The face was similar, but she didn't look like his mother and he didn't know the women in his father's family well enough to tell. He couldn't even tell for sure whether it was a current photograph. From the dress she was wearing, it could have been taken yesterday or fifty years ago. If he could hear her voice, he would know. Even as a child, she had a unique voice—a contralto, deep and sultry. He'd always imagined she would become a singer in some famous opera in Italy when she grew up.

"Any luck, Fred?" He called out to the front, hoping the postmaster had been able to find out more about the package through official channels.

"Nope," the older man called back. "I even got ahold of a buddy of mine who knew someone from Russia. I sent him a scan of a few of the words but he's never seen anything like it. You might check with your old pack. Maybe the Duchess knows something about it. Or maybe the university in Spokane has a linguist who would recognize it."

The Duchess. Alek had nearly forgotten about the elegant white-haired seer, the Alpha female of the Chicago pack. She was old Russian, somehow connected to the former royal family, back when there was a czar. It wouldn't be easy to reach the pack. Nikoli was fanatical about security since snakes had managed to attack the hotel that was their headquarters. He moved the remaining pack members with regularity, never staying too long in one place.

Alek might not love life in Luna Lake, but it was better than forever running from an enemy you couldn't see and wouldn't know was coming. The enemy was within—their own family members who were human. It was like running from your own shadow. There was no way to escape.

He shut down the computer and slid the letter and photo back into the envelope just as Fred called, "Alek? Lenny's here to see you."

Crap! He'd forgotten all about Claire. She was probably wondering where on earth he was. The search for the alphabet would have to wait.

He opened the frosted-glass door and was startled by the

furious expression on Lenny's face. But he didn't smell angry, which must mean he was using the special Wolven cologne that masked his scent. That meant he was beyond angry but didn't want to make the townspeople hide in trees, desperately trying to escape a pissed-off cougar. Most people didn't even know the cologne existed. He had found it by accident one day when cleaning out Lenny's car. It was a clear liquid with no scent, none at all, in a glass container. He'd notified Lenny in case it was an explosive he'd never seen before. Alek had a sneaking suspicion that Lenny wasn't supposed to have told him about it, so he didn't comment on Lenny's lack of scent. "What's up, Chief?" It seemed a good idea to be more formal right now.

"Our new resident seems to be a bit of a jailhouse lawyer. She's made a formal demand, before a witness, for a mentor for the Ascension." Each word was spit with careful precision . . . letter of the law wording so there would be no questions later. "You're who she's picked." He turned on his heel, apparently expecting Alek to follow. He stopped with his hand on the knob. "*Don't* screw it up."

Alek felt his eyes widen. A *mentor?* He couldn't remember the last time someone had requested a formal advocate in an Ascension challenge. Sure, it was written into the original town charter, but nobody actually requested it. It was tantamount to telling the whole town that the challenge was a fraud. Usually the mentor was a senior town member. He'd never heard of anyone short of the Alpha or Second being named.

Don't screw it up. There was an understatement if he'd ever heard one. Wait. Had Lenny said "our new resident"? Why on earth would Claire be part of an Ascension? She'd only been in the town for a day and had come from a place where she'd probably never even heard of the games. Who would challenge her, and why?

The brass bell tinkled and he realized that Lenny was already outside and looking back at him. "You coming, Siska? There's only three hours left. It took me forever to find your ass."

Alek didn't say a word, just followed at the chief's blistering pace. There was something deeper going on here and he had no intention of stepping into a bottomless pit of shit by mouthing off without knowing what was happening. But the truth was they'd known he was going to the post office . . . had insisted, in fact, that he go. One phone call or a saunter down the street and Fred would have told them he was still there.

It only took a few minutes at a nearly dead run before they reached the police station. Ray was at his desk, with a tense but sympathetic expression on his face, as Alek walked through. He had practically reached the door when Lenny said, "You have one hour for spoken instruction in human form and one hour in either form in the forest. You must be back at the meeting hall no later than five o'clock or she forfeits. Do you understand? Do you have any questions?"

"Yeah, tons. But I guess my primary concern is that I've never been a mentor. Are there guidelines or do I just play it by ear?"

"She's a wolf. You're a wolf. It's a tracking challenge. Same course as normal. The guidelines are about how to appoint a mentor, not what to do when you are one. Okay?"

"Okay." The word probably sounded a little forced, because it was. Hopefully, it would just sound like uncertainty. But it *wasn't* okay. Lenny had just told a bald-faced lie. There absolutely were guidelines for mentor conduct. He'd seen them. Was this a test to see if he'd been studying, or a trap to catch him in some sort of violation? He just didn't know. The first thing he knew he had to do was to get Claire out of here to a location where there were fewer prying ears.

He descended the stairs two at a time, checking his watch and matching it to the clock on the wall. They actually didn't have the full three hours required to be given for mentoring. Another lie. What the hell was going on?

He opened the first door and saw Rachel Washington inside. She looked at him and smiled. "Make me proud, Alek." It was a bare whisper, not because she was trying to be particularly quiet, but because the side of her face was swollen from what looked like repeated punching. But she was smiling and her eyes were bright. "Keep her safe."

Why in the world would they let her compete in that condition? Who hit her in the first place? He could only shake his head and give her a small smile. "I'll do my best." Then he shut the door and moved to the next room.

Claire was standing at the sink in one corner of the room. Judging by the strip of bandage and the paper towels she held, she had cleaned the blood off the gauze and was drying it with paper towels. *Why not just get new bandages?* She would occasionally dab at the trickle of blood leaking down from a stitch that had torn in her scalp. "Hi." Her voice was quiet and slightly embarrassed. "Sorry to drag you into this mess."

He crooked his finger for her to follow. There would be more time to talk once they were in the forest. "Don't talk. Just follow me."

Without another word, she gathered up the sodden mess of paper towels and tape and tossed it in the trash and rolled up the gauze and tucked it in a front pocket. Then, as almost an afterthought, she grabbed a handful of paper towels and shoved them in the pocket too. Together they climbed the stairs to the main office. Nobody said a word to them, not a single greeting or good luck, as they left the office.

He turned his head. "Can you run? Can you track scents?"

At her nod, he took off at a sprint into the trees. "Count to ten and then follow me! I'll run the course." He didn't look behind. The point of the challenge was tracking. If she couldn't find him, she would fail. Plain and simple. He could explain how the challenge worked until he was blue in the face, but it just made sense to see if she could even track.

The bright sunlight dappled, shadowed, and finally disappeared as he ran. The forest closed around him and the noisy modern world became primordial and silent. Scents became his world as his nose guided him along hidden deer trails where travel was quick and quiet. He let the frustration, anger, and worry dissolve as the velvety brush of leaves and pine needles slid around him. Emotions could be tracked. Fear was the easiest to follow, and frustration was a form of fear.

Only prey show fear, Alek, his mother had always said. *Fear has large eyes that predators can find in the darkest forest.*

He had always struggled to understand the nuances of fear. *But shouldn't I be afraid of people who want to hurt me?*

She would stare at him with those patient, intelligent wolf eyes and sigh. *Caution is not the same, child. Do not fear your enemies, for all they can do is attack you. If you are prepared, the attack will fail. Wolves are always prepared.*

Even to the end, she had been prepared. But overwhelming force had been too much and she had been taken down. He still remembered her last words as she gripped the back of his neck like a steel vise. *No fear, Alek. You are wolf. You are Sazi. We can be killed, but we will never be defeated. Defend your brothers and sisters. Promise me. Keep them safe.*

He'd failed to protect Vera, his older sister. Sonya had disappeared so he had no idea whether he'd succeeded. And Denis? Well, Denis was safe from outside enemies. If only Alek could save him from himself.

So many memories of happier times with Denis. Of hide-and-seek in the hotel, hunting with the pack in the trees, with the humans in their park just a stone's throw away. The scents of cars and people and fur everywhere. Here was so very different. There was no interstate, no throngs of humans rushing to and fro. No pack to call his own. Feathers replaced fur in his nose. But they were family too, those feathered children. Why couldn't he find them? He was supposed to be one of the best trackers in the town. How many times had he won the Ascension? Fifteen? Twenty?

A vibration in his pocket stopped Alek abruptly in a small clearing, where the quickly setting sun managed to reach through blackened stumps that spoke of a horrible fire in years past. Thick green grass defied the cooling weather and a few small yellow flowers poked out of the carpet of pine needles. The sound of his own heart from the hard run made it hard to hear subtle sounds in the woods. He pulled out his phone. Lenny had texted him: the first hour was over. Looking around, Alek realized he was at least five miles from town and nowhere near where he'd planned to be. Damn it! How had he gotten so lost in thought?

He'd planned to cut back and forth, go under logs and over boulders, but stay to within a half-mile of town on approximately the course that would be used for the challenge, so Claire wouldn't be hard to find if she hadn't found him after an hour. Now she could be anywhere and Ascension was fast approaching. Should he wait quietly or call out to her?

To hell with this. And to hell with him! Claire sat on a log, feeling frustrated tears nearly overwhelm her. She was utterly lost, her *mentor* nowhere in sight, and the time of this stupid Ascension test fast approaching. She'd never understood the saying, "can't see the forest for the trees" until now. But she'd never been in a forest before. Growing up in Kansas and then moving to west Texas never exposed her to trees so high that you couldn't see the tops, so dense that the branches seemed to grow into a mat of wood, and so intensely fragrant that any

hope of following someone was gone. Her head was pounding from running and she'd finally been forced to sit down so
she wouldn't fall down. Being dizzy wasn't surprising but it
wasn't good. It was hard to concentrate and blood kept dripping in her eyes. She kept her legs carefully on the big round
fallen tree as she'd been taught and pressed the last of the
paper towels to her stitches. Snakes liked to hide under dead
branches. She didn't know how many snakes lived up here . . .
and she realized she hadn't properly prepared herself for
this experience.

"What an idiot," she whispered to herself. She thought
about calling out for Alek, but asking for help wasn't exactly
the mark of a Wolven agent. This was her first real assignment, and she would be damned if being alone in the woods
was going to get the best of her. *Don't trust anyone*, Rachel
had said. Did that include Rachel herself, or the man who'd
brought Claire back from the dead?

Fine. If she had to rely on her own resources, so be it.

She stood up and had to blink a few times to stop the
ground from moving. Getting her bearings at last, she decided to turn around and head back to town. Heck, maybe that
was part of the coaching, to see if she could make a trail that
could be followed. Or maybe Alek was in cahoots with the
police chief after all, trying to get her lost up here so she'd
lose this challenge. But she wasn't going to go down without
a fight.

Her pack leaders had taught her well how to follow a trail.
She remembered hunting with the other kids for sticks of
deer jerky hidden under cacti or in the crevices of mesquite
trees. You had to move fast to get to the jerky before the fire
ants did. Nothing worse than fire ant stings on the tongue.

She knew her own scent and had made sure to break small
branches as she'd chased after Alek. On the way back, she'd
look around as she ran, to start learning the terrain. But she

would have to run, though at a slow pace, to beat the clock; she had to be at least a couple of miles from where they'd started.

On the way out, she'd been consumed with keeping up with Alek, but he was too fast. She'd panicked a little when she'd started to lose ground. Speed had never been her best thing. She was fast enough to catch food and could probably get quicker with more training, but pace had never been an issue since she had endurance. She whispered the words her Alpha used during their runs together. "Focus on the one true scent, Claire. Don't get distracted by the scenery."

And just like that, she fell into a quiet, familiar energy. She was a marathon runner, not a sprinter. She let her breathing slow, pushing air out of her mouth with each leg fall and pulling it in again with her nose to maximize the scent intake. Soon she started to be able to match scents to individual plants instead of perceiving an overwhelming rush of newness.

It wasn't like home—the grasses didn't smell the same, nor the trees. But as long as she didn't try to put a name to things, she could concentrate. Every so often she would catch a whiff of the musky maleness of Alek and she would falter and lose focus. Every time, Claire forced herself to ignore that scent, knowing that if she didn't, she would follow it as if she were a homing pigeon. His natural wolf scent was intoxicating enough without whatever the hell cologne or soap he wore. Together they turned her mind to putty and her insides to liquid.

Alek could be dangerous in more ways than one. She didn't like to admit that chasing after him, she'd wanted nothing more than to overtake him, throw him to the forest floor, and rip off his clothes. Taste his smooth skin, wrap herself around him, bury herself inside that musk, and see if it was stronger when he was sweating and excited. She felt a shudder pass over her and a rush of warmth in her gut that made her stumble. Damn.

No, she couldn't afford a distraction like Alek Siska, not with lives on the line.

It was probably better this way. Let him play whatever games he was playing. She would rise above them to do her job. It helped that she was pissed and feeling betrayed by him.

The top of the sun edged beneath the shadow of the mountain and the sky's blue dissolved into orange and fiery red, beautiful but almost too bright to look at. She remembered the old rhyme an uncle, his name long forgotten in her memory, used to recite. *Red sky at morning, sailors take warning. Red sky at night, sailor's delight.*

Tomorrow would be sunny, clear sailing. If only she could get through tonight.

She moved from a jog to a run as the daylight dimmed and the shadows grew deeper. She had to rely more on her nose than her eyes in the thick trees and that made her head hurt.

The more she ran, the angrier she got. Wasn't it just common courtesy to explain what the hell he planned to do? Alek knew she'd just arrived, that she didn't know the area. He knew they were short on time and that she had no idea what Ascension was or how it worked. Wouldn't it have been nice if he'd explained the rules?

Pushing harder to reach town before night completely stole her vision, she made her tired muscles move faster, forced her burning lungs to pull in even more air as the town began to appear in the distance.

"Ten . . . nine . . . eight . . . seven . . ."

The sound, distant but pure, filled the still air. It was a chorus of voices, young and old, male and female. It was a happy sound, like at the celebrations for the New Year.

"Six . . . five . . . four . . ."

The wall of trees finally gave way to a wide clearing and

Claire saw a crowd of people at the far end of town, gathered around a wooden stage. They were all looking at the speaker at a podium. *"Three . . . two . . . one!"*

The man at the podium was the mayor and Claire felt her feet falter and slow. "That's it!" he called out to the crowd. "The challenger has defaulted. Ascension is over and we have a new champion!" He held up the arm of a buoyant, wildly excited Rachel like she was the winner of a prize fight. A moment later she was accepting hugs and pats on the back from townspeople as she descended the stairs into their welcoming embrace.

Claire's mind buzzed and her stomach felt like she'd been punched. She'd missed it. She'd lost her first challenge in a new pack . . . by *default*. Claire felt her face begin to burn hot, partly from embarrassment and partly from sheer anger. *Damn Alek!* Damn him straight to hell! And damn her too, for believing that he would be honest and help her.

She smelled him before she saw him race out of the woods just a few seconds behind her, but her inner wolf was too shaken to respond to the musky scent. "Claire . . . I—" He touched her shoulder, his scent a wet mix of sorrow and shame.

Claire didn't want to hear it or smell it. In fact, she wanted nothing to do with him. "Go to hell, Siska. Thanks for nothing."

She strode forward toward the crowd, head high and defiant, leaving him standing alone on the dirt road. She was ready to accept whatever humiliation the mayor and police chief were likely to heap on her.

Rachel saw her first. She broke out from the crowd. Rather than the sly smile at her failure that Claire was expecting, the other woman's expression flicked between horrified, terrified, and relieved. "Claire! Where in the world have you been? Are you okay? What happened?"

Claire didn't get a chance to open her mouth before the police chief chimed in. "What happened is she missed the challenge. So she lost the challenge. We take timeliness seriously around here, Miss Sanchez."

Someone shouted out from the crowd that began to gather around them, "You snooze, you lose, newbie!"

It shouldn't bother her—the visceral glee from the town at her humiliation—but she was accustomed to a more supportive pack. It was clear that she wasn't going to be happy in Luna Lake. She'd do her job anyway, of course, but she didn't see that she had to protect the person who was really at fault. "My so-called mentor ran off and left me in the woods. I couldn't make it back in time. Congratulations, Rachel. You won fair and square." She turned to the police chief, who was nearly salivating under watchful, predatory eyes. "So what happens now? Locked in a cage? Taking a strip of hide?"

Rachel flinched visibly. She pulled Claire into a hug and whispered, close to her ear, "Not that, hon. Nothing like back then. It's not so bad, being the Omega. You'll get through it. It's only a month and you've always been stronger than me. I've done it most of the time I've been here." Rachel pulled back and gave Claire a shaky smile. It was clear she wanted to be happy she was no longer the Omega, but wasn't happy enough to wish it on her replacement.

Omega. The leaden weight of the word made Claire want to vomit. The realization of what had just happened was sinking home. She hadn't just lost a challenge. She'd become the lowest member of the pack. She'd almost rather lose some of her skin.

The mayor pushed his way through the crowd, pulling Alek by the literal scruff of his neck. "Is what Miss Sanchez says true, Alek? Did you leave her in the woods so long she missed her check-in time?"

Alek looked in agony. Embarrassed, angry, humiliated,

worried, afraid—a melting pot of negative scents. Even the crowd noticed the smells and some of the jubilant chanting and cheering faded away. "I . . ." He seemed to be ready to say a thousand things. But all that came out was, "Yes." He turned and looked straight into her eyes. "I'm sorry, Claire. I messed up."

Part of her wanted to scream at him, "Yeah, you did, you idiot!" Another part wanted to hug him and tell him it was okay. A tiny bit of her just wanted to slap him.

But she didn't get a chance to do anything, because the mayor just tsked. "Sorry about that, Ms. Sanchez. Not your fault, but the rules are very clear." He raised his voice to the crowd. "Looks like we've got us *two* Omegas this month, folks! We won't need to have a meeting tonight after all to introduce our new resident. Get your list of chores written up, folks. You'll all get to meet her as she and Alek both stop by each and every house in town until the next Ascension!" The crowd cheered and started laughing and celebrating again.

At Alek's sudden startled look, the police chief leaned in and whispered with the oily scent of dark glee leaking from his pores. "Look at section fourteen, paragraph ten. 'A mentor who shall knowingly or intentionally allow a challenger to violate a rule of the games shall share the result of said violation.'" The police chief put a tight arm around Alek's shoulders and the other around hers, appearing to be jovial and friendly. But the pressure as he dug his fingers into Claire's shoulder wasn't friendly and the words he whispered under his breath as the crowd cheered chilled her blood. "Oh, I'm going to *enjoy* making you both crawl."

CHAPTER 9

The scents drifting out from the kitchen the next day should have made Alek's stomach growl. Roast turkey, venison stew, and baking bread, seasoned and cooked to perfection. But his gut was rumbling and queasy and a band of pain enveloped his head like a vise.

Omega.

He'd never been the Omega; had no idea what it entailed. Worse, he'd inflicted it on Claire, who didn't even know how things worked in town. He'd tossed and turned all night, reliving the scene. He'd failed her, plain and simple. There was no excuse. When they'd gotten home, Claire had locked herself in her room without a word to anyone. Mom had suggested Alek not try to talk to her until the weekly dinner today.

Maybe it would help if he knew more about what being the Omega meant. He'd been alpha since he could remember—since his first change—so he'd never had to serve in that role. But his bro, Scott Clayton, had been the Omega on and off for several years before Rachel lost her first challenge.

Alek wound his way through the crowd of people who'd arrived for dinner, heading for Scott, whose blond ponytail, with its distinctive streak of white, he'd spotted from across the room. As he passed the staircase, a flood of scent froze him in midstep. Sweet, thick, warm. Chocolate in front of the fire, it filled his nose, his head; it fluttered in his chest. He tried to inhale again without exhaling, to capture more of it. He turned his head and saw those perfect features and those eyes . . . those *angry* eyes. Claire glowered down at him, fingers clutching the handrail like she was trying to squeeze the life out of it.

"Claire. I'm so sor—"

She held up a hand, her clenched jaw relaxing just enough to say, "I don't want to hear it. I didn't realize you'd be here. Tell Asylin I'm not hungry after all." She turned and stormed back up the stairs, the fresh bandage on her head brilliant in the sunlight streaming through the high windows. The door to her room slammed shut behind her.

Stunned by their interaction, Alek didn't notice Dani until she punched him hard in the shoulder, shaking off some of the fuzz in his brain. His hand automatically moved to his stinging bicep. She had a mean punch. "Ow! Dani, what the hell?"

"What did you say to her now, Alek? It's bad enough you humiliated her in front of the whole town, but you got her fired too . . . before she even started! God, you can be such a jerk sometimes!" She ran up the stairs and gently knocked on the bedroom door. "Claire? Honey, are you okay?"

Fired? Say what? The fluff in his mind returned. He couldn't seem to focus on anything. He put a hand on the bannister, intending to follow Dani up the stairs, when a firm grip on his shoulder pulled him back. "Don't do it, bro. You'll only make it worse."

He turned to see Scott shaking his head, almost sadly.

"What did I miss? What was Dani talking about?"

Scott put an arm around his shoulder, throwing up the

scents of feathers and pity in a thick cloud. The white owl shifter plucked a jacket off the rack near the front door, then half-shoved Alek out the door and down the stairs. A cold wind hit Alek in the face, clearing Claire's scent from his brain.

"Dude, you are so smart, and yet so completely clueless." Zipping up the jacket, Scott let out a light chuckle as the two men crunched through the leaves littering the ground.

Alek slammed his fists into his pockets and hunched his shoulders, shaking off the other man's arm. "I screwed up, Scott. I know it and I'm sorry about it. Do you have to rub it in? All I was asking is what Dani meant about Claire's job."

Scott stopped and threw up his arms, causing the brightly colored knit scarf around his neck to whip in the wind. "*That's* exactly what I mean. You go to the same family meetings I do. I've seen you make eye contact and nod when everyone else does." He tapped a gloved finger against Alek's forehead hard enough to rock his head back. "But nothing sinks in. You only hear what you want to hear."

Alek felt his anger rise. He pushed away Scott's hand. "What the hell are you talking about? What does this have to do with Claire?"

Scott leaned against the trunk of a tall pine tree, the lowest branch a dozen feet above his head, crossed his arms over his broad chest, and let out a sound of exasperation. "Everything. Two days before Kristy and Darrell went missing, Mom told everyone Claire was coming to stay with us because she was going to be the new teacher for Kristy's class. She even told us Claire was a red wolf. You were there, but everything with you was dispatch this and rotten Lenny that, and the all-Sonya, all-the-time channel. Dude, you obsess about shit and don't listen."

He tried to think back to before the kids had disappeared, to any mention of Claire and . . . nothing. Crap. What else had he been missing? "Okay. You're right. Maybe I was too wrapped up in other things. But that can't have been when she got fired, or she wouldn't have come here at all."

Scott scratched at the back of his head, then flipped his ponytail around to the front and began to pick bits of bark out of his hair. "Yeah, I just heard about that." He shrugged. "It makes sense. She's the Omega now. How would she be able to teach when she can't talk to anyone above her station? Even kids are above the Omega. It'd be chaos. Don't you remember Mrs. O'Donnell?"

In a flash, Alek did. He and Scott had been fourteen then. Mrs. O'Donnell had been a small woman, a falcon if he remembered right, and not very powerful magically. From the start of the school year, the class ran roughshod over her. Yelling, throwing stuff around the room, ditching class entirely. She couldn't control the kids at all. The principal had had to step in—he was a wily black bear who had run an entire human school district somewhere in the Midwest—before things settled down. Mrs. O'Donnell had moved away a month later. "Yeah, we celebrated *breaking* her. Ouch. Thanks for reminding me of one of our not-so-stellar moments."

Scott shrugged, but with a strong scent of embarrassment. "Hey, we were kids. Rowdy shifters feeling all tough and shit." He snorted and suddenly smelled of thick, wet sorrow. "At least you lived up to the *tough* part. I got a lot of swirlies when you weren't around."

Feeling abruptly uncomfortable about the direction the discussion was going, Alek cleared his throat. "But Claire *is* an alpha. Even with the Omega title, she could still control the class."

"When she's forbidden to look the other teachers in the eye, or the principal, or the *parents*?" his brother countered. "Yeah, that would be fun. And when would she do the Omega work? At night? Dude, I was *exhausted* after all the crap that needs to be done at this time of year. Even with you taking part of the load—and by the way, that part royally sucks—she would be too tired to grade papers or make lesson plans. It just wouldn't work."

At this time of year? "What sort of things need to be done?"

Scott furrowed his brow for a moment and then let out a loud, sudden laugh. "Oh, man! That's right. You're in the in-between generation. You've never *been* the Omega. Wow . . . where do I start to explain the suckitude?" He paused and really seemed to struggle to begin.

"Scott! Alek! Dinnertime!" Their mom's shout from the doorway made them both turn.

Alek didn't want to go in, didn't want to face Claire's justified anger. His screwup was far bigger than he'd originally thought. He hung back as Scott headed for the house. "Hey, do me a favor. Tell Mom I had to do something and can't make it to dinner."

Scott looked both amused and horrified. "Mom-assisted suicide isn't something I'd recommend, bro. You know how she gets."

"I'll just have to risk it. I've got to take care of something." He needed to make this right. It was time to go to the police station and do whatever he needed to do to get Claire out of this.

Scott searched his face and Alek knew his brother knew what he was planning. As he sprinted away from the house, keeping out of his surrogate mother's direct view, Scott quietly called after him, "I don't think it'll work, but I don't blame you for trying. I'll stall for as long as I can. Good luck."

"If Claire's not going to eat, I'm not either." Dani's face was firm as she confronted her mother's sour expression. "She doesn't feel well." She put an arm around Claire in solidarity.

It was nice to have someone who felt like a friend right now. There weren't many to be found. The black waves of hair that brushed Claire's face as she tightened her hug smelled of rosemary and aloe.

Asylin let out a sharp-pitched hiss, characteristic of an annoyed owl. Her eyes glowed amber with magic, bright enough to make her dark skin look golden . . . as though she should be an eagle or great horned owl instead of a snowy one. "What she feels is embarrassed . . . which won't be fixed by starving herself. Neither of you have eaten since you got here. That's more than a day ago. You're both still healing. Get downstairs and eat something."

Claire only glanced at the older woman for a moment before returning to staring at her own hands. She could smell her own burnt-metal frustration and embarrassment, blended with wet sorrow and tangy fear. "I know what I'm feeling is something I need to deal with, Asylin. But I don't think it's unreasonable to skip mingling with a big group of strangers while I absorb all this." Everyone downstairs, whether dark skin, fair, olive, or brown, was family to the Williamses, even if they were only foster placements, but they were just strangers to Claire and now they thought of her as something beneath their notice. "All I want to do is talk to someone who knows what I'm supposed to do tomorrow and then go to sleep."

The room filled with the scent of warm concern from both owls as Asylin sat down next to her and enveloped her in a hug. Her earring briefly caught on the edge of the bandage covering the stitches, but then slid away without tugging.

Asylin said softly, "Claire, the moment they brought you through the front door, you were family. The people downstairs aren't strangers. They're your brothers and sisters. When you're in pain, we'll heal you. When you're afraid, we'll protect you. When you're happy, we'll share your joy. You can trust us."

Pretty words and lovely thoughts, but Claire was here for a reason and trusting people wasn't part of the plan. Still, she did need to put aside her anger and start to make some contacts, get information. She hugged Asylin in return. "Thanks. Maybe it *would* help to get to know some people."

"How about starting with us?" Claire started and looked toward the door. It had opened so quietly on oiled hinges that she hadn't even heard it. Not good.

Rachel was standing in the doorway with another young man, not much past his teens, who was so pale he looked ghostly next to Rachel's dark skin. The streak of white in his long hair made Claire think that he might have also been an attack victim who had his first change forced on him. More warm concern wafted into the room.

"We're all the help you need," Rachel said. "Scott and I have both been the Omegas for over a year. We know all the ins and outs and tricks. We'll get you through this. One day at a time until the next Ascension."

They both smiled, but their scents didn't match their expressions and Claire could tell that they were both nervous. If Asylin noticed, she gave no sign, just patted Claire on the hand and rose to her feet. "So it's settled, then. Let's all go down to supper and the four of you can talk."

Four. That could only mean . . . "I really don't want to talk to Alek right now. Maybe in a few days, but . . ."

Rachel, Scott, and Dani nearly simultaneously let out strangled sounds that could have been muffled laughter or an indication of pain. Asylin shot them a sharp look and their gazes dropped to the floor in total deference. Her voice was strong and her deep brown eyes were serious and confident when she faced Claire and said, "In this family, we face our problems head-on. In the past decade, nearly forty troubled souls have passed through this home. Children and teens traumatized by every form of loss and abuse, physically and emotionally wounded, too damaged for nearly any other pack to take on. Every possible personality has met, clashed, and eventually, rejoiced.

"The only way that can happen is for there to be *trust*. John and I rule this roost with a firm hand. So long as you trust in that, you'll know that there's no conflict so horrible that you can't deal with the person face-to-face. I let you have last night to rest, but you can't avoid this forever. No harm will come to you from anyone under this roof. I swear that to you as I swore it to your pack leaders."

Claire nodded, neither agreeing nor disagreeing, keeping as much emotion from her scent as possible. Instead, she concentrated on the smells of the food downstairs until her stomach rumbled and she literally had to wipe drool from the corner of her mouth. It was a good distraction, because Asylin let out a small chuckle.

"We can talk more after supper."

The food was good. Great, in fact. The venison was a perfect medium rare, the turkey was juicy under a crackling brown skin. Granted, there weren't four different homemade salsas to slather on things, but Claire had to expect that not every place would be like Texas. She hadn't realized just how hungry she was, although she should have, considering the events of the past few days. Even the traveling between states to get here had been traumatic because it had been years since she'd been in airports in major cities. Fortunately, keeping her mouth stuffed with food was a great reason not to do more than raise her chin and wave a finger whenever anyone said anything to her, so she mostly could watch and listen. There were men and women, kids young and old, various species and various nationalities. Yet they all got along and seemed like a real family. She'd thought the Tedford pack was the only group out there that got along well, and only because they were bound mentally under the Alphas. She'd heard stories from visiting dignitaries from the Council and Wolven that had led her to believe that most of the problems they had to intervene with had to do with the species not blending well in the same area. The great cats didn't like living even a few miles away from wolves, the birds feared cats in their territory, the wolves hated the smell of the birds. But there seemed no such problems here. It confused her.

What confused her more, though, was that nobody was talking about the missing kids. It seemed weird. There was talk of college courses, and who was dating who, and who hated their job more, but nothing about what should be the biggest issue on the minds of this particular family.

After some minutes, Claire tapped Dani on the arm and leaned in to whisper. "So what's the scoop on the search for the kids? We haven't really talked about it since we got here."

Dani stared at her with furrowed brows and then blinked a few times, looking around the room as though searching for a memory. "I . . . I don't know. I think Mom said something about them being okay."

Say what? After her panic in the car yesterday? Claire let out a small squeal. "Really? That's amazing! Are they here? Did they say where they'd been? I'd love to meet them."

Now Dani seemed really confused. She started shaking her head, drumming her fingers on the edge of the plate on her lap. She stood abruptly. "Excuse me, okay? I need to find Mom."

Claire wanted to follow, but spotted Scott and Rachel headed her way. Even if Kristy and Darrell were safe and sound, others were still unaccounted for. She couldn't leave until she could give the Council a report on the situation here.

And that meant a stint as an Omega, as much as she hated the idea.

"Hey, Rachel." She raised her hand, inviting the pair to sit on the couch across from her. "And . . . Scott, right?"

He nodded and smiled. "How you doin'? Have you met everyone?"

Claire shrugged. "Sort of, I guess. They only have to remember one new name. I'd struggle to remember half of theirs if you quizzed me." In truth, she'd been concentrating on trying to overhear conversations. "Where's Asylin? I wanted to thank her for the amazing food. She's one heck of a cook."

Rachel chuckled. "Then you need to thank Dad. He's the cook. Mom is the galley sergeant that gets everything on the table at once, but she's not too good with a skillet."

That explained the bacon yesterday. "Good to know. Anyway, where is she? I haven't seen her since we came downstairs."

Scott rolled his eyes. "Out tracking down Alek, I think. When Mom says dinner is *mandatory*, she means it." Claire must have shown her confusion, because he explained between bites of roast, punctuating with his fork while he shifted from foot to foot with nervous energy. "Dinner is more than a meal here. It's an event. It used to be every night when we were little. It was Mom's way of making sure everyone was under lock and key once the sun went down."

Rachel nodded and added, "You know how they advertise about *family game night* on TV? Sort of like that. Everyone participates in preparation and cleanup. And sometimes we do play games. Jenga or charades or even gin rummy."

"Right." Scott started in on a big chunk of apple pie that Claire had wanted to try but was too full. "But now *dinner* is just once a week so she and Dad can catch up on everyone— since we mostly live in other houses around town. I mean, we eat supper every day, but *dinner* means the weekly family thing." He sat down on an oversized hassock and Rachel sat down beside him. "They're treating you like a guest this time, but plan that next week, you'll be helping cook and clean."

"Got it." That she understood. It was the same in her pack. The weekly tamale cooks and tortilla baking parties were part of her life. She would miss them.

Scott swallowed down half a soda and then started talking again. "Until she gets back, let's go over the Omega duties."

Claire laughed nervously, feeling a warm rush of something approaching fear. "Your voice just went up about an octave. Is this something I need to worry about?"

The two shifters, who stank of worry, exchanged wary glances. Rachel reached over and touched her hand. "This will probably be a cakewalk for you, since you're an alpha. You're stronger, faster—"

Scott added, nodding, "And heal quicker. That'll be a bonus."

Rachel nodded also. "Huge. Really, Claire. You'll be fine."

Heal quicker? Stronger? Faster? What the hell! "You guys are freaking me out. Do I need to carry a medical kit with me?"

Scott looked at her with an expression somewhere between sorrow and contempt. His voice was flat and angry. "No. They make sure marks don't show. At least, not for a few days."

What the hell was going on in this town? "Come again? Maybe you'd better give me some specifics." Because if the Omegas were being abused here it was definitely time to bring in the big guns of Wolven. Maybe even the Council.

A flash of movement in the sky, glimpsed through the picture window, made her flinch, remembering things she'd rather forget. A large white owl swooped over the yard, clutching a man in its talons. Though she'd seen him only a few times, Claire had no trouble recognizing Alek—which meant that the owl was probably Asylin. She dropped Alek from a height of about four feet. He bounced once on the thick coating of pine needles that covered the ground, then got to his feet.

The owl landed silently beside him, almost without a wing flutter, and transformed back into Asylin Williams. Though Claire knew she was naked—clothing couldn't be shifted or carried—Asylin appeared to be fully dressed, which told Claire the owl shifter was a powerful alpha. Many high-level alphas could use their magic to create the appearance and sometimes even the feel of clothing when they didn't have a stitch on. Claire might be an alpha but she didn't have anything close to that power.

Asylin didn't touch Alek, just pointed toward the house. He sprinted up the drive with her hot on his heels.

Scott and Rachel had turned to watch the spectacle. "Ooo," Scott commented with an almost painful wince. "That probably wasn't pretty. I warned him she wouldn't be happy."

"Do you guys actually wander around in animal form during the day?" Claire couldn't help but ask. The sighting of a wolf or cougar wouldn't necessarily be a cause for alarm in humans, but an owl with a wing span of a dozen feet was bound to be noticed.

"No," Rachel said, with raised brows. "Asylin wouldn't do that unless there was trouble. She wasn't just ticked off; she was *scared*."

CHAPTER 10

The minute Asylin walked through the door behind Alek, she started snapping out orders.

"Battle stations, people! We've got a rogue." Plates and cups dropped to the floor from multiple locations and all conversation ceased. Everyone turned to face the willowy, dark-skinned woman with the voice of solid steel. "A female cougar, headed toward the main road. A-team, get to the mudroom, shift, and hit the perimeter. Drive her here." She pointed at Claire. "I know you're new, sweetie, but you're alphic. You're part of A-team. Your pack said you can handle defense. Alek, take her with you. And this time, explain the process to her."

Alek hesitated before starting forward and his mother noticed. "Get past it, Alek. You too, Claire. We have a verified threat."

His stomach churning, he swallowed, nodded, and walked quickly over to Claire, holding out his hand. She hesitated only a moment before she took it, clearly not understanding what was happening. The tingle when their hands met was strong, flashing across his skin like fire, hot enough to pull a gasp from his throat. But there was no time. He pulled her with him toward the mudroom, just behind Patrick, Janet, and Cindee.

Behind them, Asylin continued setting people into motion. "B-team, get the barricades up. Dani, you're with C-team today. I don't want you flying on that wing yet. Get the kids to the basement. D-team, you're with me."

"Alek, what's happening?" Claire asked, turning her head to try to see everything that was going on. Alek knew without looking that some of his brothers and sisters were locking previously concealed metal grating into place over the plate glass windows. Others were sealing the doors, using steel plates stored under the top of the big dining room table.

"Someone in town has gone rogue. Insane. Have you ever encountered a rogue shifter?"

She nodded, swallowing hard. "Once. Not one of our pack; an eagle who started attacking humans in town. We had to hunt it down. I lost a good friend in the fight."

He nodded. "That's happened here too, but we'll try not to lose anyone today. I presume you've met everyone, but just in case . . . Claire, meet Patrick, Cindee, and Janet. Along with Mom and Dad, we're A-team. But Mom tends to stay and guard the house." Claire raised her hand somewhat sheepishly.

"We've met, sort of," Janet said. "I was in the kitchen when most of the people were doing the hellos. I'm Janet. Welcome to the chaos."

Once they were in the mudroom, Patrick stepped behind them to pull a thick steel bar out of the decorative woodwork on the wall and used it to barricade the door. He closed the heavy, extra-strong, thick mesh screen door, which latched with a sharp snap.

Janet had already taken off her boots and shifted to cougar form, shredding her clothes in the process. The rags lay in little heaps around her.

"Jeez, sis," Patrick said, pulling his sweater over his head. "Looking for new reasons to go shopping online?"

She turned her shaggy head and twitched a whisker at him. "I'd rather have the ability to shop later instead of getting shredded by the rogue while I was trying to unhook my bra. Besides, I was tired of those jeans." She leaped out the back door. "See you on the flip side. Going south toward the lake."

Patrick was a beat behind her, shifting to owl form and hopping to the door. "I'll head north to the ridge," he said, then spread his wings and was gone.

Cindee was crouched, naked, staring at the floor, with her honey-colored hair hanging loose, almost concealing her face. Her clothing was in a neatly folded stack on top of the washing machine. She was taking deep breaths and exhaling slowly. Alek knelt beside her. "You okay?"

He focused on his sister, whose nude form held no attraction for him, to distract himself from what Claire was doing. It was wrong, wanting to look as he heard the whisper of cloth, knowing she was getting undressed. It was wrong, wanting to know what her body looked like, to see her muscles moving under pale skin.

Cindee looked up at him sadly, seeming somehow small and vulnerable though she was an alpha wolf. "Will this *ever* be over, Alek? Will we forever be tracking down and slaughtering our friends and family?"

"There have always been rogues, Cindee. It's not just since the plague. It was just another secret, something most of us never heard about." He heard the bitterness in his voice and made an effort to sound encouraging. "You can do this."

"He's right." Claire's voice was lower now, with a slight growl. She stepped into Alek's peripheral vision, a fluff of cinnamon-colored fur. "There are rogues all over. I know I'm new, and you don't know me, but insanity . . . whether human or animal, happens. It sucks, but it happens."

Nodding, Cindee let out a slow breath. Her amber eyes were glowing, unblinking, and cold but her voice trembled as she said, "Female cougar, Alek. What if it's Tammy? I've worked so hard with her. I thought I had her on the mend."

Like Alek and others in the family, Cindee worked Luna Lake's suicide hotline. Tammy was a frequent caller. She'd lost her whole family in New Mexico to the snakes. Though cougars weren't terribly pride oriented, most of Tammy's family had been human. To see them terrorized and slaughtered just because Tammy wasn't alphic . . . Alek couldn't even imagine the feeling of helplessness. At least the family members he lost had been able to fight.

He sighed, knowing it probably was Tammy—she'd been close to the edge for some time. "Even if it is Tammy, she's not Tammy anymore. She's not alphic. How would she manage a full shift, in the daylight, even this close to the moon? You know as well as I do that if she's gone rogue, her magic has gone wild. The person you knew is gone and if we don't stop her, people will die. Maybe us, maybe some innocent tourist the next town over."

Cindee seemed to gather herself, raising her chin and flipping her hair back. She wiped her tears away with the back of her arm. Her eyes flashed with determination and the moist, thick scent of her sorrow turned cool and metallic. "Okay. You're right. Let's do this." As she leaped toward the door, her form shimmered with energy. She landed on the concrete stoop in wolf form. "I'll go west. You make sure she doesn't make it to the road."

Alek reached inside for the part of him that was wolf. It wasn't so much pulling the animal out as opening the cage that prevented him from taking that form permanently. He remembered the first time he shifted . . . the pain as limbs broke and reformed into new shapes. Now it felt like a spring uncoiling, easing the constant tension. Color dissolved from his view as the world shifted to a million shades of gray.

He turned and looked at wolf-Claire. She was smaller than him, but the power that glowed from within those pale eyes was startling, despite the leaking blood that was already marring the fur next to her ear. His gaze flicked to the ground, where her bandage lay, coiled. "So what's the plan?" Her voice was curt, tight, professional, but her scents didn't match. She was still mad at him, but there were other emotions that filled the air. He couldn't sort them all out, which wasn't going to make coordinated action any easier.

He let out a light snort to clear his throat, which caught her attention. "Look, I'm sorry. Okay? I didn't mean to screw things up for you. I got distracted and I shouldn't have. But I can't afford to have you at less than your best out there or questioning things I say to keep you safe. You don't know the area or the rogue. I do."

Claire looked at him for a long moment, then shook her head a couple of times before padding past him to the door. He could almost taste the beat of her heart as her magic slid past his. It scrambled his brain for a few seconds. She scanned the distant line of trees in a slow arc. "Maybe you are sorry. Maybe you sabotaged me intentionally. But you're right that it doesn't matter. I'll work with you because you have knowledge. But don't presume that means I can pretend nothing ever happened. I'll be sniffing for lies or threats." She bolted out the door, headed east, forcing him to race out after her. *Damn it! She's going to get herself killed being that impulsive!*

An arctic-chilled wind hit him as he cleared the shelter of the house. A fine mist hung in the air, making it feel colder than it probably was. There was no scent of angry cat riding the wind. Claire was already at the edge of the heavy woods, nose to the ground, sniffing back and forth. Did she know anything about cats? He didn't know much about the

Texas pack. But she wasn't looking *up*, which is where the cats liked to hunt. He headed for the other side of the clearing, carefully watching for movement and sniffing as the breeze swirled, shifting direction through the treetops. "Make sure you keep an eye overhead. Rogues can jump a long way down." He said it softly, rather than yelling, relying on the wind to carry the words to her flicking ears. She started and turned her head before nodding and scanning the treetops overhead. Either she didn't know that Sazi cats could leap from high places—ledges, mountaintops, and even the tops of trees, where they couldn't be easily seen or smelled, or she'd forgotten. Either way, it was worthwhile to warn her.

There, just a faint whiff, but he smelled cat. He let out a short bark. At the corner of his eye, he saw Claire's head rise and her nose lift. Alek bounded into the trees with Claire at his flank. Their footfalls were nearly silent on the forest floor, cushioned by fallen needles and moistened leaves. They ran with nearly identical strides, shifting direction in nearly perfect unison. They stayed in the trees, parallel to the road. Alek soon became aware of how fluid, how *easy* it felt to run with Claire . . . like they'd been pack mates all their lives. In fact, he was more in sync with her than either Cindee or Janet.

So when she slammed into his side, flipping him over a fallen log in a painful tumble, it took him by surprise. "Hey! What the hell?"

The ground under him shuddered as he came to his feet and found himself just a foot away from a large cougar that had pounced onto the exact spot he'd occupied moments before. She'd taken the lesson better than he had apparently. *Sheesh. Get your mind back in the game, Alek.* Claire was already in a defensive stance, shoulders lowered with hackles raised. Her teeth were bared in a threat that had made the cougar freeze instead of leaping to attack Alek.

One whiff of the big cat's musk told him two things: it was

Tammy, and she didn't smell right. Not only was there a flurry of negative emotions, so strong that they nearly made him sneeze, but there was also an underlying smell of decay and illness. It was sweet as rotting flesh, but with a rancid quality. He took a step forward and so did Claire. The cougar seemed undecided, not sure whether to attack or retreat. Maybe that was to their advantage.

"Tammy. It's Alek. You know me. It doesn't have to be this way. Let us get you to Marilyn. You're sick."

"Hurts." The word from Tammy's mouth was a low snarl that ended with a whine. "Head hurts."

He took another step forward. The cat's skin twitched but she didn't move away. "I know it hurts, Tammy." He knew he had to keep using her name, reminding her of her humanity. "Cindee is looking for you too. We want to help it not hurt anymore."

That made the cat blink. "Cin . . . dee?" Good. She remembered.

Alek was glad to see Claire ease into a more relaxed pose, still wary but following his lead. He continued, quietly, "Cindee told us she's worried about you. She wants to make sure you're okay. *Are* you okay?"

"O . . . kay?" Tammy shook her shaggy head. "No. Not okay. Hungry."

"We can get you food. Come back to the house. Dinner's on. There's plenty of food left. Just waiting to be eaten. Deer, pork, chicken . . . anything you want."

Tammy blinked those huge amber eyes. He was winning her over. She'd eaten at their house many times. "Dinner. Deer. Bird." The cougar turned toward home and Alek let out a small sigh. They could get her in the house, contain her in the basement, and have Marilyn see if there was anything that could be done.

It happened so fast that there was no time to react. A

swoop of white from the sky. A flash of red splashed across tawny fur and a scream from the big cat as talons opened her skin. "Patrick! NO!" He shouted the words and it was enough to make the snowy owl turn in midair. But Tammy reacted with pure instinct in a blur of frenzied motion. A paw reached up and wide hooked claws found purchase on a feathered leg. Patrick's owl form was abruptly on the ground, under the bulk of the powerful cougar.

The bird and cat began to roll, clawing and tearing at each other. Unearthly howls and screams filled the air. Alek edged toward the pair, trying to find an opening to pull them apart. Before he could leap into the fray, a hand wrapped around his tail. His *tail*! Who grabs a wolf's tail? He turned, claws and teeth, bared to find a naked Claire standing behind him.

She had to shout to be heard over the battle. "Adding claws is the worst thing you can do. Use your magic!" She threw her arms forward and then out, as though stopping elevator doors from shutting. The fighters slowed, their movements losing energy and speed. The sheer power he felt streaming out from her stung his skin. "Alek! C'mon, help me!"

He wasn't really sure what she was doing. He'd never seen an alpha use raw magic to break up a fight. He threw power toward her, hoping she knew what to do with it. But it bounced off the flare rather than adding to it. "I don't know how. What do I do?"

She was on her knees now, her hair blowing forward in the cold wind, her skin glowing with power. "Shift forms. Stand behind me and feel the flow of energy."

Tammy was writhing in the stream of magic, fighting to get to the owl. Patrick was trying to get away, but couldn't get the cougar's claws out of his leg. He was bleeding from multiple puncture wounds and was flapping in slow motion backward.

Alek shifted in a rush and edged around Claire, careful not

to get between her and her targets. He reached out to touch her shoulder and the world shifted. Flames of magic licked across his skin, electric, erotic, and so painful he could barely breathe. Claire let out a sound, something between a moan and a scream. As though hit by hurricane-force winds, Tammy and Patrick were thrown up and out in opposite directions. They each slammed against the trunks of trees a dozen feet up, hard enough that the branches swayed and the wood made a cracking sound, then dropped to the ground and lay still, stunned. Alive. He could smell that, and hear their slowing heartbeats. They were out cold.

Without a target, the flare of magic ripped through Alek and Claire. Alek tried to pull his hand away, but it was as though his skin was welded to her. He tried to use his other hand to pry the first one free and watched in horror as instead, his hand began to caress her hair. The sensation of the silken strands through his fingers made him instantly hard, hungry in a way that he'd never felt before. It was the wrong time, the wrong place, but the sound of the low moan that escaped her throat at his touch shut out all reason. Before he even realized it, he was on his knees beside her, his lips against her neck, tasting with his whole mouth, his teeth, his tongue. He slid an arm around her slim waist, pulling her tight against him.

He had to stop. There were two bodies on the ground. He didn't know how badly they were hurt. The rest of the teams would arrive any second. No way they couldn't have heard the fight. But still he didn't back away from Claire. He couldn't. He couldn't talk, couldn't ask permission or even apologize.

What the hell was happening to him?

The sensation of Alek's hands on her, his lips on her skin, was nearly too much to bear. She'd heard tales of power surges like this with mated pairs. But she didn't feel any sort of mental connection to him . . . nothing that would explain what she was feeling.

"Alek . . ." It was all she could get out. The word was a moan, a whimper, a plea. Not that he stop, but that he continue, take her to that next step. No! That *wasn't* what she wanted. She barely knew him, was furious with him. But her body was reacting without her control. She didn't want him, yet she did. . . .

As though he heard her thoughts, his hand turned her face toward him. Her mind went blank as his mouth claimed hers. Her heart raced so fast she was certain it was going to explode. This wasn't supposed to be what a first kiss was like. It wasn't supposed to *be* a first kiss. Despite the cold wind on her bare skin, she felt overheated. Everywhere his skin touched hers felt like it was on fire. The musky scent that filled her nose, combined with the cologne he wore, seemed to paralyze her. All she could do was accept his tongue, his weight, his hand gliding along her skin.

He cupped her breast, twirled her nipple with his thumb. A shock of sensation tore through her nerves and made her inhale sharply. Claire was suddenly wet, her insides contracting so hard it felt like cramps. His kiss deepened, his jaw working against hers almost frantically. Their tongues tasted and explored while their fingers clutched with increasing urgency. His twitching erection pressed against her hip, so very close to where she wanted it to be. If he pushed just a fraction more, she would let him take her without any regard for her own safety. She tried to feel the ground beneath her, the rocks and sticks that must be digging into her knees, but she couldn't. Nothing seemed to matter except the sensations he was causing.

She'd never felt so hungry to be taken, so deliciously vulnerable. It terrified her.

It wasn't until she heard rustling from the fallen cougar that she managed to collect her thoughts and open her eyes. The snowy owl, Patrick, was sprawled in a limp mass of feathers—alive and in no serious danger, judging by his scent and sensation of power Claire felt beating against her own. But Tammy's legs were beginning to twitch and the chaotic energy coming off her intensified. Fighting her instincts, Claire began to focus on the external world, smelling blood everywhere, hearing the cracking of branches in the distance.

The cougar's ears twitched; the cat apparently realized what those sounds meant—someone was coming. In a fight-or-flight moment, the cat chose flight. A blur of tawny fur jumped over Claire and Alek, heading for the deep forest. Something jerked Claire backward, past Alek, flipped her over, and smacked her head against the trunk of a tree a dozen feet away. Terror filled her as she realized that somehow she and Alek had become tin cans, attached to the bumper of the terrified cougar. The magic binding them dragged her along the ground, through brush and fallen leaves, battering her on all sides. She shrieked as her bare skin was ripped open. Blood flowed into her eyes—the stitches in her scalp must have ripped loose. Pain tore through her.

The grunts and yelps she heard from Alek as he tumbled along beside her told her he was in no better shape. She could smell sweet copper on the wind and not all of it was hers. She couldn't imagine the pain of being dragged with an erection.

"Tammy!" It was a scream. It was another full second before he could catch enough breath to talk again. "Tammy, you need to stop. You're hurting u—" Alek's plea was cut off by a pained sound and another spray of blood blossoming in the air.

Claire felt like she was falling down a mountainside. She had no control over how her body tumbled and skipped across the landscape, no hope of avoiding the jagged stones and fallen trees in her path. Trying to protect her battered, aching limbs and torso, she wrapped her arms around her chest, tucked in her chin, and tried to draw her legs up. She could tell from the pain that it would be days before some of the deep bruises surfaced and suspected she would need more stitches for some of the injuries to her arms.

Despite being constantly banged about, Claire fought for control of the magic that clawed at her, but it was like being wrapped in barbed wire. Every time she eased the pressure in one place, another would tighten. Normally, she could focus her mind like her Alpha had taught her, but for some reason, this power wouldn't bend to her will. Maybe that was why it was so hard to put down a rogue—the magic just kept slipping through her fingers.

She prayed that the cougar wouldn't decide to climb a tree. Hopefully, she and Alek weighed enough to limit the cat's options, but there was no way to tell.

Though the destruction their passage left behind would make them easy to track, they were moving so fast, Claire doubted the others would catch up to them unless the cat tired. The unfamiliar landscape was a blur as the cougar and her unwilling captives zigzagged through the trees, across rocks, and under bushes.

Apparently Alek had managed to keep his bearings and knew where they were. "Tammy. No! No, you need to turn around." Somehow he managed to yell loudly enough to be heard over the snapping of branches they crashed into. "I'm not kidding, Tammy. You can't do this."

The stink of Alek's fear filled Claire's nose and her heart pounded. She gasped until she could get enough breath to speak. "What's wrong? What's happening?"

"She's headed for the canyon. It's too wide to jump and she knows it!"

Suicide. Plus murder. Mustn't forget the two tagalongs

dragging behind. "Look, Tammy, I don't know you, but you don't seem like"—she let her body roll to avoid a tree, colliding with Alek in the process—"someone who would kill her brother. You're not a murderer."

The tortured screech from the cougar was difficult to decipher. Claire wasn't skilled at cat languages. "Not . . . a . . . murderer. Not . . . *anything*." An explosion of emotional scents hit Claire like a sledgehammer: anger, pain, sorrow, love. The conflicts dissolved hot peppers in cool water, wrapped Claire's nose in cookie spices, then burned to a crisp. She began to sneeze, losing what little control she had over her movements. Her nose broke against a rock. The pain was immediate and blinding and Claire felt like she was drowning in her own blood.

"Tammy! You don't have to give in to this!" Alek's voice was growing panicked. "Let us help you. We can get through this."

"Sorry, puppyboy—" The magical tether tying Claire and Alek to the cat released and they tumbled backward, tangling with each other, as the cougar raced up the mountainside. Had the magic been Tammy's doing all along?

"Don't!" Alek got to his feet before Claire and sprinted after the big cat. Claire followed. She was pretty sure one or two ribs were broken, and possibly her foot, but it didn't matter. They had to reach the cat, see if there was a way to save her. She counted on adrenaline getting her through, enabling her to ignore most of her injuries, and suspected Alek was doing the same.

Claire could see the drop-off ahead—the big cat was headed straight toward it. Alek poured on more speed then leaped onto the cat's back just as her front paws cleared the cliff edge, clawing at thin air.

His weight and her momentum propelled them into the canyon.

CHAPTER 11

Alek couldn't let Tammy do this. He just couldn't. Maybe she was nearly rogue. But *nearly* wasn't irretrievable. He was confident she could be saved if he could just get her to listen to reason. Maybe it would take drugs or a healer, but he wasn't willing to throw away yet another family member just because she had mental health problems.

When Tammy had said "Not anything," it spoke volumes to him. She was a cougar in a family of birds, just like he was a wolf. Alone in the crowd. His family meant well, but when it came down to it, an owl had more rights in the house than other Sazi.

The cuts and scrapes from his rough ride through the woods were nothing compared to the pain in his chest. Tammy shouldn't think there were no other options available to her.

He was embarrassed and angry with himself for giving in to such a base instinct as arousal at such a critical time. There was no excuse, and no way possible to apologize enough. Touching Claire like that had been unforgivable. He'd let himself be tempted by her smooth, curved body and a rush of energy like he'd never felt before. Even now it lingered, tingling his skin and numbing him to the serious wounds he knew he had. He could see the blood drying on his skin as he ran, and didn't even want to see what parts of him were damaged.

He was close enough to Tammy now to smell her fear, pain, and determination. That she wanted to end her life would make it far harder to fix whatever was wrong. But that was for later. Now he had to keep her from jumping. His only choice was to tackle her, drag her to the ground, and take whatever punishment she gave out.

Alek leaped forward, using his strength and his magic to push her down. It should have worked, except he was a second too late. There was no ground under Tammy's feet. Fingers clutched tight in her thick coarse fur, Alek felt the rush of wind in his face as they started to fall and his heart skipped a beat. The nearest ledge had to be a hundred feet down. Even if he survived—which was not guaranteed—he knew that Tammy wouldn't. He wrapped his arms around her heaving sides, feeling her heart beating like a trip-hammer against his skin as they dropped toward the canyon floor, far below.

Her whisper confirmed his suspicion. "Help me, Alek . . ."

He tightened his grip. "I will. I promise." He scanned the landscape in a moment that felt like all the time in the world. Maybe he could guide her toward one of the many pine trees beneath them—the branches might cushion her fall or even allow her to catch hold. "Hang on, sis."

They started to tumble. Slowly at first, then faster, the rush of wind making it impossible to hear or talk. Or steer. Tammy started flailing her limbs while screaming in fear. Her razor-sharp claws slashed at his torso, trying to find purchase.

He might have made a noise when she ripped open his flesh. He couldn't recall. What he did remember was the moment they stopped. Not because of a ledge or a tree or even the ground. They just . . . stopped, frozen in the air, the weight of powerful magic holding both of them firm against gravity.

Alek couldn't move a muscle but he could still hear the wind rushing through the canyon, feel fragrant pine needles brush across the side of his leg—they must have been closer to those trees than he'd thought.

His mind spun back to a moment, years before, when he'd stared up at the ceiling of a Chicago hotel. An intensely powerful shifter, the Councilman for the snakes, had been thrown against the ceiling by an even more powerful cat—a petite bobcat that all of the Council feared not only for her power but for her unpredictable nature.

Alek had wondered as a young boy how someone so powerful had been trapped like a fly in a web. Now he knew. He could breathe, but barely. It must be Mom. Asylin was an intensely powerful shifter. He'd never seen her do something like this, but he wouldn't put it past her.

In a moment he felt the rush of wings above them. He couldn't move his head to verify it, but he was certain that it had to be Patrick—he was closest. His brother must have woken and now was going to carry them to safety. Alek felt talons carefully close around one leg while the other set of claws encircled his bicep. Another snowy owl arrived to take hold of the large cat while a golden bird lifted Tammy from underneath. He could only see feathers. He couldn't figure out whose they were. Only then did the magic holding Alek immobile release. He began to cough from the rush of air into his lungs and forced himself to relax so Patrick wouldn't lose his grip. Tammy had wide eyes and stank with abject terror like a week-old litter box. Alek doubted she'd ever flown on the back of a bird before, judging by her stiff posture. He could hear her breath coming in tiny gasps, see her eyes flicking about. He hoped her claws, which were curved deep into downy feathers, hadn't penetrated skin.

He rose in small bursts of lift, the owl burdened with Alek's weight. "You're doing fine, Patrick. Take your time."

The owl was already tired, Alek knew, and injured. Alek closed his eyes as several fast flutters revealed quickly how his rescuer was weakening. He wished he could help but there wasn't anything he could do except wait . . . and closing his eyes made it worse because he kept imagining the ground getting nearer and nearer, too fast. He opened his eyes—they were still high, though low enough that he could clearly see a small herd of deer edging through the trees below on a well-worn path. He concentrated on the deer, trying not to think about the struggle Patrick was having, lifting him to safety. Hopefully the other two would get Tammy on the ground and then come help.

A flash of color behind the deer caught his eye. Red and white, moving slowly and carefully. It was smaller than the deer. Was that a child? It *was*! He strained to see, ignoring everything else. It was a young girl, with dark hair and skin. "Patrick, I think I see Kristy! Down at the bottom of the canyon. She's wearing that red-and-white-striped shirt you bought her last Christmas."

The owl hesitated, spun in the air like a helicopter. "I don't see her. Point where you're looking."

But she was gone. "Damn it. It was just a flash. Get me close to the ledge and drop me. I'll climb out and you can go down and look around."

It was the push the massive owl needed. He put in extra effort, expanding his wings to grab the largest amount of air possible. Alek helped by throwing a wave of magic ahead of them to literally pull the pair back to solid earth.

As soon as he was dropped, just barely on solid dirt, landing on his palms and already battered knees, the owl was off, streaking down into the depths of the trees.

Motors sounded in the distance and some of the B-team was already there. He wasn't sure how that was possible, since it felt like he and Tammy had just barely fallen over the cliff.

But here they were and the sun seemed lower than it had before.

Cindee tossed him a blanket to wrap himself in and draped another around Tammy's furred shoulders. Alek noticed Claire, in human form but still on all fours, throwing up whatever she'd eaten for possibly the last week. There wasn't anything sexy about vomit, no matter how cute she was. Plus, he was still remembering how to breathe and wanting to kiss the rocks under his feet.

His foster mother fluttered to the ground and shifted back to the smooth-skinned, statuesque woman he'd known for a decade. She ignored both Alek and Tammy, instead stalking over to Claire, who was still spitting out the last of her dinner and heaving for air.

"Fifth in line, my ass," Asylin said sharply.

Claire looked up and their gazes locked. Alek saw something pass between them—and whatever it was didn't make Asylin happy. She bent down and whispered something in Claire's ear that made the red wolf stiffen and raise her head sharply.

Alek decided that a break in the tension was needed and expressing his genuine gratitude to his foster mother seemed just the ticket. "Mom, thanks so much for the help. Oh, and great news! While Patrick was carrying me, I thought I saw Kristy down at the bottom of the canyon. He went down to look."

The owl shifter looked at him in confusion. "Kristy? She's with Aunt Patty in Louisiana."

All movement stopped. Even Tammy, back in human form, in restraints, and guarded by Cindee, stared at the matriarch.

"When did that happen, Mom?" Cindee's voice was careful, edgy, her brow furrowed above tensed muscles.

"Weeks ago. Don't you remember?" She seemed honestly bewildered by the questioning, which worried Alek.

"No, Mom. Kristy's missing. She and Darrell. We've been searching for them for days. Don't *you* remember?" He watched as the words filtered past the frown and narrowed eyes that flicked back and forth while she thought. In a moment, her eyes widened and her mouth formed a perfect O. "Kristy!" With a flash of magic that swept across him painfully, she shifted and dove over the side, wings wide.

"Well, that was weird," Cindee said to nobody in particular, with a small, nervous laugh.

"That's one word," Alek agreed. "It's a weird sort of day." He couldn't look at Claire, so he focused on Tammy, now huddled against a tree, curled in a fetal ball. "How are you doing, kittycat?"

"Been better," she admitted. She took a breath, then lifted her chin and met his gaze. "Thank you."

He nodded. "You're family. Of course I'm going to help you. Me, Mom . . . all of us. You'll get through this."

"Doubt it." Her small chuckle made him sad and worried. "You don't *get through* being rogue. Just because I got my sanity back right now doesn't mean I'll stay this way."

She was right, but they had to try. "We'll call Marilyn. Maybe there's a drug or . . ." He let the thought drift off because there wasn't really much to be said. He'd never heard of a cure for insanity in the Sazi world. He looked over his shoulder at Claire, her enticing body now safely concealed by a blanket. He pulled his a little tighter, suddenly cold. "You said you know healers, right?"

"I do, but . . ." Tammy's shoulders slumped a little more. Claire noticed and despite her obvious exhaustion, made an effort. "Y'know what? Let me call my pack's healer. He knows just about everyone. Maybe someone out there has found something that I just haven't heard about."

Tammy gave a shaky smile and Cindee ruffled her blond

hair. "It'll be okay, kittycat. And you know if it comes down to it, I won't let it hurt."

That made the cougar shifter smile. "Pinky promise?" She held up her bound hands, one finger in the air.

"Always." Cindee hooked her pinky with the other woman's and fragrant cookie spice edged out the wet, tangy scents of pain and fear. "Let's get the two of you back to the house so we can dress those wounds."

Claire stared at them with something approaching wonder. She shook her head, as if trying to figure out what she was seeing, but he couldn't figure out why. They began to walk slowly toward the house. It was one thing to walk on hardened wolf pads across the rocks and sticks. It was another thing to do it in bare feet accustomed to shoes. He couldn't help but notice Claire's snickers each time he hopped and cursed after an unprotected toe cracked against a rock hidden in tall grass.

It was long minutes before they reached the house. Alek had never been so glad to walk on smooth concrete and couldn't wait to sink into a hot bath because pretty soon, the adrenaline was going to wear off and his body was going to remind him just how badly he was hurt.

Scott raced outside as they reached the front porch, skidding to a stop when he saw Tammy, his eyes nearly as wide as when he shifted to an owl on the moon. "Hey, Tam."

She noticed that he stayed just out of reach and flinched, her gaze dropping to the polished planks underfoot. "Hey, fluffball."

Cindee put a hand on her arm. "C'mon. We need to get you settled downstairs."

Tammy nodded with a tiny movement, accepting that not only was she a prisoner, but she was unstable enough to be locked in the secure room in the basement where she wouldn't be able to harm herself or others. "'K." She looked at Cindee hopefully, her scent worried and sad. "Will you stay with me tonight?"

Cindee looked at Alek, then at Scott. "What do you think Mom would say? We used to room together."

True. But . . . "Tammy, you know I think we can fix you. I do. But do you even *remember* attacking Patrick? Do you remember trying to chew his leg like a drumstick at Chkn-N-Mo?"

To her credit, she tried. Her eyebrows dropped and bunched until they looked like one long line of blond hair across her forehead. Alek knew the truth, as did Claire. He needed to find out how close to the edge the cougar was—whether she had been suicidal and *hoping* Patrick would kill her, or rogue and outside her own mind. Her breath started to come in fast pants until she shook off whatever was trying to overtake her and set her jaw. "Lock me up. I don't want to hurt you guys. I don't know what I'll do. I hate it, but I just don't know."

Scott couldn't take it anymore. He brushed past Alek and threw his arms around Tammy, his streaked sheet of hair obscuring her face for a long moment. She couldn't hold him back because of the restraints on her hands. It wasn't long before her shoulders began to shake beneath the pale pink blanket and she broke down in heart-wrenching sobs, collapsing onto Scott.

They all stood there for long moments in uncomfortable silence until Claire broke the tension. "Ugh, I'm getting chewed up by bugs in places I really don't want to scratch. I'm going inside." Without really waiting for acknowledgment, she climbed the stairs onto the porch.

Cindee touched her shoulder as she walked past. "Really impressive, by the way. Thank you so much."

Alek had no idea what she was talking about. Claire just shrugged and curved up one corner of her mouth as she walked past. "Yeah . . . well. Tell Asylin that."

He was missing something but wasn't even sure what to ask. He figured if someone wanted him to know, they'd tell him. "See you in the morning?" There was a lilt in his voice that sounded strange to his ears. Hopeful, nearly asking permission for her favor.

She stopped, shoulders tensed with the door half open. Her finger twitched on the painted wood. "I suppose so." Her voice was . . . neutral. Not angry, thank heavens, but not really warm either, which bothered him more than he wanted to admit. She went into the house, letting the screen door slam behind her.

"She's still mad at me." He said it quietly, not even caring that the others would hear.

Scott had released Tammy, who had gotten herself under control. He clapped Alek on the shoulder. "Let it go. You're exhausted, dude. So is she. Go home. Get some sleep. It's going to be a long day tomorrow."

Tomorrow.

His first day as the Omega. He'd nearly forgotten in the rush of events. "Where do I check in? I probably need to know—"

"It's okay, Alek. Got your back. Rachel and I already talked. We're going to be your guides the first day. It's in the rules for the outgoing Omega to train the new one in the duties. I'm the last male Omega, Rachel the last female. The chief will probably have kittens about two helpers, but there's never been two Omegas before. The mayor is a wuss, but he's a stickler for the rules. Just ask for a *male* guide and they'll be stuck. Equality bites both ways."

CHAPTER 12

*P*ain seared with every twitch of a muscle. There was no way to get comfortable. The straw underneath Claire's injured body gave no relief, no matter how she tried to fluff it into a bed. The screams from other cages had lessened to whimpers and finally to exhausted, uneasy sleep. Her stomach growled angrily, but she wouldn't touch the meat on her plate. She was positive it wasn't beef or chicken, and she didn't want to imagine what else it might be. The pads of cactus, the outside scorched to remove the spines, wouldn't keep her alive for long. But she wasn't interested in being alive for long. Life meant only more torment.

Yesterday she'd been taken to The Room . . . lined with cages filled with massive birds—owls mostly, but some eagles and a few falcons. They spoke human languages and their eyes held either intelligence or insanity.

The guards would decide which cage she was thrown into. She knew from other captives that pleading would do no good. As far as they were concerned, she wasn't a terrified twelve-year-old girl from Kansas. Wasn't even human.

She was just a piece of meat. She might become a new warrior for their army. Or she might be food and nothing more.

When the guards left them alone, the other victims talked

in quiet tones. Most advised her to fake being afraid of the birds that looked intelligent and ignore the insane ones. If a bird wouldn't attack, the guards would goad it with shock sticks or spears until it scratched or bit. Even then, the attack would be shallow, just breaking the skin.

The insane ones didn't need persuasion. They considered anything moving to be food and were always hungry. Captives would have to be dragged out of those cages.

Sometimes they weren't.

She'd been thrown into a cage with a golden eagle this time. Last time it had been an owl, fluffy feathers over the eyes looking like devil horns to her. The eagle had required goading. The scratches across her torso came with an apology in Spanish and a sad expression. That helped Claire endure it. They were both victims, after all.

She heard the sound of footsteps bouncing off the ceiling. Before she was kidnapped, she would sleep so soundly that her grandmother would have to call her a dozen times to breakfast, run so late that she usually had to chase after the bus. Now, if she slept at all, it was light and fitful. The guards' footsteps were better than any alarm.

They would only enter the choking, ammonia-laced dungeon when a victim was needed. That only happened when a new bird had been created or someone had died during the process. The guards' boots were heavy, steel-toed models that echoed when they walked. They stopped at her door. She bolted upright.

Not again. Surely not so soon. Her heart started pounding. She'd thought the guards had been placated by the shallow talon wounds. Most of the other captives agreed that shallow cuts wouldn't usually turn someone unless they had shifter blood already. But the deep wounds, the life-threatening ones, those could turn nearly anyone . . . if the person didn't die, that is.

Though Claire couldn't see in the pitch blackness, she could smell the guard's sweat, even stronger than the stench of urine and feces. Maybe she would be lucky and be chosen to be a guard's girlfriend. She'd heard of that happening, and to have a guard's protection was a powerful thing. It wasn't much of a choice to Claire. But few of the guards had a liking for pale skin. The girls with the same skin color as the guards usually wound up the girlfriends.

A wave of stinging, bitter scent hit her nose, left a taste on her tongue like iodine. It was *him*. The one who had kidnapped her. Latino or Middle Eastern—she'd never known for sure. He was the black snake, the one they called Roberto. She'd heard one or two guards call him Lord Nasil. He terrified her. Not because he was violent, but because he was *cold*. Calculating, fast, and frighteningly intelligent. He was always one step ahead of everyone, like he could read minds and know what people were planning. Did he know she'd been loosening the bolts that held her shackles to the stone wall? Was he finally going to kill her for trying to run into the sunlight that one day, long ago? The fact that Roberto frightened all the guards just as much didn't make her feel much better.

The door creaked open. Heart pounding, stinging sweat dripping into her eyes, breathing shallow and fast, she did not move, did not make a sound. Noise made the guards laugh or, worse, hit her until she stopped. She had no idea what Roberto would do if she screamed.

The darkness wasn't as complete as she remembered. There was light through a window, a soft cover over her, and the scent of pine in the air. There was no cave, no cage, no silver chains on her wrists and ankles. Disoriented, panicked, she silently slipped to the edge of the bed and dropped to the floor, feet under her, ready to spring.

"Claire?"

The familiar voice, from the cave and not from the cave, pulled her back to reality. Rachel was outside the bedroom, whispering through the barely open door, careful to stay away. "Are you ready?"

Ready? Claire blinked again, trying to focus past the pounding of her heart caused by a rush of adrenaline. The house was silent except for her own harsh breathing and the whisper of fabric on the other side of the door. She remembered then—it had taken some time and scrubbing last night to remove the oil from the door hinges so it would squeak when opening. But it had been worth it. She wasn't sure what she would have done to Rachel if she'd reached the bed and had shaken Claire awake. Especially after the dream.

There was a scent of urgency from the owl shifter, but also fear. What would it be like to forever be afraid of waking someone?

"Claire? Are you dressed? We should already be there."

It was still dark outside. She twisted her body to look at the alarm clock in the corner. Muscles she didn't know she had screamed in protest. It was only three o'clock! What the hell? "What time are we supposed to be there? It's not even light out yet."

Now that Claire was obviously awake, Rachel poked her head in nervously. "Oh, sweetie . . . you can't afford to start when it's light. You'd never finish." She paused. "Although, with two of you working—Hmm. Maybe it *won't* take all day. You might get lucky. But c'mon. Get dressed. Won't know until we try."

Claire rose to standing, feeling the sharp stabbing from the cuts on her back. She couldn't put full weight on her right leg. The pounding in her thigh said the bruising probably went a lot deeper than she'd originally thought. She wasn't at all sure she wanted to turn on the light to see what it looked like.

When she looked up again, Rachel had slipped into the room, closing the door behind her. She started talking, low and soothing. "Another nightmare? I still get them too. Not a surprise, considering yesterday. Man, even my sucky nose can tell you're hurting." She didn't say anything about the smell of sweat and fear that likely overpowered the scent of pain. Claire's Alpha had never mentioned the stink of fear either. She would just open a window to let fresh air clear it out, which is exactly what Rachel did now. The little dignities helped.

"Sort of. Does it matter what I wear?"

Rachel shrugged in the pale moonlight; lace curtains rustled in the breeze like wings behind her. "Not really. You'll have different things to wear depending on where we are, so what you start and end in doesn't really matter."

Different things to wear—? "What exactly does the Omega do in town? I'd figured it was chores and such."

Now the scent that came from Rachel turned uncomfortable, making Claire look up sharply from where she sat on the bed putting on socks. "Of a sort. Every house is a little different."

"What aren't you telling me, Rachel?"

She stepped forward, glancing at the door as she bent down and whispered right next to Claire's ear. "Not here. I promise . . . as soon as we're outside. Just *hurry.*"

What the hell was going on? But she did as Rachel asked, throwing on jeans and a long-sleeved dark top that wouldn't show dirt easily and a pair of borrowed hiking boots with ankle support. She probably wouldn't need her purse or keys. In fact, she'd be afraid to lose them if she was moving from place to place in the dark. Instead, she tucked the purse under the mattress and gave it a quick spray of perfume as an extra precaution. It was expensive perfume, made of natural flower oils that were extremely difficult to wash off. Someone changing the sheets probably wouldn't get it on their skin, but someone touching her purse definitely would.

As a last touch, she grabbed her knife and a bandana off the dresser and tucked them in her pocket. She'd taken off the bandage because the stitches had scabbed over but she wanted to keep dirt out of it. She had a feeling she was going to be getting dirty and sweaty today.

Going down the stairs after Rachel was more painful than Claire expected—too many muscles that didn't want to flex after being motionless for hours. She had to hold her breath to keep from making little achy whimpers. She could already feel the itching from her stitches. Hopefully that meant tomorrow she'd be healed. But today was going to suck.

Outside, with the door shut quietly behind them and no lights on in the house to say that anyone had been woken up, they trotted down the barely lit path toward the feeble lights of the town far in the distance.

After a while, Rachel motioned Claire to walk beside her. Keeping her voice low, she spoke quickly. "Okay, so here's how it works. The Omega hits pretty much every house and all of the businesses in town every day. We do the stuff that normally city employees would do . . . if Luna Lake had any . . . plus stuff that people might hire out. That's how we keep outsiders from the town, reduce the risk of discovery. So the Omega is the Jack or Jill of all trades."

"Why not tell me this back at the house? Why the big secret?"

Rachel stopped so abruptly that Claire stepped past her without meaning to. "You have good ears. Is there anyone out there? Anyone to hear?"

She was serious. Deadly serious, so Claire gave the question the weight it deserved. As though flipping a switch in her brain, she pulled in the moon, listening like a predator— for threats, for prey. She opened her ears and eyes and flared her nostrils, then scanned in a full three-sixty circle as if she was hunting. Rachel watched, arms wrapped around herself as though freezing cold.

The night wind made Claire's skin tingle, set the hairs moving like her fur when she ran. The darkness disappeared as moonlight filled her eyes; everything looked a shade darker than in the day but she could see leaves, pine needles, a mouse moving under a log, a deer bolting in the distance. She grinned, certain the animal had reacted to her scent—not that of a human, but a wolf.

Though she didn't have much magic left—not after that stunt Alek had pulled—she pushed it out in as wide of an arc as she could. It didn't go very far, not more than a stone's throw. It had taken nearly everything she had to freeze Alek and Tammy in midair. She'd been lucky vomiting was the only ill-effect; she'd heard of more than one lesser alpha whose heart had stopped after that big of an energy drain.

Rustling leaves that stopped the moment she turned toward them. Thumps of hooves that faded into the distance. But there, floating above the trees . . . the gentle whoosh of feathers. It wasn't just a raptor looking for a meal, not unless the neighborhood birds used shampoo on their feathers. They were being spied on. But the bird was too far away for Claire to identify even the species and it kept climbing higher until it was just a dark speck against the partial moon. She shook her head and motioned for Rachel to keep walking. More and more, she believed Rachel had good reason to be worried. But of what? And why?

Pondering, Claire was silent for the rest of the journey. When they reached the chief's office, Rachel whispered a hurried, "We'll talk more after we check in and start on our rounds."

But the door was locked. She rattled the knob and then turned her head to Rachel. "It's locked. Should I knock?"

The woman's eyes took on the same wide terror that they used to in the caves. Her hand went to her mouth and only a whisper came out from behind it. "We're *late*. Lord help us. We're late."

That wasn't really an answer. "So do we knock?"

Instead of answering, Rachel pulled on her arm, tugging her away from the door. "Hurry. We have to hurry."

There was an urgency to her actions that reminded her of Dani in the car. She let herself be dragged for fifty yards before she finally dug in her heels and stopped, jerking Rachel to a stop with her. What was setting the people in this town so much on edge? "Rachel, would you just stop and tell me what's going on?" She did her best to try to push calm at the woman, much as she had in the car. Claire squeezed Rachel's hand. "Please. Try to calm down and tell me. We can go somewhere where we won't be heard."

Finally, Rachel nodded. "Okay. You deserve that. C'mon. We'll go to the school. It's right down the road. It's usually where I start cleaning anyway."

The school? Perfect! Nobody would be there for hours. It would be a good time to get the layout of the rooms.

The building was nondescript brick, like most schools Claire had seen. She remembered little of the schools in Kansas before she was kidnapped, but the one in Santa Helena in Texas was small, just like this one. She started to walk up the stairs but Rachel shook her head. "We use the back door, not the front."

"So there are different keys?"

A raspberry noise came from in front of her. "No. But the Omega doesn't get to use the front door to any building."

Claire waited until they were inside the darkened building before she whispered, "I'm not a very politically correct sort of person, but it just seems *wrong* that you're both a black woman and a second-class citizen who has to use the back door to businesses."

Rachel shrugged. "It's not a race thing. Think about it. Scott was the last Omega, and you can't get more lily white than that man. Snow has more color than him. But you're right, it's *wrong*. The whole Omega system is fucked up in this town . . . but you didn't hear that from me."

"So tell me about it. What's wrong with it?"

But Rachel had already walked away. Claire followed her down the dim hallway, lit only by the faint red emergency exit lights. It smelled like kids. Claire inhaled deeply and sighed. Young children and teens. Cats and birds and wolves and maybe a bear in the making. This was what she wanted. Just to inspire kids and help them become something amazing.

A bank of lockers lined each side of the short hallway and as Claire peered into rooms, they looked like any other school rooms. The younger-kid rooms had brightly colored letters pinned on the walls and small desks, while the older classrooms had maps, charts, and inspirational sayings over adult-sized tables. There was even a small science lab that included microscopes and Bunsen burners. She would have loved to have had an actual science lab in her high school. Instead, they had one of the micro lab units that did the experiments, but with none of the bubbling. Not nearly as much fun.

Rachel had stopped next to a janitor closet and was pulling out a rolling trash can filled with brooms and mops. "We'll have to talk while we work. We can't afford to not finish everything today. Not after being late."

"What's going to happen? Is someone going to come track us down and check on what we're doing?" Claire followed Rachel's lead and started dust mopping the hallway.

The other woman stopped and turned to her. "I can't keep being vague. It's not fair to you. You didn't earn this or even deserve it. Lenny . . . that's the police chief, he's a bastard."

"No duh," Claire said under her breath.

It made Rachel smile. "Already noticed that, did you? Well, he seems to think that the only way to enforce the pack is to hurt people. Physically, emotionally, mentally; doesn't matter to him. Yes, he'll check up on you. Yes, we're both in for a beating. I've never been late enough to have the door locked, but . . . Scott was. Just *once*."

The way she said that. The echo of the word hung in the air. "Bad?"

She shook her head sadly, but her fingers tightened around the handle of the wide cloth floor duster, her scent angry enough that Claire was betting she would like to use it to beat on the chief. "His leg was broken. The thigh bone—snapped clean in half. He was screaming when we found him. He'll probably have arthritis before he's thirty."

"When you *found* him? You mean the chief just left him somewhere to suffer?"

Narrowed eyes from across the hallway told the story. "Oh, Lenny took him to the clinic all right. Locked him in tight. And then promptly went home. He didn't bother to call the healer. We had one back then. She was livid. I don't know if she quit and left town in disgust or if he buried her at the bottom of some canyon. They were constantly at each other's throat for shit like that."

"Good God! Why doesn't the Alpha do something about him? Kick his ass or turn him in to the Council."

Rachel started moving her duster again. "The mayor's a joke. I don't know why people keep electing him. I guess because he's no threat to anyone. But Van couldn't hurt a fly and is too loyal to Lenny to fire him or turn him in. Maybe that's normal. I don't know because I've never been part of a normal pack." They'd reached the end of the hall and once they dumped the dust in the bin, Rachel handed her a plastic bag. "Start dumping the wastebaskets in these. I'll do this side, you do the other."

So, I'm in for a beating. Great. As if I didn't already hurt enough. The thought made her stomach churn. There was nothing quite like waiting for a beating. The clock always ticked slower so you got to agonize over the details. It was better not to think about it. Instead, she threw herself into cleaning. Maybe if she got tired enough, she'd be too numb to feel the pain.

When Claire tried to turn the knob to the next room, it just jiggled. She called out across the hall. "This door is locked, Rachel. Do I skip it?"

"No," came the shouted reply. "That's the office. It has a separate key." A ring of keys sailed out from the doorway to land on the floor near her feet. "It's the one with the yellow jelly around the top. There's a trash can for each desk. Make sure you get them all. The principal gets freaked out if his basket isn't emptied."

The office! Could it get any better? She unlocked the door and made sure to lock it again once inside. She limped around the room emptying the baskets as fast as she could, and then glanced out the window set in the door to make sure Rachel wasn't watching. The coast was clear.

There were more than a dozen matching gray file cabinets— far too many for a school this small. Especially since the school had only been in existence for a decade. She started opening filing cabinet drawers quickly, trying to be as quiet as possible. Squinting in the dim red light, it looked like this cabinet had the accounts payable files. She quickly moved to the next drawer. Same. Third drawer. Nope. Standardized tests. Same for the fourth. By the time she got to the second cabinet, it was too far away from the EXIT sign to read the file labels and she didn't dare turn on the lights. *Crap. Tomorrow I need to bring a penlight with me.*

A sudden tapping on the glass and rapid jiggling of the knob made her start so hard she nearly slammed the drawer shut. "You okay in there, Claire? Is that stupid door stuck again?"

It sticks? "Yeah. I'm so sorry, Rachel. I didn't realize I locked it." She spoke intentionally loud to cover the tiny metallic click of the drawer shutting. Shifting sideways to the door made a sharp pain travel from her hip all the way up to her neck. She jiggled the handle with her hands like Rachel had, then began to pull on the locked door as though she couldn't open it.

"Try turning the knob and lifting the whole door just a fraction. The building settled wrong. They didn't compact the ground right when they built this place. Don't yank it when you lift. One time the window glass shattered."

Claire turned the knob while simultaneously twisting the lock mechanism, and then lifted so the door visibly raised up. Another flash of pain in her shoulder nearly made her let go of the handle. But she managed to hold it long enough to slowly pull it inward. The door opened easily. *Oh, this will come in really handy.*

"*Voila!*" Rachel said with hands spread. "Sorry, I meant to tell you about that."

"Thanks for the lesson. I probably would have broken the door." They were several steps away from the door when Claire nearly slapped her forehead. *Fingerprints! Duh!* She turned in a panic, causing Rachel to turn too.

"What's wrong?"

What could she say? She should have left her trash bag, but it was right in her hand. "I forgot the principal's basket!"

"Oh! Crap, better get that one. I'll meet you in the boys' bathroom at the end of the hall. It's always a mess."

If Rachel could smell the lie, she didn't say anything. She raced back into the office, pulled a few tissues out of the nearest box, and squeezed some antibacterial alcohol gel from a pump dispenser near the door onto the paper. She used it to quickly wipe away fingerprints from the handles of the cabinet and then tossed the tissue into her trash bag. The alcohol would dry in minutes, and should remove her scent. Better safe than sorry.

Rachel had been right about the boys' bathroom. She smelled it before she made it inside the room. "Man! It smells like a stray tomcat sprayed urine on the ceiling."

"Not a stray, but yes. The Kain twins strike. They're bobcats in eighth grade and are getting territorial." She handed Claire a scrub brush on a long pole and a bottle of industrial cleaner.

"Gawd, that's horrible!" The combination of scents filled her nose and made her eyes burn. She waved a hand in front of her face but it didn't help. The longer she stayed in the room, scrubbing the walls, the worse it got. "It's like cat and skunk mixed with gasoline."

"Yeah, it's probably worse for you. My nose isn't that powerful. I got the eyes, but not the nose. Why don't I finish up in here and you do the girls' room? Then we just have the locker room and we'll head to the next stop."

Claire was happy to escape the stench to gulp in great breaths of fresh air in the hallway. She started for the girls' room but her eyes were drawn back down the hall to the locked office door. What was in all those cabinets? Her feet seemed to have a mind of their own as she found herself walking down the hallway. She stopped in front of the door, not even remembering feeling pain in her leg. Should she go in again? *Something very strange is going on in this town and I'm betting some of the answers are right in that room.*

A fast, firm grasp on her shoulder made Claire's head whip

around. The tall, muscular man behind her reeked of authority, but she didn't recognize him. She struggled not to lash
out in defense. Her muscles twitched with the effort. *You're
the Omega. Don't attack.* The baritone that accompanied the
grip matched the size of the hand. It sped up her pulse. "Who
are you and what the hell are you doing in here?"

CHAPTER 13

"What's Mr. Burrows's car doing at the school at this time of day?" Alek stared at the older-model Chevy, all alone in the parking lot. It was free of the dusting of snow that had started to lightly blanket the town, so he must have just arrived.

"He's the principal, Alek. I'm sure he's here at all sorts of weird hours. C'mon. We need to get over to the park and start on the bathrooms." Scott's voice sounded equal parts exasperated and frightened. He put a hand on Alek's shoulder. "Leave it alone."

A shadow appeared in one of the windows, dark except for a faint red glow. When a second shadow appeared, Alek started to move forward. Something was wrong. He didn't know what, but he had to investigate. He was in midstep when Scott grabbed his back belt loop. "Alek, I mean it. You already got your clock cleaned once today. Don't push it. You know Lenny and Nathan are tight. Whatever is going on in there isn't our business."

He reached back and pulled Scott's hand off his belt and then turned around. "Chill, dude. It wasn't that big of a deal. It was just one punch . . . didn't even loosen any teeth. I was late and I paid for it. Besides, what good is it to have an Omega if they're not going to watch out for trouble?"

Scott crossed his arms over his chest and let out a hiss. His hair fluffed like blond feathers, high enough to lift his pony-tail a fraction. "Oh, yeah. This just *screams* trouble. A principal . . . in a *school*. I swear to God, Alek—"

A scream came from inside the building. It was a woman, and Alek immediately recognized it as Rachel's. He'd heard it a hundred times in the Ascension challenges. Sometimes in frustration, sometimes in pain when she just couldn't move any faster. Alek moved instinctively toward the sound, with Scott hot on his heels. "Jesus!" he called out after Alek, "Man, no wonder you're going to be a cop. You got some sort of sixth sense about this shit."

He let Scott believe that without commenting. But this wasn't normal. It wasn't just an intuition, but a seizing of his gut, like the sensation when he was riding Tammy over the cliff.

The front door was locked. He tried twisting it to pop the lock, but it held fast. He was about to race around to the back, when Scott hissed and motioned him over to one of the windows. Principal Burrows stood over the inert form of Rachel, but he was nearly inert too. Alek couldn't help but smile at the sight of Claire holding his fist in a steady grip, seeming not to even be struggling to keep him from attacking again. Her eyes flashed with pale blue fire as she spoke in low tones. "You had no right to punch her. She didn't do a thing to deserve that."

Nathan Burrows wasn't one to be trifled with. He was as even tempered as they came, but when the black bear shifter got angry, he could do serious damage. He rose to his full height, towering over Claire's slight form, his eyes red with fiery power that made the exit lights seem dim. "I didn't punch her. She'd be dead if I had. She met my eyes in a direct challenge, Ms. Sanchez. That is absolutely *not* allowed by an omega and she knows it. The only reason you're not on the floor beside her is that you're new to town and *don't* understand how things work here. But know this—if you don't let go of my hand and lower your eyes right this second, I will drop you where you stand. You will also *never* work in this school. I don't care whether you're an alpha or the Omega, I am the principal here and you *will* respect me."

There was a long pause where they stared at each other. Alek watched Claire take a deep breath and then release Burrows's hand. She dropped her eyes to stare at his neck, then spoke through gritted teeth. "I meant no disrespect. But I don't approve of hitting an omega. It's as bad or worse than hitting a child. Alphas are supposed to *protect* the weak and innocent."

Alek winced, expecting Burrows to backhand her. He actually raised his hand, as though to strike, but then held it at about chest level. "I want you back here promptly at ten o'clock. Just you, not with Ms. Washington. Now go. Leave the dustbin where it is. I'll put it away."

He turned and walked into his office, shutting and locking the door behind him, leaving Claire staring after him with furrowed brows. Alek tapped on the window just as Claire knelt down beside Rachel. She looked up, surprised. He motioned at the door and Scott made motions like turning a knob. Claire helped Rachel to her feet and supported her weight as they limped toward the door. He was surprised Claire was able to bear Rachel's weight. She seemed to be struggling to walk.

A small vortex of snow swirled as she pushed open the door. It threw their scents right to Alek. Rachel was in pain, but not nearly to the level of the scream he'd heard, which confused him. Claire smelled . . . well, she smelled *amazing*. The intense cold-metal determination mixed with her natural chocolate-and-fire scent to make an intoxicating cocktail. If she was in pain, it didn't show in her scent. It was hard to clear his head enough to speak. He reached to take Rachel's arm and Scott quickly moved to the bench near the sidewalk, brushing off the snow so they could sit her down.

He squatted down next to the previous Omega and lifted her chin into the small amount of light from the streetlamp a dozen feet away. Burrows had hit her already injured eye, making it swell up and turn a darker purple. "Are you okay? That scream was pretty intense."

She nodded, her eyes narrowed and angry. "I'm fine. I've learned to scream like a little girl when someone hits me because it makes them stop and wonder if they really hurt me." She gave a dark smile that made him chuckle. "Fortunately, most people don't use their noses or he would have realized he barely tapped me. Idiot."

Claire gave the side of her shoulder a little slap. "Rachel! I thought you were really hurt."

Rachel reached up one manicured hand and gingerly touched her temple before saying ruefully, "Sorry. I really didn't expect you to jump in like that. Nobody else stands up for an omega." Alek flinched. Would he have done what Claire did? He wasn't sure. "And don't get me wrong. I am hurt. But I've had worse." She looked up and then reached out to touch Claire's hand. "That was really nice of you. Thank you."

Claire looked back at the building. "I don't know that I like someone like that running a school with kids, especially human kids. He looked pretty steamed. What do you think he'll do at ten o'clock?"

Rachel just shrugged. "I really don't know. He's never asked me to come to the school when the kids are in class. School is in session today, isn't it?" She turned to Alek and Scott with raised brows.

Scott nodded. "Yeah, I think so. I don't know what he wants either. Maybe a public humiliation in front of everyone? What do you think, Alek? Would Burrows do that? He's always seemed like one of the good ones. Yeah, he comes off tough, because otherwise the kids would run roughshod, but I've never seen him actually hit someone until just now. Weird."

Alek shook his head, trying to clear his mind. "I don't know." He turned and looked up at Claire. That was when she noticed his face.

"Ow! What happened to *you*? Your eye looks worse than Rachel's."

Alek hadn't really thought about the punch since it happened, but when he reached up to touch his face, out of instinct, white lights flashed in his vision. No wonder Scott had been urging caution. "I guess I hadn't noticed. I was late this morning. Lenny slugged me for punishment." Scott made a noise like a raspberry that made him look over and say, "What? That's what happened."

The owl shifter rolled his eyes, hands punched down in the pockets of his jacket. "That's not why he hit you and you know it. Just tell her. He's probably going to if you don't."

Claire cocked her head and Alek felt a sigh slip out. Scott might well be right. Lenny would probably take it out on her too. "I asked Lenny to let you out of the Omega duties. I reminded him it was my fault and asked him to let me serve as the only Omega. It *was* my fault. I really am sorry."

Her face softened and she reached out to touch his hair. Then Scott added, "Except he didn't ask Lenny, he *told* him. That's when he got slugged."

Claire let out a small exasperated sound, but didn't stop running her fingers through his hair and smelled proud of him. His scalp tingled so strongly he could barely breathe and he was pretty sure she felt it too if the fluttering of the vein in her neck was any indication.

She moved her hand from his hair to touch Rachel's shoulder. "Rachel, why don't you go home and get your eye cleaned up and then get some rest. I'll stick with Scott and Alek. Think how fast it will go with three of us working."

Rachel looked up at Scott. He nodded and shrugged. "Fine with me. It hasn't been that long since I did the job. And it will go pretty fast that way."

She smiled at all of them. "That would be great. It's been a long time since I had a day off to just laze in my jammies. I'll come back and wake you in the morning, Claire. We'll get a jump on the day." She turned her head to Scott. "You make her sit down every so often. She really hurt that leg."

It wasn't long before they were all over at the apartment building, getting in Scott's little VW. He glanced at his apartment window. Nothing seemed out of place or odd.

"I normally don't use my car to do this," Scott said. "But it's the only way we're going to be able to get out to the park and have Claire back again by ten o'clock. Hop in."

"I've got short legs," Claire said before he could offer her the front seat. "I'll get in back." Alek didn't want it to bother him that she didn't ask him to join her in the backseat. But it did. "Is it far to the lake?"

"Not too bad," he replied. "Only about ten minutes by car. Probably twenty on foot unless you jog the whole way."

After a few minutes of silence, Claire spoke again. "So, tell me about yourselves. How did you come to be here and growing up in the same house?"

He exchanged a look with Scott, wondering where to start. Scott waved a hand his direction. "You tell it better. I need to watch the road anyway."

Alek turned slightly in his seat so he could see her. "We're both orphans. I grew up in the Chicago wolf pack. Scott was part of an owl parliament in California. When the snakes attacked, my mom and older sister were killed. Denis and I survived. I don't know about my younger sister. We're still trying to find her."

"*He's* still trying. I don't know that anyone else has tried," Scott said. "He's looked *everywhere*. Trust me. You ought to see the *Sonya wall* in his apartment. Photos, letters, maps, hair and skin samples, the whole works. He's relentless. It looks like an episode of *CSI* in there."

Alek shot him a *look* and that, plus the combination of annoyed scents that likely billowed out in a cloud, shut him up.

He continued without explaining, even though Claire seemed like she was interested. But it wasn't her search or her worry. "Anyway . . . I wound up in a busload of kids from all over the Midwest. Anyone who survived got shipped to the Boulder pack facility and then sorted to this place. I don't really remember much of the first few months. It was all I could do to keep track of Denis and ask everyone I met if they'd seen Sonya."

Scott added, "I don't think anyone remembers much about the whole first year. I came on a different bus that picked up survivors along the West Coast. Not many of the original people from Cali are left here. The winters are too hard. I remember shivering constantly when we first got here and it was still summer. I hadn't shifted yet, so I was mostly human. Part of it was sort of cool—pioneer living was fun as a kid. Like camping on a grand scale. Until the cold set in, that is. Building the town kept me warm at first. I shifted that first winter . . . probably out of sheer self-defense. But I remember that finding food and clothes and building stuff ate up most of the early days."

They rolled into the parking lot of the park. Scott turned off the engine right next to the bathrooms. Claire nodded.

"Yeah, it was like that down south too. There was a lot of us victims and food and housing was a problem." She noticed when they both looked at her, not understanding what she meant. "I started out human too. I . . ." She paused and then looked out the window into the darkness. "Was an attack victim. Collateral damage of the snake war. I didn't come from a shifter family. It was just thrown at me. Dealing has been hard."

"Jeez . . ." Scott turned in his seat and reached back to touch her knee. The fog-bank scent of sympathy filled the car. The scent turned warm from her gratitude. She reached out and touched Scott's hand, giving it a little squeeze.

Alek shut his eyes. What would that have been like? To come from a human upbringing into both a massacre and a shifter society in crisis? He was amazed she wasn't insane. She must be one tough lady. He opened his eyes and tried to convey his admiration. "That had to have been rough. I'm impressed."

"Not a cake walk, I'll admit. So there's not much here that can throw me off my game." She paused and stared directly into his eyes. "Not *much*."

Time seemed to slow while he drowned in the cool blue of her eyes. It wasn't until Scott uncomfortably cleared his throat that he blinked and shook his head. He shouldn't be liking her this hard, this fast. She wasn't staying, after all. This was just a way station on her way somewhere else. "Yeah, so . . . we should probably get cleaning."

Claire blinked, feeling sound come back to her in a nearly audible *pop*. "Yeah," she replied. "We should clean." Light was edging the top of the mountain. The whole town was in the shadow, so it would be nearly ten when the sun was visible, but it was getting quickly light. She scooted out of the car with Scott holding the door. He seemed like a really nice guy, but not really her type. But it was obvious that she and Alek were tight. She'd have to corner him somewhere and ask him more about Alek's past. Against her better judgment, she was liking the gray wolf. She was still furious at him for getting her into this mess, but she was realizing that becoming the Omega would have happened one way or another. She was pissing off nearly everyone she met, and she wasn't even trying.

Scott started getting trash bags and bottles of cleaner from behind the seat. She decided to go inspect the bathrooms to see how bad they were. After the school boys' room, she didn't have high hopes. She walked in the women's room and . . . it was immaculate. The floors nearly sparkled and the scent of pine cleaner filled the air. Even the shiny metal strips that passed for mirrors over the sink, as well as the basins were spotless. "Wow, this is going to be pretty easy. Doesn't anyone ever come here?"

There was no answer from the boys. She went around the other side of the building to see what the men's room looked like. The roiling of negative emotions put her into a sneezing fit. Anger, betrayal, frustration, worry—all rising from Alek, with Scott bleeding all the worry with a healthy dose of fear. After the fourth sneeze, she was able to catch a clean breath of air. She peeked past them into the spacious men's room. It was the same, spotless. "What's up? Did someone get here before us? Will we get in trouble *again*?" She'd pretty much resigned herself that a beating was coming. Possibly more than one.

"I am getting *sick* of this shit!" Alek turned on his heel and brushed past her so fast she nearly tripped trying to get out of his way. He stormed off into the distance, headed back toward town. He broke into a run that made him just a blur of motion in seconds. She was surprised he could move that fast. He'd been pretty beat up in the accident too.

"Alek!" Scott called out after him and took a few steps before remembering she was there. "Aw, hell. He's going to die. He's an idiot and he's going to die. Get in. We need to try to stop him."

She jumped in the front seat and hurriedly buckled her seat belt, wincing as pain shot across her back from the motion. Scott started the car and threw it into gear. "Why? What's happening?"

He turned his head briefly to catch her eye. "You met Denis, right? I think you got here about the time when Dad picked him up from getting arrested."

She nodded. "He had to stay overnight because Alek was helping out with the accident."

"Yeah, well he got picked up for tagging the bathrooms . . . *these* bathrooms, with spray paint."

She was confused. "So why is it bad that the paint's been cleaned up? Isn't that what's supposed to happen?"

Scott sighed. "Alek is convinced that the mayor and police chief have been sweeping infractions under the rug . . . burying them so nobody outside of town finds out. What we can't figure out is *why*."

Should she tell him? No. Not yet. First she had to find out who could be trusted. Right now, he and Rachel seemed the most likely to have information. She wanted to cultivate that so they could help her find what she needed. In order to do that, she had to make them trust *her*. "But wouldn't you, of all people, know?"

He raised his brows and flicked his eyes toward her before looking out the window again, scanning for Alek. "Why would you say it like that? *Of all people?*"

She shrugged, trying to personalize the comment so it

didn't seem like an accusation. "In our pack, the Omega has more knowledge than anyone. Everyone talks in front of Juan like he's not there—like a waiter in a restaurant or a hairstylist. I've always been amazed at the things he hears. He knows *all* the secrets and his continued safety hinges on the fact that nobody dares tick him off or he'll reveal stuff they don't want other pack members to know."

Scott was quiet for a long moment. "I do hear stuff, and I know stuff. The problem is I don't have anyone to tell who cares. I would *love* to have an hour in a locked room with a Council member. There'd be a well-deserved bloodbath in this town."

Wow. She hadn't expected that strong of a reaction. That was *very* useful knowledge. "But you don't know why they'd want to hide infractions?"

Another silence and he tapped his finger on the steering wheel. "I have a pretty good idea. That's why we need to stop Alek. He's headstrong and way too honest for his own good. I don't dare tell him what I know because I can see him blundering in and accusing them of things. True things. And they'll just kill him."

"Ah." There was nothing more to say to that. They probably would. And knowing that the people in charge were capable of just killing him might just keep her alive.

"I like you, Claire. I think you're smart, like Alek. But you're realistic, like me. Alek is a little too idealistic. He believes that everyone should *want* rainbows and sunshine. But you and I . . . we know that a lot of people want bad things."

How well she knew. "Yeah. So playing stupid is a good idea?"

He laughed, but there was a bitter, dark edge to it. "And playing dead. Keep your head down . . . don't let them know you have brains, and play dead if they find out you're smarter than you look."

CHAPTER 14

*A*lek stared at the closed door for a full minute before raising his hand to knock. This wasn't where he'd planned to come. When he left the park, he had every intention of racing back to town and confronting Lenny in his office—demanding answers about every suspicion he'd been swallowing for ten years. But his mind kept going back to the scene in the school, with Rachel on the ground, stunned, and Claire the warrior, holding the attacker at bay. And then . . . and then, her backing down and lowering her eyes.

Why?

He knocked and it sounded so muted in relation to the screaming of questions in his mind. He wanted to pound, to kick, to yell.

But the tiny knock produced results. He heard soft footsteps inside and then the door opened. Rachel was indeed in pajamas, pale yellow flannel with tiny ducks. The color made her skin glow with an inner light. The hand not on the door held a bag of generic frozen peas to the side of her face. She seemed surprised to see him. But not nearly as surprised as he was to be here.

"Got a minute?"

She shrugged. "Sure. Do *you*?"

"I'll make time for this." She backed up, clearing the way for him to walk in. He realized he'd never been in her apartment before, even though she lived in the same building. He was on the first floor, she on the second. But that one flight of steps seemed a million miles away today.

He stood in the center of the small living room and wasn't sure where to start. Rachel seemed to smell his turmoil and touched his arm. "Why don't you sit down? Something's wrong, isn't it?"

He sat on the floral couch, immaculately clean but several decades out of style, like pretty much everything else in the room. "Why did you put up with being the Omega? Why haven't you left . . . gone home, joined another pack or just escaped? Is what I saw today *really* your life?"

She sort of fell back into the chair, her face clearly stunned. "Wow. That is *so* not where I thought this conversation was going." She tossed the bag of peas to him and he caught it. "You need those more than I do. I'll go get another bag."

"Thanks." They were still frozen and felt good in his hand. He tentatively raised the bag to his eye and felt the cold sink into the heat from the swelling. She was back in a minute and sat down in the same chair across the coffee table from him.

After a pause, her scent settled into an odd combination. Guilt, shame, pride, and hope mixed with other things. "Is that my life? Yes. It has been for the past four years. Why haven't I left? I don't have anywhere to go. Just like a lot of us."

"What about your family? Didn't you have a parliament somewhere?"

She shook her head. "Y'know, for growing up in the same house, we really don't know much about each other. Didn't you notice that it was really easy for me to talk to Claire, like we were friends from a long time ago?"

He nodded. He *had* noticed that. "I just figured you guys clicked. Sometimes people do."

"True. But sometimes, it's because you shared a common past. Claire and I were locked in the same prison, a few cells apart—kidnap victims of the snakes. That's where we met."

She was serious. He felt the bag of peas slip through his grasp, hit the carpeting before he could stop them. "But you're an *owl*, not a snake. And you grew up in a house of owls."

Rachel laughed, but not happy laughter. Bitter. "And because I'm black and the Williamses are black, and we're owls, we came from the same place? Is that what you mean?"

"No!" he exclaimed quickly, shocked by the implication enough to feel his face get hot. "I mean . . . I just . . . Oh, hell, Rachel." He threw himself back into the cushions. "I don't know. I feel like I'm coming out of a fog that I've been in for my whole life."

"You sort of are. You've always been wrapped up in stuff and don't really pay attention. It's just who you are." He felt himself sputter, trying to think of a response that didn't sound stupid, but she waved it off. "Don't worry. I know it's not malicious, Alek. Heck, half of the family didn't bother to ask my past, and I haven't asked theirs. That part of us, what used to be before Luna Lake, it just disappears into a mist. But I don't have a home to go back to. At least not one that would celebrate, or hell, even *recognize* what I've become."

"Like Claire."

Rachel flipped the bag of peas over and put it back against her eye, twisting her body so she was sideways on the chair and could rest her elbow on a pillow. "Probably. We were both raised human, not part of the Sazi world. How do you go home again and explain to a whole extended family that you're back a decade later and oh, by the way, I'm now magical and can turn into an animal? Because even as the Omega, I'm a dozen times more powerful than the toughest S.O.B. in the 'hood. It would freak people out."

He nodded, understanding finally. "Which is how the whole plague came to be. Fear."

"Exactly. Did that answer your question?"

"Sort of," he admitted. "But why do you put up with the abuse? Why not stand up and say 'no more'?"

She let out a sigh. "That one is trickier. See—"

A knock sounded on the door and it made him jump. Was it Lenny? Would he be dragged out of here and Rachel take another beating? His eyes must have conveyed the questions because Rachel slipped over to the door, checking the peephole and sniffing delicately at the edge of the door. "It's just Scott." She opened the door. "Wow, two visitors in one day. I feel special."

Scott just rolled his eyes. "I was just over two days ago for our bad sci-fi movie marathon. You're not lonely." He stepped inside and walked over to the couch and thumped Alek square on the head. Pain sang through his swollen eye from the sudden movement.

"Ow! What the hell?"

"You scared the bejebbus out of me! I thought you were going to confront the chief and mayor and get yourself killed."

"I nearly did. Where's Claire, by the way? Is she still out at the lake?"

"Duh. Look at the sunshine outside. I dropped her off at the post office for her to clean the windows. She can walk to the school for her appointment. But she insisted I try to find you before you . . . as I said, got yourself killed."

"And you thought to look *here* for him?" Rachel asked. "You do realize he's never been here before?"

"No," Scott said, "I came here hoping you could help me look for him or at least keep watch out at the police station for any dead bodies being stuffed into trunks." He paused. "Why *are* you here?"

Rachel spit out a laugh. "He just this minute realized that the Omegas are abused in this town and is asking why I put up with it."

They were talking as though he wasn't even there. Again he felt his face flush. "It's not like I didn't know that you were the Omegas, guys. I just never . . ."

"Thought?" Scott prompted.

"Looked?" Rachel countered.

"Listened?" Scott added. When he finally growled, deep from his chest, Scott patted him on the shoulder. "Dude, chill. We understand. Really. Your kind of clueless isn't bad."

He threw the bag of peas against the wall, landing with an unsatisfying *slorp* to drop to the tile next to the kitchen in a heap. "It is! How could I not notice you're being *beaten*? What the hell kind of person am I not to step in and make it stop?"

Rachel curled her legs into the chair beside her and leaned down on the chair arm. "You *can't* make it stop. You're not a big enough dog. Nobility only goes so far and then the noble die fighting. That's not to say that some battles aren't worth fighting, but really, what you saw today doesn't happen that often. It's been a long time since I took a cuff to the face. It's like, you know how you want to be a cop?"

He nodded, but, "How is that the same?"

"People abuse cops because you enforce the law. A lot of cops burn out because of the abuse. I mean, why put up with bullshit when nobody gives a damn whether or not you do the job?"

True. Ray had said as much to him.

"But you do it anyway, because *serve and protect* actually means something to you. And, well, *serve* means something to me too. My birth mom was a nurse and she was really proud of what she did. She didn't want to be a doctor and think about just medicine. She wanted to think about *people*. Caring for them, helping them stay healthy or get better when they were sick. Service was something to be proud of. And I inherited that."

Scott nodded. "Yeah. That. I don't mind cleaning or cooking or caring for old people. I'd do it anyway, even if it wasn't an assignment. Just like you'd be a cop even though you'll sometimes be abused. Eventually, I'd like to start my own business, selling herbs and health food to keep people happy and well. People will laugh and some people won't be customers. That's okay. The great part is, I've learned a ton by being the Omega—about customer service, about the kinds of products that are needed . . ."

Rachel nodded. "About family disputes and how to salve wounds, both physical and emotional. Lots of stuff. It's not a horrible life, Alek. Working as the Omega for an insane boss is like any other job where you work for an insane boss. It sucks. You get through it by thinking about the good things. The people you help, the lives you touch. It makes it better."

"Not great," Scott admitted ruefully. "But better."

"So is that the sort of abuse I have to expect, or what I've inflicted on Claire?"

"Yes," Rachel admitted with a nod. "But don't sell Claire short. She's tough as nails and resilient. She always kept up everyone else's spirits in the cave. Even when she was scared shitless. She always seemed calm and in control and it gave the rest of us a little extra courage. She encouraged me to keep singing, even when my throat was parched and people were screaming and dying. 'Don't let them take your soul too,' she used to tell me. I've remembered that to this day. My soul is my own. Everything else is fixable. Mental, physical, and emotional. I can fix those. But I have my soul. Nobody in this town has the power to take that away."

Scott grimaced just a bit. "I don't know that I agree with you. I've wondered for a long time if the souls in this town are being sucked dry. Memories, feelings, even people aren't the same now as even a few years ago. Like, have you noticed nobody is searching for Kristy and Darrell anymore?"

Rachel raised a brow. "I heard Dani say they were found. Haven't they been?"

Alek felt that creeping dread seep back into his chest. He hadn't imagined seeing the dark-skinned girl on the canyon bottom. "Has anyone actually *seen* them? Are they really back?"

"Maybe we should ask Claire when she gets back from the school, if she saw them there or if any of the kids were talking about them." Rachel flipped the bag of peas again, the thick black hair over her ear now dripping from the thawing bag.

Alek stood up. "Or maybe I just need to go there myself and ask." He walked to the door, but before leaving, he turned back to his friends. "Thanks, guys. Really. This has been . . . enlightening."

As he shut the door behind him, he couldn't help but hear Scott's comment. "And off he goes again to get himself killed. I hope he lives long enough to see a badge on his shirt."

Rachel replied, "Me too. Wanna stick around and watch *Die Hard*?"

Scott guffawed. "I can't imagine what made you think of that movie."

Their laughter followed him down the hallway to the stairs.

The bell signaling the start of class was just fading as Claire walked into the school. She could hear voices in the classrooms as she walked down the hall, nearly silent in sneakers. She wished she had been able to clean up a little more, but the best she could do was to duck into the bathroom at the post office and run a comb through her hair and scrub her face with a paper towel and some hand soap. The clerk behind the counter had been nice enough to share a couple of breath mints. He seemed like a nice person, even though he was a little sullen. Sort of the town curmudgeon, but not hostile.

She heard young laughter behind one door and couldn't help but peek through the window. The students were about the age she had planned to teach. The instructor seemed bored as he announced in a monotone to turn to page twenty-seven of the text. "And stop laughing this minute." The words were like a blow to her heart. How could you tell children to stop laughing? Tiny faces fell, their eyes lowered to the text.

"Ms. Sanchez?" Principal Burrows's voice behind her made her jump and turn away from the classroom door. She glanced at her watch. It was 10:01. Crap!

She carefully looked at his necktie, which was different from the one he'd had on earlier this morning. "Yes, sir. I'm sorry I'm late."

"This way, please." He turned on his heel and expected her to follow. She did, remembering to keep a few paces behind. *Omega. Be the Omega.*

He opened the door to what appeared to be the cafeteria and held it open while she went in. He closed the door and then swept his hand toward the tables. "Have a seat."

Why meet in here and not the office? What was going to happen? She sat at the one table where there was a wall at her back. She was surprised at the lack of smells this late in the morning. Was there not a school lunch program in place? Of course, maybe the kids went home to eat. In a town this small, that would make sense.

He remained standing, his hands clasped behind his back in what she recognized was "parade rest" in some branches of the military. "Marine?"

A short nod. "It takes discipline to run a school, Ms. Sanchez. Children are unruly in the best of times, and the natural Sazi aggression makes them even more difficult to manage as they approach puberty."

She knew that and he didn't seem like he wanted her opinion, so she stayed silent and clasped her hands on the table in front of her.

"Do you agree with corporal punishment in schools?"

She wagged her head. "Let's say I'm undecided."

"How so?" So, he was going to push it. Well, better to talk about it now than have to defend it later.

She took in the room—the pale peach cinder block walls, the tile floors, and rows of tables. "I believe that people, including children, are good for only two reasons: the desire not to harm, or the fear of retribution. I prefer to encourage the desire not to harm. But we're Sazi, and predators. The desire to hunt and kill is in our DNA. Add that to a fragile, developing psyche and there has to be some fear of retribution or the world would know we exist and we'd be slaughtering every human in a fifty-mile radius."

He nodded, actually listening to what she was saying. "So is a measure of pain reasonable retribution?"

"Sometimes," she was forced to admit. "But last night wasn't reasonable. It was excessive."

He frowned and squared his shoulders, his relaxed body stance taking on a hostile edge. "I wasn't talking about last night."

She looked him calmly in the eyes. "Yes, you were. Ultimately. You want me to agree. But I don't."

"I should hit you right now for staring me in the eyes."

Sudden understanding rushed through her. "But that's why we're here, isn't it? So you don't *have* to. In front of your staff in the office, you'd have to."

He didn't respond. Instead, he turned and walked toward the back of the room where a buffet line stood empty and dark. "You will report here every day at ten o'clock to prepare lunch for the students. We haven't had a cook for some time, and I believe a hot midday meal encourages learning. I understand from your pack leaders that you're an excellent cook."

Lunch lady? He was making her the *lunch lady?* "But—"

"You will cook and clean up the room afterward. In addition, you will have the opportunity to meet the staff and students in a nonconfrontational manner, where your status in the pack is clear." He turned back to face her. "At the end of what I imagine will be a very short period of your Omega status, judging from the stinging in my hand this morning, you will be integrated as a teacher's aide until the next term. Is that clear?"

Her head was spinning. Not beaten. Not humiliated. He had figured out a way to follow the rules while giving her a measure of dignity and a way to advance in a logical way. "*Why?*"

He let out a small sigh. "People with teaching degrees are a dime a dozen, Ms. Sanchez. But a *teacher* . . . that's a rare commodity. When you come upon one who can even teach a grumpy old bear, it's worth saving and encouraging. Now, I believe you have some cooking to do. You'll find the supplies in the kitchen."

"But what about the rest of my duties?" It would take hours to prepare the food for the whole school and clean up afterward.

"That, I can't help you with, I'm afraid. This will be in addition to your duties. It won't be a pleasant period for you. Make the best of it and strive to impress and inspire."

So, the ex-Marine was telling her to "suck it up, snowflake." It was what her Alpha used to say when she would complain about chores or schoolwork. Some things were worth paying a price for. "Yes, sir." She stood and saluted, probably botching it horribly.

He actually cracked a smile as he returned the salute. "Eyes down, Ms. Sanchez. For now. The office secretary will provide whatever information you need."

The principal left her alone in the cafeteria for her to plan a meal for a whole bunch of people that needed to be served in about two hours. Unfortunately, she didn't know how many people, food allergies, or even where all the supplies were kept.

She had a *lot* of work to do.

CHAPTER 15

*I*t was nearly nightfall when he saw Claire again. He'd watched from a distance through the window of the school cafeteria as the principal met with Claire. When he left her and she had started to prepare lunch for the school, it took him by surprise. That she was smiling confused him even more. He needed to find out what had happened. He'd left a note at the office and was relieved when she limped into the diner, scanning the room until she spotted him at a corner table.

She slid into the booth, looking utterly exhausted. "I'm glad you're okay. Scott was really worried you'd . . . well, he worried. But you look okay. Or, at least, not any worse."

"Yeah, he had reason to worry. But I talked with him and Rachel for a while and they calmed me down." He reached out and touched her hand. "Are *you* okay? You were at the school a long time."

Paula, the waitress who usually took care of his table approached with pad in hand. "Hi, Alek. What'll you have?"

"The venison roast smells great tonight. I'll go with that." He looked over at Claire. "Are you hungry? I'm buying."

She looked around the table, as though searching for something. "Could I get a menu?"

Paula's eyes narrowed. "I'll see if I can find one." She spun around on her short heels and disappeared behind the counter.

"Great. Now I pissed off the waitress. It's been that kind of day. She'll probably spit in my soup."

He shook his head. "Nah. Paula's fine. She must just be tired. Look, she's coming back and has a menu."

But instead of handing it to Claire, she tossed it down on the table. It bounced and nearly knocked over the water glass. He looked up in surprise. "Ease up, Paula. Are you okay?"

"Fine," she said through gritted teeth. "It's just been a long day."

Claire took no more than a few minutes to make her choice. "Just a burger and fries, I think. I'm too tired to chew much more than that."

"Yeah, I ran into several people who saw you today. Everyone is really impressed. I'm glad the leg and head didn't slow you down too much. I'd be happy to help you more tomorrow. Now that I know what I need to do, I'm sure I can fit it all in."

She yawned wide. "It was a lot of work and my leg is pretty sore. Being on my feet for so many hours hasn't helped the muscles heal up any."

"When I left the note at the school to have you meet me, they said you were cooking. Why cooking? I thought you were coming on as a teacher."

By the time she'd explained what Mr. Burrows had done, the food had arrived. Alek was impressed. "So you just have to cook for the rest of the time you're the Omega? Heck, that won't be too long."

"I hope not," she said, sipping on her glass of tea. "And I do like to cook, so it's not a real burden. It will make for some long days, though."

"Like I said," he said through a bite of venison. "I'll help. It's my fault you're not in a classroom already. But hey, you're probably sick of talking about chores. What was it like in your old pack? What's the biggest difference you've noticed here?"

After dipping a fry into catsup and taking a bite, she sighed and said, "The smells. Absolutely the scents. Everything is so intense up here. It must be the thinner air. It can be overwhelming. It's why I had a hard time tracking you. I'm actually a pretty good tracker."

He felt warm. "Yeah. Again, my bad."

She waved off his embarrassment. "No, I'm over that. I figured out that the stars are aligned wrong or something. I would have wound up the Omega some way. It was destined. But I will need to practice tracking before the next challenge. I can't afford to lose. I don't know how long I can burn the candle at both ends."

Paula walked back over and asked, "Will there be anything else?"

He glanced at Claire, who shrugged. "No, I think we're good. Just the check." He touched Claire's hand again. "I'd be happy to give you some tracking practice after our duties are done tomorrow."

"That would work. It might be better to learn when I'm tired. I don't think that will be changing anytime soon."

The door chime rang and a familiar scent caught his nose. He looked up to see Denis striding toward them, anger etched in his face. "There you are!" he said as he reached the table. "What the hell are you doing here?"

"Hey!" Alek snapped. "Watch your mouth. What's the problem?"

Claire pretended not to notice the interaction, focusing her entire attention on her plate of french fries and reading the back of the menu about how the diner's owner, Aiden, came to America years before.

"You promised last week that you were going to help me get my science project finished tonight. It's due in the morning and it's locked in your apartment. I can't finish it without your help."

Claire started scooting out of the booth, even as he reached to stop her. "Hey, I need to get some sleep anyway. I'll take off to the house and you guys do what you need to do."

He reached out past Denis's arm and grabbed her wrist. "Claire, wait. You don't need to go. I'm sure Denis wouldn't mind if you helped."

"Actually, Denis would mind a lot," his younger brother said. "I can only have one person help. You know the teacher can smell lies. I'd get an F."

Claire gently removed his fingers from around her wrist with her other hand. "It's okay, Alek. Go help your brother. I'm sure we'll run into each other again another day."

She carefully walked out of the diner, putting only a little weight on her leg. Was it insane that he wanted to toss his apartment key at Denis and chase after her? Support her on the way back to the house? Probably. And it wouldn't do any good. She'd said she was over his screwup, but hadn't yet said she forgave him.

He'd work on that. He had to be sure she forgave him. It was vitally important, but damned if he could figure out why. "C'mon, Denis. Let's pay the check and go."

CHAPTER 16

The chief and the mayor were waiting in the front room of the police station the next morning. Claire had been determined to be on time. She hadn't waited for Rachel to wake her up. She couldn't rely on anyone but herself. In fact, she was outside ten minutes early waiting for Rachel, just to be safe.

The mayor, dressed in suit pants and a dress shirt with the sleeves rolled up, looked like he'd just stepped away from a meeting. The chief wasn't in uniform, but was dressed all in black, similar to some enforcers she'd met in Texas, visitors from other packs.

Wolven agents weren't supposed to be a pack leader's enforcers; they were supposed to keep the pack leader in check. The chief was the Second of the Luna Lake pack, using his Wolven status to raise the fear factor. Wolven had the power to decide life and death, while a Second had to obey the rules laid down by the Council.

She could smell that Alek and Scott had already been here—and that something unpleasant had happened. Carefully, so that the two men wouldn't know what she was doing, Claire took a deep, slow breath. The scent of the bleach-based cleaner that had been used couldn't completely erase the

odors of pain, fear, and blood—blood that had been spilled
recently.

The minute the women stepped into the room, Rachel
dropped her gaze to the floor and her scent and body language
turned passive. It was a struggle for Claire to do the same,
but she managed, remembering Alpha Cara's reminder when
she was a child: *There will always be someone in our world who
is a bigger dog. There's no shame in giving credit and honor to
that power. You don't have to like the person, but you should respect the authority they have earned.*

"So, Ms. Sanchez, you're late again. It seems we need to
have a little chat." The tone said there was likely an evil smile
on the chief's face. His scent was anticipatory.

But she *wasn't* late. What did they mean? "I apologize for
being late yesterday. Rachel tried to wake me, but I hadn't
set my alarm. I thought I was on time today. Please tell me
the expected time I should be here so it won't happen again."
She kept her tone mild and tried to convey shame in posture
and scent. All she could do was try to keep Rachel out of it,
because even if this had happened in her own pack, in Texas,
she would have gotten some sort of punishment. She should
have asked the details, rather than going straight upstairs to
bed. "Too tired" was no excuse.

Out of the corner of her eye, she saw the mayor stand and
walk out from behind the big wooden desk. His tone was
neutral. "Normally, Claire, I would accept your apology and
let this go. You're new to the pack and haven't been trained
in how we work. I was surprised when I talked to your Alphas
today and learned your pack has no formal Omega." That
made her flinch. He'd called her pack leaders. "The chief
wasn't nice to Alek because he *does* know better. And I know
you can smell that he bled. Lenny is a little sensitive about
people being on time. I just don't know how he'll react to two
tardy Omegas, two days in a row."

Rachel's head snapped up. "Van, no. Please. It's not her fault. If you need to take a strip of hide, take mine. I should have told her what time."

The chief touched Rachel's shoulder and shook his head. Claire kept her chin down, but raised her eyes to watch their interaction. An odd mix of emotions flashed over Rachel's face and through her scent as the young woman flinched away from his touch. Father/daughter? Ex-lovers? Torturer/victim? Claire couldn't quite figure it out, but it was well beyond Second/pack member. He rubbed Rachel's arm lightly, seeming to enjoy touching her. She struggled not to move, twitching and grimacing. "This isn't about what you did or didn't do, Rachel. This is about what Claire withheld from us."

He turned his attention to her, lifted her chin to force her to look him straight in the eyes. She knew better than to fall for that trick. She kept her gaze firmly on his neck, no matter how high he tilted her head. He chuckled. "So, you've been disciplined before. I'm not surprised. What's your *real* rank in your pack, Ms. Sanchez? Fifth in line couldn't hold a struggling rabbit in place with magic, much less hold two adults in midair for . . . how long? Five minutes? More?"

Oh. They'd found out about that. "I didn't count." That was the absolute truth. She was in defense mode now. She wouldn't lie, couldn't afford to have him smell that. "Until rescuers could get to them."

"And your rank?"

"We don't have them." Again, it was the truth. They had a fluid pack of various animals, like this town. It was difficult to figure out how to rank a wolf against an owl or an eagle. There were so many alphas in the pack that everyone decided there was no need. "Nearly all the females are alphic. I'm in the middle."

Claire could see Rachel's jaw drop beside her. "*All* the women are alphic? How are you all *alive*?"

She shrugged. "We fight enemies. We don't need to fight among ourselves."

There was a long pause while Chief Gabriel turned her face from side to side, studying her. *Watch the neck, focus on his scent, on his pulse. Wait. Wait. Don't move.* Her Alpha's voice came into her mind, a memory rather than a current mental attachment. In fact, she hadn't felt her Alphas in her mind for nearly a day. That worried her a little.

"That's because I'm blocking them." The chief's voice startled her and she raised her eyes to meet his. The chief immediately backhanded her across the face. The pain of the blow nearly dropped her to her knees. Rachel let out a small sound but didn't move. Claire didn't raise her hand to touch her jaw, but could feel it beginning to swell. She had heard of alphas that could block another alpha's power. It took a powerful Sazi to pull it off.

"Let me explain how things work up here, Ms. Sanchez." The chief's voice grew rough, his scent angry to the point of fury. "You're the Omega. You're *nothing.* You have no rank, no prestige, no standing until you earn some. You will swear your allegiance to Mayor Monk, as your Alpha, for the remainder of your stay here and will have no contact with your old pack." She felt a moment of panic, did her best to suppress it. "You will not meet the eyes of any other pack member, regardless of their gender, rank, age, or species." In a blur of motion, her head rocked to the opposite side from a second vicious slap, and white flowers erupted in her brain. This time she did fall, her knees slamming into the floor with a shock of pain. "You don't seem to understand your station. You looked at the principal, the secretary, nearly every teacher in school today, along with the waitress in the restaurant."

Wait. What? How was she supposed to serve food if she could only stare at the floor? "You are forbidden to interact with any town resident for the next week other than the mayor, me, and Rachel, who will be your guide during your training. You will listen and do as you're told, when you're told, and how you're told. You are forbidden to refuse or disobey direct orders and will do whatever you're instructed to do by your superiors."

Within reason, surely, she thought. The chief was in her mind in an instant; she screamed and raised her hands to her ears, feeling that her brain was going to explode. The chief kicked her backward sharply, sending her sprawling on the floor, and pulled out of her head at the same time. She remained where she landed, mostly because his foot came down on her throat.

She fought to breathe and tried to turn her head so she could get air. He ground his foot on her neck in response. "You breathe when I let you, Claire. You think what your Alpha allows you to think. There is no *within reason* in this town. Do you understand?"

Claire didn't answer, wasn't sure if it was another trick. How had the chief known what had been in her mind? Who was the Alpha here? She held her breath until she couldn't anymore, keeping her eyes on the ceiling, not meeting his eyes.

He lifted his foot, seeming to be satisfied. "You may answer."

It took two tries to get her jaw to work. When she spoke, she made sure there was no fear in her voice, only anger. That seemed to both amuse and excite him. "Yes."

"You understand?"

"Yes."

"You're fortunate that we're feeling reasonable today. I'm tempering my normal reaction because you didn't understand. You do now. Any further breaches will mean a strip of hide. Do you understand?"

"Yes." No emotion. No reaction.

He put a beefy hand around her neck and pulled, using both magic and muscle to raise her to her feet. He left her enough room to breathe, but dug fingernails into her skin until she bled. The chief leaned in, close enough that she could feel puffs of air against her face when he spoke. "You are part of our pack now, Claire. But because those who are now above you would fear your power, you can no longer be alpha. Until you earn your place back, your glow must be dimmed."

She was frozen, just as surely as she had frozen Alek and Tammy earlier. She couldn't move a muscle, couldn't stop the alpha from pulling her power out from her very pores. Without ever moving, the chief siphoned off what little power she still had and she knew then that he had the ability to do it for the whole time she was here. She would be completely helpless.

That thought made him smile. "Yes. You will be. You are an Omega now."

Rachel looked confused, not understanding the interaction. Claire resolved not to think about it anymore. She couldn't afford to. How were they reading her thoughts?

She risked a glance at the window, where a clock was on the wall above the panes of glass, as though checking the time. It was nearly five. The chief followed her gaze, looking far too pleased with what he'd done. That the mayor hadn't stopped him told her all she needed to know about this pack, this town. "It is getting late. We should probably let them get started, Van. If you're done, of course." The last was almost an afterthought, as though it didn't really matter what the mayor thought.

Mayor Monk checked his watch and then stood, moving from behind the desk as though this was any normal business meeting. "True. Rachel, I gave Alek and Scott the south side of town. You'll take the north. You'll meet up with them at the grocery store at ten. We have supplies coming in today."

Rachel raised her hand. He nodded at her and she spoke. "May I ask a question?"

Oh, a double layer of submission. Good to know. Claire appreciated any hints about the proper etiquette.

"Go ahead." Chief Gabriel said.

"It's rare to have so many hands to us to help people. It might give us the chance to do some real good."

That changed the chief's whole attitude. He transformed back into a smooth politician. "Such as?"

Rachel shrugged, trying to seem casual, but it was obvious to Claire that she'd been thinking about this for some time. That the chief apparently didn't realize that was telling.

"The back of the roof of Marilyn's clinic has been leaking for a while. The shingles need work and winter's coming. I don't know how to tar roofs, but Alek does. And Polar Pops is crawling with spiders because of all the boxes everyone has stored in the basement. We could clean it all out for her and get rid of them before the cold sets in. I couldn't do it alone and you know Skew wouldn't even think about it."

The mayor pursed his lips, considering. Rachel continued. "It might mean a few regular, everyday things would have to wait a day or two, but sweeping isn't nearly as important as water damage and bugs in a restaurant." She ducked her head. "If you agree, of course."

The chief interjected. "The lumberyard *is* on the way back from the grocery wholesaler in Spokane. It wouldn't take much to throw some bug bombs and a few bales of shingles in the back. I think I still have a box of roofing nails in the storage shed, but we might need some roof tar. The stuff we have is probably dried up."

The mayor nodded. "Marilyn has been a trooper about the

ceiling. It's past time for it to be fixed. Good suggestion, Rachel. I'll call David before he leaves. You get started. The supplies will be at the grocery. Ms. Sanchez, I know you are expected at the school at ten. As soon as you're done, you'll join the others at the grocery." He clapped his hands sharply, making Claire jump. "That's it, then. Get moving. Daylight's burning." *Bastard.* She risked a glance back as they turned to leave. The chief didn't turn around or give any sign that he'd perceived her thought. Either he didn't hear or didn't care what she thought of him.

Not wanting to push things and risk more abuse, Claire followed Rachel out of the office. The other woman pulled Claire into the light of the overhead lamp near the door and turned her face, peering at it closely. "Not too bad. Your head's almost healed, so hitting the floor didn't open any stitches. It doesn't look like your nose is broken. Are any of your teeth loose?"

Claire honestly hadn't thought about that. Using her tongue, she gingerly felt around her mouth. One lower molar wiggled a little, sending sparks of pain through her head. "Yeah. One. Right lower. I'll have to be careful eating for a few hours."

"*Hours?*" Rachel let out a snort. "Days, more like. You're omega now. Healing went out the window with your magic. Think back to falling off your bike when you were little, in Kansas, and how long the scrapes lasted. Then double it."

Crap. She was right. No magic, no advanced healing. She didn't feel all that different, but the day was young. "Okay. I get it. Keep my mouth shut and my head down. What do we do first?"

Now the other woman grinned, her white teeth bright in the fading lamplight as they walked. "First are the places we get to *avoid*. Say thank you for that gift."

Claire had had a feeling there was a method to the madness of suggesting more work. "What joys are we missing out on?" She managed to grin when she said it.

"Well, at least temporarily. Devon Jones is off the list. He's scum. I wouldn't do that to you on your second day."

That sounded ominous. "What sort of scum? He doesn't hurt you, does he?"

Rachel shook her head. Actually, her whole body shuddered. "Nope. Let it go until there's no choice. We're also skipping old lady Morgan. She's evil incarnate. Would work you to death with a smile on her face and then take the whip to you because you had the audacity to die before you had finished."

"Oh joy. She sounds like fun. How do you manage people like that?"

They reached the edge of a small group of houses. Rachel stopped and set down the large black duffel bag that had been slung across her back. "Aprons and masks on."

"Masks? Aprons?" She reached out to take what Rachel handed her. It was a full-face owl mask made of nylon netting, covered with snowy bird feathers. The apron was the same. "What the hell is this about? You're already an owl. Why dress up like one? What do we do here?"

"These are the Kragan triplets. They're elderly owls—two brothers and a sister, all in separate houses. Their sight is nearly gone and they're a little . . . paranoid. We need to clean their houses but they're scared of all humans and most other Sazi. So I wear an owl mask because I can't shift off the moon . . . and I can't run the vacuum with wings. This way, I reduce the risk that any of the Kragans will have a stroke or a heart attack from being afraid." She smiled again. "Not all the duties of the Omega are horrible. The people? Some are wonderful, most are just people, with good days and bad. Some are creeps. Like anywhere." She dropped the mask over her face. The moon lit up the white feathers.

"Brown eyes in an owl. Looks weird." Claire chuckled, putting on her own mask and feathered apron.

A raspberry from behind Rachel's mask sounded like a whoopee cushion. "Not as weird as blue eyes." They stepped onto the first porch. An overwhelming smell of bird clung to the wood. It wasn't an unpleasant scent, not like the ammonia odor of feces. Claire had heard that raptor shifters tended to smell more "bird-y" as they got older.

"Follow my lead. Use any owl customs you still remember." Rachel used her fingernails like talons to claw at the wooden planks in front of the door, then let out a few low hoots. Claire was a little surprised when a woman inside yelled out in French-accented English. The way Rachel had been talking, she'd expected to have to dust off her memories of owl speech.

"Who es out there? I am armed and I have silver bullets."

"It's Rachel, Bitty. I have a friend with me today. Claire. Say hello, Claire." Rachel flexed her fingers above the wood, looking at Claire, who realized Rachel wanted her to scratch as well. Claire's nails weren't as long as Rachel's, so she was probably going to wind up digging splinters out from under her nails, but she scratched as best she could, then made friendly clicking noises. Her accent was probably more barn owl than snowy, but Bitty responded with small, happy screeching.

"Well, come in, you two. Come say hello to an old lady."

Rachel opened the door carefully, pushing Claire back against the doorjamb. Claire soon saw why, as there was a double-barreled shotgun pointed right where they had been standing. "You can put down the gun, Bitty. Just us owls here."

The woman on the couch peered at them through watery yellow eyes, her white hair looking like so many feathers, but sparse and showing pale skin between the strands. Apparently, she liked what she saw. The shotgun was lowered and tucked under the couch, still within easy reach. Rachel pulled Claire forward and closed the door behind them. The woman wrinkled her nose and waved a hand in front of her face. "You two need to use better soap before you come see me. One of you smells like you've been walking around with wolves." She made a hissing noise. "Filthy things, wolves. Not as bad as cats. But I don't have to tell you two about those hateful things."

Claire winced and glanced at Rachel, who shrugged. Apparently, she was used to the old woman's prejudices. Rachel dropped to her knees and scooted over to the woman, tucking in the apron around her legs. "What would you like us to do for you today, Bitty?"

The woman reached up and petted the feathers on the mask. "Such a respectful young owl you are, Rachel. You'll make some man a fine mate."

"Thank you, Bitty." She touched the old woman's face in return and smiled warmly. She smelled like she meant the thank you, which surprised Claire a bit. She'd never asked Rachel about her plans for the future. Maybe being a good wife would make her happy, as it did several people in Claire's pack. Being a wife and mother wasn't something to be ashamed of in her pack, but neither was being a career woman . . . or both.

She was careful not to meet the old owl's eyes. She might look blind but she had focused full attention in those few short moments. Claire had a suspicion she wasn't as frail as she made people believe. "I'd be happy to do the dishes. There are a few in the sink." Claire knew they were on a schedule and since she was the one who was supposed to be working, there was no reason why Rachel couldn't sit and keep the older woman company. Plus, Claire was starting to sweat under the mask. The house was boiling. Usually owls liked it cold, especially snowy owls, but this one had the heat set to uncomfortable.

"Did I ever tell you about how my brothers and I moved to New Orleans in a covered wagon?"

"No, Bitty. Tell me." Rachel's voice sounded eager and interested, but the wave of deceit that wafted out of her nearly made Claire sneeze. If Bitty smelled it, she didn't say anything. She just started talking.

Nearly a half hour later, the story was done and Claire was just drying the last dish. "So, tell me, how are those two little owls? I hear they're back in the nest. Hiding in the woods, were they?"

Claire stepped out of the kitchen, wiping her hands on a green-and-orange-striped kitchen towel. "Where did you hear that, Miss Kragan?" She didn't feel comfortable using the woman's first name until invited.

"Oh, heavens, where *did* I hear that? I don't get that many visitors." She peered at Rachel. "Did you tell me, little one?" Rachel shook her head. "Well, then it must have been one of my brothers." She raised a hand. "Yes! That was it. Egan told me. I don't know where he heard it, though. But they're safe and sound?"

Rachel shook her head. "He must have heard wrong. We haven't found them yet."

The old woman's face fell. "Oh, my. I'm so sorry for their mother. I don't like her very well—she's far too pushy for my taste—but to lose your little ones . . . Dear, dear." She clucked her tongue. "You've already searched the caves at the bottom of the canyon, I'm sure. Some of them are easy to get in, but rather tricky to get out of. Children are not terribly clever about getting out of trouble . . . at least not as easily as getting into trouble." She chuckled at her own joke. "When we moved here, I explored them at length, but could only fly out of a few."

That grabbed Claire's attention. "Someone mentioned they might have seen Kristy at the bottom of the canyon yesterday. But I don't think they found her . . . or at least nobody mentioned it to me."

Bitty turned her upper body so that she was facing Claire, looking across the back of the couch. The old woman peered closely at her new visitor. After more than an hour of cleaning in the heat, wearing a mask, she was dripping enough sweat that there was probably a puddle on the floor. She hoped she didn't smell too *wolf* for the old owl. If she noticed, Bitty was too polite to mention the scent. "I seem to remember that someone made maps of the whole canyon before the town was set up. We had to protect the routes to the camp from snakes, and serpents love canyons to hide and travel in. I'm sure the maps are in the town offices somewhere." She shrugged, then turned back to face Rachel. "But as I say, surely those searching have already checked."

Or maybe they hadn't—nobody yesterday had mentioned checking the canyon previously when Patrick and Asylin had arrived back from the search. It seemed it hadn't occurred to anyone, which was strange in itself.

It was another twenty minutes before they could pry themselves away from the elderly owl's home and Claire had never been so glad to get out into the fresh air. They waited until they were at the end of the lane before they ducked behind a stand of bushes and peeled off the aprons and masks. Claire sucked in a huge gulp of cool breeze, letting it wash over her soaked skin and clothes. "How do you stand having feathers on the moon? Good lord, I was baking in there!"

Rachel chuckled. "Feathers cool as well as warm when you know how to use them. The problem with the apron and mask is you can't fluff them, so they hold in the heat." She waggled her head as she carefully folded the apron to tuck it back in the duffel bag. "Actually, it's sort of both. We fluff to keep in heat too. It's sort of like when you wolves shake after coming out of the water. You're fluffing your coat to cool off." Opening a zippered pouch on the side of the bag, she pulled out an old-fashioned pocket watch, then let out an exasperated sigh. "Yeah, I figured we were running late. She was really on a roll today with the stories. It's nearly eight. We're going to have to move to get everything done and get you back to the school by ten."

She turned away and expected Claire to follow. But Claire had turned to the other two houses tucked back behind Bitty's. "What about the brothers? Don't we do anything for them?"

Throwing the duffel over her shoulders, Rachel shook her head. "Not now. They're still sleeping. They're night owls—Egan doesn't go to bed until around five a.m. and Claude is probably still up. He'll drop off around nine and then sleep until just before dark. We'll stop by right at sunset for both of them."

"Is this what you do every day? Go around and take care of people from before dawn to after dark?"

With a rueful expression, Rachel said, "It's a living . . . of a sort. Part of being the Omega sucks. It's hard, dirty work. But the rewards are cool when the chief is feeling nice. My room and board are free. I eat for free anywhere in town. People can give me gifts if they choose . . . I get clothes and gift certificates for stores and other stuff. The Omega is taken care of by the pack in exchange for service."

Claire couldn't help but notice the caveat—*if the chief is feeling nice.* "And if the chief *isn't* feeling nice?"

The dark-skinned woman paused and then stared strongly at Claire, willing her to understand without actually saying the words out loud. "He was feeling nice today."

Oh, crap.

She closed her eyes, realizing that the next thirty days were going to be rougher than she'd originally thought. "Is anything off-limits?"

Rachel lowered the duffel to the ground again and chose her words very carefully. Claire couldn't smell any emotions over the thick sweat musk that hovered in the air like a cloud. "Death of the Omega would be . . . *regrettable* because someone else would have to be selected. Another Ascension Day would have to be planned on short notice. The Council would be annoyed. But they probably wouldn't be much *more* than annoyed."

So, nothing was off-limits. *"Any* sort of abuse is allowed?" She was getting a suspicion that she didn't like and she wasn't sure what had brought it to mind.

Another sigh. "Forced sex is frowned on because there can be *complications.* But sexual humiliation is completely within the rules. Remember the scum I mentioned? Yeah. That."

Claire took a deep breath and let it out slowly, then changed the subject to something Bitty had said, partly because she didn't want to think about it. "So did anyone check the canyon when the kids went missing? Playing in rocks is pretty normal kid behavior. And why is nobody looking anymore? It's been less than a week. I don't see any posters up, haven't seen any searchers. It's more than a little weird, frankly."

Rachel just gave a little shrug. "I haven't really noticed. I've just been doing my thing." She started to walk away again but Claire grabbed her arm and held it fast. Rachel looked back at her as though expecting to be hit.

"But don't you see?! That's what I mean. You were the *Omega.* Doesn't it seem logical that they'd be having you search twenty-four/seven for those kids?" She waited for an answer. Claire didn't feel any pain in her head at the accusation. Maybe the chief couldn't read minds at a distance. Maybe he didn't pay attention all the time.

"Gawd!" Rachel's exclamation was punctuated with violent

movement as she yanked out of Claire's grasp and threw her hands in the air. "You're as bad as Alek. Everything is not a conspiracy, Claire. Just because you don't *see* people searching doesn't mean they aren't. Just drop it!" She stormed away, leaving Claire stunned at the ferocity of her reaction. Had the question hit a little too close to home? She trotted after Rachel, squinting as the sun rose over the mountain and hit her right in the eye.

"Hey, look, I'm sorry, Rachel. You're right, I don't know the whole situation. I'm just saying what I'm noticing. But we'll drop the subject if it bothers you. What's next on our list?"

The other woman let out a sigh. "I'm sorry too, Claire. I shouldn't have snapped. I just get frustrated when people think nobody cares about those kids. Of course we care about them and I know people have been searching for days. I've been hauling water and energy drinks for the searchers so I personally know people have been searching for clues and they tell me about all the places they've looked." She seemed eager to change the subject. "So what was up with Asylin yesterday? Cindee said she was acting weird up on the top of the mountain."

Claire nodded as Rachel led her toward the edge of town. "Yeah, it was pretty strange. It was like she was convinced that Kristy was visiting an aunt in Louisiana and wasn't missing at all. Everyone looked at her like she'd grown a second head. When Alek called her on it, she looked like she was trying to remember something and then bolted down into the canyon in owl form. Strange.

"Where are we off to now? Does anyone live this far out?"

Rachel shook her head and stopped just off the road to drop the duffel and unzip it. "Nope. Now we do a quick roadside cleanup. Humans dump crap out here all the time. I don't know what it is about traveling that makes people such slobs.

I mean, how much effort does it take to throw out the trash when you stop for gas?"

Claire looked down the deserted road. She hadn't seen a car all morning. "Is there a lot of traffic around here? I haven't seen much." But Rachel seemed to be right. Now that she was looking closer, Claire saw white Styrofoam cups poking out of the grass next to the dirt road, plastic shopping bags fluttering in the light breeze, stuck on a barbed wire fence.

"Nah, we don't get many visitors, for which I'm grateful. But there's still trash around." She pulled a folded black plastic trash bag from the duffel and handed it to Claire, along with a stack of bright pink strips of ribbon. "If we clean it up every day, it doesn't get too bad. I'll take the left side of the road. You take the right. It's about a mile." She handed Claire a pair of work gloves, then outfitted herself with a matching set of equipment.

Claire was amazed that the Omega position was so versatile. Cleaner, companion, road crew, cook. What would be next? Tucking the ribbons in her pocket, she started to walk down the road with the other woman. "Hey, can I ask you a rude question?"

"Um . . . sure." Rachel didn't look at her, just kept walking, occasionally picking up a bit of trash and putting it in the bag.

Claire tied a ribbon on the fence next to a discarded blown-out tire. "Were you ever a girlfriend? In the caves?"

Rachel stopped and turned to face Claire, her jaw open wide and her eyes wide in horror. "Why in the world would you ask that? No! Of course not."

She knew it was a weird question but she couldn't forget the dream. "I had a dream the other night. I was back in the caves and Roberto was opening my cage door. I was terrified. I kept thinking it would have been easier if I'd been a guard's girlfriend and got to go to the parties. Maybe they wouldn't take me to the cages so often. But they didn't like little white girls."

Rachel started walking again, nodding absentmindedly. "And they *did* like little dark-skinned girls? Yeah, you're right. They did. I was lucky that he liked my voice. Roberto."

"Your voice? You mean when you used to sing?" She picked up a plastic Slurpee cup—blue raspberry by the stain at the bottom—battling the no-longer light breeze that tried to pull the cup out of her hand and made it hard to open the trash bag.

"Yep. The guards, and especially Roberto, liked my singing. So I'd do concerts for their orgies. Roberto called me *Be-lili*. I looked it up once I was rescued. She was a Babylonian goddess of vegetation who was known as 'the goddess who weeps.'" Rachel shrugged. "I guess because I sang the blues a lot. There was good reason, y'know? So he instructed new guards that nobody was to put *anything* in my mouth. Nobody would defy him, so the rule sort of extended to the rest of my body, for which I'm grateful. I wish I could have thanked my mother for the music lessons." She turned away then, and Claire could smell sorrow on the wind. Rachel snuffled and wiped her nose with the back of her glove, then said, "Did you know you were off-limits from the orgies too? That's why you were never a girlfriend."

"Wait. *Orgies?*"

Rachel spit out a harsh laugh. "You didn't think 'girlfriend' meant wine and roses, did you? They were gang rapes. I remember the faces of those girls. They started out terrified, taken by a dozen men every night. After a few weeks, their eyes went dead and whoever they had been before they were kidnapped died. If they could have killed themselves, they would have. You should be grateful."

The reality was a harsh slap across the face of the memories of an innocent ten-year-old. As an adult, the horror of what those girls endured . . . "Why was I off-limits?"

Now Rachel shrugged. "Dunno. But you were the only white girl who never showed up. I only heard your name mentioned once. A new guard asked for you, and Carlos, the senior guard—you remember him, the fat one with the broken tooth—cuffed him on the ear and said, "Not that one. She's Roberto's."

Claire felt suddenly cold to her core. She began to shake so hard that she dropped to her knees. That moment in the tunnel, so close to the light, frozen in place while he squeezed her throat flashed into her mind, raised from a hundred nightmares. *You're mine, little one.*

She felt a hand on her arm and looked past the image of those cold dark eyes to Rachel's concerned ones. "Hey, you okay? What just happened?"

It took several tries before she could talk. "I tried to escape once. I managed to make it past the guards, all the way to the entrance. But he was there. Roberto or Nasil or whoever he was, in snake form. He turned human, fully dressed, and grabbed my throat. Lifted me off the ground and told me that I was his. What did that mean?"

Now her friend's dark face and scent held sadness and a woman's knowledge. "Probably that if you'd have stayed any longer, you would have wound up a girlfriend, and it wouldn't have been pretty. The guards were petty and cruel. But Roberto . . . he was evil. You are one lucky girl."

"Got it. I'll remember to say my thanks. So, what's next? Is it time to head over to unload groceries?"

Rachel checked her watch. "Yeah, they should be back by now. It's pretty close to the school so you can slip out while we're loading boxes. The boys might already be there. We also need to clean a lot of stuff out of the basement. You're limping again, so I might have you do the sorting downstairs. I have a chart of which family has which space in a drawer in the desk downstairs. I'll show you where it is."

Claire turned, fully intending to follow until a sound caught her ear and brought her up short. *What was that?* "Did you hear that?"

Her friend shook her head, then stopped and listened. A second strange noise made Rachel furrow her brow. "Okay, I hear it now too. But I can't figure out what it is."

Muffled and distant, it didn't sound like any animal or bird Claire had ever heard. She pointed in the general direction. "I don't know, but I think we need to check it out." Not waiting for Rachel to disagree, Claire grabbed a fence post and vaulted over the barbed wire strands, leaving her friend to either follow or go back to get help. Rachel hesitated, then launched herself over the fence.

"You must have a streak of masochism in you, girl. We're going to get beat on for wandering off on our own."

Claire picked up the pace, keeping her nose in the air and sniffing in short bursts, searching for a scent to tie to the sound. "Can't be helped. It's part of the jo—" *Crap. This won't end well.* She'd picked up a scent, one she'd smelled recently, just this morning in fact. The scent had lingered at an open doorway, princess bedspread still mussed, waiting for the young owner to come home and crawl underneath. "I think I smell one of the kids."

Rachel's eyes went wide and she started sniffing frantically. "My nose sucks. But if you're right . . ." She must have realized what the sounds might mean. "Keep going . . . lead the way."

She did. The new forest scents were becoming more familiar, and she could focus better. Claire bent over slightly, ignoring the pain in her leg and the throbbing of her jaw at the sudden movement. Tracking a scent in the air, rather than on the ground, took effort. There were wind shifts and vegetation to take into account. The grass was tall here and brush sprang up at odd angles, threatening to trip her with every step. She slowed from a sprint to a careful trot, Rachel so close on her heels that if Claire stopped suddenly, Rachel would slam into her.

The noise became more agitated, like muffled yelling. That's when she saw figures in the distance, heading deeper into the woods. "Over there," she said quietly and turned toward the two figures, one a lot smaller than the other.

When Claire and Rachel entered the woods, the sunlight abruptly disappeared, plunging them into darkness. These weren't normal shadows, from sun filtered through the pine branches above—it was more like a light had been switched off. Claire could feel the sting of magic flow over her skin. She'd met alphas who could mask an area from view during a hunt, make it an unpleasant place that humans would avoid or even run away from. This was like that, and Claire could tell that Rachel was feeling the effects. She'd slowed, her strides growing shorter and more hesitant.

Claire felt it too—a creepy, uneasy sensation that made her want to stop and turn around. Her hair started tingling and goose bumps crawled all over her. Then her training took over. Her Alphas had worked hard to prepare her for most things. In anything other than a direct fight she could ignore false signals and push past.

She smelled them then. Two people, both male. Claire pushed past her own pounding heart, ignoring her mind's intense urging to run away from the threat. She reached out and grabbed the smaller person and wrapped her arms around his torso. It was a child and she could smell it was the missing Williams boy!

Powerful magic slammed against her, trying to throw her off the child. Claire looked behind her, hoping Rachel was there to add her strength, but the owl shifter was gone. It was hard to blame her. Panic was making it hard to think. All sound vanished, along with her other senses. She couldn't smell, couldn't see. It was like being in a sensory deprivation chamber. Terror soared and Claire couldn't decide whether the fear was being imposed on her or was a natural result of the lack of sensation.

Claire locked her fingers and willed herself not to let go, knowing that with her diminished strength, she couldn't withstand more than one or two more blows. She reached inside herself for more magic. But the moon wasn't full so there was nothing to pull on to replenish herself. Her pack had found her during the wreck; maybe she could reach them, despite the block by the mayor. She had to try.

Pulling magic from someone else was like sucking soft serve ice cream through a straw. It was technically possible, but it was slow and made her head hurt. She reached out through the pack link that was always in the back of her head. The chief might have dimmed the connection, but only her Alphas could truly end it. She pulled while simultaneously yanking on the boy, trying to free him from his captor's grasp. That he didn't scream in pain said he either wasn't able to or she just couldn't hear it. She didn't see a gag, but physical bindings weren't the only kind her people were capable of. She felt a faint trace, like light under a closed door. She pulled, and with a burst of light in her head, power flooded into her body.

For a moment, time seemed to freeze. Then she started gaining ground, both physically and metaphysically. Magic flowed over her in a rush and she pulled the boy free. The magic began to fade as quickly as it started, so obviously the mayor had regained control and was locking her out again. Claire didn't hesitate; she picked up the boy and ran toward the light. He seemed to weigh nothing, his clothing drooping on him like he was just skin and bones.

Her chest was heaving with effort and she was positive the boy's captor was going to leap on her and kill them both. The sensation of hot breath on her neck wasn't a mirage. But somehow, it seemed whatever chased couldn't catch her, even though it felt like she was running in mud up to her knees.

She saw Rachel in the distance, urging her forward, hands cupped around her mouth like she was yelling, screaming encouragement that Claire couldn't hear. With her last ounce of strength, she threw the boy into the sunlit field where Rachel stood, hoping against hope he was one of the missing kids. The boy landed in the light on all fours, immediately scrambled to his feet, and ran toward the road as fast as he could. Rachel spun and followed. When she caught up to and then passed the child, she grabbed his hand and began to tow him along in her wake.

Exhausted, Claire felt herself slowing, felt claws wrap around her ankle and yank. *No!* She stumbled and started to go down. Sunlight touched her outstretched hand, warming the fingers that felt like ice. So very close, but it wouldn't be enough.

She prayed that if she died today, if this *thing* dragged her back into the darkness, that at least Rachel and the boy could reach safety in town and describe whatever it was that had killed her.

CHAPTER 17

"Dude, you okay?" Alek slowly sat up from where he was sprawled at the bottom of the stairs in the basement of Polar Pops and rubbed the back of his head. He looked up at Scott, staring down at him from the main floor. "That was a harsh fall. Should I go find Marilyn?"

His head was spinning but it wasn't from the fall. He felt like he'd been kicked by a horse. He felt weak as a kitten for no apparent reason. "No, I just lost my balance." It was a lie, but he also had no better explanation. "I need to watch where I put my feet. Missed the first step."

Scott carefully carried a case of ice pops down the stairs and set them on one of the risers. "Here, make sure you didn't sprain anything." He offered Alek a hand, holding onto the railing for balance. Alek was grateful for the help. He wasn't sure if his legs would hold him.

Once upright, he leaned against the wall, his head still fuzzy. Other than weak, he didn't feel any worse than he had the rest of the day. "Nothing broken, as far as I can tell. I still feel just as much like crap as when we got here."

Scott snorted. "Getting the shit beat out of you will do that. I told you what would happen if you didn't shower faster. Back talking didn't help either."

"I still don't think saying 'Lighten up' qualifies as *back talk*."

"Alek, I love ya like a brother, but sometimes you need to keep your lip zipped." Apparently, his face showed the surprise he felt, because Scott sighed. "Look, you weren't talking to Lenny the mentor or Lenny the fellow cop. You keep forgetting you're talking to Lenny the Second of this town, and you questioned his authority to set and enforce the rules. 'Lighten up' says, 'you don't own me' and 'your rules don't apply to me.' He then explained why he *does* own you and his rules do apply to you. Got it? You're the Omega now. Rules are about to become your life until the next Ascension. Feel lucky and fall-down-on-your-knees grateful it's *only* for a month."

There was a haunted look in Scott's eyes that Alek had never seen before and the scents that rose from the long-haired owl made his eyes burn. "What have they been doing to you?" He hadn't asked for details earlier and now felt like he should have. He felt both sympathy and outrage in that moment but he also feared for what he might hear and felt shame for what he might not have even bothered to notice until now, despite his and Rachel's saying they didn't mind. "I'm sorry."

The blue eyes turned from haunted to angry. "Whatever they want to. Whenever they decide. Nobody cares. Get used to it."

Alek had never seen this side of his brother before—this coldness—and it unnerved him. How could this have been going on without his noticing? But he had no solution right now. "Okay. So what do we do next?"

Scott sighed and shook his head, picking up the box once more. "The frozen stuff on the truck goes into the walk-in freezer in the corner. As soon as we finish unloading the ice cream, we'll get started on the grocery store. Then we can start moving boxes up. I wish Rachel would get here. This stuff belongs to at least a dozen people and I can't seem to figure out what sort of code she used for the families."

The moment he thought about Rachel and Claire, a panicked feeling clenched his gut. "I'm worried about them. We should go look for them." He started to walk past Scott up the stairs, when he felt the slap of an arm across his chest.

"Are you *insane?*" Scott's face was incredulous—dropped jaw, furrowed brow, and all the trimmings. "There's a ton of ice cream sitting up there, in a truck parked in the sun. There's milk and butter and other stuff for the grocery too. If the girls are much farther than a block away, we'll have puddles of melted stuff to clean up. After the beating you got this morning for being ten minutes late, imagine what they'd do to us for wasting the town's money."

Alek's bad feelings didn't allow for logic. He was about to try to explain, knowing that he didn't have any idea what to say, when Rachel's voice split the air, getting louder by the second.

"Help! Alek, Scott . . . someone! *Help!*"

He beat Scott up the stairs and bolted out of the shop to find Rachel running down the road at top speed, dragging a child by the arm.

"Rachel, what's wrong?" He ran up to her just as she fell to her knees, coughing and gasping for breath, revealing the person she'd been hauling. It was Darrell!

Scott let out a whoop and grabbed their little brother, spinning him around and hugging him tight. Alek knelt down next to Rachel, who was trying to breathe.

"Darrell?" Scott was no longer whooping for joy and sounded scared. He was on his knees in front of Darrell, who was staring at nothing, his eyes vacant, his mouth half open and slack. "Buddy, it's Scotty. Talk to us. What happened? Where have you been? Where's Kristy?"

Alek turned, trying to concentrate both on Darrell and getting Rachel to breathe normally. He patted her on the back until finally, after a combination cough and retch, she could breathe again. She grabbed Alek's arm, pointing toward the edge of town. "Go get her! Claire is still out there with that *thing*. She was amazing! She ran right after it, pulled Darrell away, and threw him back into the sun before it sucked her back into the dark."

Rachel wasn't making any sense. It was bright sunlight with not a cloud to be seen. There was no dark anywhere, not even in the deepest forest. But if Claire was in danger . . .

He looked toward the forest, where Rachel was pointing, and saw Claire running lopsidedly toward them. Limping again on her right leg. Alek sprinted toward her, reaching her just as the leg gave out. He caught her before she hit the ground.

"I've got you. Hang on." The flash of energy, sensations, and scents as she collapsed into his arms took his breath away. Fear, pain, adrenaline, arousal, relief, anger—a potent, tangy cocktail that made his jaw ache and his head pound. "Are you okay?" he asked, even though he knew she wasn't. He smelled blood on the breeze and saw a trail of red leading back down the road.

"Caught me with its claws. It's not too bad—I'll be okay in a few minutes." From the quantity of blood, he doubted that, but he couldn't help but admire the sentiment. "How's the boy? Is it Darrell? I thought it was, but couldn't tell for certain. My nose wasn't working right in there."

Alek nodded. "Yes, it's Darrell. In *where*? What happened?"

Her answer was more matter-of-fact than he expected, her voice surprisingly steady, her scent hot-metal determination with a healthy dose of spicy pain. But no fear. None. It both took him aback and made him admire her. "We found an area that was magically blacked out—no sight, sound, or smell. It was done by a Sazi. No question. I haven't seen the kind of power that could create that very often. A few Council members, maybe, the head of Wolven, a pack leader or two. That's all I know of. I need to call my pack. Right now."

"Is the town in danger? Should we talk to the chief or mayor?"

She shook her head, wincing as her good foot twisted on a hidden rock, sending a burst of scent into his nose. He shook his head, trying to ignore the scent of her. It filled his nose with sugared warmth, despite the crisis. "No. Not now. Whatever is out there probably stays there because of them. Sending people out to hunt it would only make it run and it could go anywhere. We need to find out what we're dealing with first and lock down the town."

It was partly the truth, but he could smell a little lie hidden in the words. But which words were the lie? He'd never heard of a *blacked out* area anywhere near Luna Lake, but he'd met some Council members who could probably do just about anything . . . including kill someone snooping into their business. What surprised him was that *Claire* also knew Council members. "Let's get you back and get Marilyn to look at your leg."

Claire didn't object, so he helped her hobble back to the ice cream shop. Scott was cradling Darrell in his arms. The crowd had dispersed, which seemed seriously odd to Alek. One of the missing kids had been found. Why weren't people celebrating?

"Mom's on her way," Scott said. "I'm going to take Darrell to Marilyn. Rachel's going to head to the city office. You two are supposed to stay here and wait for the chief. He said he'd call the school for you, Claire."

Rachel shrugged. Scott smiled and nodded. Neither of them seemed to notice that Claire was bleeding and Alek couldn't figure out how all that had happened in the few minutes it had taken him to help Claire walk back. "Was Lenny here? I didn't see his car, or did someone call him?"

It was as though they didn't hear him. "'K. See you guys later." They walked away together. Alek boosted Claire to sit on the floor of the truck. Wincing, she used the cloth of her jeans to lift her wounded leg until it rested on the cold metal.

As soon as the others were out of hearing range, Alek leaned toward Claire and said quietly, "Something really weird is going on. They should have asked if you wanted to see Marilyn."

The skin at the edge of her eyes crinkled as she thought. After a few moments, she tapped her fingers on her jeans. "No, I changed my mind. We need to let it go for now. I'll call when I know more about what's going on. And I'm not worried about my leg. I'll heal eventually. I've survived worse. The cold in here should slow the bleeding." She reached to one side and grabbed a box. "Now how about I sit here and toss you boxes and you stack them in the freezer? I get the feeling nobody is going to race over to help us unload this truck, and I'm betting someone out there is just waiting for us to screw up. This feels like a setup, but I'm surprised Rachel and Scott are helping."

He looked around, seeing empty streets that were normally filled with people at this time of day. It was hard to disagree with Claire's assessment. "Yeah. Sort of looks that way. But I don't know that Scott and Rachel are playing along. Something else is going on."

It only took a few minutes to stack the rest of the ice cream in the basement freezer. He still felt like he was coming down with the flu, but was pleased that by the time he'd finished with the last box of ice pops, Claire was back on her feet, although gingerly. She wouldn't be running any races anytime soon, but she could walk. She was a fast healer. A lot faster than most people in town.

"You heal really quick. Do you have healing talent?"

"Of a sort," she admitted. "Mostly empathic. It's not really good for much more than being sympathetic to someone's pain. But it does give me some boost when I'm hurt. I'm a little surprised myself, because the chief sucked out most of my power. Maybe he's distracted by Darrell."

Alek pulled down the roller door on the truck. "Are you up to handling stairs? We need to get the other boxes unloaded at the grocery."

She made a face. "I can, if you need me. But I could also start downstairs on getting boxes ready to go back to families. Rachel told me on the way over here where the list is."

That made sense to him. It would probably be better to put her downstairs where she didn't have to risk tripping over the little step at the entrance to the store. The basement was just a wide room with no uneven surfaces. "Let's go downstairs and see what's there. I think you'd have an easier time moving around down there. Unfortunately, I have no idea what order to bring boxes up, or what we're supposed to do with them after they're out."

"Might as well. Maybe it'll make sense once we're down there and I look at the list." Alek went ahead of her into the shop so she could use his shoulder to steady herself going down the stairs. He was surprised Skew wasn't around. She was always here, always open even if the CLOSED sign was in the window. "I wonder where Skew is. It's not like her to leave the place unlocked."

"Should we be poking around without her here?"

"No, it's okay," Alek replied. "That was part of the deal when people started storing here. People need to be able to get to their things. I've been here lots of times before without letting her know first. But she's normally here."

They got to the bottom of the stairs and looked around. The unfinished gray cinder blocks made up the main part of the area, and wooden timbers supported the floor. Other than a large hot water heater, the area was mostly bare.

Claire sat down on the bottom of the steps and twisted her leg to look at the claw holes through her jeans. "That's going to leave some new scars but at least none of the muscles were cut." Looking up and around the room, she pursed her lips and said with surprise in her voice, "Hey, it's not too bad down here. I was expecting a real mess. But there's not much to move at all."

Little did she know. "The basement is bigger than it looks." Alek moved to the far end of the front room and opened the long wooden gate to the storage area. "Here's what we need to empty out."

He flicked on the light switch and heard Claire gasp behind him. The room was thirty feet square and packed floor to ceiling with boxes of all sizes and shapes. Some were carefully sealed with tape or plastic wrap, while the contents of others bulged out at odd angles. "All the spots used to be marked and each family had their own section. I guess things got a little out of control . . ."

Noticing the variety of webs stretching from stack to stack and the insects crawling openly on the boxes, Alek began to understand why Rachel had suggested that this be done. "Man, we're going to have to bug bomb down here before winter. There must be dozens of spiders in here." Beside him, Claire shrugged and rolled her eyes a little. "What?"

"Nothing. I guess I'm just not used to getting worked up over bugs. Maybe there are some bad ones here I don't know about. But in Texas we have about six kinds of black widows and brown recluse spiders, and tons of scorpions. These just look like regular garden spiders to me. Nothing to bother with. You find them, you smush them. You get bit, put on some baking soda and move on. No big deal." He must have had an odd expression on his face, because she looked contrite all of a sudden. "Sorry. I guess that wasn't the right thing to say. I'm still getting used to how things are done here. We can bomb if you think that's best. Do you have any around? I do know how to use them."

Maybe that was why Skew hadn't done it herself. The spiders might be no big deal to her. He hated to admit that spiderwebs gave him the willies, but if they didn't bother Claire, he wasn't going to let them bother him either. "Nah. Never mind. I'll talk to Skew about it when she gets back. Let's just get started and try to figure out what belongs to which family." He thought he knew approximately where the Williams section was, but there didn't appear to be any guide marks on the floor or walls. "Y'know what? We should grab a pad and pencil from upstairs and keep records, so we can put everything back in the same place."

That lit up Claire's face. "Ooo! Good idea. And I can take pictures with my cell phone. I might as well put it to some use, since it's useless for making calls here." She pulled the slim smart phone from her pocket and started pressing buttons on the face. "It even has a flash, except that uses up the battery pretty fast."

Also a terrific idea! "Wait here." He sprinted up the stairs to get a pad from behind the counter. He'd worked here several summers while he was in high school, so he knew where everything was.

Or at least he used to know. Not only was the pad not where Skew always left it, but while looking for it, he started noticing other things that were out of place. A key ring was on the floor, nearly invisible next to the wall. The dishes in the sink weren't from breakfast. The smell of mold on unwashed plates was plain when he walked back into the sink area. In fact, he was surprised he hadn't noticed it when he and Scott first arrived. It was very unlike the uber-clean falcon who had been constantly on his ass for not sanitizing the counters after customers left. He realized he couldn't remember the last time he'd seen Skew. He'd been so busy searching and doing work for people that he hadn't been by for days.

"Alek? Are you coming back down?" Claire's voice rose up the narrow stairwell.

He stepped to the door. "I think something's wrong. Stuff is out of place up here. I don't think Skew has been here for a while." Claire came up the stairs, leaning less heavily on the rail than when she'd gone down. "Hey, you seem to be doing better. In fact, the cut on your head is nearly healed."

She reached up to touch her hair, then patted it with a pleased expression. "Is it? Oh, I guess so. Good. Maybe El Chupacabra is sleeping or something."

"El . . . what?"

"That soul-sucking chief of police of yours. A chupacabra is a south Texas legend, like Bigfoot. It supposedly sucks all the blood out of goats and little kids. That's what it felt like when he *dimmed my glow*, as he put it. Can't have me just *pretending* to be omega, after all. Jerk."

Alek couldn't disagree. "At least he didn't make you grovel on the floor, begging forgiveness." He paused. "Did he?"

She shook her head. "Unless you count him stepping on my windpipe for accidentally looking the Alpha in the eye."

Alek let out a small growl without intending to. Lenny had no right to do that! It wasn't how things were done in this town. "He's going too far. That's not police behavior and it's especially not Wolven behavior."

"Pfft," she snorted. "No doubt. But it's not like we have much to say about it. Let's just finish up here and then we'll report the owner's disappearance. Maybe there's a simple explanation, like running to the city to shop, or visiting relatives or something."

Alek didn't know much about Skew's family. She mostly kept to herself and didn't really talk about where she came from. "It's possible, I guess." He turned to follow her back downstairs but stopped. "Hey, can I see your phone for a second?"

When she handed it over, he clicked on the camera button and took photos of the key ring and the dishes. He wrapped his shirt over his hand, opened the cash register, and took more photos, showing the drawer full of cash. Something was definitely not right. When he turned back, Claire was leaning against the jamb to the stairwell, nodding and smiling. "Rachel was right. You *are* paranoid." Before he could reply, she smiled. "Good." Then she trotted down the stairs, barely touching the handrail, as though she'd never hurt her leg. Very strange.

He followed more slowly. The day was already taking a toll on him, even though it wasn't even half over.

By the time he made it down the stairs, Claire had found a stapled list that marked off the storage area by letters and numbers and assigned a family for each slot. "Tell you what," she said. "It looks like everything is out of order from the last time Rachel updated this. I think we should go unload the groceries and tackle this tomorrow. I don't trust the police chief to call the school and the last thing I need is to make another enemy."

Alek agreed. "I think you're right. There's more than a day's worth of work here, and I'm worried about Skew and Darrell. If we have to take another beating, so be it."

He felt suddenly out of breath and reached for the stairwell railing for balance. She noticed. "Hey, are you okay? You don't look so good."

His heart was pounding and he felt cold. "I don't know. Maybe I'm getting the flu or something. I felt fine earlier, but now I feel like all the energy has been sucked out of me."

"Maybe we should get you to the nurse too. Let's head over that way. I'll drop you there and check in at the school. Maybe they'll let me store the refrigerated stuff in the school fridge. Is the truck a rental? Is there any rush to get it back somewhere?"

Alek shook his head, feeling light-headed and slightly dizzy. "No. The town owns the truck. I don't know if there's enough room in the school for the dairy stuff, but it's worth a try."

He let her help him up the stairs. "Actually, why don't you drop me at my apartment? I'll use my landline to call around and check up on people. I'll call Marilyn too. She makes house calls."

"Are you sure? You really don't look good."

He shook his head. "I'll be fine. Don't worry about me."

Claire made it to the cafeteria with just minutes to spare. She was grateful that she'd started a pot of chili the day before to simmer overnight, because it gave her time to get Alek to his apartment. Rachel had spotted her helping Alek inside and promised to keep an eye on him, including calling Marilyn herself. She had agreed that Alek would probably try to tough it out. Still, she needed to check up on him later. He'd said not to worry, but she did. He could have a concussion after that punch to the temple.

The spicy scent of chili filled the air and she had no doubt the whole school was drooling by now. There was nothing quite like fresh ingredients cooked slow.

She'd barely filled the trays and turned on the heat lamps before the room was crowded with kids and adults alike, clamoring for a bowl. The microwave had to do for warming the tortillas—store-bought, which her Alpha would have shuddered at. But it was quick and easy and filling.

"Oh, my gawd!" a woman about her age who worked in the

office said after swallowing a spoonful. "Are you sure you have to be a teacher? Couldn't you just stay and cook?"

Was an Omega supposed to acknowledge compliments? She didn't know. But she kept her eyes at neck level when she answered. "Thank you. But I want to be a teacher. Cooking is just a hobby."

"Well, it's great." She held out a hand. "I'm April, by the way. You're Claire, right?"

Again, she didn't know enough about protocol. "Should you be talking to me? I don't want to get you in trouble."

"Nah. We can talk to you. You just can't speak without being spoken to."

Ah. She figured there had to be a set of rules somewhere. Time rushed by as she passed out bowl after bowl. The room was soon filled with laughing children and chatting adults. She could get used to this atmosphere.

The chili all dispensed, she started to gather the pans that needed to be cleaned. She glanced up to see Denis. "Hi, Denis. How's Darrell? And how are you doing? Did you get your project done?"

Denis stared at her with a level of hostility she didn't understand. "Why did you come here? You're screwing everything up!" He stalked away, leaving her staring after him open-mouthed. What the hell was wrong with him?

April stepped in front of her, blocking Denis from her view as he left the cafeteria. "All gone? Damn. I was hoping for seconds."

"Sorry. All out. But hey, what's up with Denis Siska? He seems to have a real chip on his shoulder."

April turned toward where he'd just exited the room and then shook her head. "I don't know. He's been like that for a couple of years now. Maybe growing up in Alek's shadow made him angry. It's hard to live up to the standard of the golden child."

"Alek is golden?" From everything she'd seen in the past two days, it seemed more like he was on everyone's shit list.

April turned back to face her. "Oh, yeah. Best grades, best athlete, multiple Ascension champion, going to be a cop, does hours of community service stuff. Blah, blah. It's no wonder Denis acts out. He can't compete with the attention. Alek is the oldest by a few months. All of the Williams kids have had to find their own specialty to break out of his shadow. But it's tough when Alek was good at *everything*. Denis is just sort of average."

Interesting. It did make a lot of sense. But it didn't explain why he was mad at *her*. "By the way, did you hear that Darrell has been found?" She didn't want to talk about her part in rescuing him, but she thought people in the school would be happy to know.

"Who?"

That made Claire look up sharply, but not meet the other woman's eyes. Instead, she looked past her left ear. Her platinum-blond hair was cut in a bob and her furrowed brows matched the color. It must be natural. "Darrell Williams. One of the missing kids."

"Darrell's not missing. He and his sister have been staying with their aunt in Louisiana for a couple of weeks now."

"Are you sure? I've been staying at the Williams house and I got the impression they were missing and there have been search parties." This was getting very odd.

The other woman shrugged. "Nope. No kids missing around here. In fact, Darrell is in the class where I help grade papers, so I know for certain. He was really excited to take some time to go visit New Orleans." April wandered off, using her finger to get the last bits of chili from the plastic bowl.

Curiouser and curiouser. She picked up the stack of metal pans and carried them to the sink. After pouring the last of the chili into a bowl for herself, she put them in to soak and then started back out to start collecting plates.

When she turned around, Principal Burrows was standing in the doorway. She was careful not to look at his face, but she noticed he had shed his suit jacket and had rolled up the sleeves of his snow-white shirt. "An excellent job, Ms. Sanchez. Everyone is raving about your cooking."

"Thank you sir. I wasn't sure I'd be able to make it on time after the excitement earlier. I presume the police chief called you?" It was a test and by the scent of confusion that rose from him, she had her answer.

"No. What excitement?"

"Darrell Williams was found earlier out in the woods." She paused, waiting.

Confusion was replaced by excitement and joy. "That's *wonderful*! I'll have to call his mother. What about Kristy?"

So, not everyone had the same story. That was worth checking into further. "I don't know. I was going to head over to the house after I left here. If it's okay, I'll come back later to clean the building."

He nodded hurriedly. "Of course. I understand fully. You have the key, I presume?"

Claire nodded. She had the key all right. And with everyone distracted by Darrell's homecoming, tonight would be the perfect time to do some sniffing around.

CHAPTER 18

*A*lek woke from a fitful sleep in a cold sweat. It was pitch black in his room so the sun must have already gone down. Yet it felt like he had just laid down for a minute. He ran his fingers through his hair and sat up on the edge of the bed.

Rachel had apparently gone after Marilyn made sure he didn't have a concussion. She thought he might have a virus, but did a throat swab and took some blood to check out back at the clinic.

He was feeling a little better but had been having the strangest dreams and couldn't seem to quite shake it even now—that he was skulking around the school searching for something. He didn't know what he was looking for, but it felt terribly important that he find it because there was a ticking clock. He could never find the clock, but it kept ticking, always ticking, like a bomb was going to go off at the end.

He had no idea what it meant.

Maybe the clock was Kristy. Darrell had been skin and bones, even though he'd only been gone a week. And he'd been in the woods, not at the school. Kristy was younger, and not as tough. What if they didn't find her in time?

Could there be a clue that had been missed? Had anyone

even checked her locker or desk? Everyone had been concentrating on the park. Why? At the time, it seemed logical because he presumed other people were searching other places. But were they?

Maybe his subconscious was trying to tell him something. He shook his head and wandered to the bathroom to use the toilet, unable to shake the feeling that he should be at the school.

Indecision beat at him as he drank a glass of water. He'd left a whole town full of chores for Claire to do. She hadn't complained—had in fact insisted that he stay home and rest—but it wasn't fair. She was probably still out there somewhere, cleaning or tending to someone. Exhausted like he always was.

He called the house, intending to both check on Darrell and Tammy and see whether Claire had made it home yet. But there was no answer, even after eight rings.

There was no way he was going to be able to get back to sleep until he made sure everyone was safe.

It only took a few minutes to throw on a black turtleneck, change pants, and brush his teeth; then it would just be another few minutes out in the cold wind to get to the Williams house. *Man, I miss my motorcycle.* The insurance was another thing he was going to have to deal with soon. But not tonight.

He was nearly to the house when pain erupted in his back and a crushing blow sent him sprawling into the snow. A cracking sound filled his ears. Weight pushed down on him, so heavy he couldn't move. He pressed his palms into the snow and tried to lift himself to throw off whatever was holding him down, but it was no use. He was pinned. Fingers clutched at his face, covering his mouth and plugging his nose. He couldn't breathe. He grabbed at anything he could, finally grabbing onto what he presumed was a pair of pants on muscular legs. He ripped at the cloth, trying to get some sense of who was attacking him.

Harsh words whispered in his ear. "Leave this alone. Or else!"

The weight was suddenly gone, along with the hand on his face. His ribs ached as he struggled to his feet. Lying next to him in the snow was a two-by-four that had been used to club him.

I'm on to something, but I don't even know what. Still, the piece of wood was a clue, as well as the few threads still under his fingernails from where he'd ripped open the attacker's pants. He carefully sniffed all the way down the length of the board. He didn't recognize the scent, which was odd because he knew the scent of everyone who lived in town. So could it be someone from *outside* of town? It couldn't be Claire. She didn't have the weight needed. But did she come to town *alone*? He needed to talk with her, and with Dani. Taking the board with him, he fought off the pain as he walked the rest of the way to the house.

The moment he walked through the door, he smelled blood. He dropped the board next to the staircase. "Where is everyone? Is someone hurt?"

He heard his mom's voice in the distance. "In the kitchen, Alek. Come on back."

Walking quickly down the hallway, he pushed open the swinging door. Asylin was wrapping a broad roll of snow-white gauze around Dani's arm. It was still bleeding in stripes that looked like scratches. "What happened?"

Dani looked stricken and smelled worried and scared. "I was taking Tammy her dinner. She lost it, Alek. She shifted right there in the cage and slashed my arm." She stopped Asylin's wrapping and dug fingers into her hand. "I'm scared for her, Mom. Isn't there something we can do?"

Asylin's voice was cold but calm. "No. There's not. We'll have to put her down soon."

"Mom! No!" Dani started to cry. "It's not fair. She needs help."

Alek hated it too, but his mom was right. "The kind of help she needs doesn't exist, Dani. The plague messed a lot of people up. It's *not* fair. But nobody can heal a rogue."

Dani stood up in a rush, nearly knocking over the heavy wooden chair where she sat. "Maybe nobody *here* can help her. But surely someone in the world has found a way to fix this. Just promise you'll keep her alive until the full moon. I'll find someone, somewhere to come here and fix her. I'll drive to where they are, pick them up and bring them back."

Asylin shook her head. "I can't promise you that, hon. I'll do the best I can, but if she gets any more unstable, she'll break out of that cage. I can't have her attacking the rest of the family." Dani crossed her arms over her chest angrily, glaring at her mother until she threw up her hands. "Fine! I'll do what I can. But I don't think she'll last until the moon."

Dani turned to him. "You agree with me, don't you, Alek? There must be someone out there who can fix her. What about Claire? Doesn't she have healers in her pack?" Her desperate brown eyes seemed to drill into him.

Alek nodded but felt it was a hopeless cause. "She said she would call them. But I doubt she's had time. In fact, I was looking for her. Have you seen her tonight? And how is Darrell? Is he okay?"

Dani shook her head. "Darrell's upstairs sleeping. He's still not talking, but we're hoping he was just shaken up. Scott's sitting with him, but don't go up 'cause you might wake him. Claire called earlier, saying she wouldn't be home for dinner. She said she had more chores than hours today."

Now he really felt like a heel. "I'm going to head out and

look for her and help her get caught up. But hey, maybe you could answer a question. When you picked her up to bring her here, was she alone? It's important."

Dani didn't hesitate. "Yeah, she was alone. She was waiting for her luggage to come out at baggage claim at the airport. She wasn't talking to anyone or anything like that. Just standing next to the carousel, waiting. Why?"

"I don't know. I'm just trying to figure some stuff out. I need to talk to her. She's got to be somewhere around town."

Asylin clucked her tongue. "Then at least make yourself up a burger. Everything's on the counter. I'll bet you forgot to eat again today."

She was right. Everything was still warm so it only took a second to put a meat patty on a bun and slam it down before he was completely to the door. He hadn't been eating very well lately. He'd have to fix his diet pretty soon or he was going to be fighting with his gut for a month. That's when he spotted Scott's key ring. Having a car would be very useful in tracking down Claire. And he had been told to not go upstairs to disturb them.

He won't mind. I'd do the same for him.

The little black VW wasn't roomy, but at least it kept him out of the wind. And it was a lot quicker to get out to the Kragan place. He had bet himself she hadn't been here yet, but discovered he was wrong. Claude and Egan were playing checkers when he arrived. They'd seen the *pretty new wolf* just an hour before. She'd made them a nice bowl of soup and even buttered the crackers when they asked. Claude offered, "I think she said something about going to Fred's next."

"No, no," Egan said as he jumped a red checker over two of his brother's black ones. "She was going to the school first and then to Fred's. Remember? She said she had to stir the soup."

"Oh, yes. That's right. She was simmering soup for the

kiddies for lunch tomorrow. Nice girl. Bet she makes good soup too. Probably better than this canned crap."

Alek thanked them and started on his way. Claude called out the door after him. "Tell her to come back tomorrow and bring us good soup, boy! No more canned crap."

He couldn't help but smile as he closed the door. "I'll tell her."

Fred's or the school? Where next? The nagging feeling that he should be at the school wouldn't leave, so he headed that way and parked in the empty lot. As he approached the building, he noticed a flicker of light in one of the rooms. It was a flashlight. *Now, why would someone be using a flashlight instead of the overheads?*

He crept up to the edge of the window and was shocked at what he saw. Claire was in the school office, digging through the filing cabinets! A penlight was held in her mouth and she was pulling file after file from the drawers. What the hell?!

He quickly went to the back door and started trying all of the keys on the ring. The tenth key slid into the lock and he heard the tumblers trip.

It was hard to open and shut the door silently, but he did the best he could. Warm air rushed at him and the scent of rich beef stew filled the air, making it impossible for him to smell emotions. To his advantage, though, she wouldn't smell him coming either.

He crept down the hall, listening for anyone else who might be in the building with her. He focused all his attention to his ears. But the only sounds were crinkling paper and the heated air coming through the vents.

Would she be armed? She didn't seem the firearm or knife type, but he couldn't put it past her. It would be better to stay in a defensive position. Moving to the doorway, he made his first noise. "Claire! What are you doing in here?"

The flashlight fell from her mouth and she let out a little yip. "Alek! I'm . . . I mean, I can explain."

He moved through the door, still keeping most of his body behind the bulk of the file cabinets near the door. "Then you should start. I'd rather not hurt you or turn you in. If you're armed, you need to drop your weapons."

She shook her head, her hair flipping in the breeze from the heater. "I'm not armed." She held her gloved hands up and out. He turned on the overhead lights. She squinted in the sudden brightness. "You might want to turn that off."

He motioned toward the open files on the copy table. It looked like she'd already copied half a ream of paper. "What are you looking for?"

"It's . . . complicated."

He pointed to the nearest chair. "Sit down and start talking or I'm calling the station. I think I'm smart enough to handle the explanation."

She sighed and sat down. "Something really strange is going on in this town. I've been talking to people here at the school. Did you know that only a handful of people know Darrell and Kristy are missing?"

That threw him off guard. "What? No, everybody knows. We've all been looking for them."

She shook her head, slowly. "No. They haven't been. At least, nobody from here. Most everybody thinks they're visiting their aunt in Louisiana. Do you remember that even Asylin thought that after the thing with the cougar?"

Alek moved to sit on the edge of the nearest desk, careful to be able to watch her and to keep an eye on the open door. He did remember, but that didn't explain this. "So what are you looking for in here?"

Claire started to stand and he instinctively moved toward the counter, watching her movements. She stopped. "Can I show you what I found? Please, Alek. Trust me. I'm not trying to steal anything or hurt anyone."

He stared at her for a long moment, taking in the sincerity in her eyes, her relaxed posture, even the scents of worry and concern that were stronger than the bubbling stew. Maybe he was crazy, but he believed her. "Okay. Show me."

She did. File after file of children that didn't match other school records. She had open yearbooks that showed photographs of kids he knew. But the official file showed they had either been expelled from school or had transferred. He couldn't remember a single incident of an expulsion. If there had been, Denis would be one of them. Yet, when Claire showed him another list, the children appeared on the school roster as attending classes. "What the hell?"

"I know! You see what I mean?"

"But why would you be looking at all these other kids? What's the connection?"

She pointed to the file label. "Darrell's and Kristy's records are in files with green striped labels. I didn't think much about it at first, but there aren't that many in a whole decade that have that color of file. And look here." She used a fingernail to lift up a corner of the label. "These didn't used to be green, and see how white the white part is? The other files with green striped labels are more yellowed in the white part."

Alek shook his head. "I'm still not getting it. I'm missing something here."

She grabbed the stack of yearbooks again and pulled out a file folder from the green label stack. "Okay, look at this name—Sammy Havens."

"I don't know a *Sammy* Havens. April Havens works here in the office, and she has a younger brother, David."

She opened the yearbook from the year he was in sixth grade and flipped pages. Right there, in black-and-white, was a photograph of a Sammy Havens. In his own *class*! "But that's *my* graduating class. How could I not remember someone in my own class? It was only a dozen people."

Claire lifted her hands, punctuating her point. "Exactly. Why don't people remember? When I asked Dani at the family dinner how the search was going, she didn't remember they were missing. I've only been here a few days, Alek! She was in a panic about searching for them when we were driving here."

"Nobody left, nobody died." But the more he stared at the picture of the smiling boy, the more it seemed familiar. Memories started sputtering back in snippets of images. Those eyes, peering intently over a handful of cards. "We played Pokemon in the schoolyard. His grandparents always gave him specialty cards from the city for Christmas. He was unbeatable."

Her brows raised. "So you *do* remember him?"

Alek fought to remember more, but it was gone. "That's all I remember. Pokemon. And I could be wrong."

She opened the seventh grade book. No Sammy Havens was pictured. Nor in eighth grade, but he was in fifth. Alek grabbed another file from the stack. Carol Nickerson. He didn't know any Nickersons. This time, the picture disappeared after fourth grade. Another file, another name. No photo after seventh grade. He was in school with all of them, but remembered none of them. "What the hell is going on?!" He slammed shut the yearbook of his senior year. All the faces, smiling, happy. But not *all* of the faces.

"I don't know," she said softly, putting a hand on his shoulder. "But I think there's evidence I need to get back to my pack leaders. Someone needs to look into this further. Someone *not* from this town."

He agreed. He reached across his chest to put his hand over hers. "Thank you."

She shrugged. "I haven't done anything yet. Thank me when we track down these kids."

"You breathed life back into them. That's something. It's a lot." He reached forward to brush away a few strands of hair that had fallen across one eye. She shivered at the light touch. Unable to stop himself, he let his fingers glide through her hair. A small sound escaped her throat. He leaned in and she let him. Electricity shot through him as their lips met, so strong it nearly hurt. He needed more. Standing up, he pulled her closer, wrapped his arms around her tight. A moan slipped out when she did the same. She tasted like honey and mint. It mingled with the cooking in the air and turned into something amazing. The kiss grew fevered, desperate. Their jaws ate against each other, and her fingers dug into his back. When he reached his hands under her shirt to caress bare skin, she jumped. Panic filled her scent. She pushed him away, her eyes wide. "We can't. Not here. Not now."

His fingers ached when she pulled away. But she was right. There was too much at stake and it would be far too easy for someone to know they'd been here . . . doing exactly what they were doing. Any Sazi with a nose would know. He struggled to get his breathing under control. "You're right. Yeah. We have to get these cleaned up. But this isn't done."

She didn't answer, couldn't get words out. But the look was enough. It wasn't done for her either. Claire changed the subject instead of answering. "Is there somewhere I can go to get a good signal to talk to my pack leaders? Somewhere that nobody will overhear?"

He nodded. "There's an okay signal in Republic. But at the top of the mountain, you have a clear shot to several towers. Here, let me draw you a map."

It was somewhat crude, but as he drew, he explained it. When he was done, she nodded and tucked it in her pocket. "Thanks. I'm sure you understand why I can't take you along."

He raised his brows and then sighed. "Yeah. You probably can't." It was so matter-of-fact that it took her aback.

Her mouth dropped in surprise. "Excuse me?"

He raised his hand, looked around the room. "Whatever is happening, it's happening to the whole damned town. Memory loss, missing people, weird darknesses, and creatures that attack cars. None of this is normal, even for Luna Lake. I can't tell you for certain that I'm not involved, even if I don't think I am. Until you got here, I thought everything was normal. Now that I know it's not, I could easily be poison to you finding out what's going on. Someone has to, and you might be our best hope."

She didn't seem like she knew how to respond. "I appreciate your honesty. I am going to try to figure this out. I promise."

"I know you will. Go stir your stew again and let's get going. I'll take the papers out to the car."

CHAPTER 19

*I*t took a few minutes to wipe down the files and get them back in order in the cabinet. But they had copies of everything. "Let me give you a ride back to the house." She shouldn't be alone on the road. Maybe what she was uncovering was what his attacker had meant. "You should know I was attacked on the way over here. Hit in the back with a chunk of wood and told to leave this alone. But I didn't have any idea what *this* meant. I think maybe now I do."

She locked the school door and pushed against it to be sure it was shut tight. He held out his hand to help her down the icy step. No tingles with both of them wearing gloves. "Good to know. We'll both have to watch our backs until we can notify someone on the Council or higher up in Wolven than . . ." She faded off and he quickly realized why.

He heard the growl just a second too late. A blur of fur ripped Claire's hand from his as she was knocked a dozen feet away by a pissed-off female wolf.

Claire's first instinct was to grab the wolf by the scruff of the neck and toss it . . . no, toss *her*, up and over her head. Then she shifted, tearing her clothes to ribbons in the process. Fingernails were no substitute for claws and teeth. The wolf twisted in midair, landing on all fours and came toward her again, growling. The wolf's snarls became strangled as Claire got her jaws around the black-and-tan beast's throat. Claws ripped at her fur, found purchase, and tore open one foreleg. Claire tasted blood as she bit deeper—not sour, so not a rogue. But the scent of jealousy was strong, with anger, hurt, and hate enough to make her eyes water. Why wasn't she surprised that Alek had failed to mention a girlfriend?

Alek ran forward in human form and grabbed both wolves by the scruffs of their necks and used brute strength to pull them apart. Claire also felt that he was trying to push them apart using his magic, learning from her example the previous day. But the stream of magic was dim. It had been a long day. "Paula! Stop it! What the hell are you doing?" He moved his grip to hold Paula around the chest, using his legs to heave her away from Claire. *Paula? The waitress?*

When Claire sensed that Alek had a good grip on the other wolf, she released her bite and pulled away. She moved off a few feet and paced, staying alert in case he couldn't hold her.

"Stay the fuck away from my boyfriend, Texas trash!" Her strong accent was unfamiliar to Claire. She writhed in Alek's arms, obviously eager to get at Claire again.

Above Paula's head, Alek looked thunderstruck. "I'm not your boyfriend, Paula. What the hell?! We went on *one* date. *One!* And it was two years ago!"

That stopped the wolf cold. She stopped wiggling and turned her muzzle toward Alek, leaning back against him as though he held her in a loving embrace. "But we see each other every day. You come to the diner, we sit, we eat and talk. How could you not think of them as dates?"

Claire watched Alek try to figure out what to say. It was apparent that this whole scene was a surprise to him. At the very least, there was serious miscommunication going on, and it was more than she could solve right now. At worst, she was mated to him and he was going to have to find a way to let her down. He was an available alpha and she was an unattached female. It happened fairly often, from what she understood. It was seldom pretty or fun. "Look, I'm going to let you two work this out. I still need to tell the police about the woman from the ice cream shop. And I do have to tell them you attacked me. I won't press charges, but I have to make a report." Maybe it was coincidence. Maybe not. But she couldn't afford to presume that the whole police force was corrupt. The missing kids might have something to do with the school instead. The only way to find out if the police were corrupt was to file a report and see what they did.

She picked up the remains of her clothes and pocket items, and trotted toward the police station. Just before she opened the door, she heard Paula shout, "Stay away from him, bitch!"

The last thing she needed was to get in the middle of a love triangle. He might make her feel crazy with lust, but apparently she wasn't the only one.

It wasn't until she was opening the door to the police station with one paw that she realized she hadn't picked up the map Alek had made for her. She pulled the door so it hit her forehead, a quicker method than finding a wall to beat her head into. *Sigh.*

The police chief was waiting for her in the entry. "You're late."

She dropped the clothing in a heap on the floor. "I am?" It was an honest question because she didn't know she had to report back at any specific time in the evening. "When was I told to stop?"

His face went through a few contortions as he recalled their conversation, trying to figure out how to blame her. Finally, he put up a lie to cover his trail, but it was so blatant that the pepper scent nearly made her start sneezing. "Rachel was supposed to tell you there's a six p.m. stop time. I'll have to deal with her later."

"What Rachel told me was that the job had to be done, no matter how long it took. It took this long to finish everything. So just go ahead and take it out on me. I know that's what you want to do anyway." She couldn't hide the frustration and disgust in her voice. She blocked her mind as much as she could. It took work and had to be a conscious effort, so the less she thought the better.

His boot tip caught her square in the chest, right between her front legs. He was quicker than she'd expected. Her back and head hit the wall next to the door, knocking the air out of her lungs. She fell in a heap and had to relearn how to breathe. He stepped to stand over her. "You don't know when to keep your mouth shut, do you?"

She coughed and spit out blood. Great. Hopefully it was just from biting her tongue. "You're the Second. I would think you'd be accustomed to people expecting the worst of you." Having no experience with Seconds in other packs, she had no idea whether his method of enforcement was common, but it was unacceptable for her own pack.

Dropping into a crouch and sitting back on his heels, he grabbed the fur between her ears and lifted her head until he could look into her eyes. She didn't fight, as hard as it was. *Undercover work is hard*, she remembered her Alpha telling her. *Sometimes you're the cop, sometimes the robber. Either will get the bad guy if you embrace the role.* "I saw the little scene outside. You attacked a resident. Should I consider you a rogue?"

An idea came to her and she said it quickly, trying to keep him from seeing it before he heard it. "No, but I think protective custody would be a good idea. Aren't Omegas supposed to be kept safe from people who want to kill them?"

He glared at her. "You're asking to be locked up for the night?"

Worked for her. "For the night, until she cools down." After a second, she added, "I'll need clothes. I had to shift fast."

He nodded once. Good. "So I saw. You're a good fighter.
I'll remember that." Damn. Not as good. "I'll call Dani. She'll
bring what you need. The first door on the left downstairs is
the Omega quarters. You should remember. It's where you
woke up yesterday."

She didn't remember if there was a bed in the room, but
the floor would probably be more comfortable than the couch
she'd been lying on. "I haven't eaten today. I was working."

He shrugged and pulled her by the scalp to her feet. "Guess
you'll know better tomorrow."

So . . . wounded, tired, and no food. At least there was a
sink to get water. She wouldn't starve for one night. She'd
learned only too well how to live on very little food, and
she'd eaten well last night. "Guess I will." She worked hard to
keep any hint of sarcasm or whining out of her voice and scent.
It wasn't easy. All she could think was how much she would
enjoy going home to Texas.

He didn't offer to help her carry the ripped clothing. She
was pretty sure he enjoyed watching her struggle with everything in wolf form. She wouldn't give him the satisfaction of
shifting. He followed her to the stairs and unlocked the door.
She kept an eye on him the whole time so she'd have warning if he tried to push her down again, but he didn't even try.
Apparently, her being submissive had made an impact.

The door locked above her with an audible click and then
a sharp clang echoed through the hallway as the iron grate
was slammed into place. It was time to get a few hours' sleep.
Once everyone had gone to bed she would do a little explor-
ing and see what she could learn about this town and the
people who lived here.

CHAPTER 20

*P*aula, what's going on? We're just friends. We've never been anything else. Have I said or done something that made you think there was more between us?" Once Claire had left, the black-and-tan wolf had settled down and was now sitting next to him on a park bench across from the police station. He didn't feel right leaving until he was sure Paula would not be a danger to Claire when she left the police station. Hopefully, Lenny would understand his staying outside instead of coming in to report was a public safety issue.

"You've always been so nice to me, Alek. You smile. You touch my shoulder, give me hugs. We've grown up together. I know all your quirks and what you like. I'm the only woman you talk to. Why *wouldn't* I think you were interested?" She seemed honestly confused. Her jealousy had faded and her scent had taken on some of the warmth that made him enjoy stopping at the diner when she worked.

The only woman? "What about Tammy and Dani and Beth? I treat them the same. I talk to them and hug them." This wasn't making any sense.

She cocked her head and her ears twitched back. "They're your *sisters*. You grew up in the same house. That's not the

same thing." Her scent was growing more frantic as understanding settled in. She didn't want to hear the words that he
needed to say.

Alek took a deep breath and let it out slowly. He didn't
even have to think about it. "It is to me, Paula. I'm just not
attracted to you that way. Not like . . ."

Now her eyes hardened, began to glow with an amber light.
She wasn't a powerful alpha, but she must be more powerful
than he'd believed since she'd shifted off the moon. Or was
it her strong emotions that had tipped the balance? Emotions
he hadn't even realized she had. "*Her*. I smelled the lust when
you touched her hand, Alek. Her scent is on your skin, your
mouth. I'm not stupid." She put one front paw on his arm.
Her gaze was intent on his, earnest. "Don't you see? It's just
lust. It doesn't last. We know each other, like each other.
That's what lasts for the long haul."

Was she right? He'd never thought of her as a romantic
partner. Was that fair? Could it just be that Claire was new
and different? There was attraction, no question, but she'd
never actually said she was interested. Yet he was holding on,
hoping for more. Wasn't that exactly what Paula was doing?

He found himself shaking his head, his emotions in turmoil. The fact that he didn't remove Paula's paw from his arm
said something too. But *what* did it say? "I have to think,
Paula. It's been a long day and I'm tired."

"I know you are." Her voice was soft and kind. That was
the way she sounded when he went to the diner to sit and
watch people come and go while she waited on him, her dark
hair in a high ponytail that swished as she walked. It was just
business. Wasn't it? "Just don't rush into anything. That's all
I ask."

He touched the side of her face and she leaned into his
hand. He felt nothing more than soft fur. No tingles, no sense

of passion. "And all I ask is that you not bother Claire again until I do decide."

She stiffened and a tiny growl slipped past her lips. She nodded. "Deal."

He heard a loud thump in the distance, like someone dropped a heavy weight from a height. "Okay, look. I have to get in and report to Lenny. We'll talk more another day. I don't know for sure when because of the whole Omega thing. My schedule is really up in the air."

"I'll be waiting. But I won't wait forever." She got to her feet and padded off into the darkness.

Just frigging great! He didn't need this kind of stress. He raised his hands to his head and ran fingers through his hair. Could this day get any worse? Oh, right. It could. Because he had to go deal with Lenny now. He'd been explicitly told to check in at the end of the day.

He glanced at the station and realized that the light in the window was off. That seemed odd—Claire had just gone in and neither she nor Lenny had come out. A quick glance down the street confirmed it wasn't the power. All the other lights were on.

And then they weren't.

Blackness closed in around him like a tight glove. Even the stars had disappeared. He couldn't see his own hand, even when it was close enough to touch his eyebrows. He stood and sniffed around carefully, feeling his way to the edge of the bench. There were no scents . . . none. It was as though the trees and rocks, the whole town, had disappeared. Was this the "darkness" Claire and Rachel had talked about? If so, it was disorienting and more than a little unnerving.

He pulled the wolf inside him to the surface, feeling the weight of cloth shred and fall away. But even his wolf eyes couldn't find enough light to focus. Every hair on his body told him that there was something out there, something large and imposing. His lips pulled away from his teeth and a low growl came from deep in his chest. He could feel it, but not hear the sound.

Panic began to rise from his gut, speeding his heart and making his breath come in shallow gasps. How could he fight something he couldn't see, hear, or smell? The attack could come from any direction! He turned in circles, snapping his jaws at nothing, feeling helpless.

Helpless? Nyet! The voice of his old pack leader, Nikoli, rushed into his mind. *No wolf of mine will ever be helpless so long as he has a mind.* Was it a memory or the barest hint of a still-existing attachment to the pack mind?

Alpha? He pushed the word out as though shouting into a crowded room.

There was no answer.

But there was no need for one. He *did* have a mind. He gathered his will around himself, let the senses he usually relied on drop away, and opened up his mind. What other ways were there to find a threat?

Haptic senses, echolocation, passive receptors. The new words in his brain startled him. They weren't his thoughts, nor his Alpha's. He didn't know whose they were. Each sound made a spark of light appear behind his eyes, like tiny green fireflies. He had heard the term *haptic* before, but couldn't remember where. He wasn't even positive what it meant.

There was a breath like a sigh in his inner ear that vibrated his eardrum. It made him cock his head and scratch at the ear with his rear leg until he stopped being dizzy. *You know . . . haptic?*

More lights appeared and the fireflies became a thousand sparklers, then skyrockets, as if with each passing moment, the light grew stronger. *They're proximity sensors, like blind*

*people use to identify objects. Didn't you ever take science class?
Like how you avoid trees when you're running; chasing prey. Try
to find the source of the magic by feeling where on your body it's
the strongest. Then turn until your nose is pointed at it. Passive
receiving.*

With more words came the realization that the voice in his
head was Claire's. *How are you in my head?*

The voice sounded confused, as though she'd thought she
was talking to herself. *I . . . don't know who you are, so I don't
know.*

Alek.

There was a long pause. *I'm leaving now.*

"Wait!" He said it out loud because he wasn't sure how to
project a shout in his mind. The air stilled and the flicker of
light remained right at the corner of his senses. *How do I get
out of the darkness?*

No pause this time. *Attack or retreat. Those are the options.
I retreated because I had to save the boy, but I didn't like it. You're
a wolf, like me. Seek it out. Hunt it down.*

There was an intensity to the words that made his whiskers and fur vibrate and want to start the chase, to feel the
rush of wind that brought the scent of prey. His whole body
became a receptor for powerful magic and he realized it was
strongest on his left flank. He spun and planted his feet. His
chest lowered instinctively and his lips pulled back to bare
his teeth.

The flickering in his mind urged him on, not to defend,
but to attack. The being in the darkness—the one he knew
was there though he could not see, hear, or smell it—sensed
this and didn't like the turn of events. It tried to move to
flank him again, seeking a weak point to press its attack, but
Alek spun again. Now that he had the flavor of the magic sting,
he could follow it. After a third unsuccessful attempt, the
being retreated, taking the darkness with it.

Starlight returned, as did sound—with a pop that made his inner ear hurt like it did when changing altitudes.

He could let the darkness go, let it retreat to wherever it came.

He *could*.

But he wasn't going to.

Digging into the turf, he chased after the dark, focusing on a moving area of blackness surrounded by the normal landscape.

The sound of distant glass breaking nearly made him stop, but he didn't dare risk losing the scent. Or whatever it was that was allowing him to follow the dark. A blur of movement made him risk flicking his gaze sideways. A second wolf was easing up on his right. Claire's cinnamon fur smelled like cigar smoke and blood. "Are you okay?" he asked.

"I will be after we catch this bastard."

There was a venom in her voice he hadn't heard before. "Okaaay . . ."

She dug in her claws, expanded the reach of her front legs to keep up with his sprint. "I don't want to talk about it right now. Let's just finish the hunt."

Whatever they were chasing was fast. Racing after the darkness became more about avoiding barely seen obstacles at blinding speed than actually catching up. An hour passed, then two. Claire moved like a shadow at his side, two dancers on a stage gliding to music they were hearing for the first time. Unfortunately, the farther north they ran, the farther ahead the darkness got. Alek had no idea where they were. Were they even in Washington anymore or had they crossed into Canada? Claire's breath didn't seem to be as harsh as his, but was still faster than normal. They'd both been beaten down so much and lost so much energy running that there was nothing left. "We have to stop. We're not going to catch it." He slowed to a lope and then to a trot and Claire did the same. His chest was burning from trying to get enough air and his legs felt like rubber.

She shook her head and ruffled her fur in annoyance. "I know. Damn it! And it's not an *it*. It's a him. I think I know who it is."

What the hell? "Who is it? Someone in town?"

A small growl came from her throat. Not as though she was angry with him, but annoyed with herself for saying anything. Her scent changed to the melted plastic smell of regret and frustration. "I can't say. Not yet. The first thing I need to do is get ahold of someone who can help." She turned her head back and bit at her back leg, like chewing on a sting. But he heard a ripping sound and she winced just before pulling a cell phone into sight.

"You taped a phone to your *fur*? Ow! And where did you even get a phone?" He winced just thinking about tearing off the hair of his inner thigh. "Who are you going to call out here? There can't be a signal this far down in the valley."

She put the phone on the ground so she could see the screen. "Some phones don't require a carrier. And I had it in my purse, which was recovered from the wreck and was in a filing cabinet." Using her nose to navigate, she opened an application, then spoke directly into the phone. "Best shoes in my area."

"Voice print confirmed," said a tinny, mechanical voice from the phone. "Let's go shopping."

Alek sat down in total disbelief. *Shopping?* She was really going to go shoe shopping right now? No, it had to be more than that. He stood up and padded over to where he could see the screen.

A world map appeared with different kinds of shoes all over the screen. As the app worked out their location, the aerial map began to shift on the screen, closing in on the United States, then Washington, then their county and finally their location, which was still in America. But only just. A pair of fluffy bunny slippers and a red stiletto shoe appeared. A blinking arrow appeared, pointing to their left. "What the heck is that? We're really going shoe shopping?"

She ducked her head and pressed the fuzzy slippers with just the tip of her nose, and then the red heel. Then she lifted the phone by taking the tape in her mouth and talked out the side of one lip. "Of a sort. C'mon. Trust me." She looked funny, with the phone dangling beside her jaw, but Alek knew better than to laugh.

She trotted away without another word. He only had two choices . . . try to find the way back to Luna Lake or follow her.

The scent that hovered in the air behind her was a blend of warm chocolate, citrusy happiness, and anticipation. After a second Alek flicked his tail before bolting after her. *What the heck. At least shoes are a start to clothes . . . or no clothes.* "Wait up, Claire!"

The information she'd found had shocked Claire to her core. This was so far beyond a few missing kids that it needed to be dealt with by someone far above her pay grade. While she didn't think Alek was involved, she couldn't figure out whether he'd been compromised. There was mind control going on in Luna Lake and she was fairly certain that the townspeople didn't realize it was happening. Because no way could this level of sick go on in such a small town without someone noticing.

But she couldn't just openly accuse another Wolven agent of having BDSM relationships with children. Yet, there was no other explanation of the photos she'd found behind a heating grate in the police station. She was horrified by what she'd seen and now she understood what Rachel had been talking about. If it wasn't sex, it was certainly humiliation. Photo after photo of her and other people, posed as though they were mannequins. The police chief was in every photo, naked, not touching the other people, but just on the verge. His hand about to touch a nipple, his erection about to enter an open mouth, his hands touching himself while he stared at them in bondage. It was hard to tell from the photos, but Claire was pretty sure his magic was holding the victims in place, frozen and forced to submit as surely as if they'd been given a date rape drug. Because in many pictures, Claire could see their eyes . . . haunted, terrified, resigned. Fully aware of what was happening, which made it far worse.

Rachel was an adult now, but in some of the photos, she looked like she was still in her teens. But there were both boys and girls, which wasn't common in pedophiles. Claire had seen both Scott and at least one of the kids in the green files. Claire hoped that the chief wouldn't find where she'd hidden the stack of photos before she got back to Luna Lake to retrieve them, but consoled herself with the thought that it would take him some time to return, given how far she and Alek had chased him.

Because the darkness was the chief. She had no doubt. He was powerful enough. He'd proven that. How easy it would be to black out an area to take a victim, take his photos and do . . . well, she hoped it was just photos, and then destroy the memories.

Were the missing kids the ones whose memories wouldn't wipe? Who threatened to go to the human police or even Wolven command? She didn't know, but she was sure as hell going to find out.

The temperature was dropping like a rock and freezing rain was trying to glue her eyes shut every time she blinked. Alek trotted alongside silently, but it was all she could do not to sneeze from the emotional cocktail of scent that surrounded him like a cloud. Curiosity was top of the list, which was the only reason she wasn't having an allergy fit. Suspicion reminded her of cedar tree pollen and made her sneeze horribly. Happily, the swirling emotions distracted her from his normal sweet, spicy musk. If she paid too much attention to that scent, all her plans would go horribly wrong.

"I'm not seeing any signs of a mall out here, but I wouldn't mind a food court about now." The teasing in his voice said he knew she hadn't really been using a shopping application. Though he didn't know what it might be, he was coming along. Claire tried not to think about why. If he was a plant, this safe house would be compromised. She crossed her fingers that her instincts about Alek were right.

"It probably won't be *much* of a mall, I'll admit." They came to a clearing and she saw what she'd been looking for, an old wooden cabin that blended into the trees so well that it was nearly invisible. The old pine timber that supported the covered porch and made up the four walls retained enough bark that it was hard to tell where the forest began or ended. Dried lichen covered the weathered roof.

Alek edged to where he could stick his nose out of the edge of the brush line and sniffed, then whispered, "Who lives here?"

"Us, for now." She pushed through the last of the tall grass and trotted through what used to be a flower garden. The bars on the windows on either side of the door were decorated to look like designer grates. Once she reached the porch, with Alek close on her heels, she set the phone down on the wooden planks, glad to get the tape out of her teeth.

"Hey, where's the doorknob?" Alek asked. Claire looked up to see that he was right—there was no way to open the door.

"Hmm, good question. Could you look around back, see if there's another entrance?"

While he was gone, Claire carefully checked the porch,

looking for a way in. The wind picked up, beginning to lash at her face, freezing her nose hairs with each breath and making the tips of her ears burn. She inspected both windows and the strange handle-less door and even pressed each board in turn with increasing urgency to see if there was a hidden switch. Nothing. She wasn't made for this temperature. She was a desert wolf and her skin was cooling fast.

Alek returned from the back of the house, his head frosted with sleet. The cold didn't seem to bother him much but his thick coat had fluffed out to fend off the wind.

"Nothing around back," he reported.

At that moment the penny dropped and Claire knew why the cabin seemed impregnable. She let out a sound and shook her head. "I'm an idiot. I forgot the security system." She went back to her phone and once again pressed her nose to the screen. A new screen popped up, blinking words: *Style of shoe?* "Bunny slipper."

The application responded instantly and she heard a snap from inside the house. "Voice print confirmed. Please answer the security question below."

"Hey, something happened." Alek stepped forward and pushed against the door with his forehead, and then stood on his hind legs and leaned on the door. It moved fractionally.

Claire read the question and furrowed her brow. *An owl lives in a tree outside a college classroom. What does the owl say at sunset?* Surely there was some sort of trick to this. It couldn't be that simple!

"What's wrong?" Alek asked, dropping back onto all fours and joining her to look at the screen. "What sort of question is that?"

"A very silly, very old joke." She shook her head in dismay, then spoke as clearly as she could into the phone. "Why, why, why."

Another metallic snap and the front door eased open a

crack as a single light came on inside the cabin. Alek stepped in front of Claire, blocking her way, and nudged the door open with his shoulder. She used her magic, along with her eyes and nose, to confirm that there was no one else present. There was no scent except for pine, snow, and the delirium-inducing musk next to her.

The door opened wider and they heard another click, tiny but loud enough to make them both jump back and off the porch to land a dozen feet away on the cold ground. Claire shivered anew in the icy wind.

There was no explosion, no gunfire or people yelling, just a slight hissing sound and the smell of fire.

"Oh, for heaven's sake. Just go in." A new voice made them start and turn as a single unit. A bobcat stood at the edge of the garden, its eyes twin golden stars that bored into Claire's head like lasers. "C'mon, it's freezing out here."

"Who are you?" Alek's voice held a threat that Claire had no doubt he would act on if needed. He stepped slightly in front of her, shielding her. It amused her, because she was pretty sure she was the better fighter. She'd been trained by some of the best.

The cat made little snarling sounds—laughter, Claire realized. "Oh, you've grown up well, young Alek. Strong chest, coat like your mother's, but with your father's starry eyes. Nikoli would be proud."

Alek started. "Who *are* you?"

"My sister put a snake on your ceiling and you got beaned by a metal lighter from his pocket. The cut should have needed stitches, but it healed while I watched. I knew you'd be an alpha. Do you remember that?"

Alek stepped forward a few paces, and when he spoke, his voice was filled with wonder. "You're the French doctor, the Council's doctor. Why are you here in the woods?"

"Please, call me Amber." She stepped closer and brought

the light scent of cat with her. It wasn't an unpleasant smell . . . not like the police station. "I presume one of you called me. I got a flag that someone needed stilettos."

Claire backtracked and picked up the tape attached to the phone with her teeth. "I did," she said, a bit muffled with her jaw closed. "But what are stilettos? I know the others."

"Doctors, or healers if you prefer. I would have picked sneakers, but the messengers got those. And the heels sort of look like needles. But can we *please* go inside? I'm sure the fire has warmed at least a bit of the great room."

"Fire? Do you live here?" Alek's head cocked slightly and his ear twitched.

The cat shook her head as she stepped past them. "Just visiting. My husband is in Alaska visiting his family. It's cold enough *here*, much less going to the Klondike." She ruffled her fur, shaking off the crystals of ice. "Polar bears and their ice . . ."

She didn't add anything else, but it was enough for Claire to realize just who this person was! The wife of the Chief Justice was inviting them into her home. At least, it was hers while she was here, and she'd gotten here first.

Amber sprinted through the cabin door and planted herself next to the wide fireplace that held a gas-fired log set. "Ahh . . . fire. I love fireplaces." She turned her head, licking her paw to clean her whiskers as she did. "This converts easily, if you need to use logs. Where are you headed and who's hurt?"

Claire let Alek go inside first and checked her six before closing the door behind her. The latch inside the door automatically sealed with a solid, sharp *thunk* that drifted a faint odor of oil to her nose.

"First I need to know that the area is secure." Claire had no choice. The Four Corners battle had proved to her that nearly anyone could be compromised. There were alphas who

were mind controlled, just like the lesser animals. Not everyone was fighting against the snakes. Some were fighting *for*
them.

Amber looked closely at her for a long moment. "Well, you
do have the phone and the door opened for you. I'll show you
mine if you show me yours." She glanced at Alek, who looked
confused. He remained standing but not sure what to say or
do. "I don't suppose you're part of this, are you?"

He let out a snort of air. "I'm not even sure what *this* is."

The small cat nodded once and came toward Claire. Once
she had blocked Alek from seeing, she lifted her right front
paw above her head to show Claire the brand under her foreleg. It was the only way Wolven could go forward after the
plague. Nobody could take anyone's word for anything because lies were truth if people believed them under mind
control. So once the Council was confirmed clean by the
seers, who had special abilities to see auras that could confirm truth, or into the past, or even the future, every Wolven
and Council member had been branded with a hot silver iron
to show their affiliation. Amber's had both the flying *W* sym-
bol for Wolven along with the reverse C that showed she was
a Council member. Claire likewise lifted her arm and held
out a paw and touched Amber's. The cat looked at the single
flying *W* in Claire's armpit and nodded. "Okay, so you
are . . . ?" Amber trailed off, waiting.

She glanced at Alek, then back at Amber. "Can you make
sure nobody is listening in before I begin? The Second of Luna
Lake seems to have deep claws into people's minds."

"The *Second*? Interesting. Well, that's easier in human
form. The shift shuts down some of the sensory input I'll
need to clean the area. Give me a second. And I have some
clothes that should fit you both, so you don't have to stay in
wolf form the whole time." She turned and left the room,

heading through a back door. Claire saw a flash of light through the doorway that didn't seem to be a light.

"Everything okay in there?"

"Yep," came the reply. "Just changing into fluffy clothes. Be right out."

Still watching the door, she asked quietly, "What was that flash of light?"

He nodded and came over to whisper next to her ear. "The really powerful ones do that sometimes when they shift. My mother explained once that so much power is hard to hold in either form. They have to consciously not glow. But it bursts out between forms, which is why they don't often shift around other people. You'd feel the sting of it, like being shot with a fire hose in the chest."

Oh. She'd never had it explained like that, but she had noticed that when Council members visited her pack, they tended to change forms away from the rest of the pack. She'd never known why. She turned to look at him, saying, "Thanks. I didn't know that," and found herself staring at the most amazing eyes she had ever seen. Alek's eyes were glowing, shining like twin stars, filled with bright white fireflies. Mesmerized, she couldn't look away.

"Your eyes are amazing." The words came out in a whisper, nearly breathless. He seemed equally lost, standing still, inches from her, just breathing.

"That was a little tougher to untangle than I'd imagined." Amber's voice preceded her into the room. "And I see you have your *power* back." The redhead's twinkling eyes had a knowing quality. She wasn't a tall woman, standing about the same height as Claire. She was lean but compact, yet had feminine curves and a quick smile with her canines a little longer than normal, even in human form. She added, "Don't make me open a window. The pheromones are getting a little thick in here." The pair of jeans she threw at Alek hit him in the muzzle, causing him to blink and back up abruptly. "Those should fit if you shift and take a cold shower first so you can close the zipper." She threw a shirt at him as well, to back him up a little farther from Claire.

With an effort, Claire looked away as Alek shifted. She could tell from the sounds that he was in human form. He scooped up the clothing and sprinted into the bedroom.

"And these are yours." The healer tossed garments into a pile in front of Claire: a pair of soft flannel pants with a drawstring and a heavy sweater. Claire wasn't sure she still needed them. It seemed warmer in the room than it had a moment before. "The area is secure. And whatever your name is, I need to know right now if you're doing it intentionally. Remember that I'll know if you're lying."

Feeling better than she had in days, Claire had already shifted to human form and started to dress by the time Amber's question registered. "Doing *what?*"

The healer looked bemused. "Yet another interesting . . ." She stepped over and lifted Claire's chin with one manicured finger. "I don't think you know yet." A chuckle escaped her. "Never mind. I'll let you figure it out."

"Figure what out?" What did the healer know? "You said you untangled the mess. Is that why I feel like myself again?"

The other woman pursed her lips and walked across the room to sit in a recliner. "Mostly. But let's cut the last tie and see what happens."

A flare of magic hit Claire full in the chest, dropping her to her knees with a cry of pain. The healer didn't blink. It was the strongest burst of pure magic Claire had ever seen, and it took Amber no more effort than raising an eyebrow.

Claire struggled to breathe, to think while the searing that started in her chest spread to her arms, legs, and head. She screamed then, or thought she did. She wasn't sure what was real. A part of her felt, saw, tasted Alek race in from the other room, heading for the healer, who casually tossed him to the side with her magic.

He hit the wall and then was on all fours, trying to get to Claire. She was clawing at her throat, trying to breathe, but the air stayed just out of reach.

Alek screamed across the room, trying to get somewhere but being held in place. "For God's sake! She can't breathe! Stop it! Why are you doing this?"

Amber smiled . . . *smiled*! "I'm not doing a thing. You guys are doing all this. Want it to stop?"

If crawling, groveling, pleading with the healer would help, she'd do it, because her lungs were burning for oxygen and it felt like she was being sliced with razor wire.

Alek fought against the power that kept him motionless. "Fine. Whatever you want. Just stop it!"

Amber picked up a cup and filled it with a tiny individual bottle of wine. "Okay, if that's what you want. Reattaching."

The pain stopped. Just stopped. Air filled her lungs so fast that she coughed. "What is *wrong* with you? Do you get a kick out of causing pain?"

"You really don't get it, do you?" She made a tsking sound with her tongue.

Claire looked over at Alek. Where she was feeling better, he seemed to be dragging tail. He'd dropped to his knees and while not in pain, he looked like he had in the basement when she'd insisted he go home and sleep.

"Are you okay?" Her words came out hoarse, choked.

He shook his head. "Just tired. I felt fine a second ago, but now I feel like I did in the basement."

"Okay," Amber said from her comfy seat. "You guys are being pretty clueless and she's becoming a health risk to you, Alek, so I better tell you."

That raised her brows. "I'm *becoming* a health risk? To *who*?"

Amber pointed at Alek. "Think about it, little wolf. When I said I was untangling the mess, I meant Alek, not you. His problem is that he has too many draws on his magic. He's actually a pretty strong alpha, but you'd never know it because of the siphons that've been draining him dry. You feel good, he feels like crap. He feels good, you feel like crap." She shrugged and raised her hands. "And let's not forget the stink of lust in this room. You do the math."

Claire felt her eyelids open so wide her eyeballs felt cold. She risked a look at Alek but didn't dare sniff. He'd apparently already figured out what she was just coming to understand. He was mated to her. Mated. Crap. How could she not have noticed that when she noticed Paula being mated to him? *Idiot!*

Alek was crouched on the balls of his feet, leaning against the wall, beating the back of his head slowly into the wood. The panic scent that rose from him was muted, as though he either wasn't thinking about it too much, or was resigned to the situation. Rather than say the word out loud that there was no choice but to say, she asked a less obvious question. "Who's the *other* draw? I only met him a couple of days ago. I mean, don't . . ." Nope. She couldn't say the word. Not this soon. ". . . Attachments like this generally require . . . physical contact?"

Alek sighed. "Our first meeting was me giving you mouth-to-mouth when you were nearly killed by that wreck. Then we kissed at the school."

Amber raised one shoulder, noncommittal. "It's happened with less, and not happened with more. A kiss isn't usually enough. But him breathing for you and keeping your heart going? That isn't far-fetched."

"But that was just a few days ago. Who else?"

"You caught that," Amber said with a smile. "Good. That's been tricky. There seems to be more than one draw besides you. You were just the last straw on the camel's back. Totally not your fault. His old pack is one, his new pack is the other."

Alek shook his head. "No. That's not right. My old Alpha released me when I moved to Luna Lake. Everyone said so. And our town's Alpha doesn't bind pack members."

The strawberry-blond healer chuckled. "I am shocked, *shocked*, I say, that Nikoli lied about that. You were young when you left, but how many times did you hear him say, 'Once my pack, always my pack'?"

Alek sighed. "Nearly every day, when someone wanted to move away or get a job somewhere other than the hotel."

A quick nod from Amber. "His attachment has been passive—all he's done is keep tabs on you and infrequently, it seems, until recently. Have you done anything recently that might have caught his attention? Tried to contact him or anyone from the old Chicago pack?"

He dropped his head to his chest. "My sister, Sonya. I've been trying to find her and got a letter from the Siberian pack that I couldn't read. I put in a call to the last number I had for them to see if anyone back there could translate it. I thought the Duchess or Yurgi might be able to help."

Amber stood and walked over to Claire, offering her a hand up from the floor. While the younger woman wasn't sure whether it was safe to touch the alpha, it would be rude not to accept the help. Amber said, "That would do it. You became interesting to him again. Probably he's checking on you through that old, familiar connection before deciding whether your call was a trick just to find his pack."

Once Claire was on her feet, she released Amber's hand, but the healer didn't let go. "Now, on to you. I can peel apart your head if that's what you want, but it would be simpler, and far less painful, to just tell me who you are and why you're here."

There were things in her head that she wouldn't want a Council member to see. "Let go of me and I'll tell you what I can."

"Actually," Amber replied, "you'll tell me everything I want to know." She paused for effect. "Whether or not it's by choice."

CHAPTER 21

*A*lek watched the interaction between the two women carefully. They were staring at each other with intensity, neither giving an inch in the battle of wills. Amber spoke first. "You know I can strip it from your mind."

Claire didn't flinch, just raised her eyebrows slightly. "Then you also probably know that it's illegal to do that."

He had to say something. The sting of magic and nose-twisting explosion of scents were giving him a headache. "Guys, can you ease up a bit? Claire, just tell her what you know. She's a Council member. I can vouch for her. I have literally seen her *at* a Council meeting."

"That's the thing," Claire said. "If she was part of the current Council, I shouldn't have to introduce myself. She should have gotten a picture of me, along with the cases I'm working on. The current Council knows that anything or anyone from before the plague is suspect."

Cases? "What are you talking about? Why should she have a picture of a teacher in a little town in Washington?"

Amber released Claire's hand, sighing before she stepped back a pace and regarded Claire with arms folded over her chest. There was both surprise and suspicion in her voice when she spoke. "You're absolutely right. I *should* have. Now I'm wondering why I didn't. Who's your direct?"

"Will Kerchee," Claire responded, seeming to know what Amber was talking about.

"So you're part of the Texas pack?" When Claire nodded, the bobcat shifter pulled a cell phone out of her pocket. "That should be easy enough to check." She pressed a single number on the keypad and hit the green call button. She put it on speaker so they could all hear it ring.

"Hello?" The man's voice was sleepy, the word a bare growl.

She didn't bother to introduce herself, so apparently the person would know her voice. "Care to tell me why I don't have the current roster of Wolven agents?"

Now there was confusion in the voice, but it sounded more awake. "You do. Or, at least, you should. Why?"

It suddenly sunk in to Alex's brain. Cases. Agent. He stared at Claire. "You're *Wolven*? But you're so young." Or was that a lie too? "Or are you young?"

Amber spoke into the phone at the same moment that Claire seemed to freeze in place, like a statue that had moving eyes. "I have a person shopping for slippers who says she's one of yours. But I don't know her. You'll need to vouch for her to me or she won't leave here to reveal the location."

The voice on the phone was all business now. "Name?"

Claire didn't open her mouth, just glared at Alek and Amber. Amber stared back, brows lowering. Alek knew they were running out of time. He had to speak. "Claire Sanchez."

One word came from the phone. "No."

"That's what I needed. Thank you, Lucas."

Lucas? Lucas Santiago? Crap. "Claire, that's the head of Wolven. You have to talk. She'll kill you. I'm not kidding here. You need to tell them what you know."

Claire let out an annoyed sound. "Fine. It's Clarissa Evans, not Sanchez."

Now the voice on the phone swore. "Oh, goddamn it! I just remembered you're in Washington with Charles. Amber, this is my fault. You caught me still asleep. Claire's brand new. She was supposed to be in deep cover, even from Wolven and the Council, so it was need-to-know only."

She really was Wolven, and high enough to be secret *from* the Council? Who or what was she investigating? Alek felt a stabbing in his chest. Who the hell was this person?

The caramel scent of burned coffee mixed with ticked-off cat made it smell like the cabin was about to burn down. "And the only healer within two hundred miles of the location of a deep-cover operative wasn't considered *need-to-know*? Are you stupid, Lucas, or just getting careless? I swear to God that I'm going to examine your brain next time I check how you're healing. This paranoia of yours is going to get us all killed!"

"It's not paranoia," Claire said quickly. "You were right, Lucas. There's something going on here." The whole timbre of Claire's voice had changed. She looked pleadingly at Amber. "Could you please ease up on the magic? I can't feel my fingers anymore." Alek looked. They were clenched into tight fists, the knuckles bloodless and white.

"Oh. I suppose." Amber made a slight gesture, and the sensation of biting insects eased on Alek's arms, but the rumble in his gut didn't stop. He was mated to a liar, and to a Wolven agent. He wasn't ready for any of this, didn't even know what to think. "So what exactly are you investigating?" the Councilwoman continued.

Lucas and Claire spoke in chorus. "Is the area clear?"

Amber rolled her eyes. "Well, at least I know who trained her. Yes. The area's clear. The only thing I left intact was the mating."

"What?!" Lucas exclaimed. "When did *that* happen?"

"Single sided," Claire said, a little too matter-of-factly for Alek's taste.

"So far . . ." Amber added, with a knowing smile. "Only a kiss so far . . . plus mouth-to-mouth resuscitation."

The sharp tang of worry, not quite fear, that she gave off didn't match her words. "Shouldn't be a problem."

"Report." One word. Curt and commanding. That was how Alek remembered the Wolven chief.

"They hold elections for the power positions. Sort of interesting. The mayor is the Alpha, the Second is the police chief. The town doesn't hold challenges. They have some weird contest they call 'Ascension,' that's like tracking and races. I . . . *lost* by default on my first day. I'm the Omega right now." She paused for a moment.

"The *Omega?*" Lucas sounded surprised.

Claire struggled to contain the annoyance in her scent and voice. "The town operates on a caste system. The Omega is a nonperson. That explains how the corruption has worked without being noticed."

"I knew it!" Alek didn't intend to say it out loud, but it just slipped out.

"Who else is there, Amber?" The suspicion in Lucas's voice was plain.

Amber replied. "Alek Siska. Remember him? He grew up in Nikoli's pack and lived in the hotel. He's the mate."

The mate? "I have unique insights into the town. I've lived there for ten years and am planning to apply to Wolven Academy as soon as I finish the police academy."

Amber shook her head. "You're compromised, no good to us." She spoke into the phone. "He's got a pack binding to both Chicago and Luna Lake, plus the mating binding. I've unraveled all but the mating tie, but he all but has strings above his head."

Lucas let out a low growl. "Van Monk didn't apply for permission to do a pack binding. We've been cautious about that since the plague. Only the Council members have clearance to bind members."

"We're not bound," Alek protested.

Claire interrupted. "I think people don't know they're bound. Everyone has memory lapses and the Second has proven he can read my thoughts. With effort and not all the time, but it's been a struggle to keep secrets."

"Lenny?" Lucas asked. "He's involved in this too then?"

Claire's scent turned to a pepper so strong that it burned Alek's nose. "Oh, he's involved all right. I'm pretty sure he's the real Alpha and Monk is just a puppet. I also have evidence that he's . . ." She paused and looked right at Alek. "I'm sorry, Alek. I didn't want this to be the way you found out. It seems like you were friends."

He felt his brow drop until he could see the tiny hairs at the edge of his vision. "Find out what?"

She took a deep breath while Amber shifted her footing, keeping the phone held so it had the best angle for Lucas to hear Claire. "He's been using his position to abuse kids in town. Torture. Bondage with photos."

Alek's jaw dropped so fast he felt air on the back of his throat. "What?!"

She continued, her voice more uncomfortable with each passing word. "I found the photos. It's obvious the kids are magically frozen. Pretty disturbing stuff. I've got no idea what might have happened to the missing kids, but I'm afraid it's really bad. As far as I can tell, not a soul in town even questions that they're gone. Ten years, eleven kids that I've found evidence of. I managed to get one back this morning, Darrell Williams, but I haven't had a chance to talk to him yet. I think his sister's still out in the wild somewhere."

Amber's voice held barely contained fury. "Why haven't

you questioned the boy yet, agent? They could be destroying evidence right now, or worse, disposing of the boy."

Claire didn't wither under the press of emotions or magic lashing at her. "At first, I trusted that the boy was getting medical attention because his AP siblings said they were taking him to the local nurse. They don't have a healer, by the way, and haven't for over a year. The townspeople honestly believe that the Council and Wolven have abandoned them. It wasn't until late in the day that I realized I didn't know where the boy was, and then things were moving too fast.

"I found the pictures in the police station's basement after I was locked in, then Alek and I chased what I think is the perpetrator after I broke out."

"Wait," Alek interrupted, his scent mingled confusion and anger. "How did you break out? The basement is completely secure; unbreakable."

She shrugged. "I suppose it's meant to hold people without tools. My pocket knife has a screwdriver. I crawled up through the heating vents." She turned her attention back to Amber. "He has enough power to do a full-out blackout of all senses over a wide area. I think that's how he's been taking kids. And he's *fast*. We lost him just an hour or so ago; that's how we wound up here."

She let out a frustrated growl from deep in her chest. "Everything came to a head today. Like my arrival was a lit match to a powder keg."

There was a pause while everyone took in the information. Long minutes passed. Finally, Lucas said abruptly, "You need to go back. And Amber, you need to leave."

"What?" Claire sounded shocked, though Amber's magic held her so firmly that her expression didn't show her emotion. "My cover is blown in a dozen different ways. You'd be sending me back to my death. And Alek's . . . and probably the kids.'"

"Not if Amber puts all the connections back the way she

found them, with one exception. She's going to be listening in. I know you've done that before."

"It won't work," Amber said to Alek's great relief. "The Second will already know that the tie has been broken. He's probably looking for them right now. Even if we could think up a good enough cover story on why the pack tie was interrupted, he'd notice a new thread. He's likely discounted the old pack thread as a remnant. But this would be too obvious to miss."

There was a slyness to the Wolven chief's voice when he replied. "It would be, so we make it even *more* obvious. We exploit the mating binding and hide the passive tie inside."

Exploit the mating binding? "Um . . . say again? What do you mean?"

For the first time Lucas spoke to him directly. "Look, Alek. None of this is your fault. When we sent Claire to Luna Lake, we thought she was a strong enough alpha to handle whatever came up. Van Monk is a solid leader. But apparently this Second of yours has managed to slip through the cracks and mess with his mind.

"Your link to the Chicago pack has made you at least somewhat immune to whatever's happening. Nikoli is strong enough to resist being shut out. Claire is linked to the Texas pack, and they were already planning on trouble by letting her go undercover. You say you want to be a Wolven agent. With that responsibility comes the occasional order to do something uncomfortable. Sometimes our agents have to hurt or even kill someone for the greater good."

He nodded. "I understand that. Wolven agents have to go into danger."

"All I'm asking you to do is let a mating play out . . . have sex with a beautiful woman you're already attracted to." Alek felt a fluttering in his chest and buzzing filled his ears. He looked at Claire and found her likewise shocked at the implication, or at least as surprised as she could look while still held in place.

Amber looked both amused and impressed at the idea. "The binding will tighten and will hide the lesser tie. I can listen to whoever is attaching and gather evidence the Council can use. My memories can be directly accessed by any of the seers."

Lucas agreed. "Correct. Right now, even with photographs, we don't have enough. It's too easy to digitally alter pictures. It would be simple for them to argue that the evil new-comer, Claire, is besmirching their good names." They heard him sigh through the phone. "The Council is split on many things right now. If we vote to remove a pack leader from command, it has to be unanimous."

Claire sighed. "A mating *would* explain why we disap-peared. People in town have already noticed how we look at each other. Alek's brother told me to leave and I was attacked tonight by another woman in the pack who noticed Alek's unusual attention to me."

Sounding worried, Amber interjected, "They just met a few days ago, Lucas. They might not be ready to hop into bed together on command."

Lucas's reply was almost gentle. "Not even to catch a pred-ator who might also be a murderer?" When he didn't get an immediate response, he added, "Amber, you sifted through Siska's mind. Anything that would make him unworthy?"

Unworthy? Of *what*? It was such an odd question that he didn't know what to think. The revelation that Amber had been sifting through his mind was harder to take. How long had she been doing that? Since they'd arrived? *What the hell!*

"Other than the puppet strings, not a thing. I know I said he wouldn't work, but he's intensely honest, to the point of constant self-adjustment. He'd be a good pick overall once he's clean. I'm sure Nikoli would vouch to the rest of the Council. It would take a little work and maybe some shiny tribute to get him to release his ties, but Charles could convince him."

"Great. Alek Siska, as Wolven chief, you're officially appointed as a new field agent for Wolven."

"What?" Just like that? For years, Alek had been focused on joining Wolven. He'd hoped that someday he'd have enough knowledge, meet the right person, and somehow get an audience with someone high enough in the organization to even *apply* for Wolven. And now, here he was, a field agent? Surely this was a dream. He had to be about to wake up in his own bed.

"Your first official assignment is to help Agent Evans catch the bastard who is hurting kids in your town. It'll be an undercover job. If you don't want to actually be mated to Agent Evans—and trust me when I say I understand that—I'm ordering you to *pretend* you are long enough to find out the truth."

He raised his voice so everyone in the cabin could hear him clearly. "Listen carefully: I don't want him or her dead. I want them to stand before the Council and be forced to admit every sordid detail, so *they* can make the person dead. If that bastard is your own Second or the Alpha, so be it. If they're being framed, find out who's guilty. Amber, if they need to have some memories wiped, take care of that. I have some calls to make. Amber will be your local contact from the cabin. Just think what you need and she'll handle it."

Without saying good-bye, Lucas disconnected the call; the phone beeped quietly and the screen went black. Amber tucked the phone into her pocket and quickly moved toward a pair of boots drying by the fireplace.

"Okay, then. I hadn't planned on staying here for an extended time. I'm going to need to pick up some things at a grocery store. Not much around here, but there's a truck stop on the interstate near the Canadian border. You two need to figure out what you have to do to make this work. Once you have a plan, tell me and I'll take care of the rest. But if Lucas says I can't come back to Luna Lake, then I won't. It would be easier with me there, but he has some plan in mind and I don't want to mess with that." She continued as she pulled on knee-high boots with laces. "I can make you forget this whole conversation, even forget you're mated. I've done that a few times before. But you'll still know who you are and what you need to do." She finished tying her boots and looked up to see them staring at her.

"Wow, those are big eyes. Yes, I'm leaving, even if you give me that deer-in-the-headlights look. You're Wolven agents. Own it. Decide what you want and then tell me. When I come back, you'll have to leave. Figure out where you need to go." She got up and pulled on a heavy parka hanging on a carved stand near the door. She twisted the knob and tried to open the door, but it didn't move. Amber braced herself and yanked. The door budged slightly, letting in a frigid wind—the door must have frozen shut. The healer pulled up the furred hood of her jacket and buckled it tightly across her neck. "God, I hate driving in ice. *Bon chance*, you two."

The door opened after another yank, admitting swirls of tiny ice crystals that sparkled for a few seconds before melting into rain.

Amber stepped into the storm and shut the door.

Alek and Claire were alone.

The ticking of the grandfather clock in the corner seemed to boom louder with each passing second. He hadn't a clue what to say. His mind was putty.

"So . . ." Claire said, dragging the word out. "*Congratulations?*" She sounded unsure. "Welcome to Wolven."

He grabbed a chair from the dining room table next to him and sat down heavily. "Can he just *do* that? I don't know the first thing about being a Wolven agent. I haven't even gone through the academy."

Claire shrugged and then turned to walk toward the kitchen, saying over her shoulder, "Lucas Santiago is the chief and a former Council member. I think he can do whatever he wants."

As the rush of adrenaline faded, the enormity of the situation fell on him like a lead weight. "What the hell am I going to do?" He put his head in his hands and tried to remember how to breathe.

The scent came first, spiced chocolate and musk. When he opened his eyes, a beer bottle had appeared on the table before him. Claire clinked the one in her hand against it. "Wing it. Like me." She took a long drink and then put a hand on his. The tingles threatened to overwhelm his brain. "I'm sorry. For everything."

He couldn't do anything other than stare at that tiny hand, so pale, perfect. He wanted to lick it, taste her skin. "What's everything?"

"Oh, I don't know. Siphoning your magic, lying to you, exposing what's happening in your town . . . ruining your life? Pick one."

Those eyes. So earnest. So very blue, like the ice swirling against the window. He could drown in those eyes. She'd said words, but they didn't make sense in his brain. "What?"

Claire kept staring at him and her jaw went slack, her lips parting just a bit. He leaned forward. He had to touch them. Couldn't help himself.

She jerked back her hand like it was on fire and pushed back her chair, nearly tripping over it to back away. "I'm sorry. I keep doing that."

"What?" His brain was clearing. The farther away she was, the more he could think.

"You're mated to me. You're going to be attracted to me. I keep putting you in a position where you can't think. You'll be distracted and won't be able to investigate." She stopped in front of the fire, keeping her back to him. "That's not fair to you."

He slipped off the loaner shoes, which were killing his arches, and padded across the room on stocking feet until he was only inches behind her. He slipped his arms around her waist. She flinched so hard she would have fallen into the fire but for his grip on her. He whispered into her ear, slow, letting his breath raise goose bumps on her skin. "Let me decide what's fair to me. Maybe I don't want to think right now."

"Alek . . ."

She smelled of musky desire and fear. The desire was stronger, enough to make him instantly hard. She moaned when he pulled her tight against the weight of his erection. The pressure of her body against him was intoxicating. When he nosed her hair aside and began to lick her neck, a small sob crept out of her throat. Her fingers dug into his arm and one hand lifted to slide across his hair and pull his mouth tighter to her. He felt a surge of some emotion well up inside him. It was more than lust, but different from any version of love he'd known. It was . . . completeness. It spread through him, urging him on to include her, needing her to be part of this. Not just as a recipient, but a participant.

He didn't remember turning her around. Maybe she'd done it on her own. But he remembered the instant their mouths met. She tasted of hops and honey and chocolate fire.

There was nothing beneath the zippered sweater except her skin, soft and warm under his roaming hands. But he needed more. His mouth still on hers, tongues tangled, he gently lowered her to the Oriental rug in front of the fire. Her gasp, her tightened fingers on his back, emboldened him. He raised his head to look at her face as he unzipped her sweater, then lowered his gaze to stare at her perfectly formed breasts, just large enough to fit in his hand. Her nipples were already taut and the rush of cool air made them pucker, looking like they were begging to be kissed.

He obliged.

The gasp turned to a moan. She tugged on the back of his shirt. "Off."

He sat up long enough to pull the shirt over his head. Claire's hands glided over the skin of his chest, setting his mind on fire. He let out a little growl. She lingered on his shoulders and then pulled him forward. He found her mouth again, then settled his weight between her muscled legs. The pants would have to go next, but this was good for now.

Alek kissed her slow and deep. He couldn't get enough of the taste of her, feeling her tongue explore his mouth and her harsh breath next to his ear. His heart beat even faster, if that was possible. His hands explored her body, noting every curve, every place that made her moan or gasp.

He moved his head abruptly to one breast, pulling it into his mouth as far as it would go. She responded by grabbing one of his hands and taking his fingers into her mouth to suck on, one at a time and in pairs. If his mind had been putty before, it was hot butter now. He began to tug at the drawstring that held up her pants, kissing his way down to her belly button and shoving in his tongue. Her hips began to writhe. "Oh, God. Alek. Please. I want you."

Oh, she was going to get him, all right. The bow that held the tie finally loosened and he slid her pants down as far as he could reach. Her thighs already glistened with wetness and he knew what he would find as he slid a hand down to rub the hardened nub of her sex. His mouth followed and when he slid his hands beneath her buttocks to raise her up so he could lick and suck her, she let out a sound that was part cry and part scream. He eased his thumb inside her while he licked and her back stiffened. "Let yourself go over, Claire. I want to feel you squirm under me."

Her head began to thrash from side to side on the carpet, blond hair sparkling in the firelight. "Please, Alek. Take me. I want you inside me now."

Alek chuckled. "In good time. I want to take you over the edge first. Let go, Claire. Let it happen." He moved his thumb inside her faster, harder, and moved his mouth back to her nub, sucking it in and flicking it with his tongue. Seconds later her fingers tightened on his back and then dropped to the carpet to clutch frantically at the weave. She cried out as her back arched. Muscles clenched around his thumb, and he couldn't stand it anymore. He pulled down his pants and slid inside her, causing a second series of spasms and another cry that made his whole body clench.

Claire's eyes snapped open. They were as bright as the sun, so filled with magic fire that he couldn't look at them directly. He dropped onto her and kissed her, his tongue moving in rhythm with his hips.

The magic that flared in her eyes flowed into his mouth, then down to his chest and limbs until he was on fire.

Time seemed to be going too fast, yet was utterly stopped. The climax took him by surprise. One moment he was building, hard, fast, pushing into her, and then fire consumed his mind and cock. He drove in one last time and it felt like he was pouring lava into her. She moaned and clenched around him again, her fingernails buried in his shoulder muscles while magic lashed at them—her nails like tiny stakes holding down a tent caught in a hurricane.

This is really happening, isn't it?

He could feel her heart beating in his chest, like an echo of his own, then a door blew open in his mind, one only she could see. A single word echoed in his mind as his jaws closed lightly around her neck, feeling her pulse beating against his tongue. *Mine.*

She pressed her cheek against the side of his temple and spoke out loud. "I think so. God help us both, Alek, I think so."

CHAPTER 22

Claire woke from a dream in which she was making love to Alek, *as* Alek, looking down at herself. Her eyes opened slowly, feeling the delicious weight of his body on hers, snuggled into the couch cushions. Every touch of his fingers felt like fire and ice, tingling her skin.

How many times had they explored each other since the first time? Four, five? The sky outside the window was still black, painted with a layer of ice, so it had happened faster than she'd thought. "What time is it?"

He lifted his head and twisted to peer at the clock on the kitchen wall. "I think it says two-thirty. Why?"

"I'm wondering where Amber is. Shouldn't she be back by now?"

He chuckled and the light scent of citrus filled her nose. "Are you eager to have her walk in and find us naked on the couch?" He went back to nuzzling her neck, then stopped and raised up onto his elbows to see her face. "You're worried, aren't you? Do you think something happened to her?"

She shrugged her shoulders as best as she could under the weight of his chest. "She's a Council member and a healer. I don't really know what *could* happen to her, but yeah. A little."

"Do you still have a charge on your phone? Won't it show the stiletto heel wherever she is?"

It was the very thought that had occurred to her. Coincidence, or something more? She tapped his shoulder blade . . . his very firm, muscular shoulder blade. Yum.

She felt, rather than heard him chuckle against her chest just before he rolled off onto one knee, which hit the floor with a thud. Her face felt abruptly hot, and doubly so when he leaned over and whispered into her ear, "Is *yum* an observation or a memory?" Then he licked her ear. "Mmm. Good memories."

Claire wanted to be playful with him. She did. But she felt so awkward. . . . "Why is this so easy for you?"

Now he laughed out loud. "Oh, it's not. I think I'm still in shock. But it was *really* good sex, so I'm running with that for now."

Oh. Well, she'd had a few one-night stands. She wasn't a virgin, and it had been amazing sex. "I agree. Let's go with that for now." She started putting on her clothes and had just pulled on socks when there was a flash of light through the window. "We have company."

Alek was already dressed and at the window, using the cuff of his shirt to wipe away the layer of steam. "It's Amber, and she's alone. Get the door. She's loaded down with bags."

Fully clothed by then, Claire opened the door and gasped as the icy wind stole her breath away. She started coughing, doubling over as she struggled to breathe. Amber raced past her, clapped her on the back a few times, and kicked the door shut so hard it vibrated against the frame. "What a mess out there. Breathe slow and easy. That cold will make your lungs seize up." Her words were muffled behind a thick multicolored scarf that she hadn't been wearing when she'd left.

Amber unwound the scarf, which seemed impossibly long.

As her nose came free, her eyes grew wide. She covered her mouth and nose again and nearly leaped across the room to reopen the door. "Wow, you guys. Are you wolves or bunnies? I guess I know how you spent your time while I was driving that death-trap clunker on the skating rink outside."

The cold wind didn't bother Claire the second time. The ice cooled the fire under her skin that was likely making her face beet red.

Alek didn't look embarrassed in the least. Grinning at Amber, who shook her head and rolled her eyes, he said, "You missed a good show."

She shoved one of the bags toward him. "I've seen that show. Not impressed. Do you know how to cook? I'm starving."

He picked through the bag, which appeared to be mostly cans. "Man, this is an eclectic mix. It's like a *Chopped* mystery basket. But yeah, I can whip up something out of this."

"Well, there's also a deer. It's in the trunk."

Claire's jaw dropped. "You went *hunting* in this storm?"

This time it was Amber who grinned. "It jumped in front of my car, which is now an accordion. But it still runs, and it seemed a shame to waste the meat or have another driver run over it and wreck."

In the kitchen, Alek was opening cabinet doors and drawers. "Wow, real spices, and a good set of pans. I think we're going to feast."

Amber handed Claire a heavy coat from a cabinet next to the door and they went out into the wind. Still on the porch, the healer stopped Claire with a gentle touch and asked, staring into her eyes, "Is it a double mating?"

She shook her head. It was only during the orgasm that she could feel his heart, read his thoughts. But she was fairly convinced he felt hers all the time.

"Thought so. But he thinks it is. It'll feel real to him at first, like a double bond, so you have to keep the secret for now. He needs time to adjust. It would be a huge blow to his emotional state to find out otherwise. Early mating emotions are tricky." Amber tucked her face back into her scarf and said, "Let's get that deer."

Claire tucked her chin into the zippered collar of her coat, trying to keep out most of the chill, but her exposed ears felt like they were going to shatter and fall off any second.

Amber hadn't been kidding about the front of the car. It looked like the deer had jumped right into the corner, next to the tire. "The frame's probably not sprung, but you'll need to replace that marker light and turn signal. We can probably whip up something temporary with a flashlight, some plastic wrap, and a red or yellow Magic Marker."

Amber laughed, caught a gust of wind, and started to cough. "That's what I like about the Texas pack. Always a low-tech solution to any problem."

"No high-tech for a hundred miles in any direction. We've learned to improvise." Speaking of improvising, the keyhole to the trunk was iced over solid. Claire had recognized the brand of the car, so she opened the driver's door, reached in, and pulled the trunk release.

"Improvising is good. You'll make a good agent." Closing the door and returning to the rear of the car, Claire hauled up the trunk lid to reveal a nice two-year-old mule deer buck. Judging by the raw break, one antler had snapped off in the wreck. The meat had been nicely refrigerated, but it was also stuck to the carpeting.

"I'd expected this," Amber said, producing a good-sized pocket knife from the pocket of her coat. "Besides, I really don't want the smell of that staying with the car for the next two weeks."

She cut through the carpet all around the deer and the

blood. Then it was Claire's turn. Lifting the carcass was no problem thanks to her supernatural strength, but the legs stuck out at odd angles and forced her to be careful with her footing.

Alek met them on the porch, holding a clean bowl and a set of knives in a wooden block. He was smiling at her. Claire was pretty certain they could have been holding a rabid skunk and he still would have been smiling.

It wasn't long before he'd butchered several fresh steaks, which he took inside. Amber joined him after asking Claire to clean up. She began carrying the skin and bones far out into the bushes for other hungry animals to feast on in the cold, and using a chunk of ice to soak up the rest of the blood, which she tossed out into the brush with the skin. As she scrubbed, she could hear Amber and Alek talking in the kitchen.

They didn't sound happy.

"The hell you say!" Alek whispered so Claire didn't hear, almost hissing between gritted teeth. "There's nothing wrong with me. I don't need you putting any kind of block in my head." He flipped the steaks with more force than necessary, causing hot oil to splatter out of the pan and onto Amber's hand.

She didn't move, didn't even flinch, which made him nervous. "Of course you'd say that, but you have to understand that you're not being rational right now."

He put a cover on the pan to avoid the temptation of smacking her with it, in sheer frustration. "So being happy isn't rational? The Council hasn't done enough damage in Luna Lake, now they have to take away the one thing that's finally making my life better? And besides, didn't Chief

Santiago say to *exploit* the mating so you could hide your
listening link?"

The healer let out an exasperated sound. She also kept her
voice low. "That was before you actually mated. He's not here.
I am. This is a very strong link, Alek. Trust me, I know. You
about cut off your finger outside just now because you couldn't
stop staring at Claire." Moving so quickly he could barely see,
she grabbed his wrist and lifted his hand until it was inches
from his face.

"Take a good look. That's a deep cut. I haven't healed it
yet because I wanted it to sting for a few minutes, give you a
taste of the damage you could do to yourself and to Claire, if
you can't think straight. The fact that you haven't noticed the
pain is *not* a good thing. Ignoring pain when you're in a crisis
is one thing. Not realizing you're wounded is dangerous."

The splash of color caught his eye first. Then he focused
on the wide gash that ran nearly the width of his left fore-
finger. The white of bone visible in the center was disturbing.
The wound was still bleeding, tracing red rivulets down the
side of his hand. He hadn't even noticed it. He glanced at
the stove and saw that it was peppered with crimson drips.
The gravity of what she was saying started to hit home.

"I didn't even realize I was cut." He reached over and tore
off a piece of paper towel with his free hand and tried to wipe
up whatever blood was still wet. Unfortunately, the hot stove-
top had dried much of it and he was going to have to scrub the
metal once it cooled down.

Amber's voice softened. "That's what I've been trying to
tell you. Not noticing things can get you dead in this job." She
put her other hand on top of his. Warmth coursed through
his hand, making the skin tingle, then burn. He winced a
little and tried to pull back, but her grip was like iron. When
she released his wrist, the finger was completely healed. Pale
pink skin covered the wound, which looked as though it was

weeks old. "Let's eat first. I'll think about how best to go forward once we have full stomachs."

The food was nearly ready. Claire came in from outside and washed her hands, then set the table. The only sounds for the next several minutes were the *tink* and scrape of metal on china and chewing. The venison tasted as good as it smelled. In fact, he couldn't remember the last time he'd had such a great meal.

As Claire was using a slice of buttered bread to sop up the last of the gravy, she sighed contentedly. The sound made his heart race. "That was *amazing*, Alek. Are you sure you want to be in Wolven? You should open a restaurant. I thought I was a good cook, but I would absolutely pay money for that meal."

He shrugged and when he finished chewing, said, "I just play around with cooking. I don't have the sort of time management skills it takes to be a chef."

Claire was taking a drink of water when she let out an abrupt laugh; she almost sprayed everyone at the table with the liquid. "Are you *kidding* me? I can't imagine how you do all you do!" She turned to Amber. "You should have been there for the earlier part of today. They've set up the Omega position in town so they do all the stuff nobody wants to do—clean the city bathrooms, do home health care for the elderly, pick up trash on the roadsides. It's actually not a bad system. But every single place I stopped after I dropped him off at his apartment, someone was trying to pull more out of Alek: 'Don't forget to tell Alek he promised to work on my computer,' 'Oh, I'm so glad you're here. I thought Alek would be over last night to help me chop wood for winter,' 'I've been looking all over for Alek to help with the next Ascension route.' Every single house! You may not have ever been the Omega, but you might as well be. Do you ever *sleep*?"

He didn't really have an answer for her. "I just help out where I can."

Claire just rolled her eyes. "For the record, I think you have excellent time management skills."

Amber was sitting, staring into space, tapping one manicured finger on the edge of the table. "Time management . . . that just gave me an idea. The problem with time management is that too many things of equal importance can make the mind muddied. That's what we need to do."

He looked at Claire. She was wearing the same confused expression that was probably on his face. "I have no idea what you're talking about."

When Amber's eyes finally focused again, she smiled. "Your town is about to get a Dennis the Menace. Or, more precisely, three of them." He was still confused and Amber noticed. "Wow. I can understand Claire not getting my comment, but you should know precisely what I mean. They must have really gone low-key." Still not getting whatever reaction she was looking for, she continued. "If there was ever a real-life model for the character of Dennis the Menace, it was Claude Kragan. His brother Egan was no better. The great fire of San Francisco? Claude Kragan's handiwork. He was powerful enough to cause lightning in a clear sky.

"The *Hindenburg*? Egan Kragan. Not as powerful, but he loved to play with exploding things. He thought it would be funny to play with skyrockets and see if he could let the air out. He didn't realize hydrogen burned. Nobody could ever pin anything on them, though. Those boys were clever, and only Charles could keep them in check.

"Bitty was just as bad. They were never malicious, just mischievous to insane levels."

Claire gave Amber a sideways smile. "She was a card when she was talking about the 1800s in New Orleans."

Amber smiled freely. "Oh, that *was* fun. I was there. It was quite a time." Then she sobered, looked more concerned. "But they're older than me. Did they seem like they really needed help when you visited? Or worse, have they been compromised?"

Claire waggled one hand in the air. "I was in Bitty's house for a while and all she did was sit on the couch and talk. Rachel Washington told me that she has a bad leg and doesn't want anyone to look at it. But I'm not really sure that's true. She seemed more competent than she tried to make me believe. And the men are downright spunky. I'm pretty sure they're not under any control but their own."

"Hmm. Okay. Maybe this won't work, but we're going to try it. I'm going to put a partial block on your mating, so that you don't get yourselves killed." Claire didn't react the way Alek had. She just nodded. "Once we have enough to prosecute your Second—and I agree that's probably who's behind this, I can take it off. You'll still feel the mating during the block, but it'll be like a watercolor versus an oil painting."

Amber stood up and picked up her plate, flatware, and glass and started toward the kitchen. "You need to visit the Kragans again. If they don't shoot you first, give them your phone so I can talk to one of them." Her smile turned to a grin. "I don't think I'll have to work hard to convince them."

Alek knew she wasn't going to tell them any details, in case the chief got hold of them, but he wished he knew what she had in mind.

Claire cleared her own place, then reached for Alek's, seemingly out of habit. He grasped her hand, letting the tingles flow over him, arouse him for possibly the last time for the foreseeable future. She didn't pull back, but the look in her eyes told him she wasn't feeling what he was.

Are you okay? He spoke to her mind, but she didn't seem to "hear" him. Yet, hadn't she been first to contact *him*, on the park bench? He didn't understand. Could a mating unravel?

"Is this okay with you?" he asked aloud.

She gave him a tired smile. "I'll do whatever I have to do to bring the kids home. That's what I'm here to do."

He felt a stabbing in his chest. It was *all* she was here to do.

CHAPTER 23

*I*ce and snow were things to be avoided in Texas. Where she lived, the county didn't even own a plow. Alek not only seemed comfortable driving in conditions that scared her half to death, he was also almost *speeding* in the thin, pre-dawn light. Claire kept a firm grip on the door handle and checked—again—that her seat belt was cinched tight. She'd been in one wreck already this week.

There needed to be so much going on in Luna Lake that the chief of police and mayor couldn't keep up. Claude and Egan, along with Claire and Alek, would be responsible for causing a lot of the trouble they were planning—and likely would bear the brunt of the chief's response. She wanted to tell the former Omegas what was going on, but she was pretty certain they were being controlled. Amber had explained that Claire and Alek were probably the only two, plus the Kragans, who were too powerful to be mind controlled.

Amber continued laying out her plan on the phone. "You need to keep him so busy that he doesn't notice that things are going wrong. Make lots of little, obvious mistakes. He's going to be more interested in beating you down than any-thing else."

It was hard to ignore the sting in her ribs each time she

took a breath. She'd been too aroused during sex to notice the pain, but once that was done, and especially out here in the cold, it came roaring back. "No problem there. He's been having a great time beating on me. Missing the curfew by five minutes got me a couple of cracked ribs."

Alek turned his head so quickly that his hands on the wheel followed. She let out a little screech as the tires left the pavement to bump through the pile of ice left by a plow. He righted the car quickly, with a few fishtails. "What do you mean, cracked ribs?"

She shrugged. "He kicked me in the chest while you were dealing with Paula, so hard it lifted me off the floor and bounced me off the wall. Still hurts like hell."

Amber sighed. "I wish you would have told me that while you were still here. I'd have fixed it." She paused and Claire could almost hear her shake her head over the speaker. "But he'd spot that immediately. Better for you to have some bumps and bruises, like nothing happened, when you get back. You'll want to shower too. You both smell like sex . . . and each other. Although, that's not the end of the world. Like you said earlier, being in lust would explain a lot. Keep in mind," she said in a rueful tone, "that'll probably get you a beating too. Sounds like most anything will."

"Breathing is probably enough," Claire commented, rubbing her left side again.

"How did I not feel that . . . Amber?" He seemed uncomfortable to be calling her by her first name. Claire understood. It took time to think of the Sazi hierarchy as *equals*, or at least coworkers. "Aren't mates supposed to feel their other half in danger? Shouldn't I have known she was getting her ribs broken?" Alek sounded confused. Claire didn't really understand either. Her Alphas were double mated and the whole pack was joined. She felt more of the daily aches, pains, and joys of her adopted family than she did with Alek.

Amber let out a little snort. "You've been hearing too many fairy tales. Mating is different for everyone. For some, I admit, there is that level of attachment. You know everything about the other person—their wants, needs, heart, mind, body. For others, it's more of a longing . . . a sense of missing something you know you can't have. Sort of like being told you can never again eat red meat or drink alcohol or have a peanut butter sandwich because you're allergic. You miss the taste, the texture, the experience. Tofu and near-beer will never be as good, but you can get by. And occasionally, if you give in and play with fire, you'll pay a price. It can be worth the price, but there's usually pain involved."

"How do you get over the guilt?"

"By realizing that people aren't just the animals we become. We're more complex. A single mate can happily love someone else. Double mates can fall in love with two different people, even though they'll never have the same level of intensity as if they were together. For example, I'm not mated to my husband. I'm mated to someone who is mated to someone else. I *want* him every time I think about him, but I don't love him anymore, so I don't think about him very often. I love my husband, who's not mated to anyone to my knowledge. We have to work it out as best we can. Look, I need to make some calls. You guys let me know when you get there. Okay? Bye."

"Bye." Silence dropped over the car, broken only by the crunching of snow under the car. Claire closed her eyes so she didn't have to watch the ice and snow rushing past. Should she tell him it wasn't double? Amber had said it would be bad for his psyche, and she needed him logical. Yet . . . she was sure he suspected, and wouldn't that be worse? They drove in that silence for a time. She opened her eyes again to see the snow blowing right at them, tiny bullets of white that stuck to the window almost as fast as the wipers pushed them away. It was easy to lose herself in the mesmerizing pattern of snow against the windshield, tapping a staccato beat on the glass.

When they reached Republic, the streets were bare of cars; the main street had just a few tracks in the snow. Alek pointed to a church steeple set high on the hillside. "We'll leave the car up there. Amber said it's where she picked it up when she got here. It belongs to a friend of hers. We'll shift and go into Luna Lake by different routes. If you're okay with people knowing we've been together, then make it obvious. Find people almost immediately but don't say a word. The scent will tell everything. Remember that the goal is to keep them busy. Make errors that people complain about. Do the best you can as far as withstanding pain. I'm going to poke my nose where it doesn't belong but not enough to get killed. Just keep them off balance."

Claire snorted. "The pain part is nearly guaranteed. Remember that I also jumped through a window at the jail and it's probably been snowing on someone's desk. That'll cost me a strip of hide."

"I'm sorry." Alek sounded miserable. She had to look at him then, for the first time in half an hour. There was a haunted look in his eyes and the wave of cool wet scent—sorrow, depression that hit her was strong enough that she had to immediately raise shields against it. But she couldn't avoid it.

She remembered Amber reaching into the car just before Alek had come out of the cabin to get in the driver's seat, putting a hand on her shoulder. "He'll start to feel the separation from his mate soon. Pining is normal. It's temporary, like an energy crash after an adrenaline rush. Try to keep his spirits up. Be bright and cheerful. Smile at him. Just do your best and remember the mission. Stay focused and he won't notice it so much."

When he'd stopped the car in the parking lot and turned

off the engine, Claire reached out and put a hand over his. His skin was cool to the touch, yet gave her the slightest tingle. Just the barest pulsing, as though it was hidden behind a thick curtain. He flicked his attention to her, gave a small smile. "I'll be okay. We'll get through this." The words didn't sound cheerful. They were sad, and the guilt stung her again. A part of her was glad she wasn't out of her mind in lust with someone she barely knew, but the other part of her wished she was. Even jealous, like Paula, might be better.

The phone rang again and Claire punched the button quickly, just as she was opening the car door. The rush of cold wind made her breath turn white. "Before I forget, get those pictures, Claire. Take them to Bitty's house and hide them somewhere. Bitty will know how to get them to me." She disconnected the call, this time without saying good-bye.

They were alone. Again. She couldn't stand the sadness next to her. She shut the door again and looked at Alek.

"I'm sorry, but you need to know. It's not a double mating. You're mated to me. But I'm not mated to you." She felt horrible about everything. He had every right to hate her.

There was a pause and then he nodded, his face a blank slate. "Not your fault." But the words were stiff, tense. "Just tell me one thing."

She looked at him. His eyes were cautious, so her response was as well. "Okay."

"Was the sex out of guilt? Did you feel anything at all?"

She couldn't read the expression in his eyes but it might have been pain. He was guarding his emotions so tightly she couldn't sense them. She had to tell the truth. "It wasn't out of guilt. I wanted to at that moment. But I don't honestly know what I felt."

He nodded, a tiny movement of his head. "Okay. That's fair." He paused, but it was obvious he wanted to say something else. She waited until he continued. "Paula thought we

were dating and I'm not positive we weren't. I enjoy spending time with her. We're friends. And the more I think about
how she responded to you, I wonder now if she's mated to me.
At the very least, she wants me."

Claire felt a peculiar sensation inside her. She wasn't quite
sure what it was. "Okay."

"I thought you should know. So you don't have to feel
guilty." He got out of the car then, shifting without removing his clothes. "Luna Lake is straight north from here. Just
stay along the road and you can't miss it." He bounded off into
the forest.

She looked down at the shreds of clothing littering the
ground and felt nauseous. Her eyes started to burn and tears
threatened. She started to wipe her eyes angrily, but then
remembered *Abuela* Carlotta, the matriarch of their pack,
telling her once that she scheduled time every week to cry.
That tears cleansed the soul, focused the mind.

She could use a little soul cleansing right now.

Reaching for a tissue from a box between the seats, she let
choking sobs claim her, alone in the darkness where no one
could see.

The rushing wind slowly cleared Alek's mind. So much made
sense now that had confused him for years. But the knowledge
wasn't what he'd imagined. He might have known Lenny was
corrupt, but a torturer? A killer? That left him stunned and
disgusted. He wasn't sure how he was going to keep the knowledge out of his face and scent the next time he saw the chief.

As the lights of the town neared, he had to decide where
to go first. His apartment for a shower, or Mom and Dad's
house? Or even the police station to turn himself in and take
the punishment for being out past curfew. Did he want people
to know he'd slept with Claire? He just didn't know. He

wanted people to be happy that he'd found the woman of his dreams, not pity him because he was in a single mating with a woman who didn't love him. He'd heard of strong alpha males who had multiple females mated to them—like his old pack leader. Nikoli loved the attention and felt it his duty to give each and every one of them at least a little of what they wanted and needed. His body was available to all, his heart only to a few. It didn't bother Nikoli that the women all loved him and were hurt by his indifference.

But Alek wasn't like that. He wanted *one* person, not dozens. He wanted Claire.

Or was that an illusion? How could he want only her when he'd just met her?

Paula was stable, kind, patient. She showed up on his doorstep with chicken soup when he had the flu, she spent time with him on the suicide hotline to help people who needed a friendly voice. Why not Paula? Why not other women in town who he liked enough to date?

He didn't want to do this. None of it. He just wanted to curl up in bed and not think about anything or anyone.

That's the depression part of pining. Push past it. He heard the bobcat healer's voice in his mind and realized it wasn't a memory. She really had implanted a link into his head when she put up the wall between him and Claire.

And if I don't?

He could feel reality grow still around him, felt a distant thrum like a tension headache starting at the front of his skull. He stopped running so he could "listen" for the voice in his mind. *Then you'll die. You won't want to bathe, eat, or move. You'll literally curl up in bed and pine away. I know. I've been there and I barely survived. Get past it now while it's new, before it grows any stronger. It's a lot easier to do while you're still you. You still have your life, your friends, your family. Living alone is nothing new.*

She paused in his mind and it felt odd to be alone in there suddenly. *Whether or not you think you've somehow earned this pain, get past it to help the kids who didn't do anything to deserve what's happened to them.*

Somehow earned this pain. The words resonated with him, struck something deep inside that he hadn't realized was there. Images of the past flooded over him, memories long locked away. Hiding in the closet with Denis and Sonya while his sister Vera and their mother fought the snakes. The women hadn't uttered a single cry of pain as the snakes had repeatedly bitten them, spreading venom through their bodies. They had killed the snakes, but the snakes had killed them too. When he'd crept out of the closet and saw them on the floor he'd been overwhelmed with the thought that it should have been him. He was supposed to be the man of the house, even though he was only eleven—Darrell's age. But he'd obeyed his mother and guarded the younger kids . . . and sacrificed his mother and sister in the process.

He had earned this pain.

No. Amber's voice was clear, bell-like, firm. He didn't realize she could see his memories, hear his musings. *Their deaths were the fault of others. You saved lives that night. Whether or not you believe it, you did. And not just yours and your siblings'. Your mother's sacrifice allowed you to be here to save the people in this town. Your job now is to live up to that sacrifice.*

Her words made sense. If Alek had fought alongside his mother, he would have fallen, and quickly. Denis and Sonya would have been short work for the killers and nobody in Luna Lake would be questioning what was happening to the town's children. He was really the only insider who *could* do this.

It was enough to push him past the depression for the moment. He turned and edged along the house line until he reached his apartment. He needed a shower and a shave.

Then it was time to get to work.

Just as he was climbing up the back stairs to the patio door of his place, he heard the flapping of large wings. Alek looked up to see a snowy owl, swooping among the treetops. It climbed higher and higher until it was just a speck, circling like a vulture under the bright spot on the clouds. Then it hurled down like an arrow, flattening and spreading wings just over the tips of the highest pine.

As the bird cruised past, Alek recognized the pattern of spots on the wings' underside. It was Scott! How many times had he flown above Alek while they ran the Ascension course, practicing for the next challenge? Alek knew that pattern— the one that looked like the Big Dipper—like the back of his own hand.

But Scott wasn't an alpha. How could he be out flying days before the full moon? Alek was tempted to call out to his brother and ask about his new ability. But then he'd have to explain what he was doing outside on a snowy night at nearly dawn.

Alek waited for long minutes, keeping to the shadows, until Scott finished sky dancing among the trees and flew up and above the tree line. Once the owl was gone, Alek quickly shifted forms and managed to unlock the door with the spare key he kept in a hidden spot before his toes froze off.

By first light, he had replaced the broken window at the police station and replaced the grate cover over the air duct. He was a little surprised nobody had been to the station to notice. Where was the night shift? There should be someone around. He had to admit that had been clever on Claire's part. Lenny had obviously locked her in the basement after he'd kicked her. She'd used a pocket knife to unscrew the grate in the meditation room and had crawled upstairs through the ducts. That must have been where she found the photos—by sheer accident. But she'd found a way out. It took some doing to make both grates look like they hadn't been touched. Nobody ever cleaned the baseboards in this place, so it was painfully obvious that someone had been fiddling with the duct. Some dust from the back of a file cabinet in the basement, carefully crusted in the screw grooves and around the edges made it look unkempt once more. Then a few minutes with a pipe wrench to carefully unscrew a joint in the pipes in the ceiling to explain the water on the floor and desk. When he was done, it looked like nothing but a frozen pipe had caused the damage. Only time would tell whether the ruse worked.

He'd hoped that Claire would show up so he could lock her back in downstairs and she could avoid that particular beating. He ran his fingers over the bulge in the metal door to the basement. They were bulges he'd caused when he was about Denis's age. But unlike Denis, he could shift and was already showing alphic signs. He hadn't done anything wrong when he'd been locked in. It was the only place to hold someone unstable, before the cage in the house was built. He thought again about Tammy, alone in that cage. Was her mind like his right now, in turmoil? Would he be the next occupant of that cage, when this *pining* made him insane?

CHAPTER 24

Claire stood under the hot water for a long, long time. Her muscles felt like they couldn't hold her up. Of course, racing a dozen miles at top speed to get here hadn't helped. But sitting in the car after she'd finally stopped crying, she'd felt a sense of foreboding. She was being stalked and was in no condition to fight. Retreat had been the safest course, so she'd run. She'd decided to run in human form. The boots Amber had given her fit well and were broken in. And the clothes kept her warmer than her thin fur would have. These winters would be a problem . . . if she stayed.

Climbing the tree and jumping to the windowsill hadn't worked right away, but on the third try, she'd caught the wood and thankfully, the window hadn't been latched since Rachel had opened it to air the room the previous day. If the sounds of her arrival had woken anyone, nobody had come to investigate.

She was just rinsing the bubbles from her hair when there was a knock on the bedroom door and Dani's voice rang out. "Claire, get out of the shower! You're using up all the hot water. Other people live here too."

She laughed. She'd gone from a guest to a resident just that fast. "Sorry!" she called out. "Just finishing. Be right out."

Dani came in without asking and, from the smell, brought Rachel with her. Claire heard the other women gasp. The clothes! Crap, she hadn't disposed of them yet. Even omega noses would be able to smell what she'd been doing.

Taking a deep breath and steeling herself, she wrapped herself in a towel and opened the door.

Yep, Dani had the sweatshirt in her hands and both of them were slack-jawed in amazement. Dani recovered first, whispering, "O. M. G. You are *kidding* me! You and *Alek*?!"

Rachel elbowed Dani's ribs and said, in a barely audible tone, "Told ya so. When two people fight like that, lust is in the air. That's where you've been, huh?"

It was easy to let them jump to the conclusion they wanted, so Claire nodded. "It just sort of *happened*. The chief is probably going to beat the crap out of us for it."

Rachel let out a sigh and sat down on the edge of the bed heavily. "Yeah. He will. Omegas are forbidden from having relationships. Plus, I heard at the diner what happened between you and Paula. She's going to try to chew your face off when she finds out about *this*."

Just like at home—news travels fast in a small town. She wasn't surprised that everyone already knew about her encounter with Paula. It had been happening her whole life, so why would now be any different? "Nothing I can do about it now. All I can do is try not to get killed before the next Ascension."

Dani pursed her lips. "If you want to keep him, you might have to challenge Paula to a mating fight. The loser would have to leave town."

She heard Amber's voice in the back of her mind, causing an immediate headache that made her eye twitch. *That would be a good distraction for later. But for now, you need to bring Rachel to see Bitty. Find an excuse. And bring the other girls along too.*

"Maybe. I don't know for sure that I want him." That was the honest truth.

Sighing, Dani leaned against the dresser and crossed her arms over her chest. "He's my brother and I love him. But he can be the world's biggest jerk, so think carefully. Life won't be easy with him. I've always thought that the reason Paula chased him is because she thought she could change him." She laughed. "You can't change Alek."

Rachel nodded vigorously. "He can be super sweet, but sometimes he doesn't think, y'know? He says shit all the time to people and doesn't even realize it's offensive."

No arguing with that, so Claire didn't try. Instead, she walked across the room and started taking her clothes out of the suitcase to put away in the dresser drawers.

Dani let out a little laugh. "Do you remember the time Alek helped decorate the Christmas tree?"

Rachel rolled her eyes. "And said, 'Gosh, I hope you got the right kind of tree this time. We just barely got rid of the smell of cat pee.' In one swoop, he offended Tammy, who had just moved out a week before, every other cat in the room, and Mom and Dad."

"Plus Scott, who'd cut down the tree the year before. And he didn't even realize what he'd said." Dani shook her head. "Gotta love him."

In unison, they continued, "So you don't kill him!"

That was just like him. She realized that her first impression of him was what everyone else saw too. "But he can be nice too." The other girls nudged each other and wiggled eyebrows as she buttoned up her shirt and tucked it into the black jeans she'd put on. "By the way, speaking of offending, would you mind coming out to the Kragans' houses with me this morning, Rachel? I stopped by Claude and Egan's house at sunset like I was supposed to, but I didn't know what all you do there. I just made them some soup and told them

I would come back in the morning to clean. They said they get up early on Saturday. Dani, maybe you could come too?"

The other woman slapped her own forehead. "Oh, man! I'm so sorry! My bad totally. I don't know where my head was yesterday afternoon. The whole time from lunch to dinner was a blur. I absolutely should have stuck with you for the rest of the day. I don't even know what happened after we brought Darrell back to the house."

Dani asked, "Why do you want me to come?"

Claire shrugged and lied, hoping Rachel's fuzzy memory would cover it. "Bitty asked to see you. Don't know why."

Rachel didn't react, even though Bitty had said no such thing the previous day. Dani sighed and said, "I guess I'll come. But I thought she didn't like our family."

Claire shrugged again in response, then asked, as lightly as possible, "How are Darrell and Tammy? Any change?"

"Dunno. Let's go down and see," was Dani's response. "I haven't been downstairs yet and it's time for breakfast."

Reaching for her lipstick, Claire put on a splash of color that she hoped would distract from the dark circles under her eyes.

What the hell was her subconscious doing to her? Why did she care what she looked like right now? And worse, why wasn't she stopping herself?

Closing the door firmly behind her, Claire followed Rachel and Dani downstairs. Before she reached the kitchen she could hear Asylin, sounding nearly frantic. "You have to eat something, Darrell. Please, honey. Just a little scrambled eggs or some toast."

The boy Claire had rescued was sitting at the far end of the table, surrounded by other family members who watched him with worried expressions. The child's brown eyes were distant, unseeing; his mouth open just a touch and his breath was coming in great gasps like he was struggling for air. His white-knuckled hands clutched the edge of the table for dear life. The scents in the room were similar—ranging from fear to worry, sorrow to joy. But it wasn't the emotion scents that caught her attention most. It was the wave of actual emotion that hit her in the chest. While her empathy wasn't developed yet, she could feel *this*. He was terrified.

"We need to get him back to Marilyn," John Williams said, his voice showing his anger and frustration.

Denis lowered his eyebrows, his nervous energy filling the room with more tension. "Just let him be. He's freaking out because we're pushing him. He's not even here."

Surprisingly, Denis was exactly right. Darrell wasn't here. But Claire knew exactly where he was. She'd been there. He was having a waking nightmare, likely of his captivity. She had to try to bring him out before his mind broke. In order to do that, she would have to go to where he was. This wasn't going to be fun.

She pushed aside all of her own drama and found the place in her mind where she could project a wave of calm at the boy. She spoke to him mentally, using the wave of terror to slide into his mind, pressing positive emotions against him, hoping the words behind them would sink in. *Darrell, look at me.* It was both request and command. *You can stop screaming.* That was what the great gasps of air were. He was screaming without sound. *The darkness is gone.*

The gasping stopped and his head turned toward hers. Everyone in the room fell silent.

Claire took one of his hands with both of hers, wrapping his dark, chapped skin with her pale smoothness. She petted his hand and his breathing slowed.

Closing her eyes, Claire let her emotions flow through her fingers into his. She'd never tried to project. Mostly she'd received and interpreted. But it was important she try. She felt her breathing slow until she could feel her heartbeat vibrating her lungs. A trickle of magic pushed past barriers that had been erected in Darrell, likely to keep him from talking. Time to deal with that later. Now she needed to pass them, find any tiny break into his mind. "I think I can reach him. Bring him out of this."

Inhaling deeply, she tasted *his* scent, so close that she couldn't ignore it. Cloves, fresh cut hay, and spiced musk. A flicker of green light burst at the back of her eyes. Alek was in the room. Did she dare draw on him to reach the boy?

She had to. "I'm sorry." The words were a whisper. If he answered, she didn't hear. *I'm here too.* Amber's voice was distant, miles away. *Go slow. Take what you need.*

A hand grabbed her arm, then was taken away. The voice she heard was John's. "Asylin, let her do this. She's a healer. Maybe she can help."

Another voice. Was it Dani's? "Darrell's calm, Mom. Look. Whatever Claire's doing, I don't think she's hurting him."

Then the voices faded and she was alone on a dark path. Alek's green flickers were like fireflies, lighting her way enough to take a step, then stop when they went dark between flashes. *Darrell?*

Dripping water and the scent of wet clay. The scrape of metal chains on stone brought back memories she had to quickly suppress. She repeated his name, louder.

A tiny whisper, far in the distance. *Who's there?!* The sound increased and came closer. *No noise, no noise, no noise. Quiet, quiet, QUIET!!!* The scream in her mind startled her, made her flinch and drop his hand. Because it wasn't Darrell's voice saying those words—it was the other, the Darkness! Claire pulled back as quickly as she could, coming back to herself in the kitchen in a rush, praying that she hadn't accidentally made a connection that could be traced back to her.

Everyone in the room gasped or let out a startled yip when she yelped and fell backward in her chair.

Alek was instantly at her side, his arm around her shoulder, one hand lifting her chin so he could stare into her eyes with his glowing, starlit ones. "Are you okay?"

She leaned into his touch, blinking repeatedly, trying to get used to the brightness, as though she hadn't seen light in days. That was another memory she didn't want to relive. She nodded, trying to collect herself. "It's in his head. The creature that attacked our car. I found it, but I don't think it knew I was me."

Dani's face paled to the color of coffee with double cream. "The creature? It's in his head? Oh my god!" She backed up until her shoulders were pressed against the cabinets, fingernails chewing at the wood. The stink of her fear filled the room, soaked into the paint and wallpaper. "Get it out of him!"

Alek turned to her with confidence. "We will. I promise you."

Darrell had stopped screaming and was sitting quietly. As an experiment, Claire filled a spoon with some scrambled egg and put the spoon in his hand. She guided it to his mouth. *Eat. You're hungry.* She didn't try to enter his mind again, just pressed the spoon to his lips.

He opened his mouth and bit down on the spoon. Like feeding a toddler, once he had the food in his mouth, he remembered to chew and swallow. Claire turned to Asylin. "It's the best I can do for now. We need a real healer to get him back to normal."

Alek squeezed her shoulder and she looked into those starry eyes once more. "Thank you. It's something. He's not in pain right now." He'd felt it too, through her.

Claire got out of the chair and Asylin took her place, petting the side of her son's face while she fed him. Tears rolled down her cheeks but Claire couldn't tell whether they were from joy or sorrow. There were too many scents in the room.

Doing his best not to tear up, John cleared his throat and squared his shoulders. "Okay, everyone. Let's let them finish eating. You all have chores to do."

Once they were out of the kitchen, Claire stopped to catch her breath. Too much, too soon. Alek gathered her into his arms without a word and just held her. She leaned into him, took the comfort for what it was. When he let her go, he didn't say a word, just walked into the living room to talk to his adoptive father.

Denis darted up to Claire, lowered his voice, and glared daggers at her through the hair that shaded his eyes. "Stay away from my brother. You're screwing everything up!"

He slammed a palm against her shoulder so hard it hit the staircase painfully, then stalked to the living room too. Okay, what the hell was that about?

In a few seconds, she knew. "Alek, what the hell did you say to Paula? She spent the whole night in the diner crying. And Fred said you left the letter about Sonya at the post office. Said you never came back to get it. What is *wrong* with you?" He raised a finger in the air sarcastically. "Oh, wait. I know. You're sniffing after that new wolf. Stop it! You're acting like an ass!"

Claire eavesdropped shamelessly, edging forward until she could see into the room without revealing herself. Alek blinked a few times and looked at his brother. "That's right. I need to find someone to translate it. I'll see if I can track someone down."

Denis's voice rose to nearly a shout. "Sonya's our *sister*, Alek. Our real one! She might be alive, waiting for us to get her. What the hell is wrong with you?"

Alek and John were both visibly stunned by the ferocity of the teenager's outburst. Alek laid a placating hand on his brother's shoulder. "Denis, calm down. It's only been a couple of days since I got the letter. I've already spent hours trying to find someone to translate it. It might take time. It's been ten years. Another day or two won't make a difference."

Denis slapped Alek's hand away. "Oh, it makes a difference. That bitch has made all the difference in the world."

"Denis!" John's voice was stern, unyielding. "You'd better shut your mouth right now, before you say something you can't take back."

The boy let out a sound that was part laugh, part spitting rage. "I don't plan to take it back, but I'll shut up." He spun on his heel and headed toward the door. Claire just managed to duck behind a pillar so he didn't see her watching.

After he slammed the front door, she heard Alek say with befuddlement in his voice, "What the hell was *that* about?"

John sighed. "He's feeling jealous, Alek. He's always been the center of your world. Now he's not. It's pretty obvious you have feelings for Claire. He's trying to adapt. Give him some time."

Claire felt Dani move up behind her. "Denis has always been a hothead. He'll get over it."

She wasn't so sure. The look in his eyes wasn't just jealousy. There was a lot of anger in him. "I really don't want to start a family war, Dani. Maybe I should find somewhere else to live." Living here might prove too distracting to her goal. She didn't have time to pussyfoot around a petulant teenager.

Dani sighed. "Actually, I was coming out to get you. Darrell won't eat for Mom. As soon as you left the room, he disappeared into himself again. She can't get any reaction. Please, could you help us feed him? He's so thin and weak. We're really worried. Then we can run over to see Bitty and find out what she wants."

Claire leaned her head back against the staircase. She'd forgotten all about Bitty and Amber. Worse, she still had to go submit herself to the police chief's tender mercies, if he had any. But the look in Dani's eyes won. "Sure. I'll be happy to."

It didn't take long. He seemed to respond best to the press of emotions, not words or even thoughts. That was for the best, as she was confident the Darkness couldn't sense them. While it was much like spoon-feeding a toddler, once Darrell started to eat, it was obvious he was ravenous. The first scrambled egg led to two and to chopped-up bits of toast and spoonfuls of fruit smoothie.

"This is so wonderful, Claire. I don't know how to thank you!" Asylin hugged her from behind, nearly knocking the last spoonful of strawberry liquid from her hand.

She accepted the hug. "I'm glad I've been able to help. It's rare my empathy gift has any practical use. But if it calms him and keeps the nightmares away, it's worth the effort to connect with him."

Asylin froze and then asked quietly, "Have you ever tried to connect with a rogue?"

"You mean Tammy? Could I?" She asked the question both out loud and in her mind. Was it possible that empathy was the key to reversing the insanity? *It's never been tried to my knowledge,* came Amber's voice in her mind. She would know. *But I could envision a scenario where it could work. I'd be willing to shield your exit if you're willing to try.*

But could she afford to be distracted from the task at hand? She looked up at Dani, to her hopeful eyes, and then she looked at a calm Darrell who could finally blink again. It might be a long road coming home for him, but there was potential.

Amber apparently agreed. *You're not the only empath in the world, and this Tammy I see in your mind isn't the only rogue. If there's any chance this could work, you could help hundreds of others.*

"Let's try it."

This time it was Dani who hugged her. "Thank you! Maybe it won't work, but at least we tried. I can't *not* try. She's my sis." Claire understood that. She was determined to do her best.

"I'll stay with Darrell," Rachel offered, sitting down in the seat Claire was exiting. "We came through at different times, so I don't really know Tammy all that well."

The stairs to the basement were solid metal, driven deep into the surrounding stone. At the bottom of the stairs, Tammy was propped up on a wicker bed painted bright turquoise and purple, surrounded by pillows, her feet tucked under a fluffy throw. Wires drooped from a pair of earbuds that drove a thumping bass into the air. Her head was bobbing and her foot tapping while she read a dog-eared paperback novel. Posters hung behind her head—one of a band Claire didn't recognize and another of a hummingbird, caught in midflight above a morning glory blossom. It looked like a typical teenager's room. Except for the thick steel bars that separated her from them. The bars were as thick around as her wrist and, like the stairs, were driven straight into the bedrock below and surrounded by concrete above.

She looked up when she spotted their movement. She popped the headphones out and spun to set her feet on the ground. "Yay! Visitors. Come to see the freak show?" She was smiling when she said it, but there was an underlying edge in the words.

Dani let out a frustrated huff and put her hands on her hips. "You're not a freak show, Tammy. We're going to try to see if we can fix you."

She gave them a skeptical look. "*Fix me?* What do you have in mind? I won't take drugs. I already told you that."

Claire shook her head. "Not drugs." She sat down on the floor next to the bars. "Do you remember me?"

Tammy stood up and walked over toward the bars. "Claire, right? Yeah, I remember you. Are you a healer?"

She shrugged. "Sort of. I'm an empath."

The tawny-headed girl let out a harsh laugh. "Then you know I feel like shit."

Claire knew better than to respond lightly to the frustration. "I do, actually." Emotions rolled off Tammy like pulse waves, widening then contracting. There were too many scents to even attempt to sort out. "If it's okay with you, I'd like to explore why."

Tammy looked at her askance. "Like therapy? I'm pretty sure wild magic doesn't give a shit about couch talking."

Now Claire did laugh. "I'm not much of a talker. What I'd like to do is connect with you, like with a mental link. What my magic gift does is let me sort of *see* emotions and follow them like scents backward to figure out where they start."

Tammy laughed and sat down on the floor, cross-legged. "Cool. Mind-meld me, Mr. Spock." But the flippant words covered over a fear of what Claire would find.

"Do you want to know what I find?" It was an honest question. Not everyone who was tested for cancer wanted to know for sure it's what they had. Some people liked to remain ignorant except for good news.

She thought about it for a good half minute before finally shaking her head. "You can either fix me or not. I'd rather not know that I'm going to die. Give me the illusion that it's fixable."

There wasn't more to say to that, so Claire simply started. It was far easier to push through a willing subject's emotions. It was like cutting through hot butter. Likely Tammy never even noticed she'd slid inside.

The cell that surrounded Tammy on the outside was duplicated inside. Claire realized she was using music and books to keep the chaos at bay. Colors that weren't colors swirled and collided behind that carefully constructed layer of normality. In her mind's eye, she reached out and put her hand on the heartbeat of the chaos.

It had a familiar taste. It felt distinctly . . . male.

Could the insanity not be within Tammy but being pressed upon her? *The Darkness?* Amber's thoughts flowed with her own. *It is insanity.*

But to be insane presumes there was sanity once. "Maybe there was."

She hadn't realized she said it out loud until Dani said, "Was what?"

Trying to focus on the question pulled her out of the maelstrom too abruptly. She began to heave deep gulps of air, trying to come back to herself. But she only wound up hyperventilating. Like being caught in a riptide, her emotions were heaved in all directions, twisting and turning in on themselves. Snippets of memories, not her own, began to flash through her head. Chaos. Order was needed. Yelling, screaming, crying in the distance. Nobody would listen. Nobody would stop long enough to *think*. Hate would only breed hate. Something had to be done.

She watched words appear on paper, written by a ballpoint pen held in large, thick fingers, in a leather-bound journal. *Today I'm starting the Great Experiment. Heaven help me if I fail. Heaven help us all . . .*

What does that mean? Claire asked whoever was listening in her head. *What experiment?*

I don't know, Amber responded. *But I'll ask around until I find out. Maybe someone remembers something from that time. Ask whoever you meet. Now get out before we're both stuck here!*

"Claire! Snap out of it. C'mon, hon. Breathe!" It was Dani's voice. She felt pounding on her back and with a gasp, she was back in the small basement with what was now a fully shifted cougar pacing on the other side of the bars. A paw reached out sideways from behind the bars, the animal snarling, hungry. She gasped and backed up, helped by Dani and Asylin each grabbing an arm, but even then, the claws were only inches from her face. "Wow. That was close. She turned so *fast*. Are you okay?"

Claire stared at the big cat, snarling and leaping from inside the cage. Then she nodded. "Yeah. I got caught in the middle of her going rogue again. It was a pretty wild ride." She thought again about the man's hand, writing. "Hey, have either of you ever heard the phrase 'the Great Experiment' about Luna Lake? Or know a man who handwrites notes in a bound journal?"

Mother and daughter looked at each other blankly, then back at her. "No," Asylin said. "No idea. But since you're going out there anyway, you might ask Bitty. She was one of the first people in charge of the town, back when it was just a refugee camp."

Alek lay with bent knees on the wooden glider on the porch, trying to gather his thoughts. The wind had died down but there was a bite in the air that went nicely with the lightly falling snow. What the hell was wrong with Denis? Could it really be jealousy? Of *what* exactly? He didn't buy it was just Claire. Something deeper was going on. He'd dated before and Denis had never had this reaction. Maybe something was going on in school or with his friends. He needed to sit down and talk to him as soon as this mess was done.

Dad came outside just then and sat down in the rocker next to the glider where he was sprawled. No sweater, no coat. He was a winter bird. Loved the cold. He started rocking, like he always did when he was waiting to hear whatever one of the kids had to say. Alek didn't even know where to start. For the first time, there were things he couldn't tell his father. He'd always been able to tell his father anything and get good advice. Keeping secrets was new and he wasn't sure how to deal with it. He picked a safe topic, staring at the side of his adoptive dad's face. Just like always. "Jealous, huh?"

"Partly," his dad responded. "The anger makes it worse."

"What's he angry about?"

The rocking got a little faster. "Lots of things. He'll graduate next year and hasn't a clue what he wants to do. His girlfriend dumped him and he's not positive he cares. His grades are in the toilet and he's been hiding the notes from his teacher from me and his mom. Of course, there's always getting caught vandalizing the park and having to go before a real judge, with the possibility of actual jail time. And while Darrell is back, he's not *really* back, and Kristy is still missing. As much as he ragged on her, she's always been Denis's favorite sis."

While Alek had been aware of each thing individually, when they were all strung into a list, it was pretty overwhelming. The anger he'd been feeling at his little brother was swept away in sympathy. "Jeez. It sucks to be him right now, doesn't it?"

Dad just kept staring at the moving leaves on the trees, rocking quietly. That was the one thing that made talking to him easier. He never looked at you when you were spilling your guts. Even though he was right there, it always felt sort of anonymous, like a confessional. "You've always had your act together, Alek. You knew what you wanted, even when you were little, and went out and got it very methodically. Fixing *his* life has been the one thing Denis has always relied on. Now he's old enough that he has to take responsibility for what he does . . . and what he doesn't do, and you can't fix it anymore." His dad paused. "Yeah, I guess it sucks to be him."

The front door opened and Dani came out, followed by

Rachel and Claire. She spoke while she adjusted the hood on her down jacket. "We're off to check in on the Kragan triplets, Alek. Want to come along?"

No, said Amber's voice in his mind. Claire must have heard it too, because she said, "Nah, we don't want to overwhelm them. Three's probably as many visitors as they need."

Rachel nodded in agreement. "Yeah, they wear out pretty quick. With three of us, we can finish up and be out of there fast. It's Saturday, so nobody's really expecting us anyway."

It *was* Saturday. No wonder everyone was hanging out at the house. It might mean no beating from the chief. Omegas typically got the day off to be with their families, and all of the city offices were closed. It would be a perfect opportunity to start making some noise.

The women walked off down the drive, chatting about music, one of Rachel's favorite things. It didn't really seem like Claire's sort of discussion but she seemed to know all the bands that Rachel liked. Then again, he really didn't know her all that well . . .

After a few minutes of staring out into the forest, Alek asked, "Seen Scott today?"

The chair beside him stopped rocking. "Now that you mention it, no."

"Have you ever seen him shift off the moon?"

John let out a chuckle. "Lord, no. I have to help him shift every month. There's a reason he's spent about the same time doing the Omega duties as Rachel."

Doing the Omega duties. The phrase, so common in the house, made him sick to his stomach now. "Could he *fake* not being alphic?"

"No. Of course not. Why would you ask that?"

"No reason," Alek replied. But his dad was good at smelling a lie.

"Try again. Why?" John scooted the chair around so he

could see Alek's face. The interrogation position. Alek could nearly feel the light being turned on his face.

"I saw him last night. Well, actually this morning, before dawn. He was flying."

His dad waved off the suggestion with a flop of one hand. "You must have been mistaken. It's days until the full moon."

Alek nodded. "I know. It's why I was asking. But I'm not crazy. Nobody else has the Big Dipper pattern under the wings."

"What about my Big Dipper spots?" Scott walked out of the house just then and hopped up to sit on the railing. He looked like he always did and Alek felt no rush of power that might signal that he'd suddenly become an alpha.

Might as well just come out with it. "I saw them this morning." He paused for effect. "*Over* my back porch."

Scott paled until his skin was the same white as the streak in his hair. His smile was shaky. "You're confused. I can't shift without the moon."

John pivoted the rocking chair to face away from Alek. "Never have been able to that I know of. But you didn't actually say Alek didn't see you, son."

Brows lowered, Scott went on the defensive. He flipped his ponytail off his shoulder and stood up. "Look, I'm twenty-one. It's none of your business what I do at night." He stormed down the stairs and toward the road, stuffing his fists into his pockets as he walked.

Alek shook his head, surprised yet not surprised at Scott's reaction. His brother wasn't strong enough to be the Darkness and Alek couldn't imagine he was involved with the missing kids. Plus, Claire had said he was one of Lenny's victims. What did it matter if Scott had learned how to shift off the moon? He shouldn't give Scott a hard time for having a little fun. "He's right. He gets to do what he wants. It's none of my business." He sighed and laid his head back against the armrest. "This doesn't seem to be my week for talking to people."

"No, it's a very good question, Alek. You did the right thing, asking him. There are strange things going on in this town. Maybe it's time to start being suspicious."

The sound of distant banjo music made Claire pause. She looked at Rachel and Dani, who shrugged. "I've never heard music out here," Rachel said. It made all of them start looking around them more carefully, sniffing the air and watching the bushes for movement.

They reached the turnoff where the Kragans lived and crept up to where they could see the clearing in front of Bitty Kragan's cabin. Claire was surprised to see Bitty sitting on a rocking chair on her porch, clapping her hands while two elderly men straddled the railing, playing instruments.

The one with the fiddle was singing in a rich baritone, "Picayune Brown's a 'comin, a 'comin, ol' Picayune Brown's a 'coming, aha, ayah."

"Is Bitty *smiling?*" Rachel asked, sounding stunned.

Dani added her astonishment. "I didn't know Mr. Egan could play the banjo."

The music stopped abruptly as all three Kragans sniffed the air. The men reached with their free hands for the shotguns leaning next to the front column.

Bitty raised a hand. "Put down those guns, boys. It's the little owl and her friends. The sweet one who sings." She motioned them forward. "Come, come, join us."

One of the men peered at them, still suspicious. But when he saw Rachel emerge carefully from the brush, his eyes lit up. "Oh, it's *you*." His voice had a thick accent, like Claire had heard from people visiting from Louisiana. "Well, get on up here, girl. Let's hear that pretty voice to music for a change."

Claire looked at Dani, who shrugged and whispered, "I *guess* it's okay. I've just never seen them standing up and moving around before. Not ever."

Rachel went onto the porch, touching each of the elderly people, like she couldn't believe her eyes. "Miss Bitty, you're *outside*. It's been so long! And you're walking, Mr. Claude." She beamed from ear to ear. It was obvious she really cared about these people.

"Ayah," the one Dani called Egan said with a nearly toothless grin. "Too long. But there's a snap in the air today. Makes a person want to make some noise."

"Make some noise, girl. Give us a smile." Egan made a show of strumming the banjo and rolled a hand, inviting Rachel to sing.

"Well, you've heard about jambalaya, crawfish pie, and gumbo too. But have you heard about boudin? Down in Louisiana, it's an all-American food." Her strong soprano picked a fast beat and the men jumped in with their instruments. Bitty started clapping again, and stomping one foot on the board as Rachel sang a song about, of all things, sausage. "Take it home and eat it to the temperature of the moon."

Everybody laughed as she sang, putting her own personality into the song. That she could still sing songs so full of life after everything that had happened to her amazed Claire.

When Rachel finished, Bitty went inside and came back carrying a tray with a pitcher of lemonade and glasses for everyone.

Rachel stared at the old woman in awe. "You're *standing*. But . . . but, *how?*"

Bitty Kragan patted the seat where she'd been sitting and guided Rachel into it. "Darling girl, I told you all we needed was a little magic and we'd be fine. We have the new little wolf there to thank." She winked at Claire slyly. "Yes, I've always known you were a wolf. But the costume made me smile."

"Claire, you're a *healer*? I didn't know that!"

"No." She shook her head, thinking fast. She had to explain somehow. "I'm not. But I know one. I asked her to see if she could come temporarily, to help out."

Bitty patted Rachel's thick black hair. "She's not here right now, left to go find more sick people."

"Some of the people who are sick don't know they are." Claude's voice was more of a tenor than his brother's and had less of the thick French accent. "Like you and Danielle there."

The women looked at each other and back at the old man.

"We're not sick," Dani said.

"Right now, you're right," Bitty said. "But you've had a mental illness. It's not your fault, girls. Not at all. Someone bad is making you forget things." She stared right at Rachel, making it obvious to Claire she knew what had been happening. "Making you *do* things against your will.

"It stops here and now," the old owl said firmly, her eyes flinty. "I promise you. But to do it, you'll have to trust me. Trust *us*." She waved her hand to include her brothers.

Dani shook her head. "I don't know what's going on here, but it's making me nervous. I think I should go home."

Egan Kragan touched her hand. "Girl, your sister is out there with a madman. He got your whole family in his clutches. You know sometin's wrong with your momma and papa, don't ya? We hear talk, and there ain't no talk of your sis. No search parties, no posters. Don't it seem strange to ya?"

She paused, and her whole body seemed to be trembling. "They never called me to tell me. I didn't even know they were missing until I called a friend in town. Last night, when we were feeding Darrell, she called Kristy to dinner. I had to remind her that Kristy was missing. She didn't even *know*. What's wrong with her? What's happening?" She broke down into tears. Claire let her collapse into her arms and cry.

"We can keep your minds clear and free of the sickness. The more people we can keep the sickness from, the less powerful it is."

Dani shook her head. "You're not making sense."

Claude spoke up. "The sickness isn't a virus. It's a *person*. A very powerful Sazi is attacking Luna Lake, hurting people mentally and taking the children. The more people we can pull away from him, the less powerful he is. The trouble is, we don't know for sure who's pulling the strings."

"I do," Claire heard herself say. "All we have to do is catch him in the act."

"Afraid you're barking up the wrong tree, little wolf," Claude said with an annoyed look in his eye. He wasn't upset with her. She could tell from the push of his emotions that he wished she was right. He didn't like having to be . . . an *alibi*? "While you were chasing that black hole, the person you're thinking of, and I know everything you told our friend, was in a diner filled with people, including me."

Claire felt cold air on the back of her tongue as her jaw dropped open. It wasn't the police chief? But then . . . *who*?

"Oh, that man is far from innocent. He's going to hell for what he's done, no question. We have the photos. Egan went and looked around at the station this morning. And if I have any say, he'll get there quicker than he planned. But he's not the Darkness. And I don't know who is."

"You have the photos? How?"

Egan smiled. "I did a stint as a policeman, early on, and I never did give back the key. Wasn't hard to find where little wolf prints had been left. Don't worry, he'll never know you found them. By the way, you need to work on your covert work, girl. A little sloppy. I had to clean up after you."

Rachel's eyes lifted and she moved forward in her seat. "Photos? You mean . . . ?"

Bitty bent down slightly and gave a gentle kiss to the top

of her head. "Nobody will ever see them. They'll be destroyed just as soon as the Council is done with him."

Dani was confused, being the only person who didn't understand what they were talking about. "What photos? What are you . . . ?"

Claire put a hand on her shoulder. "Let's just say that a man was taking advantage of Rachel's Omega status."

The other woman's eyes widened with realization. She rushed to the porch and dropped to her knees in front of the rocker and pulled Rachel into a hug. "Oh, honey. I had no idea! When? Who?"

Rachel shook her head. "I don't want to talk about it." Then she looked up at Bitty over Dani's head. "Yes, if you can make it stop, I'll do anything. I don't ever want to go there again. But I have nowhere else to go."

Bitty held out her hand and Rachel took it. The old woman held out a second hand, offering it to Dani. "We'll need help to get your sister back, along with your brother's mind."

Dani looked at Claire and then at the two somber men on the porch. "I don't know what's going on, but if Rachel trusts you, I'll give it a shot." She took Bitty's other hand.

Bitty motioned with her head for Claire to move back. "You're already attached. Don't need anything more on your plate."

She stepped back a dozen feet and was surprised when Claude and Egan joined her. Claude bent down to whisper in her ear. "She's always been the Alpha of the family, but don't tell no one. The boys down at the VFW would never let us live it down."

It made Claire smile. "Your secret's safe with me."

Claire *was* attached, so she knew what was going to happen when Bitty joined the two new owls to her own parliament.

The same light that wasn't a light began to form around the old woman, then spread to surround Dani and Rachel. She watched as the faces of the girls moved from nervous to calm and then took on an expression of awe. They looked up at the old white woman like she was a long-lost grandmother. It wasn't more than a few moments before tears began to trace down their cheeks and they reached arms around each other in sheer joy. It made Claire smile. She remembered that first sense of belonging, the utter acceptance of *familia*.

Claude and Egan began to slip away, but she pulled on Claude's sleeve before he left. He turned and she spoke quietly. "Have you ever heard of 'the Great Experiment' in Luna Lake?"

The old Cajun nodded, and her whole body began to vibrate with energy. "Sure. That's what we called the town at first. The whole thing was an experiment: could Sazi of different species live in harmony? Nobody had ever tried to put wolves, cats, raptors, and bears in the same tiny territory. The animal parts don't normally share well. But we only have fifty acres here, so the rules had to be harsh. I'm still not quite sure how the city Council pulled it off. But we're all still here, and alive."

Were they? Maybe there was more to the experiment than most people knew. She followed the brothers while the pack attachment was still forming on the cabin porch. They began to slip off toward the edge of town. "Where are you two going?" she whispered to their backs.

They turned their heads and grinned, nearly in unison. Egan let out a little cackle. "We're going to give the chief a few things to keep him busy on this quiet morning."

Claude added, "And the town Council, and the mayor too." Plenty of *busy* to go around. You best stay here, keep out of the line of fire."

"Hey . . . *fire*. Another thing to add to the list!" Egan said happily. They slipped into the forest like a pair of schoolboys, chortling and whispering.

Oh, lord. She could only imagine what hell was about to be unleashed on the town.

There was no point in staying here until the pack attachment was complete. It didn't take too long, but a few hours was pretty common. She wasn't halfway back to the house before she heard the first alarm coming from the direction of the city offices. Next an alarm went off at the other end of town. Moments later, she heard a whooshing sound and saw a geyser of water rise over the treetops. She sprinted back to the Williams house. John Williams was packing his truck with firefighting gear. "There's a fire over at the community building. Dinner's going to be late."

Patrick came racing out of the house, pulling on a second yellow-and-orange bunker jacket. Smoke was beginning to rise above the trees. "C'mon, Dad. The tanker truck's loaded up. We'll meet at the city building."

A third alarm rose into the once-quiet morning and John pulled a walkie-talkie from a holster on his belt. "Lenny, John here. There's *another* alarm. Might be at Polar Pops from the direction."

"Ten-four," came the harried voice of the police chief. "I'll add it to the list. Nearly every alarm in town is going off. I'm not sure which ones are fires, which are burglaries, and which are pranks."

Alek touched his dad's shoulder. "Let me and Claire check that one out. It's close." He motioned to Patrick, who tossed a radio to him. "If there's a fire and it's too much for an extinguisher, I'll call you right away."

John clapped a firm hand on Alek's shoulder. "Thanks, son. Be careful."

As soon as they drove away, Alek moved up beside her and leaned down to whisper. "Kragans?"

She nodded. "Kragans. They are little spitfires. Whatever Amber did, they're back in the game. Dani and Rachel are part of their pack now. Once the connection is firmed up, they can be trusted. We should probably get Scott and maybe Tammy over there too. I've got a lot to tell you about what's happened in the past few minutes."

He put an arm around her as another alarm bell, just slightly off counterpoint, added to the din. "You can tell me on the way. I really would prefer not to put out a *real* three-alarm fire."

They took off at an easy jog toward the ice cream store.

Alek turned off the alarm by entering a code.

"How do you know the code?"

"Used to work here. It's never been changed."

A new voice, high-pitched and female, made her spin around. "Three three two seven. Three three two seven. Cubed is cubed."

Alek turned and looked around, and Claire saw his eyebrows raise. "Skew?!"

A woman was standing behind the counter, moving her head around like a parakeet. "Skew? Skew! Who's Skew? Youse Skew." She burst out laughing.

Alek approached her carefully, like he expected her to bolt. "Skew, you know me right?" The bright bird eyes blinked and then she nodded.

"Know? Alek. Sure. Hi!"

"Where have you been, Skew? We've been worried about you."

She looked at the counter again, then across the room and finally back at Alek, but Claire thought only because he was waving his hand, trying to catch her attention.

"Where have I been? Where am I normally?" While she sounded nuts, there was a logic behind what she said. Three times three was nine. Nine times three was twenty-seven. So three cubed was twenty-seven. Cubed is cubed. Cute.

"Here," Alek said. "You're normally here. But you weren't yesterday. Where were you yesterday?"

There was no response. She just blinked and looked around. "It smells clean in here," Claire said.

"I know. It's confusing." Alek nodded. "It looks like the dishes have been washed and put away, the cash register is turned off, and everything smells strongly of bleach and cleansers."

"Could she just have been out of town?"

Alek frowned. "I don't think so. It doesn't smell like her in here. It doesn't smell like anything except cleanser."

"Skew?" The constantly tipping face turned her way. "I'm Claire. Tell me about the Great Experiment."

The effect was startling. Alek stared open-mouthed as the parakeet became a falcon—intelligent, logical, and calm. Even her voice changed, dropped nearly an octave and took on a professional quality. "After clinical trials, the experiment appears to have significant flaws. I would recommend to the Council that it be terminated."

The Council? What the hell! She was talking like a scientist, which made Alek lean over and whisper, "What did you do to her?"

Waving off the question because she needed to concentrate, she asked the newly clearheaded shop owner, "Did the ages of the test subjects differ intentionally?"

Skew shook her head. "The subjects were chosen randomly. Results can't be verified without randomness."

It was finally occurring to Alek that Skew was answering questions about the students in the green files. He whispered to Claire, "What does the Council have to do with it?"

"I don't know," she admitted. But maybe it was why her presence here was a secret from all but the highest members of Sazi hierarchy.

Alek got tired of waiting for her to think of the next question. "Where are they, Skew? Where are the kids?" He rushed forward and grabbed her shoulders. Claire couldn't stop him in time, just catching the edge of his shirt as he blazed past.

It was too late. Her eyes glazed over again and she tipped her head, her clarity leaking out like it dripped out her ear. "Kids will be here soon, Alek. Clean up and get ready. Ice cream for the kids. Chocolate, vanilla, extra nuts."

"Damn it!" He let her go so abruptly that she fell back a step. She barely noticed. Skew just turned around and started to wipe down the counter with a white cloth smelling of bleach.

She threw up her hands. "Thanks a lot, Alek! I was getting somewhere with her."

"I'm sorry. It's just so frustrating! I didn't understand what you were talking about and I just jumped in."

"I didn't have a chance to tell you a bunch of stuff. If you could please just give me a few minutes to explain what's been happening?"

He sighed, sat down on one of the round stools padded with white vinyl, and held his arms out, palms up. "I'm sorry. Please. Tell me so we can decide what to do next."

She did. It was fast and at times, he had to hold out his hand to ask questions to understand, but after a few minutes, he just began to nod as she explained. "So now what?" he asked. "People are busy dealing with all the alarms, but that won't last. How do we take advantage of it?" It seemed like he was asking not only her, but Amber, who was hopefully listening in.

Start searching. Look where you first found Darrell. He

couldn't have run far from wherever he was being held. Let me
see if I can help you get there faster than running.

That was actually a good suggestion. Alek must have heard
it too. He reached out and pressed some buttons on the alarm
keypad. At her questioning look, he explained. "Changing the
alarm code. It'll take longer to shut off." Then he put the radio on the counter and pulled the alarm again. "Let them
wonder for a bit. At least someone will find Skew."

It would be better if nobody could track them, but she
couldn't figure out how to manage that. The answer came
from the air. She looked up to see two great horned owls
circling the shop like tan vultures. They smelled like the
Kragans, like fish, rodents, and salt marsh—a surprise, since
Rachel had said the triplets were snowy owls.

"I hear you need a lift," Claude said, circling lower and
opening his talons, offering them for her to grab. "Noses can't
track what doesn't touch the ground."

Alek said, "Is that you, Egan? You seem to be feeling
better."

The other owl let out a few hoots of laughter. "Haven't felt
this good in years. Saddle up, youngster."

Claire took Claude's talons and Alek took Egan's and the
wolf shifters were smoothly lifted a dozen feet off the ground.
Claire tried not to look down as the massive bird soared on
the currents, rising and dropping ten or twenty feet at a time,
as he used the wind to help carry her.

"Can you put us over there, near the tree line?" The owl
looked down at her with large amber eyes and then looked
where she was pointing before nodding.

It wasn't more than a few minutes before they were passing over the meadow where Alek had met her after she'd
thrown Darrell out of the dark. She tugged on one talon to
get Claude's attention and he slowly lowered her. She let go
a few feet above the ground, landing on all fours. Actually,

that wasn't a bad idea. "We should shift. We'll cover more ground in wolf form."

Alek hit the ground beside her and nodded. "But let's leave our clothes somewhere. I'm tired of showing up places naked."

She agreed. Turning her back, she started to strip. It wasn't until she was down to her underwear that she felt Alek's eyes on her. She turned her head and he was staring at her, so hard that his gaze felt like hands flowing across her skin. "We have kids to find."

He closed his eyes, clenched his hands into fists, and nodded, backing away a few steps. "Yeah. We do." He shifted and raced into the forest. She could feel his arousal and frustration beat against her like twin clubs, making her want to chase after him and tackle him to the ground.

With a sigh of frustration of her own, she picked up their clothes, folded the garments, and hid them under a bush, heavily weighted down with snow, but dry underneath. Shifting, she ran through the woods, soon passing Alek. She'd found Darrell. She knew where to go.

The trees closed around them and the temperature dropped a dozen degrees though there was no snow on the ground under the thick forest canopy. The scent of ice and pine filled her nose and made it difficult to find the scents she was looking for. Clay, metal, probably urine or feces. The cave didn't have to be in the mountainside. It could be under a tree or rock. "How far did you guys search up this way?"

Alek shook his shaggy head. "Never made it up here. The thinking was they were playing at the lake and fell in. Someone found a fishing pole, but as far as I know nobody identified it. We dragged the water, though, and searched for tire tracks. I searched up and down the main road and in the park. I presumed others were looking in other places."

Claire turned around in a circle, trying to get her bearings.

Looking back the way they came, she thought they were pretty close. "This is about where the Darkness was holding him."

"Was it in human or animal form?"

"Human, definitely." She turned toward the mountainside. "He was big. If it wasn't the police chief, the man was of similar size. Maybe even taller."

Lowering her nose to the ground, she started snuffling in the leaves, trying to pick up a scent. Before the light had disappeared, the boy had been pulling to get away. "Look for a struggle in the leaves."

Alek moved away from her, head lowered, eyes moving from side to side.

Long minutes passed with neither speaking a word. Claire concentrated her whole attention on sniffing and looking. Unfortunately, she wasn't finding anything. Nothing here looked like it had been touched for years. No broken branches, no disturbed leaves or pine cones. The farther she walked, the less she found. Maybe this wasn't the spot after all.

"I'm not seeing anything unusual, Claire. Are you sure we're in the right place?"

She sat down on her haunches. She was exhausted and getting more thirsty and hungry by the second. Even the pine bark was looking edible. "No, I guess I'm not. Maybe I ran farther than I thought after I got Darrell out. But I could swear we're close." She yawned so wide she felt her ears pop. "I'm getting too tired to see anything right now."

It's been a long day, came Amber's voice in her head, causing a shock of pain that made her eyes throb. *Get some food and rest. We'll start up again tomorrow.*

"Tomorrow? I thought we were going to finish this today. What do we do about the chief? I'm honestly surprised he wasn't on the doorstep at the Williamses' waiting for us to beat us senseless." She was asking both Amber and Alek.

Alek nodded. "Yeah, me too. I've been waiting for the other boot to drop all day."

Amber's voice eased into her thoughts again, more gently this time. *I can't give you a good answer for that. You'll likely have to take a beating until I can get some Council members together to review the evidence. They're scattered all over the world right now. It'll be a few days.*

A few days. Great. She'd just have to do her best not to get killed while getting the Omega work done and searching for the kids. "I need to visit the school tomorrow if we can. Maybe the kids know something they don't realize they know."

Alek let out a frustrated breath. "Why don't we just march over there and confront him? Tie him up and interrogate him until he cracks."

While it sounded like a great idea to Claire, Amber's voice was quick and firm, feeling like a sledgehammer against her brain, so strong that she had to lay down on the ground to keep from falling. *Absolutely not! He has the whole town linked, except for the few I've disconnected. He can draw power from every person in town to fuel a battle. He would bleed them virtually to death. I don't have the power to separate everyone at once. Even the few I've done have been tough. Fortunately, he'd already disconnected the Kragans since they're elderly. I imagine they were drawing on him, so he cut them loose. I was able to heal them without being noticed.*

The little omega owl was beneath his notice, so he'll never miss her. I'm a little worried about severing Danielle. She was middle of the pack, but he'd severed her enough to go to college, so I'm hoping she'll slip by without notice. But anyone else will raise alarm bells and we'll have a war—one we might not win without help.

"Well, shit." Alek's frustrated swear matched what she was thinking. "I guess we're back to being the Omegas. The plan failed."

"I guess so."

Amber disagreed. *It didn't fail. We separated several people from him. It will lessen his power. The Kragans will work on bringing more in to their own group. This isn't a war. Not yet. Today's battle was won.*

It was a good point. Claire started back toward where they'd left their clothes, Alek trotting beside her. "We should probably go back by different routes. Make sure you pick up the radio and turn off the alarm at the ice cream shop if nobody's been there yet. We'll meet up there tomorrow after dark and see if we can get any more information out of Skew before we start to search again."

"Works for me."

Once he had his clothes back in his teeth, he sprinted off into the brush, leaving her alone to dress and get back to the house.

She was not looking forward to tomorrow. But there was no helping what had to happen.

CHAPTER 25

*A*lek woke in the darkness with a sense of foreboding pressing against his chest and head. The phone rang. He grabbed it quickly.

"I have her," a deep bass voice said. It was a voice he'd never heard. "And you're next." The phone went dead and then to a dial tone. There was no caller ID on the display and the last-number-called function didn't dial a number.

Panic began to fill him as he put on his boots. He wasn't sure who'd called or who the "her" was that he "had" but it was real and it drove him to move faster and faster. He'd just put his keys in his pocket, ready to leave, when searing pain raked down his face from temple to chin. It felt like someone was dragging a hot poker through his flesh. It happened so suddenly that he didn't have time to react, to prepare. He fell, screaming. The pain was breathtaking, so intense he threw up bile on the floor.

He reached up to touch his face. The skin was smooth and his fingers came away clean, but in his mind, he saw blood.

More pain now, doubling him over as his chest and ribs exploded in agony. He couldn't breathe, couldn't think. He choked again and expected to spit up blood. But he didn't. What the hell was happening?

Light exploded in his vision, as though it was projecting onto the backs of his eyeballs. He felt choking pain again and realized it wasn't his—it was Claire's! But where was she?

Amber! You have to wake up! Claire's in danger! There was no response.

Alek dragged himself to his feet, trying to ignore the blinding pain, and opened the door, breathing hard. Moving on sheer willpower he went out into the snow, hoping against hope she was at the police station. That she was being punished and he was along for the ride.

Snow was falling again. The flakes melted against skin that felt superheated. His breath came out in a thick fog of white that enveloped his head and made it hard to see. There were no lights on in the police station but it felt like that was where she was.

Pain drew him forward. He felt himself kicking in a door he couldn't see. Despite the barrier Amber had set in his mind, he tried to push power toward Claire's pain, tried to find a way to help. Racing through the station, he slammed into the door to the basement. To his surprise, it wasn't locked.

He walked downstairs cautiously, aware that there was movement in the darkness. Flicking the switch brought no light. Whether the power was out or the bulb had been removed, he didn't know. He felt his way forward. Only when he was tapping on the handrail, trying to find the end, did he realize this was no ordinary darkness. *It* was here, and it had Claire!

"Claire!" he called, but did not hear himself. In his mind, she was screaming. Pain lashed across his body. His leg, an arm, his face again.

Checking each room brought no answer. She had to be here, but she wasn't.

Where are you?! He shouted it in his head as loud as he could, hoping she would hear.

A spark. The faintest green sparkle behind his eyes. *Alek!* It was a call, a scream, and prayer and his heart raced. *Secret . . . room. Behind the stairs.*

He shifted forms to have better use of teeth and claws and slammed his shoulder into the wall behind the staircase. It was solid as stone. He hit another spot and felt the answering pain sing through his shoulder and chest.

Close! came the pained gasp. He moved and hit the wall again. This time, it gave, so slightly that he almost wasn't sure it had moved at all. He slammed the spot over and over and felt the stone shifting; the door opened so fast he fell into the room, struggling to keep his footing. The Darkness pushed him farther into the room and pulled the door closed with an ominous thud.

Claire struggled to think past the pain. She'd expected to be disciplined—had even known that taking a strip of hide was a possibility. But it was always done on a leg or arm, a major muscle so it would be a painful reminder but allow the person to keep working for the pack. She had never anticipated anything like this.

How could she have been so stupid? She knew people in town were connected, but she hadn't expected the people where she lived to betray her. But it was a glazed-eyed Asylin who had been holding the two-by-four that clubbed her over the head. Just before she blacked out, she saw the Darkness descend. And then the pain began.

The Darkness had taken great pains to shackle her with silver irons, bringing back the worst memories of her time with the snakes. She couldn't move, couldn't see or hear or smell a thing.

Then it began to strike. Punching, clawing, then stopping. Then more, for what felt like days. Then one claw that felt as long as her forearm touched her at the temple. Just a touch, but it terrified her. It had slowly drawn the claw along the side of her face, almost lovingly. She felt the curved sharpness bite into her skin, dig until it met bone. When the slicing began, the pain was beyond what her mind could take. She'd screamed over and over and knew no one would ever hear. She would die in this room, flayed alive slowly.

When she felt the spark of power, she couldn't believe it. She hadn't felt Alek's presence since she was sifting through Darrell's mind. She called to him, screamed at him, and prayed he would find her.

Now he was here, holding her in the pitch blackness, feeling the same pain as her. "Claire, can you hear me? Can you talk?"

That voice, so soft, so concerned. "Yeth." Her mouth wasn't working right.

He reached up and grasped the shackles, pulling back and hissing when the silver burned his skin. He tried again and the scent of burning flesh filled the air before her arm finally dropped to her side. She couldn't move it very well, but that was probably the ribs. More hissing and stink and then her other arm dropped. Everything hurt so badly that she could barely think.

Alek held her, stroked her hair with his burned hands, rocked her softly. He did his best to pour power into her. But there was so much pain, so many things hurt.

She didn't know how long they were there. There were gaps in her memory that meant she must have passed out. But she was grateful for it. All she knew was that sometimes she was resting on Alek's lap and sometimes on the floor. She could hear pounding in the background that said he was trying to get out. But the door opened *in*, so he was only sealing the wall tighter when he threw himself at it.

It was probably good she couldn't see. She could feel the

stickiness of her shirt and where it was glued to her skin when she moved. Alek was beside her again. "I'll get you out of here. I promise."

"'S okay," she mumbled, the swelling in her jaw and neck making it impossible to open her mouth fully. "Talk t' me. Need stay wake."

"Shit. You probably have a concussion. Yeah. I need to keep you awake. Okay, we've probably been in here for half a day. I've been listening at the door but can't hear a thing. Maybe there's nobody upstairs. I hope he hasn't killed off the whole town."

She would have laughed if she'd had the energy. "H'ppy things, lek. Tell 'bout you."

Claire heard a slap that was probably him hitting his own forehead. "Duh. Yeah. Okay." He paused for a moment. "I guess there's some happy stuff. I was happy in Chicago when I was little. We had it pretty sweet, living in the hotel. It wasn't really a hotel, like people stayed there. But Nikoli . . . he was the pack leader, he hosted events for other Sazis. Council meetings, Wolven meetings; he set it up as neutral territory so people would come there to settle disputes. One week it might be all different kinds of snakes, the next, bunches of wolves or even birds. The condors were pretty cool, from California. They were mostly surfers, which we didn't see often in the Midwest."

She touched his hand and nodded, encouraging him to go on.

"Yurgi and Pamela took care of us when Mom was working. He was the Omega and his wife was human. They were nice. We had another Omega for a few weeks, also married to a human. But he didn't stay the Omega long. He was tough. Went up through the ranks fast. He was cool, I guess. He kept me and Denis from getting beat on by one of the wolves who didn't like kids."

She listened while he rambled. It really did help her forget the pain and so long as she didn't move, it was like they were talking—getting to know each other. "Mom never really noticed when people were picking on us. She did a lot of stuff in the hotel, so we didn't see her except late at night before bed. Cooking, cleaning rooms, laundry. She was tough on us. We had to be fluent in Russian and English in every subject, grammar, math, science, and she'd quiz us every week. But there was lots of time for fun too. We got to play hide-and-seek in the rooms, and slide down the bannister of the staircase. Nikoli didn't mind if we made tents out of blankets in the conference room, so long as nobody was using it."

He paused. "After the snake attack, which isn't on the happy list, we came here. I was twelve. Mom had taught us to speak only Russian when people asked questions, so they stopped talking to us pretty quick. But we could understand them, so that was sort of fun, like Denis and I were secret agents."

You and Denis are close then? It occurred to her that she could speak into his mind, a little late, but at least she remembered.

He bent down and kissed the top of her head, which was probably covered with blood. He kept talking out loud and she could tell it was so it wasn't so quiet in the darkness. She couldn't smell him. From the throbbing, her nose was broken. That was okay with her since fear and worry weren't the best scents. She could pretend he was happy from his stories. "For a long time, yeah. We were the Two Musketeers. I kept hoping to find Sonya so it could be three again."

Sonya? I was wondering about her since Denis had mentioned it.

"My little sister." His voice was both sad and happy. "She was almost seven when the snakes attacked. She'd already picked out her birthday cake—cherry with white icing. I know she survived the attack. I kept her safe. But afterward, Wolven and what was left of the Council swooped in and gathered up everyone. We were all taken to buses and shipped off. Sonya was with me and Denis, I had her by the hand when we were boarding, but after I got our luggage stowed and got Denis settled in, I turned around and she was gone. She was so tiny that she could have wound up anywhere, on any bus. And she would have spoken only Russian to strangers."

So that's what he was talking about at the house? That I made you stop looking?

Alek shook his head. She could feel it because his chest moved a little, where her head was resting. "No. You didn't. I've been checking every pack in every country for the past ten years. My last hope was the Siberian pack. I'd hoped that since she spoke Russian, she might have wound up there. But they're hard to find. It took time. Years. I got a letter from them the first day you were here, but I can't read it. It's in a language nobody recognizes. I was looking it up when Lenny came to get me for the challenge." He stopped and let out a slow breath. "I can't begin to tell you how sorry I am about that, Claire. I was daydreaming, just got lost in thought, thinking of Sonya and Mom and the rest of the Chicago pack."

I didn't know about her. If you'd have told me, I probably would have forgiven you right then. But I was scared. Had never been in a forest and got lost. It made me angry. I'm sorry too.

She was starting to feel better and realized that the better she felt, the worse he did. *Please don't give me any more power. You need to conserve.*

"You're hurt really bad, Claire. Let me at least keep you stable."

She pushed his hand away from the side of her face, which was starting to regain feeling.

No. You're trying to heal me. You need to stop. You're not a healer.

He leaned back against the stone wall. "Okay. But I keep hoping Amber's out there somewhere and might be able to find us if I keep using magic."

A new but already familiar voice in her head made the pain both more and less. *It was a good hope, little wolf. But I can't help you personally. It would be seen as a direct intrusion by the Council. But I can send help your way. Hang tight.*

The golden sparkles in her head brought more pain, but she didn't care. *There's a secret room behind the staircase in the basement.*

Really, Amber replied. *Interesting.*

A new voice joined in, male, strong. *There doesn't seem to be a basement. He must be using magic to hide it. Okay then, we'll do it the hard way. Is there something you can hide under down there?*

"There's a desk," Alek said out loud.

He tried first to lift her, which caused her to scream, and then to drag her, which was worse. One leg still worked, so she rolled onto that side and began to kick along the floor. He guided her to a hole under a thick wooden desk.

The whole room seemed to vibrate and shake. Finally there was an explosion of dust and chunks of stone fell, hitting the desk with a rumble so loud it felt like her eardrums would burst. Light came through the hole in the ceiling as a high-intensity flashlight dropped to the floor. Alek grabbed it. Two glowing eyes appeared at the edge of the hole and then a massive owl hopped down from the floor above, holding a second flashlight in one talon. He remembered what Amber had said about the Kragans and explosions.

Claude Kragan winced. "Oh, he did a number on you, little wolf. Worst I've seen for some time. Frankly, I'm surprised you survived it. Good thing you're mated to an alpha." He poked the flashlight toward Alek's chest. "And you should be grateful Amber put in that block. You probably would have died of shock when he started to slice up her face."

"I very nearly did," he acknowledged. "Just heal her. Please. Take whatever you need from me."

He was already doing just that. "I'm a healer, but not powerful magically. Fortunately, my sister took a liking to this young'un." Claire felt the warm rush of magic flow through her body. The pain intensified, then lessened as organs stopped bleeding. She still looked five months pregnant from the blood pooling in her gut, but that would eventually sort out. Claude shook his fluffy head. "I'll heal what I can, but she's going to need some time in a hospital. We'll have to air-lift her to one of the Sazi facilities. I'll hop up to the main floor and make some calls."

Claire shook her head, happy to be able to do so. "No. Just patch me up. We need to get to the woods by moonrise. I know where the kids are. And I know what the Darkness is going to do next."

CHAPTER 26

Claire tried to stand and Claude helped. He wanted to put the shackles on her again, if only they weren't silver. "For God's sake, Claude, quit helping her. She needs to stay still."

The ancient owl looked at him with cold, unfeeling eyes. "She has to get out of here somehow, Alek. If you know of another way than standing so I can carry her out, please tell me. Would you rather I wrap my talons around her wounds?"

He looked around the tiny room, barren of furnishings except for the desk. He made an exasperated sound. "Fine. But once she's upstairs, we wait for an ambulance, right? She needs a doctor."

Now Claude smiled, just a bit. "I *am* a doctor, Alek. That's how I met Amber. I'm not just a healer. I have medical degrees and licenses from three different centuries."

He stopped and closed his mouth, forced himself to take a deep breath. "I didn't mean to insult you. I mean she needs to get to an emergency room."

Claire said, "No," at the same moment that Claude said, "Yes."

Now the doctor turned to his patient with raised brows.

"He's right, little one. You're not going anywhere except a hospital. But we do have to get you out of this room."

What was left of Claire's jaw muscles were set tight. "You're a Wolven physician. I'm an agent. Patch me up and let me get back to work."

He danced a little, his talons clicking menacingly on the floor. "Yes, I am a Wolven doctor. That means I get to decide whether or not an agent is fit for duty. You're *not* fit for duty. The knife cuts both ways . . . *agent.*"

Claire closed her eyes. "I'm one agent. There are six children in the woods who are going to die tonight. Die horribly and painfully. This is only a tiny sample of what he's capable of. He's insane. Let me do my job. If it costs me my life doing it, that's still six kids saved."

Six? Who were the others? Alek wanted to scream at her, tie her up, knock her out. "No, it just means *seven* people will die. You can't fight that thing in this condition. You *can't.* And I won't be much more help. I can fight, but it's stronger than I'll ever be . . . than either of us will ever be."

Amber had gone quiet in his mind as he ranted at Claire. When she finally spoke, it made his jaw drop. *That's because he has the strength of the whole town behind him. But with some help, I might be able to shift those odds.*

"Let's see if we can get you out of here." It was tricky and Alek could see the pain on Claire's face when he pulled her up through the hole. Claude had healed her enough that the bleeding had stopped and he guessed that some of the internal damage was repairing itself. But her face was still a mess. She looked like she'd been in a fire. Skin was missing all along her cheek and one ear was partially severed. It was hard to even look at. He couldn't imagine what she must be feeling.

"Yeah, it hurts." Claire must have noticed the look on his face. "But don't look so horrified. I'll heal."

He wasn't positive about that. He'd never seen anyone recover from having their face flayed. But he did his best to put on a smile. He just wished she wasn't going to do this. Yet he knew she was. He knew it without question. Her fire to end this was burning in his chest. It wasn't something he was going to be able to stop.

Claude lifted one talon and held it out to her. "We'd better get over to Bitty's and get this thing started."

Claire forced herself to move as normally as possible. It was the only way she could keep Alek from trying to help her. It was sweet but she knew he was only doing it because he couldn't help himself. The mating took away his free will. That was no way to live. Maybe she could love him. Maybe she liked him. A lot. But once this was done, she would have to find a way to let him down gently. He deserved someone like Paula, who was mad for him. She might be mated to him, which was even better. And he liked her. He'd said so.

It was a short flight to Bitty's over rocks and stones that she was grateful she didn't have to walk across. When Claude set her down with a fluttering of wings that left her hair a mass of tangles, they'd gasped as one and quickly guided her to a chair.

"What in the world happened to the little wolf, Claude? You leave her in this condition? Poor little pup."

He bowed his head and kept his eyes at her neck. "I must leave her in this condition for a time, alpha. She will heal on her own once we start. The one you call the Darkness has grown too powerful. Our only hope to stop him before he leaves the area to claim another, larger pack is to sever the tie from his people."

Egan gasped audibly. "What you're proposing is extremely

dangerous. Not a one of us would be safe. Elizabeth, I can't participate. I'm old, weak . . . as are you."

Bitty stood up, rose to a height with her back straighter than Claire would have believed possible from the elderly woman. She slammed the tip of her cane down on the floor so hard the board cracked. "We are healthy enough. You are more healthy right now than this young wolf who is eager to fight on. Are the owls of our family less Sazi than a mere *wolf?*"

Alex exchanged a look with her. Well, that was nicely insulting. But it had an effect.

Egan lowered his head. "Forgive me. I had no right to question you."

Claude flapped his wide wings, stretched across the whole room. "With age comes experience. We might not overpower, but we can *outsmart*. If you can sever his magic, we can make sure nobody can get to him to fight at his side. Egan, where's that case of nitro?"

Yeesh. She raised a hand. The enthusiasm was nice, but wow . . . "Can we maybe not blow up the whole town? If we survive this, people might need somewhere to live and we really don't need the state police descending with SWAT teams."

Egan puffed out his lower lip in a pout. "Fine. No explosives. But we have a few tricks up our sleeve that'll slow people down."

Bitty had sat down on the couch while they were talking and had begun to glow. Her hair floated in the air like electricity was coursing through her. "Let us begin.

"My pack to yours," Bitty said as she touched Claire's hand. The old owl gasped as her hand caught fire with golden flames that licked up her arm but did no damage. Bitty scooted sideways to sit next to Claire.

"What are you doing?" Electricity shot through her, making her mind clearer than she could ever remember.

Bitty began to speak in a singsong voice. "You and Alek are part of other packs. I plan to attach them to my own family for a brief time to give us the power to end this. I have no more time to explain. Give me your hand, Alek."

The alpha owl stretched out one arm. "Please. Your hand. Lend your power to save them all." Her eyes were unfocused, shining like stars.

It took a few tries before Alek could slip his hand into the flames. Claire understood—it was unnerving to look at. At last, he balled his hand into a fist, then closed his eyes and reached forward. "My pack to yours." A loud yelp escaped him as the flames licked across his arm and over his chest. "Ow, ow, ow. Man, that smarts."

The Kragan men chuckled. "Wolves. Can't stand to fly near the sun."

Well, Claire was no lesser being. She straightened her back and stared right at the two men as she took Alek's hand. "My pack to yours."

Fire shot through her like a high-voltage wire. Her hair crackled with flame and she could see the blood flowing golden in her veins just under the skin.

Bitty mumbled "Let the pathways open." The barrier between Claire and Alek vanished, so suddenly that she let out a cry. She could hear his breathing, smell his intoxicating scent, and the touch of his hand on hers did far more than make her tingle. It stirred things deep inside her, a hunger and longing that were both painful and intensely erotic. He felt it too, she sensed, and when he kissed her, still holding Bitty's hand, the world split and reformed.

As his mouth ate at hers, she could feel her pack. Adam and Cara, Rosa, Grandma Carlotta and the others. *Chingado*, as Rosa would say! They were all there, the whole pack. At the center was Will Kerchee, the fierce bald eagle, binding the force of her pack into a single flow of energy that filled her to overflowing.

Alek's pack was there too, their heat a cold blue flame compared to the warmth of the Texas pack. Intense, dangerous, and not to be trifled with. She'd never felt pack members who were more of a single fighting force than a family. The contact strengthened and that coldness flowed over Alek, filling his eyes and changing his face as he took on his Alpha's purpose and strength. There was power written in that face. This was a man who could become a leader to be feared, and followed. The sheer majesty of him made her shiver.

The magic of three packs filled the room until the room was too small to hold it. She felt the golden energy expand to cover every business, every home in Luna Lake. Wherever the magic went, it encountered other lines of power, red and angry, touching nearly every person in town, sucking them dry. The golden glow sliced through the red, severing the Darkness from its power source. Bitty's eyes opened. No longer stars, they had become windows on the sun. "Go now. This is your best chance."

Claire released Alek's hand and Alek let go of Bitty. His eyes opened wide and he touched her face. "Your face is nearly healed. I didn't think that would be possible."

"It's a day for impossible things." She smiled at him. Maybe there was more than *like* inside her for this man.

The two wolf shifters ran out of Bitty's house into what should have been a dark, moonless night. But the world glowed with the light of a thousand candles. She couldn't imagine how she was going to be able to sneak up on anyone. She was lit up like a bonfire.

Alek pulled a cell phone from his pocket and jabbed at the screen. She wanted to ask what he was doing but the call went through before she could speak.

"Patrick, we're getting back the kids tonight. *All* of them. Bring whoever you can, whoever can fight, and meet us at . . . Where are we going?" he finished, looking at Claire. He'd been running alongside her but didn't know their destination.

"There's a clearing in the woods a few miles from here. I saw the place in his thoughts once when he thought I was passed out. There's a rock shaped like a couch."

"Pat? Rocking Chair Ridge. Come on foot and follow my signal." He didn't hang up, just put the phone back in his pocket with the line still open.

"What if he turns them back? Will they fight *against* us?"

Alek turned his dark eyes back to her, now filled with blue fire. "They won't. He won't turn them back. I won't let him."

She believed him. Her heart was pounding as they ran. The three-quarter moon was just rising over the tops of the trees. They skirted trees and leaped over rocks under the snow as though they knew where each one was.

By the time they arrived, the glow had faded. Claire worried if that meant that Bitty couldn't keep up the energy flow, worried more when she realized she felt tired again, though without the pain she'd felt earlier.

Moving carefully through the underbrush, they crept up on the clearing. A thrill of excitement coursed through Claire at the sight of the semicircle of trees around the couch-shaped boulder. Then she stopped, shocked by the sight of a young girl, suspended by her arms from one of the trees. The girl looked like she was no more than ten and from this distance, reminded Claire of herself at that age.

Alek must have spotted her too—he gasped and started to move forward. She pulled him back, hard.

That's Frannie! His voice in her head was nearly shouting. *I thought she'd moved away with her family, nearly a year ago. Let's go get her!*

Claire shook her head and kept a tight grip on his arm. *No. It's only one child. We have to wait for the rest.*

The girl started to whimper past the tape over her mouth, and kick, trying to free herself from the shackles that dangled her high above the ground. *How do you even know there are more? You're not a seer or a healer.*

He wanted to race forward and she wanted to let him, but that would ruin everything. *I'm an empath. I told you that.* She yanked on his shirt to get his attention. *Listen to me!* He turned, finally, and stared at her with flashing, angry eyes. *He was happy when he tied me up. I wanted to know why, so I opened myself to his emotions. His feelings were tied to particular thoughts, so I could read them. He was happy because one of the children had* shifted. *That was important.* She dug her fingernails into Alek's arm to keep his attention focused on her; he kept glancing at the child in the tree. *He was annoyed because we had ruined his timeline. It's the northern lights, Alek. This is all about the solar flares feeding the moon magic. He has to finish before they end and this is the last night. He couldn't wait anymore and had to eliminate the* other five. *Then he got mad . . . and you saw what he did.*

He took a deep breath. *Five more.*

She nodded silently.

Starlight disappeared, signaling the Darkness's arrival, then reappeared when it left, revealing a new child, hanging from a different tree. Again and again and again, just a few moments each time. The place he kept them couldn't be far. It was a battle of wills for the Wolven agents to wait, to resist rescuing the little ones, most of whom were crying quietly.

Claire assumed they'd learned not to make a lot of noise. She remembered that feeling: noise was the enemy. Claire could nearly feel the weight of the shackles around her own, rail-thin wrists, feel herself dangling, suspended from the cave wall. The weight of her own body caused her agony; she swore she could feel her arms separating at the joints. But they never did.

Alek spoke into her head, startling her out of the memories. *Your Alpha said, 'not again.' You've been tortured before?*

She didn't know how to begin to answer him. He'd shared his past, but could he be ready to hear hers? Nightmares still chased her when her eyes were closed.

Where was the fifth child?

I grew up in a small town in Kansas. My mom got pregnant too young, didn't want me. Put me in a Dumpster, but someone found me and the court put her in family classes instead of taking me away. She was afraid of being punished, of going to jail, so she did what they told her, but she didn't care and never did much. She didn't love me and I knew it. When I was kidnapped, I wasn't completely sorry. She scanned the trees again, avoiding the horror she knew would be etched on his face. *The snakes were creating an army. Whether any individual child lived or died didn't matter much to them. There were always more kids.* She stared out at the four swinging forms. They were so very young. Had she really been so small?

Most of the wounds were healed the first time I shifted. But there are some deep ones that still show.

Alek brushed her hair with a kiss. She could feel her pack in the background, surrounding her with support. Alek's pack offered not sympathy but revenge, if she ever needed it. One in particular felt like another attack victim, the cold fury sprouting memories of similar attacks before rebirth as a wolf. Like her, he wanted no sympathy, no pity. What was, was.

A flicker of moving darkness caught her eye. *There. The last one.*

But it's only five.

The sixth must have shifted. No need to kill that child.

It was time to fight.

CHAPTER 27

They raced forward, straight toward the Darkness. Surely the Sazi had to be at the center of that black hole, which was smaller than Alek had ever seen it. Hopefully Bitty's power net had had an impact.

Gusts of cold wind, like bitter daggers of ice, hit him in the face as they entered the blackness. There was no light inside, but they carried their own with them. The glow of a dozen eyes—no, a hundred—lit the space: golden birds' eyes, the cold blue of wolves', bright green cats' eyes, and even red, snake slits. The power cut through the dark and revealed the man, the shifter inside.

Van Monk! Alek tackled him below the waist and threw him to the ground, then was rocketed up and back by a blow of magic like he'd never felt before.

Monk shifted, became some kind of small cat, glowing red with stolen power. In the trees, the children screamed, distracting Alek. A blur of teeth and claws, Monk lashed out, cut through Alek's skin in dozens of places.

Claire darted in, teeth bared. She caught a back leg and was quickly kicked to the side.

"You can't possibly think you can win," the mayor said. "Do

you have any idea how many people I control?" The Darkness appeared again, then disappeared.

A massive cougar stalked out of the trees. Judging by the size of the beast, it had to be Lenny. Alek fleetingly wondered if Lenny was being controlled or if he'd thrown in with Monk to protect himself and his supply of child victims. Claire leaped onto the back of the big cat and began to bite and tear at the cougar's neck, channeling the fiercest warriors of both of their packs. The cat rolled, tried to throw her off. Alek spun around, searching for the mayor, but he'd disappeared.

Tammy appeared then, a second cougar, her eyes glowing red with flickering edges of gold. Whose side was she on?

Alek hoped she was on the right side. He yelled, "Help Claire! Please, Tammy. She's family. At least to me. I love her."

The snarling cat paused, stared at him with glowing eyes. "Fam . . . ly?" Then she pounced into the middle of the battle between wolf and cougar. When Claire realized Tammy was fighting *with* them, she rolled away and ran for the trees. Wolves weren't good climbers, but she could jump just fine. She hauled herself onto the branch the first child was hanging from and began to bounce, using her weight and magic to crack the wood.

The cats yowled, screamed, and snarled, rolling over in the snow as they fought. The scent of fresh blood sharpened Alek's senses.

Finding the Darkness was like searching for a black cat in a dark room. He moved as quickly and quietly as he could, alert for any movement. But the Darkness descended on him so fast that there was no time to do anything. Claws slashed, teeth gripped, and raw power held him so tight that he couldn't fight back. Yet Alek felt a difference. This wasn't the awe-inspiring force he'd experienced before. It felt more . . . normal, in a way, like any really tough, powerful Sazi.

Pulling power from the web he was attached to, Alek felt a swirl of energy flow through him, becoming a vortex that threw off his attacker. The sensation was intoxicating. It fueled a frenzy of motion; Alek lashed out, caught an arm, a leg, a torso, forcing Monk back until he was a black blob pressed against a tree. The trunk vanished into the Darkness and the upper branches appeared to be hovering in midair.

The blob lassoed him and sucked him inside. If he could still do that, Monk had to still be getting energy from somewhere. Alek had to force him to expend more energy faster. He fought free of Monk's grip, then turned to attack—and missed. Another jump, another miss.

Alek became a whirling dervish, slashing and biting at the Darkness, occasionally catching flesh. He could tell it wasn't enough and exhaustion was beginning to drag at him. He hoped the others were getting the kids to safety.

He thought he felt a presence pushing against his skin, raising the hairs uncomfortably. He lashed out with an arm but the move left him vulnerable and Monk was fast. Claws raked across Alek's stomach and pain washed over his brain so fast, he couldn't process what had happened. Instinctively, he clutched at his gut, and found that what should be inside was out. Blood was rushing out of him fast. Too fast. It was all he could do to keep his intestines from spilling out onto the ground.

He dropped to his knees, his body going into shock. He tried to reach for the pack, but they fell away from him like the wetness that was flowing over his fingers.

Another sharp pain—the claws were driving through muscle and bone, reaching for his heart. Somehow he managed to roll away, still clutching his arms around himself, but he was still trapped in the Darkness. Nobody knew what was happening to him. No one would be able to hear him scream, if he had a throat left to scream with.

Claire! he called desperately.

The face of his attacker flickered into view above him, smiling coldly.

Then the mayor disappeared, leaving Alek alone in the cold and dark.

Claire had broken the last branch, but she couldn't get the children to run. They'd been captive too long—they were too afraid of the Darkness to seize a chance at freedom. She would have to do what she'd done with Darrell.

She grabbed two of the children by the hand and dragged them through the forest. When they weren't able to keep up, she lifted them, one under each arm, and started to run.

Two. But there were more. She wouldn't be in time. That's when she heard a flutter of wings above. A massive snowy owl was flying beside her. He opened his talons, fluttering in mid-air, and she held up one of the nearly catatonic children. He took hold of the girl's shackles in his talons and rose higher and carried her toward the house. Her arms might be hurt, but she would live. With a start, she realized it was Kristy Williams. Without the weight of the extra child, she quickly made it back to Bitty's. Just as she turned to go back, a scream in her mind made her stumble and crack her head against the couch. Claire!

It was Alek! But where was he? She looked around frantically. She could feel his energy dimming. And while she'd taken energy from him before, she had no idea how to give it back.

She picked up the girl again and held her up to a waiting Scott. "Where are they?!" She grabbed a man by the shirt and shook him. "Alek! I can't find him!"

Egan, yes, it was Egan. She recognized him now; he grabbed her arm and pulled her forward and down a flight of stairs.

The doorway at the end of the hall had a bright glow seeping through. She threw open the door and grabbed Bitty's hands. The healer's eyes opened wide in panic as Claire threw herself into the stream of energy. Like a battering ram, she pushed her way into the net of people, searching for the dimming thread.

The light was its own form of darkness—there were so many threads, so much brightness, that she couldn't see, couldn't hear past the humming energy. But she could *feel*. She searched for the memories imprinted on the emotions, calling out to Alek. *Think about Sonya and the hotel and playing hide-and-seek! Help me find you!*

The memories came from the other end of town, from Denis Siska. A shared memory of sliding down the bannister, laughing and screaming, chasing each other, not two of them, but four, flowed into her mind. Alek and Denis, and a raven-haired pair of girls, one older and one very small, smiling and giggling.

Like flashes of lightning, the children ran through the memory, buoyed by the emotions of family and home.

A spark. The tiniest green spark, far in the distance. She'd found him.

Weak. So very weak. Cold and tired. His body was shutting down from shock and blood loss.

When Claire opened her eyes, she saw Bitty's face, looking unbearably sad, as though there was no hope. Acting without thought, Claire slapped the old woman, then recoiled in horror, pulling away and racing back into the forest, toward Alek.

She knew where he was. The only question was if she could get there in time.

Every step was agony, but she couldn't stop. Wouldn't stop.

She passed a cougar's still form. She hoped it was the police chief. She couldn't seem to smell who it was through the myriad of scents from the fight. If not, she was still in danger. The other cat was gone and the clearing was utterly silent except for her frantic footsteps and harsh breathing.

Alek had been stuffed inside a hollow under a tree, where he wouldn't normally have been found for weeks, or years. The slashes across his stomach were horrible. His lips were blue. He barely had a pulse.

She wasn't a healer, but there were people in the net who were. She pulled him out, laid him on his back, and did her best to put the slippery squishy body parts back inside the ripped flesh. Then she closed her eyes and opened herself to the net of packs. *One of you, help me make this work!*

You are utterly insane. It was Will Kerchee's voice in her mind.

Amber's voice was next, incredulous bordering on amused. *Gotta give her credit for Texas innovation.*

Magic began to flow into her, guided by skilled minds. Her arm was throbbing, pulsing in time to the beating of her heart. She began to press the ripped flesh together, keeping it over his organs. She didn't dare do CPR. His lungs needed to stay inside the skin until it could be sealed.

At first, there were no tingles. Nothing more than the slap of flesh on flesh as she force-fed magic into him. But without warning, a tiny flash in her mind, like a firefly at dusk. It sped up her heart and made her push even more energy into him. She pushed everything she could into one command, *Don't leave!* Not part of the command, but equally true, was the final word—*me.*

His mouth opened of its own accord, choked in a great gasp of air.

As she leaned back in utter relief, she felt, rather than saw, claws descend. Without even thinking about it, she reached to the ground next to her, feeling for what she had seen moments before—a broken limb from the old dead tree. Her arm shot up and the stake of wood drove itself into the chest of a patch of darkness with glowing red eyes.

A scream of anger from above her made her cover Alek to protect him. But there was no need. A familiar snowy owl with a constellation of stars on his chest streaked down from the sky, talons open, filled to the brim with bright white energy. The talons dug in tight to the skull of the cat, who was struggling to pull out the piece of wood impaled in its chest. The cat screamed as the talons closed and squeezed. Claire jumped in the air and aimed for his neck.

The bird twisted hard and fast in midair. The cat's neck snapped and the darkness dissolved like smoke and starlight filled the sky again.

The owl landed on the ground and made a few hops to peer down at Alek. Scott's voice boomed, heavy with power, in the sudden silence. "Nobody picks on my big brother but me."

CHAPTER 28

The squeaking of dry-erase marker on a white board made Alek's teeth grind. But the healers had told him that it would be several more days before his vocal cords healed enough to talk. *Explain it again?*

Scott sighed and flipped his hair back from his eyes for the tenth time in the last few minutes. Frustrated, with a few quick flips, he twisted it around and tied the long strands into a knot. "There are a few alphic people in town, like the Kragans, who sometimes change me at night. Hurts like hell but it's worth it. When I fly really high, I get more powerful. I don't know why. I figured it out by accident. Then, if I come down really fast, it lasts a few seconds before it's gone again. Makes me feel like a real Sazi every so often, y'know?"

More squeaking. This time in blue marker. He was getting tired of red and black. *Powerful enough to kill Monk?*

Claire touched his hand. She'd been sitting beside him since he'd been brought home from the clinic. "Well, not him alone. It was more like three packs channeling through both of us. But he was pretty amazing. You should have seen him glowing, bright as a full moon. And I've never seen a bird twist in midair like that."

"That wasn't planned," Scott said with a self-conscious shrug. "But when I saw you stab him in the heart, I had to give it a try. I just figured I'd piss him off, maybe wound him. I never expected what happened."

The door opened and Amber walked in, clapping her hands lightly. "Okay, you two, scoot. He needs to get some rest. I can't stay here forever, you know."

He wrote again and showed her. *Thank you.*

"Thank your insane girlfriend. Weirdest operation I've ever seen."

Claire smiled. "A low-tech solution to every problem."

The healer let out a snort. "Bare hands. Yeah, that's low-tech, all right." She touched Scott's arm. "You, out." Then she pointed at Claire. "Five more minutes. No more. You need sleep, young lady. You've been hovering here for three days with nothing more than catnaps."

Scott saluted her and then gave Alek a pat on the leg. "Get better, bro. We've got a mess to clean up when you're up and around. You haven't heard all the scuttlebutt yet." He shut the door behind him.

Claire looked down at Alek, pale but not nearly as ghostly as he had been when they'd brought him here. She touched his hand. "I'm glad you're feeling better."

More squeaking on the board. *Worried?* He didn't smile with the word. Was he the one who was worried?

"You've been in a magically induced coma for a few days. Yeah, I was worried. And, I've had a chance to do some thinking and some talking to people."

A few short strokes produced black letters. *About?*

She sighed. "About you . . . me . . . *us*. And whether I'm the right person for you."

He grabbed her hand firmly and brought it to his lips, eyes closed. "Yes." The word croaked out of a throat that shouldn't be talking yet. The magic had healed a few things oddly.

"Paula is mated to you. But you probably already figured that out."

His nod was sad. Alek lowered her hand and picked up the marker again. *Not in love with her.*

"Yeah, she figured that out. She's not a happy wolf. But at least she's realized it's not my *personal* fault. No more attacks so far."

Good, came the word, this time in red. He kept writing. *How are Darrell, and Tammy and . . . everyone?*

Now she could smile, even though she knew he was changing the subject. "Both better. Tammy's insanity was an offshoot of Mayor Monk's."

Alek frowned and raised an inquisitive eyebrow at Claire. She sighed. "So much news, so little time."

The door opened again and Dani poked her head inside. "Shh, don't let the doc know I'm here." She slipped inside and leaned down to give Alek a quick hug. "What'cha talking about?"

Claire lowered her voice. "I was telling him all the news."

"Whoo, baby. How much time you got?"

He raised his eyebrows, encouraging them to continue.

"Wolven and the Council have descended on the town and are starting to dig into the records," Claire said. "Seems Van Monk used to be a really great guy."

What happened? squeaked onto the board.

"As far as they can tell, there was so much fighting between species when Luna Lake was founded that he started attaching people so he could keep everyone calm. That was the Great Experiment—trying to *make* everyone get along. Maybe all the voices in his head overwhelmed him. We don't know, but he decided that to keep the town safe, he had to kill all the humans, including the kids. We haven't figured out what Skew knew about it. Since I didn't know her before, I can't judge, but she's somewhere between the parakeet and the falcon we saw that day.

"Apparently, he kept really detailed journals in the early days," Claire continued, leaning on his bed's rail and stroking his arm. "One of the agents going through them says they really show how absolute power corrupts."

"The kids are all back home, but not all the parents remember they had kids in the first place. That's a mess. On the plus side, it means the town will be getting a permanent healer."

"Except," Dani added, "we can't afford one." He must have looked confused, because she said, "The town is flat broke. If the town didn't own the land, we'd probably have been evicted by now. The life insurance that has kept the town running has been gone for at least a year from what I gather from listening to Mom and Dad. Mayor Monk ran up close to a dozen credit cards just to keep the store full. We're going to have to get *jobs*. Or open the town to visitors. Or *something*. Everyone's freaking out. Dad's talking about re-upping for another stint in the Air Force, maybe as a trainer, so he can get a promotion and retire on a higher pension. Rachel is doing a *lot* better, though. People around town have already offered to pay her to clean house for them, but she's thinking she might go back with me to college, if I can figure out how to pay for it myself. No more free tuition from the town." She let out a little shudder but shook it off. "She had pretty good grades and could probably get a scholarship, or maybe we could both work at the pizza place just off the quad. And I already had bunk beds in my dorm. It would be nice to have a roommate that I know and could sneak out to go flying with."

• • •

Jobs. Alek took that in. Nobody his age or younger had ever worked a real job. Crap! Was he still a Wolven agent, or was that just for show, something to placate him during a crisis?

Wow! went on the board next.

"Definitely wow," Claire said. "So even if I wanted to stay to teach, I'd have to do it for free. I don't know if I can do that."

His head turned so fast his neck throbbed and he reached up to touch the bandage. Even though a part of him knew she hadn't planned to stay, he'd . . . well, *hoped* she might. He reached out to touch her hand.

Dani noticed. "Well, I'd better get out of here before that little cat pounces on this little bird. You heal up quick, big bro."

Alek hesitated before turning the board to show Claire the single word he'd written there: *Stay?*

"I don't know if I can," she replied after a long pause. "There's going to be a lot to do first. We are still Wolven, and there's a lot of cleanup to do. I don't know where that will be or if we'll wind up in the same station."

He reached out for her hand, pressing the words into her mind. *I don't want you to go.*

She kept talking. "See, at the very least it'll take time to get the passports and visas and then there's the packing. It's a pretty long trip."

She was *leaving?* Leaving the country? *Where are you going?*

Claire touched his hand and smiled, then eased words into his mind. *Not me. We. I had a few long talks with Denis at your apartment over the past couple of days. We've worked things out. He showed me your research on Sonya. I did some checking of my own and called a few Council members. But the real kudos go to Amber. Turns out the reason you couldn't find anyone to read the letter from the Siberian pack is that it's not written in a Russian dialect at all. It's ancient Inuit. Your letter wound up in the Klondike. And it's just possible that your sister is somewhere on an island in the Bering Straits. I sort of figured you'd like to go with Denis and me to find out.*

He couldn't figure out what to say. His mind was spinning. *So you're not leaving me?*

She laughed and leaned down to kiss his forehead. "I think Luna Lake is going to be my home for a while . . . give or take a few trips to Russia. I came here to teach, but it seems I got taught instead. And a certain principal told me recently that degrees are a dime a dozen, but *teachers* . . . they're a rarity and you should grab them and hold on. I think that's wise advice."

AFTERWORD

Welcome back to the world of the Sazi! For those of you who read the original eight books in Tales of the Sazi, thank you! As you may have noticed, some things have changed in this reality versus that one. Ten years have passed in the reality since the events of *Serpent Moon*. Many of the characters that you came to love in the old series will reappear eventually in this new world, but you'll meet many new people who were just children when the drug that removed the magical shape-shifting abilities of the Sazi called "the cure" caused havoc among Wolven and the Sazi Council.

The cure has become "the plague" to those who survived, a term that can be used freely around humans, because the thousands of deaths around the globe were spun into a tale of biological terrorism that made every front page. The world simply couldn't help but notice. It taxed the limits and imagination of Wolven and the Council hierarchy to keep the press from digging too deep. But thankfully, the sheer scope of the massacres of men, women, and children, and the random nature of the attacks by "cells of multinational terrorists" helped keep the secret of the Sazi . . . barely. Government investigations quietly died behind closed doors due to timely intervention of those still in power.

Families worked to salve the physical and emotional wounds of surviving parents and children, sisters and brothers. Orphans were gathered together and closely guarded to ensure their survival. Luna Lake began as one of the secure emergency compounds to protect those who remained. Set deep in the forest of northeastern Washington State near a crescent-shaped lake, Sazi of all species went there, expecting it would be a temporary refugee camp—a place to hide and lick their wounds. But they discovered something they didn't expect. They found peace from the horror of the plague and the threat of attack from enemies. They found plenty of food, fresh air to fly in, and space to run.

The compound began as a melting pot of the injured and desperate. But it soon became a colony and then a town. It became home.

But secrets abound, as well. Not everybody is who they seem. Like the Old West, the plague created a vehicle for many to escape an old life and create themselves anew. Still, escaping the past seldom changes a person's nature. A predator can't pretend to be prey forever . . . Welcome to Luna Lake and a whole new chapter in the Sazi reality!

(P.S.—Yes, if you think you recognize the names of the hero and heroine in this book, you have seen them before! Alek Siska and his brother Denis were the mischievous boys in *Moon's Web*, and Clarissa Evans was one of the girls kidnapped by Nasil in *Moon's Fury*.)

READ ON FOR A PREVIEW
OF CATHY CLAMP'S

Hunter's Moon

CHAPTER 1

Nick's Tavern is in the worst part of town. The front door opens onto a back alley and the back door dead-ends inside another building. The Fire Code wasn't in effect when the building was built. Nick's has been there that long. My Dad remembers going there after work for a schooner of beer—twenty-four full ounces—and a plate of cheese. A buck bought both in the 40s. It was big enough for lunch for two or dinner for one. They don't do cheese plates anymore. Pity.

One time I went around the back of the building just to see what was on the other side. It's an upholstery shop. Big frigging deal.

Most of the buildings that surround Nick's are vacant now. Multi-colored graffiti scars plywood-covered windows. God only knows the last time someone cleaned the trash from the sidewalks.

I'm known as Bob to my clientele. That's not my real name. I'm the kind of person you would expect to find at Nick's. Call me a businessman who works the wrong side of the street. All sorts of people have need of my services: high class, low class, quiet suburban mothers, good church-going men. At one time or another all of them give into their primal instincts and call me. I meet them here at Nick's to talk details.

I'm not a hooker or a drug dealer. Too many risks, not enough money. There are no drug deals at Nick's. You'd get bounced on your ear if you even thought about it.

I'm an assassin. A killer-for-hire. If you have the money, I'll do the job. I like puppies, kids and Christmas, but I don't give a shit about your story—or your problems. I'm the person you call when you want the job done right the first time with no sullying of your name. Yes, I am that good. I apprenticed in the Family.

Oh, there's one other thing I should mention. I'm also a werewolf.

Yeah, I know. Big joke. Ha. Ha. I never believed in "creatures of the night" like vampires, werewolves, or mummies. They're the stuff of schlock movies and Stephen King novels. I'm not.

The door to the bar opened and the figure silhouetted in the doorway almost made me laugh out loud. I stifled the laugh with a snort of air. Then I let my face go blank again. Talk about stereotyping. The woman wore an expensive black pantsuit, odd enough in a low-class part of town. But the part I liked was that she wore a dark wig-and-scarf getup like something you'd see in the 60s, and huge round black sunglasses. Oh yeah, she'll blend right in with the steel workers and biker babes. Sheesh.

My client had arrived—and she was early. No big deal. We'd only set the appointment a few hours ago. I hadn't even unpacked from my last job. The quicker we finished, the better I'd like it.

The woman in the doorway was forced to take off the sunglasses to look around the darkened bar. I got a look at her face. Nothing special. Deep, green eyes looked out from a relatively plain face. She stood about 5'5". I felt like I recognized her, but she was like me—a blender. She could probably get dolled up and look pretty but she would never be stunning. She was a woman that a man would fall in love with for her mind or personality. Or maybe her body, which was on the good side of average. She was probably a size ten—Maybe a twelve. She carried it well and comfortably. The suit spoke of money. Good. She could probably afford me. The rest of the get-up spoke of nerves.

She scanned the bar, looking for someone she had never met. You can't mistake the look. The person just stands there, hoping that someone will wave or pick them out. I let her feel uncomfortable for a moment, just long enough to size her up. She wasn't a plant or a cop. Nobody can fake that level of nervousness. She wasn't wringing her hands, but close.

I was sitting in the back booth—my usual table. I looked around the bar while I counted slowly to ten. It's a comfortable, familiar place. A Family hang-out. See, it hasn't been too long since the Mob ran this town. Nick's was one of the neutral taverns. Not upper-class. Nick didn't run "no hoitsy-toitsy gentlemen's club." His words, not mine. Nick's son Jocko runs the place now. Yeah, really. Nick actually named him Jocko. Poor guy.

The bar looks old. Not elegant old, just old. Dark wood covers the floors and walls and surrounds a real marble-topped bar. Remnants of old sweat and stale cigarette smoke cling to every surface. You can't see through the nicotine haze on the windows. Jocko doesn't do windows.

I finished counting, raised my hand, and caught her eye. She walked toward me, both hands clutching her purse like someone was going to lift it. A pleasant jingling reached my ears. Jewelry of some sort. When she reached the booth she looked at me, surprised. Apparently I wasn't what she expected.

I don't wear an eyepatch or have a swarthy mustache. I even have all of my teeth. I look absolutely ordinary. Collar-length black hair, blue-grey eyes the color of gun metal, and a build that shows I work out but not to excess. I was dressed in a blue cotton long-sleeved business shirt with the sleeves rolled up, grey slacks and black sneakers that look like dress shoes as long as I keep them polished. The jacket that matched the slacks was folded on the bench next to me. I look like I could be a lawyer, a writer, or a mechanic. I don't look like someone that would as soon shoot you as look at you. That's the idea. I gave her my best mercenary look; cold, uncaring. I wouldn't want her to think that I was just some guy hitting on her. She looked away, rattled.

Her scent blew me away. I notice smells more since the change. Nice term—"change". Her scent was stronger than it should be, but not perfume. This was just her. The woman smelled sweet and musky, with overtones of something tangy. I learned from Babs that means she's afraid. Fear reminds me, although Babs said I'm nuts, of hot and sour soup. Every emotion has its own particular scent. And lies! When someone lies, it smells like black pepper. I don't mind; it helps me interview clients.

Most scents are soft and not particularly noticeable. They rise off a person's skin like ghostly presences, only to disappear into unseen breezes. I have to concentrate to catch a person's real scent.

My client slid into the opposite side of the booth. I didn't stand. She didn't expect me to. Good thing. She sat with her back to the room. Another good indication that she wasn't a cop. Cops, like crooks, have a thing about having a wall at their back. Nobody can hit you from behind or pull your own gun on you.

"Um," she began when I just stared at her without saying anything. "Are you Bob?"

I nodded but still made no sound. It unnerved her and amused me. She was having a hard time looking at my face, whereas I looked straight into her eyes.

"I'm hoping you might be able to help me," she tried again. It required no comment, so I didn't make one.

My nose tingled. The client smelled like blood; like prey. But that's true of most people. Especially near the full moon. I never used to think much about the moon phases. Now I plan my life by them.

People didn't used to smell like food. Some days it pisses me off. But I didn't get a choice in the matter. A hit went bad. The woman I was stalking stalked me back. I wasn't prepared for a being with superhuman speed and strength. She ripped my throat out of my body and left me for dead. I should have died. She said so later. Guess I was too damn stubborn to die.

The wash of emotions from the client overpowered my nose. I could handle the fear and the blood. I was used to them. I don't meet with clients until after I've had a large rare steak for lunch. But this lady smelled of heat and sex. Heat, not sun—heat and something that I couldn't place that reminded me of a forest. Warm, dewy, sweet, salty. It was a safe, comforting smell unlike anything I've ever been in contact with. It was a smell that I wanted to soak into my pores. Breathe in, roll in. I had to blink and sneeze to clear my senses. Then I returned to staring quietly at her.

She couldn't meet my eyes but kept scanning the room. Her fingers tapped restlessly on the table, then on her lap, then on the table again while she bit at her lips as if looking for something to say or do. The hot and sour smell of fear, the burnt metal of frustration overwhelmed me as if they were my own. That was new. My muscles tensed against my will. Suddenly she stopped fidgeting, took a deep breath and looked right at me.

"Would you please say something?" she asked in frustration. "I'm drowning here."

That won her a quick smile. "Would you like something to drink? It's not much cooler in here than outside. That dark suit has to be hot."

She looked at her outfit and had the good grace to blush. "It's a little trite, isn't it? I didn't even think about the heat. I was trying to be inconspicuous." She smiled a bit as if she felt my amusement the way I was feeling her emotions, but she smelled embarrassed. A dry smell, like heat rising off desert sand, mixed with other things I didn't recognize yet. I don't know a lot of the emotions yet. Babs told me that I'd get the hang of identifying them. I'm in no hurry.

I didn't believe it at first. Didn't want to. But Babs followed me around for three days, and taped me with a camcorder. I avoided her like I avoid everyone, but she filmed enough to prove that she was telling the truth. Babs was a sadistic bitch about it, too. She made sure she immortalized all of the most embarrassing moments of a dog in living color. Pissed me off. I stopped returning her calls after that.

"I don't exactly blend in, do I?" The words brought me out of my musing.

Lying to save her feelings would be diplomatic, but I try to save lies for important things. "Not really."

I raised my hand to signal Jocko. He moved out from behind the bar, wiping his meaty hands on a snow white bar rag. Jocko's a big 6'8". He looks beefy but it's mostly muscle—he was a pro wrestler for a few years. Jocko wears his waist-length black hair in a ponytail because of state health regs. A scar cuts his left eyebrow in half. He's second-generation Italian but he looks Native-American because of the hair.

Jocko smells like bad habits. Whiskey and cigarettes and sweat. He walked slowly toward the table—almost lethargically. Jocko moves slow because he threw his back out in the ring years ago and since there isn't any worker's comp insurance in wrestling he came home to run the family business. But he's hardly a cripple. Jocko can still throw a man through the front window if he puts his mind to it. Everybody knows it. Like me, he doesn't talk much. He just stood at the table waiting for our order.

"Draft for me." I turned to the client with a questioning look.

"Um—rum and Coke, I guess." Jocko started to walk away. She raised her voice a little bit to add, "Captain Morgan, please." He nodded without turning or stopping. "And Diet?" a little louder still. Anyone that didn't know Jocko would presume he hadn't heard her. I knew he heard her and that he was chuckling softly under his breath. The mild orange smell of amusement drifted to me. A rum and Coke is not the same thing at all as a Morgan and Diet. Not to a bartender.

She glanced at me. "Do you think he heard me?"

"He heard. Now, what can I do for you?"

"I want you to kill someone," she said calmly. "I can afford to pay whatever the cost."

Well, that was direct! I shut my mouth again, closed my eyes and reached my hand up to rub the bridge of my nose. It eased the tension behind my eyes.

"Is something wrong?"

There's a certain code in my profession. The client doesn't actually ask and I don't actually admit what I do for a living. It's just sort of understood. Money is discussed but only because both parties know what transaction is being, well, transacted.

I lowered my voice. "I would appreciate it if you could be a little more *discreet* about our business here."

That stopped her cold. She suddenly realized what she had said, and that she had said it in a normal tone, in a place of business. Her face flushed and her jaw worked noiselessly. The blend from the combination of emotions made me giddy.

"That was stupid, wasn't it?"

"Well, that sort of depends whether you *want* to spend the next twenty or so years in prison. It's called 'accessory before the fact'."

She shrugged. "Actually, for the job I'm proposing, I'd never see the inside of a prison."

"That might be a little overconfident," I replied, "There's always the chance of getting a very good investigator. I always make it clear to clients that there is risk involved. I'm good. I'm very good. But there is always a risk."

She shook her head. "You couldn't know since I haven't explained. But it's not an issue."

I believed her and I didn't know why. No black pepper smell of deceit, maybe. I shrugged my shoulders. "Fine. You've been warned." I drew a breath and began my list of conditions. "I'll need the name of the mark, a photograph, and home and work addresses. I work alone. I will choose the time and place of the job. Not you. If you want it public, I'll pick the time. You can pick the method if you want. If you don't specify, it could be by a variety of methods. I vary them to fit the situation and the mark. I don't do extras like rape or torture for the same money. There will be an additional charge for that kind of thing."

She listened intently and without comment. When I

mentioned rape and torture, she grimaced slightly. I could feel her disapproval beat at me like heat from a furnace. I shook off the feeling and proceeded on.

"If the mark meets his end without my assistance, there are no refunds. I require payment in advance. Cash only, small bills. If the money is marked or traceable you will forfeit your life at a future time of my choosing. Don't presume that I can't find you. I can."

She nodded, as if she had heard my speech a million times. She leaned forward, eyes intent on my face—focused. Good. I like it when people listen.

Jocko arrived with the drinks so I stopped speaking. He put them on the table, then looked at me. "That'll be four-fifty."

I motioned for him to ask the lady. He turned his attention to her and she opened her little purse quickly. She extracted a ten dollar bill and held it out to him. "Keep it."

Jocko pursed his lips in approval and moved off silently.

"Go on," she said.

I tried to remember where I left off. I hate to get interrupted mid-stream. "If the police somehow get wind of me through you, I will make sure that you never live to testify. If there are family members involved and they get in the way, I will remove them. I don't charge for removal of witnesses. That's for my benefit, not yours. However, if there are potential witnesses that you do not wish removed, make sure they are kept out of the line of fire until after the job is complete. I won't be held responsible for mistaken identity, so if the photograph is not absolutely clear, or up-to-date, there could be a mistake."

The client sipped her drink as I spoke. It's a long spiel. Now's the only time I ask questions like whether she needed proof that the job had been accomplished. She smiled. "No,

I think I'll know." That meant that it was someone close to her; possibly a husband or boyfriend. Her amusement smelled sweeter, more like tangerines than oranges.

When I finished, my beer was almost gone. "Do you have any questions?" I asked.

She had a mouthful of complimentary peanuts and she didn't respond immediately. Jocko puts out peanuts to increase drink sales. It works, so I don't indulge.

"No," she said when she'd swallowed, "That about covers it. When do I have to get the cash to you? And how much?"

"How much depends on who. Public figure or private? Who is the mark?"

She spread her hands out, showing her chest to perfection. It was a nice view but, "I don't understand."

"*I'm* the target. The mark. Whatever."

I raised my eyebrows. "Excuse me?"

"I'm hiring you to kill me. The time and place don't matter. But soon. How much will it cost?"

Alarms started ringing in my head. "There are a lot less expensive ways to do yourself in,"

She nodded her head once. "Probably. But this is the method I choose. Is there a problem?"

There was something wrong with this situation. I couldn't think of what specifically was bugging me. I really don't want to know a person's story but I was missing something. Something important. I needed to dig.

I leaned back in my seat. "Who are you and why do you need to die?"

Her eyes shifted. Yeah, there was something there all right. "Does it matter?"

"Normally, no," I admitted, "But this is a first for me and it's making me nervous. So, give. Why do you need to die in such a way that it *doesn't* look like a suicide?"

Intense emotions washed through my nose, blending and

then splitting. I couldn't identify them all. I'm still new at this shit. I suppose a little part of me is annoyed that I haven't picked them up faster. It's been almost a year. But I'm not curious enough to contact Babs.

"I don't need to die. I want to. But you'd need to hear my story and you told me on the phone that you didn't want to hear it. I'm a nobody. No one special. Just take the money and do the job." Her eyes were bright, too bright, and her voice too intense. I didn't like it.

"What's your name?" In any event, I'd need it if she turned out to be the mark.

"Wh—" she began and then corrected herself. "Oh, that's right you need the name. Quentin. Sue Quentin."

Sue Quentin. That name rang a bell. I leaned forward and put my arms on the table. "Take off the wig," I ordered.

She looked around her nervously. Yeah, it probably wouldn't do to have her reveal herself in full view of everyone. That sort of thing is remembered.

"Fine," I crooked a finger and slid out of the booth. "Follow me." She stood and followed me down a hallway to the bathrooms. It was dark but my eyes are exceptionally good—funny thing. I knocked on both doors and waited. No response. I turned around to face her. "Take it off."

She slid the black wig with attached scarf from her head. Underneath were medium-brown permed ringlets that reached her shoulders. The hair changed the shape of her face. Even in the dim light of the hallway I instantly recognized her. The disguise was better than I'd credited. With the wig, I hadn't had more than a vague recognition. Fortunately, no one else in the bar would probably make her, either. I knew her but couldn't imagine why she would want to die.

I shook my head. "Huh-uh. No way. You're a *very* visible lady. I'd have to wait until the heat surrounding you dies down."

She stood very still, eyes closed. The hot blanket of sorrow pressed on me and tightened my throat. A single tear traced silver down her left cheek. "How long?" Her voice was barely a whisper.

I turned and walked back into the room, not able to answer right away. I had to get away from that distress. She got under my skin way too easily. That alone made me nervous. Some instinct told me if I didn't run from her, she was going to change my whole life. I didn't want this job.

I slid back into the booth. She followed me a couple minutes later, in control again. The wig was back in place and she had wiped the tear from her face. She looked relatively calm but her hands trembled a little. She folded them in front of her and held herself stiffly, as if hanging onto her control by her fingertips.

I'm not moved by tears. I've turned down jobs before. But she'd asked a question and I could at least give her an answer. "I don't know," I replied. "With all the publicity—a year, maybe more."

Her gaze was steady on me but the unshed tears made her eyes shine. "So I can count on that? A year from now you'll do the job?"

I held up my hands in front of me. "Whoa, lady. I didn't say that. I said, 'a year, *maybe more*'. I can't judge that. You could be in the papers again next week and it would start all over. I don't predict the future. No. I can't take the job."

"If you only understood," she began.

"Stop." She did. "You were right the first time, Ms. Quentin. I don't want to know. I don't *care* to know your story. I'm not a psychologist. I'm not a social worker." Except this time, I *did* want to know and I couldn't explain why.

Her eyes went cold for a moment, almost as though she could sense my thoughts. "Fine. How much?"

I felt my brow wrinkle. "For what?"

"To listen." She leaned forward a bit. "You're absolutely right. You're not a psychologist or a social worker. You're a mercenary. How much will it cost me for you to listen to my story?" Her anger bit at my nose. It smelled like coffee burning.

"It won't change anything," I said. "I don't want the job."

"So don't take it. There are other people out there with less *scruples*. I just want an ear. I just want you to shut up and listen to my story." Her voice tightened as she spoke—colder, harsher, more brittle. She was blinking back tears again. "You don't have to care. Just make the right noises in the right places. How much for a couple of hours?"

"It's not scruples that would stop me from taking the job, lady. It's self-preservation. Too many people know your name. Investigators would work a lot harder because you're newsworthy. And I'm not for rent on an hourly basis."

That was supposed to be it. The end. I don't know why I said the next. "But, fine. If you want to buy my ear for the night, it's for sale. A thousand up front and I'll let you know how much more when the story's over." I half-stood and half-slid out of the booth. "Let's go."

She looked startled. "Just like that?"

There I go again—being impulsive. I should walk out. My gut told me I should run. I've learned to trust my wolf instincts even when I don't understand them. And yet, I shrugged and smiled tightly at her. I had nothing better to do right now. I had no reason to fear this person. No logical reason, anyway. Money's money. It's just another job.

"Just like that. You're driving. But I have to make a call first. So finish your drink, go to the john or whatever. I'll meet you out front in a couple of minutes. What are you driving?"

Her eyes got wider. I could smell the hot tang of fear, the soured milk smell of disbelief and rising under both, the lighter smell of hope. She had been expecting me to walk out. Probably thought I was playing a cruel joke. Not a chance. For once I'd be able to indulge my curiosity. In my position, the less I know about a client or a mark the better. Except this time I wanted to know more. Maybe I'd find out how many people had walked out on her in the past. Or why she wanted to die. Maybe I'd walk out too. We'd see.